Praise for *New York Times* bestselling author Brenda Jackson

"Brenda Jackson writes romance that sizzles and characters you fall in love with."
—*New York Times* bestselling author Lori Foster

"Jackson's trademark ability to weave multiple characters and side stories together makes shocking truths all the more exciting."
—*Publishers Weekly*

"There is no getting away from the sex appeal and charm of Jackson's Westmoreland family."
—*RT Book Reviews* on *Feeling the Heat*

...AY

...ennett

"Jules ...   ...l passionate characters guaranteed to grip your heart."
—*New York Times* bestselling author Lori Foster

"Jules Bennett is the queen of small-town romance."
—*New York Times* bestselling author Maisey Yates

"Jules Bennett has a gift for creating warm-hearted, emotional stories of love, friendship, and romance set in small towns readers will want to return to again and again."
—*New York Times* bestselling author JoAnn Ross

Praise for USA TODAY
bestselling author Jules B...

Tender wines, heartwarming and...

NEW YORK TIMES BESTSELLING AUTHOR

BRENDA JACKSON

DUTY OR DESIRE

If you purchased this book without a cover you should be aware
that this book is stolen property. It was reported as "unsold and
destroyed" to the publisher, and neither the author nor the
publisher has received any payment for this "stripped book."

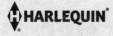

ISBN-13: 978-1-335-40998-0
Duty or Desire
First published in 2019.
This edition published in 2021.
Copyright © 2019 by Brenda Streater Jackson

Recycling programs
for this product may
not exist in your area.

Single Man Meets Single Mom
First published in 2014.
This edition published in 2021.
Copyright © 2014 by Jules Bennett

All rights reserved. No part of this book may be used or reproduced in
any manner whatsoever without written permission except in the case of
brief quotations embodied in critical articles and reviews.

This is a work of fiction. Names, characters, places and incidents
are either the product of the author's imagination or are used fictitiously.
Any resemblance to actual persons, living or dead, businesses,
companies, events or locales is entirely coincidental.

This edition published by arrangement with Harlequin Books S.A.

For questions and comments about the quality of this book,
please contact us at CustomerService@Harlequin.com.

Harlequin Enterprises ULC
22 Adelaide St. West, 40th Floor
Toronto, Ontario M5H 4E3, Canada
www.Harlequin.com

Printed in U.S.A.

CONTENTS

Brenda Jackson is a *New York Times* bestselling author of more than one hundred romance titles. Brenda lives in Jacksonville, Florida, and divides her time between family, writing and traveling. Email Brenda at authorbrendajackson@gmail.com or visit her on her website at brendajackson.net.

Books by Brenda Jackson

Harlequin Desire

The Westmorelands

The Real Thing
The Secret Affair
Breaking Bailey's Rules
Bane

The Westmoreland Legacy

The Rancher Returns
His Secret Son
An Honorable Seduction
His to Claim
Duty or Desire

Visit the Author Profile page
at Harlequin.com for more titles.

DUTY OR DESIRE

Brenda Jackson

Acknowledgments

To the man who will forever be the love of my life
and the wind beneath my wings, Gerald Jackson Sr.

To all my readers who love the Westmorelands
and their friends.

To my sons, Gerald Jr. and Brandon. Please continue
to make me and your dad proud. I love you guys.

To my family and friends
who continue to support me in all that I do.

Ask, and it shall be given you; seek, and ye shall find;
knock, and it shall be opened unto you.
—*Matthew 7:7*

Prologue

The doorbell sounded and Bane Westmoreland wondered who the latecomer could be. All his family and friends who'd been invited to celebrate his and his wife Crystal's housewarming party were accounted for.

Upon opening the door he found an older couple, in their late sixties, standing there with a baby in their arms.

Bane was certain he did not know the couple. "Yes, may I help you?"

The man spoke. "We hate to impose but we were told Peterson Higgins was here tonight. We are the Glosters, his deceased brother's in-laws."

Bane nodded. "Yes, Pete is here. Please come in."

The man shook his head. "We prefer not to, but we would appreciate it if you could tell Peterson we're here. We would like to speak with him. We will wait out here."

Bane nodded again. "Okay, just a minute." He circled around the room before finally finding Pete in a group in the family room.

"Excuse me, guys, but I need to borrow Pete for a minute," Bane said to the others. Once he got Pete aside, he told him about the older couple waiting outside. Pete placed his cup of punch aside and quickly moved toward the front door.

When Pete returned about half an hour later, he was carrying a baby in one hand and a diaper bag in the other. Everyone's attention was drawn to him when the baby released a huge wail.

It seemed all the mothers in the room hurried toward him.

"Whose baby?" Bane's cousin Gemma was the first to ask, taking the baby from a flustered-looking Pete.

"This is my nine-month-old niece, Ciara," he said, noticing how quickly the baby girl quieted once Gemma held her. "As most of you know, my brother, Matthew, and his wife, Sherry, were killed in that car crash six months ago. This is their daughter. Sherry's parents were given custody of Ciara when Matt and Sherry died. But they just gave me full custody of her, citing health issues that prevent them from taking proper care of her. That means I'm now Ciara's legal guardian."

Pete looked around the room at the group he considered family and asked the one question none of them could answer.

"I'm a bachelor, for heaven's sake! What on earth am I going to do with a baby?"

Chapter 1

Five months later

"I hate that I'm leaving you like this, Pete, but my sister needs me."

Sheriff Peterson Higgins stared at the older woman standing across the kitchen. He'd known something was wrong the minute he walked through the door.

Well, he had news for Bonnie. He needed her, too.

Pete suddenly felt like a class A bastard for thinking such a thing after she'd just tearfully explained that her sister had been diagnosed with breast cancer. Of course he understood her wanting to go be with her only sister during this time. Even if her leaving would put him in a bind, the last thing he wanted was for Bonnie to feel guilty about going to her family. Somehow, he would find the right person to live-in and keep his fourteen-month-old niece while he worked.

Of course, that person couldn't really replace Bonnie.

Bonnie McCray had been his mother's best friend. When Renee Higgins had died, Pete had been sixteen and his younger brother Matthew twelve. Renee had asked Bonnie to always be there for her sons and Bonnie had kept that promise. And when Pete's father passed away three years later, Bonnie wouldn't hear of Pete not fulfilling his mother's dream of him completing college. Bonnie and her husband, Fred, agreed to look after Matt while Pete studied.

It had been hard going to college full-time and making sure the cattle ranch his father had loved remained productive. Luckily, his two best friends, Derringer and Riley Westmoreland, had a huge family of cousins and brothers who'd pitched in and helped out. They also made sure Pete hired the best people to help run things while he attended university.

After he completed college with a degree in criminology, he discovered ranching wasn't in his blood but a career in law enforcement was. He found out ranching wasn't in Matt's blood either when his brother went into the military immediately after high school.

Even so, Pete refused to sell the ranch that had been in the Higgins family for generations. Instead he leased part of the two hundred acres to sharecroppers, and for the other parts he hired a foreman and ranch hands. That freed Pete up to work for the sheriff's office, a job he'd secured after college thanks to Riley's oldest brother, Dillon Westmoreland.

Pete loved his career, and the ranch was making

plenty of money, which he'd split with Matt before Matt's death.

A pain settled around Pete's heart when he remembered the phone call almost a year ago telling him Matt and Sherry had been killed in a car crash. Luckily, three-month-old Ciara hadn't been with them. It had been Matt and Sherry's "date night" and the baby had been at home with a sitter.

Sherry's parents, who lived in New Hampshire, had wanted full custody of Ciara and Pete had seen no reason not to give it to them. Matt had adored his in-laws, thought they were good people who treated him like a son instead of a son-in-law. Besides, Pete knew with his bachelor lifestyle, the last thing he could manage was taking care of a baby. When Sheriff Harper retired a few months before, Pete had been selected to replace him. That meant his plate was fuller than ever.

Things had been working out and he'd made a point to call and check on his niece every weekend. He enjoyed hearing about the development of her motor skills and how much she liked to eat.

But five months ago, out of the blue, Sherry's parents had shown up in Denver to say that health issues meant they needed him to serve as guardian for his niece. They assumed his bachelor days wouldn't last forever and they thought a much younger couple would have more energy to raise their granddaughter.

At thirty-six, marriage was the last thing on Pete's mind. However, he gladly gave his niece the love, attention and care he knew Matt would have wanted him to.

Now at fourteen months, Ciara Renee Higgins was ruling the Higgins household, and Pete was glad Bonnie had been there to help out as a full-time nanny. Her husband had passed away a couple of years ago and with her only son living on the East Coast, Bonnie had welcomed the opportunity to take care of others again. As far as Pete was concerned, she'd been a godsend. He honestly didn't know what he'd have done without her and wondered what he would do now that she would be leaving.

"May I make a suggestion, Pete?"

For a minute he'd been so deep in thought he'd forgotten Bonnie was standing there, waiting for him to say something. "Yes."

Bonnie smiled as she placed a serving tray on the table with soup and a sandwich. His lunch. He made a habit of swinging by the ranch at noon each day to spend time with Ciara. Although Bonnie's job was to take care of Ciara, she always prepared lunch and dinner for him, as well. Where did she find the time to do such things? On the days when Bonnie returned to her own home, Pete took care of his niece by himself. Ciara required his full attention and would let him know when she felt she wasn't getting enough of it. It was only during her nap time was he able to grab a nap of his own.

"Hopefully, I won't be gone any more than two months, and I know of someone who could replace me."

He doubted anyone would be able to replace Bonnie. "Who?"

"A woman I met a couple of months ago at church. She recently moved to the area and she and I have become good friends."

He nodded as he walked over to the table to sit down and eat. "Where is she from?"

"Charleston."

He chuckled. "Good grief. Don't tell me we have another Southerner invading these parts. Bella is enough."

Bella was married to his friend Jason Westmoreland. Everyone thought of her as a real Southern belle. From the time she'd arrived in Denver it had been obvious that she was a woman of refinement. It didn't take long for word to spread that she was the daughter of a wealthy business tycoon in Savannah, Georgia. Although Bella had adjusted well, at times she still looked out of place amidst the bunch of roughnecks in these parts.

Bonnie placed a small salad near his sandwich. "Yes, another Southerner." She then poured iced tea into his glass.

He looked up. "Thanks. And what makes you think she will be good with Ciara?"

"Because she taught prekindergarten for a few years and before that, she worked with younger babies in a nursery at a hospital in Charleston. She's had us over for tea several times. I always take Ciara with me and the two of them hit it off. You of all people know how Ciara can be."

Yes, he knew. If his niece liked you, then she liked you. If she didn't, she didn't. And she normally didn't take well to strangers. "What makes you think she would be interested in keeping Ciara until you return?"

"Because I asked her," Bonnie said with excitement in her voice. "I didn't want to leave you with no one at all, and then not with just anyone."

He appreciated that. "When can I meet her, to see if she'll be a good fit?"

"I invited her to lunch."

Pete paused from biting into his sandwich. "Today?"

Bonnie smiled. "Yes, today. The sooner you can meet her, the better. I would worry sick the entire time I'm in Dallas if you and Ciara weren't taken care of properly."

At that moment the doorbell sounded. "That's probably her," Bonnie said, smiling, as she swiftly left the kitchen.

Pete began eating his sandwich, curious about the woman Bonnie was recommending. He figured she would be around Bonnie's age, which meant she could probably cook. Having home-cooked Southern dishes once in a while was a nice thought.

"Pete, I'd like you to meet Myra Hollister. Myra, this is Sheriff Peterson Higgins."

Placing his glass down on the table, Pete stood and turned to offer his hand to the woman, then froze. Standing in the middle of his kitchen beside Bonnie was the most gorgeous woman he'd seen in a while. A long while. And she was young, probably no more than twenty-two or twenty-three. She had a petite figure and was no more than five-three. She appeared even shorter than that when standing across from his six-three height.

She had skin the color of rich mocha and features so striking he felt like he'd been struck in all parts of his body. Perfect hazel eyes stared back at him and a smile curved a pair of delectable lips. Fluffy dark brown bangs swept across her forehead and a mass of curly hair fell past her shoulders. When he finally moved his gaze from her face it was to check out the legs beneath her dress. They were as gorgeous as the rest of her.

He couldn't ignore the spike of heat that caught him low in the gut. The power of her femininity surrounded him, actually made his heart skip a couple of beats. He wanted to groan in protest.

"It's nice meeting you, Sheriff Higgins. I've heard a lot of wonderful things about you," the woman said, offering him her hand. Her Southern accent was just as perceptible as Bella's.

"Thanks," Pete replied, fighting back a curse. The moment their hands had touched, a hard hum of lust had rushed through his veins.

Bonnie wanted him to hire this woman as a live-in nanny? She had to be kidding. There was no way he could do that, even on a temporary basis. This was the first woman he'd been attracted to since Ellen.

That placed him in one hell of a dilemma.

Myra Hollister tried hiding her excitement at possibly being hired as Ciara's nanny. She adored the precious little girl she'd gotten to know. And when Bonnie mentioned her need for a replacement, Myra had been glad to help. It would certainly solve some of her own problems for a while.

First off, she would get a salary, which meant she wouldn't have to touch her savings. And since her lease ended next month, moving in here was great, too. Hopefully without her own address, her brother wouldn't be able to find her. The latter was the most important thing and would definitely buy her the time she needed before returning to Charleston for a face-off with Baron.

"How old are you?"

Sheriff Higgins's question reeled her concentration back in. "I'm twenty-four but will be turning twenty-five on Christmas Day."

Myra studied his very handsome features, which she'd noticed the moment she'd walked in. She figured he was either thirty-five or thirty-six, which would put him at Baron's age. She'd encountered good-looking older men before. Her brother's friends were all eye candy and, like him, they were all womanizers who thought women were good for only one thing. Long ago she figured it must be an age thing. Even Baron thought that way and he'd been married to Cleo almost four years. She loved her sister-in-law and regretted how Baron and his mother, Charlene, were treating her. Myra was convinced Cleo would have left Baron long ago, but he swore he would fight her for custody of the kids if she left him.

Pushing thoughts of Baron from her mind, Myra placed her concentration back on the man standing in front of her. He had chestnut-colored skin, broad shoulders and long legs that looked good in his pants.

He also had a gorgeous pair of dark brown eyes that seemed to be staring at her in disapproval. Why? Although this was what she considered an informal interview, she had dressed appropriately. She was wearing one of her church dresses with heels.

And why had he asked about her age? Hadn't Miss Bonnie given him a rundown of her credentials and experience? What was the issue? She could tell by the frown on his face that there was one.

Automatically, she slid her hands to the back of her hair and fluffed it away from her neck, something she did whenever she was nervous. And she shouldn't be feeling nervous, not when she was qualified for the job. If truth be told, probably overqualified.

"You're a lot younger than I thought you would be," he finally said, after staring her down. "Sorry, but I don't think you'll work out."

Myra blinked. He didn't think she would work out?

She was being dismissed because of her age? Maybe now was the time to remind him that there were such things as discrimination laws, but then she figured that would only make the situation worse. She glanced over at Miss Bonnie, who was giving the sheriff a shocked stare.

Deciding to reassure him, because she truly needed the job, she said, "I don't consider myself too young to care for your niece, Sheriff Higgins. I've worked at a day care and also in the nursery at the hospital. And once I finish my thesis, I'll have my PhD in child psychology."

If Myra thought that information would impress him, then she was wrong. He remained expressionless when he said, "All that's nice, but I regret you wasted your time coming here today."

Although she didn't understand what was going on, all she could do was take the man at his word. Besides, he might think of her as young, but she was strong. Only a strong woman could have put up with her brother's foolishness for the past six months and not have broken. Fighting back the anger she felt, she said, as politely as she could, "I regret wasting my time coming here today, as well. Good day, Sheriff."

Giving Miss Bonnie an appreciative smile, she added, "I can see my way to the door." Then Myra turned and walked out of the kitchen.

"Would you like to tell me what that was about, Peterson?"

It wasn't the tone of Bonnie's voice alone that let Pete know she was upset with him. She never called him Peterson. "I stated it already and there's nothing more to tell. I thought the woman you were recommending was an older woman, closer to your age. She's way too young," he said, before sitting back down to the table to resume eating his lunch.

"Too young? For heaven's sake, she's nearly twenty-five. Women her age are having babies every day. How can you think she's too young when you've gotten Charity Maples to babysit for you a few times and she's only seventeen?"

He shrugged. "The key word is *babysit*. I don't need a young nanny working for me. Have you forgotten I need a *live-in* nanny?"

"At the moment what I think you need is your head examined. Myra Hollister is more than qualified to be a nanny, and what's the problem with her living here while taking care of Ciara?"

He didn't say anything and then he wished he had come up with something. If he had, Bonnie might not have slung out her next accusation. "You're afraid, aren't you? You're afraid that a young beautiful woman will remind you to live again."

He glanced over at her, which wasn't hard to do since she'd come to stand by the table. "I don't know what you're talking about. I am living."

"No, you're not—you're breathing. I, more than anyone, know that a part of you stopped living the day Ellen died. It's been twelve years, Pete."

Every muscle in Pete's body tensed. He, of all people, knew just how many years it had been. A man would not forget the day his fiancée died when she was thrown from the horse she'd been riding. Pete doubted he would ever forget that day for as long as he lived.

A man had come into the dress shop where she worked a month earlier and tried flirting with her. She'd told him she wasn't interested and was engaged to be married. He had begun stalking her and Ellen hadn't told Pete anything. Then the man had intentionally thrown a firecracker to spook her horse. At least he'd been arrested and was still serving time for Ellen's death.

"I know how long it's been, Bonnie. What's your point? You act as if I don't date."

"Yes, you date, though rarely."

She was right. However, his excuse was a good one. He was too busy. Besides, some women saw a man in a uniform as a trophy to win and he didn't intend to be a prize in any contest. He sighed as he shifted his gaze from Bonnie to the window.

Bonnie moved around the table to stand by him, intentionally blocking his view. She stood there, a force to be reckoned with, her hands on her hips, giving him that infamous Bonnie McCray glare.

"You've just dismissed your best prospect for a nanny. I didn't even know about that thesis for her PhD. That makes her more than qualified."

He drew in a deep breath. "What do you even know about her?"

"She's living in Denver temporarily, trying to deal with grief. Her parents died a few months ago while vacationing in Morocco. The tour helicopter crashed."

"That's tragic," he said, shaking his head, feeling bad for the woman. Losing both parents at the same time had to be hard on a person. He recalled years ago when the same thing had happened to his best friends, Derringer and Riley Westmoreland. The cousins had lost both sets of parents the same day in an airplane accident. He recalled how devastating that had been.

"Yes, it was tragic," Bonnie was saying. "Her family owns a huge corporation in Charleston, but she's not in the family business or anything."

"How did she decide on Denver?" he asked,

"Someone she knows from college owns a house here and she's leasing it for six months."

He nodded. "Well, I wish her the best, but like I said, she's too young to stay here. I'm sure there are other women out there. An *older* woman I can hire to live here as a nanny."

"Myra could live here as Ciara's nanny, Pete. Don't think I don't know why you're behaving the way you are. I've got eyes. I knew the moment she walked into the room that you were attracted to her."

He wouldn't bother denying anything because he'd learned long ago that Bonnie didn't miss a thing. "And what if I am? I've been attracted to women before."

"Yes, and the few you've dated were women you deemed safe. For some reason you're afraid if a pretty young woman like Myra got underfoot that she might thaw your frozen heart."

First she accuses him of breathing instead of living and now she's saying he has a frozen heart.

His heart wasn't frozen. He just wore a thick protective shield around it. Pete refused to ever go through the pain he'd felt when he lost Ellen. Pain that could still creep up on him even now, twelve years later. Had Ellen not died, they would be married by now with a bunch of kids and living in this very house where he'd been born. They would be happy, just as they'd been that day when they'd been sixteen and had decided to be boyfriend and girlfriend forever.

Forever...

For him, forever was still going on. It hadn't died the day Ellen had.

"Have you forgotten about that dream you shared with me, Pete?"

He didn't have to wonder what dream she was talking about. "What does that dream have to do with anything?"

She sat down in the chair beside his. "Because in that dream you said your hands had been tied and Ellen was untying them for you. Not only did she untie them but then she tried to push you out some door."

A part of him now wished he hadn't shared any details about that dream with Bonnie. But he had done so mainly because it had bothered him to the point where he'd awakened in the middle of the night in a cold sweat. He'd gotten up to go into the kitchen, needing something to drink and found Bonnie in the living room, sitting in the chair, rocking Ciara back to sleep. While downing a glass of lemonade, he had told Bonnie about his dream and she'd listened and said nothing.

It had been the next morning when she'd told him what she thought the dream meant. Ellen was trying to release him, free him from all the plans they'd made together. She wanted him to enjoy life. To live and love again. To do more than just breathe.

Pete sighed deeply. He hadn't accepted Bonnie's interpretation of the dream then and he wouldn't accept it now. "I don't want to talk about that dream, Bonnie."

"Fine, Pete. But you need to accept that I'm leaving and your niece needs a nanny. I honestly don't think you're going to find another person more qualified than Myra Hollister, especially not in two weeks."

He slid back his chair to stand. "I intend to do just that, Bonnie. I'm determined to find someone more qualified."

He had to.

Chapter 2

Myra looked up from reading the morning paper and sipping her herbal tea. She tipped her head to stare at her cell phone. It was ringing and she didn't recognize the ringtone. Granted, she hadn't assigned a specific sound to everyone who called her. Only those that mattered. She was about to ignore the call and then remembered it might be Sheriff Higgins.

She had run into Miss Bonnie and Ciara at the grocery store two days ago and had been so glad to see them. Ciara's chubby arms had automatically reached for her and she'd been happy to hold her. That had been the first time she'd seen Miss Bonnie since that day a week ago when the sheriff had turned down her employment as a nanny.

According to Miss Bonnie, the position hadn't been filled and she felt the sheriff would come to his senses soon enough and realize Myra was the best candidate.

Deciding to appease her curiosity, she clicked on the phone. "Hello."

"Gosh, Myra, you had me worried there for a minute."

"Wallace? Why are you calling me from another number? One that I don't recognize?"

Wallace Blue had been her father's protégé. The man Elias Hollister had groomed for years to replace him at the company whenever that time came. At least her father had the good sense not to make Baron his successor, recognizing at an early age that her brother lacked the skills, knowledge and compassion to ever head a company the size, depth and magnitude of Hollister Enterprises.

Her father thought his only son's lack of character stemmed from Baron having been raised by his mother, who'd been Elias's first wife. He thought Charlene had raised her son to be just as callous, calculating and cruel as she was. Myra hadn't known just how true those allegations were until her involvement with Rick Stovers.

She should not have been surprised that Baron's behavior would get worse after her parents died unexpectedly. The first thing Baron had done was go after Wallace, who'd been in place to head the company. Rumor had it that Baron, along with his devious mother, had gotten to the stockholders after obtaining damaging information on their pasts. Baron and Charlene had threatened to expose the information if the stockholders didn't vote Wallace out and put Baron in as Myra's father's replacement.

"It's a burner phone and I wanted to check to make sure you're okay," Wallace was saying. "Your brother is more devious than ever and I think he might have put a tracker on my regular phone. He's desperate to find you."

Myra could believe that because in two months, when she turned twenty-five, the entire company became hers and there was nothing Baron or the stockholders could do about it. It was Baron's intention that she not show up at that meeting where she would take control of the company, appoint Wallace as the CEO and show Baron the door. How he planned to stop her was anyone's guess, but she didn't want to take any chances.

"I can't understand why you're still working there," she said.

"Because while I'm here I can make sure Hollister Enterprises stays profitable until it's time for you to take over. Otherwise, Baron will bankrupt it. All Baron's friends are working here and they don't know what the hell they're doing."

Myra believed Wallace. Her father had said often enough that Baron had no business sense and as far as Myra was concerned the men he hung out with, mostly frat brothers, were just as bad. "Well, let Baron continue to look for me. I think this is the last place he'll think to look. According to Cleo, he thinks I'm somewhere in Spain, which is why Charlene tried to have my passport revoked so I couldn't return to the States."

"Don't put anything past her, Myra. Over the years she's been known to have bed partners in some pretty high places."

Myra could believe that. Baron even bragged about his mother's past lovers and how she could get some of them to do just about anything for her. Baron and Charlene disliked Wallace because they saw him as taking Baron's place in Elias's life. Baron and Wallace were nearly the same age, and yet as different as day and night. Wallace, whose father had been Elias's best friend

since childhood, always carried himself with profession-
alism and honesty.

"So, what's going on with you?" Wallace asked her,
breaking into her thoughts.

She shrugged, not surprised he'd asked. She considered him the big brother Baron had never been. "Not
much. Paula needs to turn this house back into an Airbnb
for the holidays, so I'll be moving out in a week."

"And going where?"

"Not sure. There's a woman I've met who relocated
from Savannah," she said, thinking about Bella Westmoreland. "She owns a private B and B. I plan to talk
to her about moving into one of the rooms there for two
months. Just till Christmas. I told you why I'm avoid-
ing hotels."

"Yes, because Baron could trace your whereabouts if
you don't," Wallace said. "I just hate you're on the run
like this. If your father was alive, he—"

"But Dad isn't alive, Wallace, and we need to carry
out his wishes like he would want us to do. I'm fine, just
a little inconvenienced."

She and Wallace knew the truth. She was being inconvenienced a whole lot. It was never her desire to get
tied to the family's business. Her father had always re-
spected her decision. But she'd known, because he'd told
her, that if anything happened to him and her mother
simultaneously, the company would become hers. He'd
instructed her to make sure Wallace was CEO so he
could run things. And that was what she intended to
do. Her twenty-fifth birthday couldn't get here soon
enough. Now, if she could only stay hidden from Baron
until then.

"You still working on your thesis?" Wallace asked her.

She moved back to the table to sit down. "Yes, but not as much as I should." Then, because she wanted to share her disappointment with someone, she said, "I interviewed for a nanny position last week."

"That's great. How's that working out for you?"

Knowing Wallace figured she'd gotten the job, she said, "I wasn't hired. The guy thought I was too young."

"Too young?"

"Yes. I think he was looking for an older, matronly woman."

"Too bad, it's his loss. You're good with kids and would have been a great nanny."

She believed that, too. At that moment her doorbell rang. "Thanks. I have to go. Someone is at the door."

"Okay. Make sure you check to see who it is before opening it, Myra."

"Okay. I'll talk to you later." She clicked off the phone and headed for the door.

Pete couldn't believe he was here, but it had taken his best friend Derringer Westmoreland to help make him realize that just like Bonnie had said, Myra Hollister was the best person to be nanny to Ciara. Besides, he was running out of time.

Bonnie would be leaving town next week and so far, the women he'd interviewed had been so lacking in certain skills he'd quickly shown them the door. Then there had been Ciara's reaction to each of them. She had taken one look and started screaming her dislike.

According to Derringer, Jason's wife, Bella, and Myra Hollister had become friends. Bella had invited Ms. Hollister to one of those Westmoreland family chow-downs, something the Westmorelands got together for every Friday, and the one thing they'd all been amazed about was how the Westmoreland kids had taken to Myra and she to them. It was as if she was a modern-day Mary Poppins.

Something else Derringer had said had helped Pete see reason. If he truly wanted what was best for Ciara, then he would get the best. It would be up to him to keep things professional between him and his nanny. He had to agree with that. All he had to do was remember his relationship with Ms. Hollister was strictly business.

He intended to make sure it stayed that way.

So here he was on Myra Hollister's doorstep with Ciara in tow. It was his day off and he hoped Ms. Hollister was still interested in the job. He glanced down at his niece who was smiling happily at him.

Suddenly the door opened and Myra stood there with a surprised look on her face. "Good morning, Sheriff Higgins."

He was about to ask if he could come in when Ciara released a happy scream and all but jumped out of his arms into Ms. Hollister's. He tightened his hold on his niece as she tried twisting out of his arms.

"You can let her go. I have her," Myra Hollister said. Ciara not only went to the woman but wrapped her arms around her neck as if Myra Hollister was her lifeline.

He'd seen the interaction between Bonnie and Ciara numerous times and had seen the bond developing between them over the months. But he hadn't been prepared for this, although he'd been forewarned.

"Hey there, Ciara, how are you, sweetie?" Myra asked her, and that's when Ciara pushed back to look up at the woman while smiling brightly.

Myra Hollister lifted her eyes over Ciara's head to look at Pete, who could only stare back at her. Today she looked even younger. The legal drinking age in Colorado was twenty-one, and he could see her getting carded easily. Few would believe she was twenty-four without proof. She was wearing her hair down and around her shoulders as she had the other day, and he wondered if the curls were as fluffy as they looked.

"Would you like to come in, Sheriff Higgins?"

"Yes, if you don't mind."

"Not at all," she said, stepping aside for him to enter, propping Ciara on her hip.

"She's heavy," he said, reaching for his niece once they were inside. Again Ciara rebuffed his outstretched hands and clung to Myra.

"She's fine. Come in by the fireplace. Glad to see you have her dressed properly."

"Of course," he said, taking off his Stetson and hanging it on the hat rack by the door.

It was October and the temperature was below freezing. Did she think he didn't know to dress his niece for the cold weather? Granted, he would admit Bonnie had made it easy for him by laying Ciara's clothes out the night before.

"Would you like something to drink, Sheriff Higgins? I have tea, hot chocolate and coffee."

When she sat down on the sofa with Ciara, he sat in the chair across from her. "No, I'm fine."

He knew from Bonnie that Myra was leasing this home. He liked the community and recalled it had once been his area to patrol when he was a deputy. The people were friendly and because of a neighborhood watch program, crime had been practically nonexistent.

"I want to apologize for my behavior the other day. I didn't mean to offend you." He decided to get it out there.

He wished he wasn't noticing how good she looked sitting there in her leggings and pullover sweater. Or how at eleven o'clock on a cold Monday morning she reminded him of a bright ray of sunshine.

After removing Ciara's coat, hat and mittens, she adjusted his niece in her lap, looked him dead in the face and said, "Yet you did offend me, Sheriff."

He blew out a slow breath. He needed to explain his actions as best he could while leaving out a couple of vital details. Like his intense attraction to her. He'd hoped it had been a fluke, but when she'd opened the door just now, he'd seen that it hadn't been. At least he was doing a better job of controlling his reaction today than he had last week.

"I apologize for offending you. When Bonnie told me about you, I assumed you were an older woman. I hope you can understand my surprise when you walked into the kitchen."

"Even if I wasn't what you expected, I'm sure Miss Bonnie told you about my qualifications. I still don't understand why there would be a problem even if I'm considered *young* to you. I used to work in a day care. I worked in a nursery at a hospital taking care of newborns and I'm getting my PhD in child psychology. What else did you need, Sheriff?"

He had to tighten his lips to keep from saying he didn't need anything else, but it would help tremendously if she didn't look like a goddess. And then, as if things needed to get more interesting, his niece took hold of the front of Myra's sweater. That caused a dip in the fabric, exposing a generous portion of Myra's cleavage. He nearly swallowed his tongue when he said, "I don't need anything else. I think that would do it…if you're still interested."

She didn't say anything for a moment, like she was mulling it over, trying to decide. Then she said, "Yes, I'm still interested."

He felt relief at that. "Good. However, there are a few questions I need to ask to finish the interview process."

"Ask away."

"First, I want to offer my sympathy in regards to your parents. Bonnie told me what happened." He saw the sadness that appeared in her eyes. She and her parents must have been close. A cop was trained to read people even when they didn't want to be read.

"Thanks, Sheriff."

He wished he didn't have to ask the next question but there was no way around it. She needed to know what her working environment would be like. "You will need to move in with me for two months." He paused, deciding he didn't like the way that sounded. "Let me rephrase that."

"No need," she said, smiling. "I know what you meant. And yes, I'm aware that because of your un-orthodox work hours, I'll have to move into your place as a full-time nanny to Ciara. In fact, moving into your place works better for me."

He lifted his brow. "Why is that?"

"Because my lease on this place expires in a week, and I would have had to find someplace else to stay. I won't have to do that if I move into your place to take care of Ciara. Then around the time Miss Bonnie will be returning, I'll be heading back to South Carolina."

He nodded. She was right. It would work out well for her. That meant she would leave Denver around the holidays. She'd mentioned her birthday was on Christmas…just like his.

She shifted positions on the sofa and Ciara shifted with her, without taking her eyes off the flames in the fireplace. Funny, she'd never been so attentive to his fireplace. Then he saw the colorful flames emitting from the logs. He smiled his understanding about why such a thing was holding his niece's attention since it was now holding his.

"Did you know, Sheriff, that babies have the ability to recognize colors at eighteen months?" Evidently she noticed he was staring at the flames as much as Ciara.

He glanced back at her. "Is that a fact?"

"Yes. However, I suspect Ciara has a jump start since it's quite obvious she can detect colors now. I also suspect it won't be long before she notices similarities and differences in shapes, sizes and texture of objects."

He nodded again. "She's already begun talking and thinks I'm her daddy. She's even called Bonnie Momma a few times."

"Does that bother you? That she calls you Daddy?"

He had to be honest that yes, it did. "I don't ever want her to forget Matt and Sherry."

She shifted in her seat again, in a way where Ciara could still keep her gaze on the flames. "Can I be blunt with you, Sheriff?"

He nodded his head. "Yes."

"Chances are she's already forgotten them."

His jaw clenched and unclenched. He preferred she not say such a thing because he definitely refused to think it. "You don't know that."

A hint of sadness appeared in her eyes. "Yes, I do.

She was only three months old at the time of their accident, right?"

"Yes."

"Then what she remembers most is their scent."

Although he didn't want to agree with her, he knew what she said made sense. "Like I said, I don't want her to forget them."

"What you mean is that you want her to remember them."

As far as he was concerned, it meant the same thing. Evidently she didn't think so, but he refused to spar with her. Besides, there was one other thing they needed to cover before he felt totally comfortable hiring her.

"When Ciara gets older," she continued, "around three years old, that would be a good time to begin establishing her parents' likenesses into her memory with pictures. There's nothing wrong with her calling you Daddy. When she's old enough you can tell her the truth."

He didn't say anything for a moment. Instead of appreciating her insight, he resented it. He was hiring her as a nanny, not a social worker. He and Ciara would do just fine without her dotting every *i* and crossing every *t* for them.

"There's another matter I want to discuss with you."

"Oh?" she said, moving her gaze from his to smile down at Ciara. His niece had finally gotten bored of the fire and was glancing around the room. Myra Hollister held Ciara firmly in her arms and he was amazed that Ciara hadn't given her any pushback. Usually, she was ready to get on the floor and move around to see what she could get into. The Higgins household had gone through a lot of changes since his niece began walking three months ago.

"And what matter is that, Sheriff?"

"Our relationship." When he realized how that sounded, he quickly said, "Our *working* relationship. I think I need to define it."

He saw the way her brows scrunched up. "Why?"

Her words pretty much confirmed she honestly didn't have a clue. Maybe that was a good thing. But still, he needed to make sure they had an understanding about a few things.

"Why do you think you need to define our working relationship, Sheriff?" she asked again.

Pete drew in a deep breath. "We will be living under the same roof. I'm a single man and you're a single woman."

"And?"

"People might talk, Ms. Hollister."

She looked even more confused. "Why would they? I'm sure people around here know your profession. You're the sheriff. You're also the guardian to your niece. Why would anyone have anything to say about you hiring a temporary nanny until Miss Bonnie returns?"

He shifted in his seat. "Like I said. I'm single and so are you."

"So is Miss Bonnie."

Pete frowned. Was she deliberately being obtuse? "I've never had a *young*, single and beautiful woman living under my roof before."

She stared at him for a moment and then cocked a brow. "Although I don't consider myself one of those real proper Southern belles, I was raised to adhere to conservative protocols. Is there something about your reputation that I need to be concerned with, Sheriff?"

Her question threw him. "Why would you think that?"

"Because you're evidently worried about my reputation and what people will think with me living in your house."

Is that what she honestly thought? "I assure you there's nothing questionable about my character."

"And I assure you there's nothing questionable about mine. And as far as anyone suspecting something going on between us while we're living together, that is the craziest thing I've ever heard."

"And why is that?"

She rolled her eyes. "First of all, you're not my type. Second, you're older than anyone I normally would date."

Well, damn. She'd pretty much put him in his place by telling him she was not in the least attracted to him. There was only one thing he could say. "I'm glad because you're not my type either, and you're younger than the women I'd typically date."

"Great! Then we don't have anything to worry about. I honestly don't care what people might say or think about me living with you. However, if you're concerned about what they might say, then I suggest you find yourself another nanny."

Myra meant what she'd said, although she could understand why someone would think she could fall for the sheriff. After all, he was a very handsome man. Instead of being dressed like a lawman, today he was wearing jeans and a Western shirt. When she'd looked out the peephole and seen him earlier, standing on her doorstep, tall, broad shouldered, ruggedly built with a Stetson on his head, she'd drawn in a deep breath to slow her pulse. He was her idea of a Denver cowboy ready to go off and tame a bunch of wild broncos.

But the bottom line, handsome or not, she could not and would not be attracted to him. She could appreciate a man's good looks without losing her mind over him; especially an older, good-looking man, thanks to her bad experience with Rick.

But she couldn't deny the sensations that had gone off in her stomach when Pete had described her as young, single and beautiful. Did he really think she was beautiful? And why did the idea of him thinking such a thing give her a warm feeling? She couldn't let his words, or her reaction to them, go to her head.

Her time in Denver was limited and like she'd told him, she would be returning to Charleston in a couple of months. But she'd stay there just long enough to boot Baron out of the company and return Wallace to his rightful place as head of Hollister Enterprises. Then she intended to take a monthlong vacation in Paris. She would definitely deserve it.

"I see I've offended you again."

She glanced over at him and her stomach contracted. Why did he have to look regretful and sexy at the same time? "Yes, you have. I'm beginning to think you enjoy doing that."

"I assure you I don't. I just didn't want you caught off guard. You're new here and I know this town."

She nodded. "And I guess that means you have a reputation to uphold, and I understand that. Well, guess what? So do I. But obviously you think your reputation means a lot more than mine."

"I never said that."

No, he hadn't insinuated such a thing, but she also hadn't given much thought to them sleeping under the same roof until he'd made such a big deal out of it. "Like I said. If you're worried about what people think, then I'm not—"

"I'm not worried." He stood and she watched how he easily slid out of the chair to stand up to his six-three height. "You will work out fine if you still want the job."

He then offered her an amount that was a lot more than what she had figured on earning. That would certainly help keep her tucked away from Baron until she was ready to return home. "I accept your offer, Sheriff. Will I be expected to do laundry and cook, as well?"

He lifted a brow. "Can you cook?"

She lifted her chin. "I can hold my own. I can't cook as well as Miss Bonnie, but considering how *young* I am, Sheriff, I might surprise you."

"You're not going to let me forget about the big deal I made with your age, are you?"

"No time soon," she said, unable to hide her smile.

She looked down at the little girl she held in her arms, deliberating over placing her concentration on Ciara before she looked back at him. "But that's your hang-up, Sheriff. I'm sure you will get over it. I'm looking forward to taking care of Ciara until Miss Bonnie returns."

"I'm glad."

He smiled for the first time since she'd met him. All she should have seen was a friendly smile, but when his lips had curved, she was struck with a spike of feminine awareness. Why had his smile caused that reaction in her?

She didn't know. The best thing to do was to get rid of him to ponder the reason in private. She stood after putting on Ciara's coat, hat and mittens. "So, I guess that's it. I will be reporting to your place on Friday. That will give Miss Bonnie a chance to help me get acclimated to Ciara's schedule and my duties while she's gone."

"Do you need help moving out of here?" he asked, glancing around. She watched him while every hormone in her body seemed to sizzle. And all because he'd *smiled*?

"No, I don't need any help. Most things here belong to the owner, who is a college friend of mine. I just need to pack my clothes."

"Okay." The sheriff reached for Ciara and seemed disappointed when his niece's head dropped back against Myra's chest, as if she wasn't ready for Myra to relinquish her.

He tried again. "Come on, Ciara. We need to leave before the weather gets any worse."

When his words wouldn't budge his niece, he then said, "We'll have cookies to eat when we get there."

Evidently mentioning *cookies* had been the magic word since Ciara extended her arms out for him. The sheriff threw his head back and laughed while cradling Ciara close.

Myra's heart skipped, and she knew why. Baron had twin girls and he'd never shown them that much compassion. Yet he hadn't thought twice about threatening to take custody of them just to hurt Cleo.

"Looks like you know how to handle her, Sheriff Higgins."

He chuckled. "I do my best. And from here on out I prefer for you to call me Pete."

She nodded, swallowing the lump in her throat caused

by the deep, husky sound of his voice. "And please call me Myra. I'll see you to the door."

At the moment, she didn't care if it seemed as if she was rushing him out. Mainly because she was. All the man had done was smile. She didn't quite understand her reaction, and she was never good at dealing with unknowns.

But when they reached the door and Ciara looked at her beneath her fluffy little cap, Myra was a goner. In truth, the little girl had captured Myra's heart the minute Myra had held her. She refused to think about what could happen to Ciara if she was left with the wrong nanny. Unfortunately, not all nannies were dependable and competent.

"We will see you on Friday."

Myra met Pete's gaze over Ciara's cap. "Yes, you will see me Friday. I should arrive by noon."

"Good. We'll be waiting."

Once again his deep, husky voice played havoc with her ears, sped up her heartbeat and tempted her to close her eyes. Moments later when the pair had left and Myra had closed the door behind them, she leaned back against it and drew in a long, deep breath.

"I will *not* be attracted to Sheriff Peterson Higgins," she said aloud, issuing the command to her brain and expecting her body to cooperate. Opening her eyes, she drew in a deep breath, confident that her brain and body now understood each other.

Pete had barely made it inside his house before Bonnie began grilling him. "How did it go? Did she still want the job? Do you feel comfortable about her being here? Did you hire her?"

He placed his Stetson on the rack before turning with Ciara in his arms. Bonnie didn't waste any time taking his niece from him.

"Things went well, and yes, yes and yes to your other questions."

Bonnie smiled. "I knew things would be all right once you talked to her yourself."

Pete wasn't sure things would be all right, but he'd gotten tired of unintentionally offending Myra and figured he needed to stop while he was ahead. Bottom line, she was qualified to take care of Ciara and anything else would be up to him to keep in check. He knew now more than ever that doing such a thing wouldn't be easy. Sharing space with her even with Ciara with them had been hard. He'd been aware of every breath and every move. How would he handle her being here with him in this house alone?

If anything, what she'd told him should help. He wasn't her type and was too old for her liking. He shouldn't be offended by her comment since he was the one who'd made such a big deal of the age thing. But he had news for her; the twelve-year difference in their ages didn't mean a damn thing. Bonnie had reminded him that his own father had been ten years older than his mom, and old man Arnold was fifteen years older than Ms. Viola and they'd been married for close to seventy years.

Pete wondered why he was wasting so much thought on this issue. The important thing was that he and Myra had an understanding. Well, sort of. Deep down he believed she felt the entire subject had been ridiculous since she wasn't the least bit interested in him, and he shouldn't be the least bit interested in her.

But he was, though. The best thing to do when she moved in was to stay out of her way and make sure she stayed out of his. His home didn't have split levels. His master suite was at the end of a long hall and Myra should have no reason to venture that far down the hall since the bedroom she would be using had its own private bath and Ciara's room was next door to hers. There was another guest room and his office next to Ciara's room.

On the other hand, he would have to walk down the hall and pass by both bedrooms to get to the living room and other parts of the house.

"When will Myra be moving in?"

"We agreed on Friday. That will give you time to pack and take care of things you need to handle at your place since you'll be gone for a while. If you need me to do anything while you're gone, let me know."

"I will and I appreciate it." Bonnie glanced down at Ciara who'd fallen asleep in her arms. "Let me lay her down. It's not even her nap time yet. What did you do to her to tire her out?"

"I didn't do anything. In fact, once she saw Myra Hollister, Ciara forgot I was alive."

Bonnie chuckled. "You sound jealous."

Did he? Was he? Possibly. He wasn't used to Ciara being so taken with anyone she wasn't accustomed to seeing on a regular basis. "I have no reason to be jealous, Bonnie."

"Oh, by the way," Bonnie said as she headed down the hall, "Zane's here checking on the horses. Told me to tell you he would stop by before leaving."

"Fine." Zane was one of Derringer's older brothers. Although he was a married man now, Zane once had a reputation as one of Denver's most notorious woman-izers. But then so had Derringer and Riley. Only differ-ence was that Zane's reputation had been a lot worse. He'd also been dubbed an expert when it came to women and was known to give out advice on the topic.

Pete removed his jacket before walking over to the window. Snowfall was predicted tonight. He couldn't wait until Ciara got older and he could build a snow-man with her like he'd done with Matt while growing up. Those had been fun times when both of their parents had been alive and their only worry was making sure their homework was done before going to bed.

He saw a movement out the window and recognized Zane walking toward the house. Zane, Derringer and their cousin Jason were partners in a lucrative horse breeding and training business, along with several of their Westmoreland cousins living in Montana and Texas. The partnership was doing extremely well fi-nancially, with horse buyers extending all the way to the Middle East. One of their horses, Prince Charm-ing, had placed in the Kentucky Derby a few years ago. Since then, potential clients had been coming out of the woodwork in droves. As a result, they'd needed more land to hold the horses. Since Pete had more property than he knew what to do with, he'd leased a portion of it to the Westmorelands.

Pete had never sought out Zane for advice on the topic of women before, but maybe he should run this situation regarding Myra by Zane. Hell, doing so couldn't hurt.

Myra glanced around her bedroom. Although she had four days to pack, there was no use waiting until later.

Like she'd told Pete, she didn't have much stuff and the majority of her items could fit into her luggage.

Pete.

She couldn't stop remembering the exact moment he'd suggested she call him Pete instead of Sheriff. She knew his real name was Peterson but that he had been called Pete since he was a baby. That information had come from Miss Bonnie, who'd told her a lot about him.

Myra also knew he'd been engaged once and his girl-friend from high school had died just weeks before their wedding. She'd been participating in a local parade when she was thrown off her horse.

Myra had been saddened by the story and a part of her heart had gone out to the man who'd lost the love of his life so close to their wedding day. That had been twelve years ago and she wondered if he was now seriously involved with anyone.

She picked up her phone when it began ringing, recognized the ringtone. "Hello, Bella."

"Myra, how are you?"

"I'm fine. What about you?"

"Doing okay but I hear there will be a snowstorm beginning tonight. I hope you're prepared," Bella said.

"I am. Besides, staying inside will give me a chance to work on my thesis."

"How is that coming?"

"Great. I'm hoping to turn it in around this time next year."

"That's outstanding. Another reason I'm calling is to invite you to the Westmorelands' chow-down on Friday night."

"Oh, thanks for thinking of me again, but I'm moving on Friday."

"Moving?"

"Yes. I've been hired to be Sheriff Higgins's temporary nanny while Miss Bonnie is away."

"That's wonderful. You'll be perfect, and Pete will go to work each day knowing Ciara is in good hands. The girls will be disappointed not to see you on Friday."

Myra laughed when she thought of Bella and Jason's twins. She had won them over, along with a few other Westmoreland kids, with her magic tricks when she'd attended their Friday night chow-down a few weeks ago.

"Well, I'm going to have to pay them a visit once I get settled at the Higgins place. Then I can bring Ciara along."

"Oh, they will enjoy that, and we'll look forward to your visit."

"So, what's on your mind, Pete?"

Pete glanced over at Zane Westmoreland, whose long legs were stretched out in front of him as he took a sip of his beer. His wife, Channing, was expecting their first child and yet Zane had just finished telling Pete that *Zane* was the one craving stuff.

"I need your expert advice on something."

Zane lifted a brow. "What?"

"Not sure if you heard that Bonnie's sister has cancer and she needs to be in Texas for about two months."

"Yes, Bonnie mentioned it when I first got here. I told her that I was sorry to hear that."

"Her leaving means I have to hire a nanny until she returns. I found one, a woman name Myra Hollister, but I detected possible problems."

Zane raised a brow. "What kind of problems?"

"She's a very beautiful woman."

Zane nodded. "I met Myra a couple of weeks ago when Bella invited her to one of the Westmoreland chow-downs, and you're right, she's a beautiful woman. She's also single and so are you, so what's the problem?"

"She's younger than me by twelve years."

"And?"

Pete took a sip of his own beer. "I want things to remain professional between us while she's living here."

Zane lifted a brow. "Why wouldn't they? Or, why *should* they if you're attracted to her?"

Pete frowned. "Who said I was attracted to her?"

Zane chuckled and then shook his head. "Oh, you want to be one of those, do you?"

"One of what?"

"A man in denial."

"I'll admit to being attracted to her. A little."

"A little?" Zane shook his head, ginning.

"What if I told you that she's not interested in me?"

"And how do you know that?"

Pete took another sip of his beer. "I warned her that people might talk, with her being young and single and living under my roof. She told me not to worry about it since I wasn't her type and that I'm older than the men she would normally date."

Zane snorted. "At twenty-four she's probably not sure what type of man is her type, and maybe it's time for her to date men your age to see what she's been missing. If I were you, I'd see that as a challenge and prove her wrong on both accounts."

"Why would I want to do something like that?"

The room was quiet for a moment and then Zane said, "You know what I think your real problem is, Pete?"

In a way, Pete was afraid to ask because the great

know-it-all-about-women Zane Westmoreland was known to tell it like it was and not sugarcoat anything. "What?"

"Your problem is denial, plain and simple. You desire the woman, so admit it and stop trying to fight it."

Pete didn't say anything, then he said, "I have to fight it, Zane."

"Why?"

"Because I don't want it. I'm not ready for it."

Zane frowned. "I'm sure you've dated and desired women before, Pete."

He nodded. "This is different." He met Zane's intense gaze for a long moment and only someone who knew him as well as Zane did would feel the depth of his turmoil.

"Ellen would want you to move on with your life, Pete."

If another person told him that, Pete would be tempted to ram his fist into the nearest wall. "You don't know that."

"I do know it and I'm wondering why in the hell you don't. Have you forgotten that Ellen used to be one of Megan's best friends? She hung around our place just as often as you did. She was a wonderful girl who didn't have a selfish bone in her body. There's no way she wouldn't want you to move on with your life. I think the problem is one you're bringing on yourself."

Zane took another sip of his beer and then added, "Apparently Myra Hollister is capable of making you want to move on and—"

"Hey, wait a minute. Things aren't that serious. We're talking about an attraction and nothing more."

Zane shook his head. "But there *is* more, Pete. Attraction and desire aren't the same. A man doesn't desire every woman he's attracted to."

When Pete didn't say anything, Zane said, "If you're trying to stop desiring her, don't bother."

"Why?"

"Because you can't get rid of something you won't acknowledge having. You have a thing for the woman, so admit it. You desire her, too, so admit that, as well. And if you don't want either, then don't hire her as your nanny because the more you're around her, the more you're going to desire her."

Pete met Zane's gaze. "Too late. I have hired her." He paused a moment and then said, "I don't want chaos in my life, Zane."

Zane drew in a deep breath. "Any chaos will be of your own making. Desiring a woman is a healthy part of being a man, Pete. If you want to waste those emotions, go ahead. Doing so won't eliminate this problem you have but will only increase it. If she stays here and you try to fight your desire, then eventually you're going to snap."

Pete frowned. "I'm a lawman—I don't snap."

"You're a man first and you will snap." Zane stood. "I'm going to give you the same advice I gave myself a few years ago."

"What?"

"Stop trying to fight emotions you're supposed to be feeling. Sooner or later you're going to have to accept there's a reason Myra Hollister has the ability to make you feel things that other women can't."

Chapter 3

Myra slowed her car and took a deep breath when she came to the marker for the Golden Glade Ranch. She thought the same thing now that she'd thought when she came this way for her initial interview. Sheriff Pete Higgins's ranch was simply magnificent.

It sat on what she figured to be over two hundred acres of land. On one side of the ranch house were rows and rows of pear trees, which fared surprisingly well in Denver's cold weather. On the other side she saw herds of beautiful horses running in a gated area.

Inwardly, she asked herself—for the umpteenth time since putting the last piece of her luggage inside the car—if she was making the right move. Now it went beyond just her personal finances. She was dealing with her peace of mind. A part of her had hoped Wallace would call so she could tell him the change of plans. That she'd been hired as a nanny after all. Then she would tell him about her misgivings.

Knowing Wallace like she did, he would probably find it amusing that she had finally met someone who interested her...even though she felt the man *shouldn't* interest her. Not only was it bad timing, it was a bad situation all around.

It was days like this that she missed her parents more than ever because she would have talked to them, as well. They had never tried forcing her to date anyone. What made her happy had made them happy and she'd appreciated that.

This would be her first holiday season without them and instead of celebrating like she knew they'd want her to do even without them, she would be returning to Charleston to fight her brother for the company he was trying to take away from her.

As she continued down the long drive, her thoughts returned to her present predicament, which was being nanny to Ciara. It would only last two months, and chances were Pete would be gone most of the time. After all, he was the sheriff of Denver. And when he was at home, they probably wouldn't see each other much.

If she really believed that, then why was she feeling like she was about to have an anxiety attack?

Finally, she brought her car to a stop in front of Pete's home and drew in a deep breath. She would take care of Ciara and then she would be gone. Why was she suddenly feeling like these would be the longest two months of her life?

Pete was convinced that when it came to women, they had a language all their own. And it was one they'd de-

liberately created so a man couldn't understand. He'd
always thought that while hanging around the Westmoreland ladies. Now he was even more convinced, seeing
how Bonnie and Myra interacted. He had a feeling that
if Ciara was older, she would be right there, too.

Just like she'd said she would do, Myra had arrived
at lunchtime. He'd been standing at the window staring
out when he'd seen her car pull up. He wouldn't deny it;
he'd been waiting for her. Mainly to help with any items
she might need to get out of the car. At least that was
the lame excuse he'd told himself. She hadn't needed
help and the one piece of huge luggage had been easy
for her to roll inside. He had looked forward to helping
her get settled and showing her around, but Bonnie had
appeared. She'd let him know she would be showing
Myra around and that he wasn't needed.

He had escaped to the basement where his man cave
was located, although now it mostly resembled a baby
cave. Ciara's toys, along with her playpen and swing,
took up a lot of the room. Derringer had recommended
the swing. It was great on those days when a football
game was on. All Pete had to do was wind it up every
twenty minutes. And thanks to Flipper, one of Bane
Westmoreland's Navy SEAL friends, who was a master diver and a tech wiz, Pete had a remote for Ciara's
swing. He could rewind the swing without moving off
the sofa. How sweet was that?

However, today Pete wanted to move around. Specifically, he wanted to go upstairs to the main floor to
see what was going on. Footsteps were constantly grat-
ing across the ceiling and he figured Bonnie was showing Myra around. It was his house so shouldn't he be
doing that?

He glanced over at Ciara in the swing. She looked like she didn't have a care in the world. She didn't. She wouldn't. Not even when she reached the age of twenty-one, thanks to the trust fund he and her grandparents had established from the proceeds of her parents' insurance policies.

She did look sleepy, though. Maybe he should take her upstairs and put her down for her nap. Pete rubbed a hand across his face. It was pathetic that he was looking for any excuse to leave the comfort of his man cave and go upstairs to see Myra Hollister.

If he didn't know any better, he'd think it was a deliberate ploy of Bonnie's, to keep him separated from Myra. Had Bonnie picked up on his attraction to Myra again today? Had she felt the heat while he watched Myra get out of her car wearing a pair of skinny jeans, knee boots and a dark gray pullover sweater? She'd looked good. Too good. If he hadn't been desperately in need of a nanny, he would have backed out of the arrangement. Too late. The plans were finalized. Myra would be in his home, under his roof, sleeping in the bedroom down the hall from his, starting tonight.

Over the next two months he would try like hell not to notice her. Other than being courteous when he saw her, he would pretend she didn't exist. Her goal was to take care of his niece. His was to bury his head in the sand and refuse to acknowledge he was attracted to her.

That he desired her.

There, he had admitted it. According to Zane, the first step in fighting your desire for a woman was admitting it. Until just now, Pete had refused to do so. But it had become clear to him when she'd gotten out of the car today.

How could he desire a woman this much? He wished he could blame it on something he ate or drank, or on his lack of sleep. He knew it was none of those things.

When he heard footsteps coming down the stairs to the basement, he quickly straightened up on the sofa, rested his arms on his thighs and leaned toward the huge flat-screen television on his wall. He needed to present the impression that the football game had been holding his attention for the past hour and a half.

Glancing over at Ciara, he saw she was wide-awake and looking at him. If he didn't know better, he would have said she'd known what he'd been thinking a few moments ago. He was tempted to say, *Yeah, kid, your uncle wants your nanny, but she's off-limits and needs to stay that way, so don't worry—I got this.*

"Peterson?"

He cringed. Why was Bonnie calling him by his full name again? Heck, he hadn't done anything. She had no idea about the naughty thoughts that had crossed his mind. If she had, she would have reminded him Myra was there for Ciara and not for him.

He turned to the two women, giving them a look as if he was annoyed being interrupted. "Yes?" he said, standing to his feet.

Bonnie gave him the same kind of look his niece had given him just seconds ago. It was one of those I'm-onto-you looks. "I've shown Myra around and will leave you to cover the rest."

The rest? What else is there? Instead of asking, he said, "All right. I can do that."

"Great! I'll put Ciara down for her nap while you do." Bonnie took Ciara out of the swing.

"I would hate to interrupt you watching the game," Myra said.

He looked at her and wished he hadn't. Standing in the middle of his man cave she looked like that was where she belonged. That didn't make sense. They called it a man cave for a reason. Women didn't belong.

"No problem. My team is so far ahead I doubt the Gators can make a comeback."

She crossed her arms over her chest and frowned at him. "I guess that means you're for the Buckeyes."

"Yes, that's what it means."

"Too bad. I'm Florida all the way."

He lifted a brow. A woman who liked football? "That's too bad."

"We'll see."

Bonnie chuckled. "I think the two of you need to take it outside, and while you're out there, Pete, please show her around."

"Yes, ma'am." He watched Bonnie climb the stairs with a sleeping Ciara in her arms. He then turned back to Myra. "After you."

He couldn't help feasting his gaze on her curvy thighs and delectable-looking backside in her jeans as she climbed the stairs. Drawing in a deep breath, he gave himself a second to compose himself before he followed.

"All this land is yours?" Myra asked, glancing over at Pete.

He nodded. "Yes, every single acre we covered is mine. All two hundred of them. My great-grandfather bought it back in the early nineteen hundreds. He, Raphel Westmoreland and another man by the name of Titus Newsome all settled here together."

Pete had given her a walking tour of the area around his house, which included a huge barn and several smaller houses. They had saddled up and were now on horseback, covering the outer areas. He told her he leased the majority of his property to others, preferring to spend his time on law enforcement.

"How close are you to the Westmoreland property?" she asked him when they brought the horses to a stop near a creek.

She looked at him and there was that smile again, the one that curved his lips while making her acutely aware of him as a man. He sat beside her on his horse, a huge chocolate-brown bronco he called Satin, and she knew why. His coat was so smooth and shiny it looked like satin. Although she'd assured Pete that she was a pretty good rider, he'd still given her a docile mare named Tally. She'd tried keeping her eyes off Pete during the ride, but he looked more cowboy than sheriff today, wearing a Stetson, sitting on the back of a horse.

"Do you see the roof of that house through the trees?"

She leaned forward and squinted. "Yes, I see it."

"That was the Newsome property. In a way it still is since Dillon Westmoreland's youngest brother, Bane, married Crystal Newsome. The Westmoreland spread begins where the Newsome property ends. However, because of the shape of my property, there is Westmoreland land that backs up to my line in the north pasture. That's owned by Riley Westmoreland and he's built a monstrosity of a house there. The Westmorelands own so much land in this area that we call it Westmoreland Country. I'm just a neighbor."

She heard what Pete said but knew he was more than

just a neighbor. "I heard you're best friend to both Derringer and Riley Westmoreland."

He chuckled. "Boy, how did I get so lucky?"

She smiled. "I've met most of the Westmorelands."

"I understand you've been to one of their chow-downs."

"Yes. I enjoyed myself. They were kind and there are so many of them."

"Yes, they're a huge family. I'm close to all of them since we grew up together. I can recall clearly the day the cousins' parents died. I was hanging out with Derringer when he got the news."

Myra could just imagine. She knew how hard it was to lose both parents, but to lose your parents and your aunt and uncle at the same time had to have been devastating for all of them.

They continued riding and he showed her a lake on his property. "This was originally called Magnolia Lake, but Derringer's great-grandfather Raphel renamed it after the woman he loved, Gemma. Now it's Gemma Lake and it runs through the properties owned by five neighbors."

"Why did the landowners keep the name?"

"I'm told Raphel Westmoreland wasn't the only one who loved Ms. Gemma. Everybody in these parts did. She had a big heart."

"Thanks for giving me such a personalized tour." Myra checked her watch. They'd been gone for almost two hours.

"You're welcome. You'll be here two months so it's good that you know your way around. Even when I'm at work I'll only be a phone call away. Ciara is my family.

I want to do right by her and take care of her the way I know my brother would want."

Myra nodded as they trotted their horses back toward the ranch. "You and your brother were close."

"Yes. Extremely close. When our parents died, all we had left was each other. I was four years older than Matt, and he thought I was his hero. I tried not to let him down."

"I'm sure you didn't."

He didn't say anything for a moment, then, "I understand you have an older brother."

She wondered where he'd gotten that information. It wasn't something she had mentioned to anyone in Denver. But then, she figured she didn't have to mention it. Pete was the top cop in Denver. Regardless of Miss Bonnie's recommendations, he would still check her out. She couldn't blame him. She was thankful a routine background check wouldn't tell him everything. It would definitely not reveal her deep, dark family secrets. She knew publicly Baron was trying hard to make it seem like their relationship was a close one. It was just the opposite. Definitely nothing like the one Pete had had with his brother.

"We're okay," she finally said. "He's my father's son from another marriage and because his mother was always bitter about my father divorcing her, she tried turning Baron against Dad."

Why had she told him all that? She could have easily lied. Not wanting to think about Baron, but feeling the need to keep the conversation flowing between her and Pete, she said, "I understand Ciara's grandparents found it difficult to keep her."

"Yes, and after having her here with me for almost

six months I can see why. They're an older couple and Ciara can be a handful. Their intentions were good but I'm glad they decided to bring her to me."

He didn't say anything for a minute and then added, "Granted I wasn't in the best position to take on a baby either, but thanks to friends and Bonnie, I made it work. I had a lot to learn. I am still learning. Ciara keeps me on my toes and you will see there is never a dull moment around her. It seems she learns something new every day."

Myra could feel the love he had for his niece in his words. "I don't want you to worry when you're away. I will take good care of her."

"And that's all I ask."

And she had no problem doing what he asked. She enjoyed Denver, and she was far from Baron's ruthlessness.

He had teamed up with Charlene's present lover, who had somehow convinced him that if he kept Myra away that he could run the company without interference from her. Thanks to her sister-in-law, Cleo, who'd overheard the two men talking, Myra knew of those plans. And she knew about how he'd planned to get Rick to help him keep Myra away.

Did Baron really think she would let Rick back into her life? Still, she didn't need drama in her life. That was when Myra decided to leave without Baron knowing where she'd gone. Her plan was to return after her birthday when she could take over the company. With the help of friends, she'd faked a trip to Europe and that was where Baron was presently looking for her. She was safe as long as he continued to be misled. She'd been careful about using a new phone and not using her credit cards.

"Ciara and I are dining with the Westmorelands later.

It's chow-down Friday," he said. "I would ask if you want to go but I'm sure you have a lot of unpacking to do."

There was no need to tell him about Bella's invitation, which she had turned down for that very reason. Besides, Myra was certain the only reason he'd mentioned it was to be nice. "You're right, I need to unpack."

Moments later, when they walked back inside the ranch house, they could smell Bonnie cooking dinner in the kitchen. "Did you forget to tell her that you and Ciara are going to the Westmorelands for dinner?"

He removed his Stetson to put it on the rack by the door. He looked at her with his eyes a charismatic shade of brown.

"I told her, but it wouldn't matter with Bonnie. Besides, you have to eat. Any leftovers go to the freezer for another day."

A loud cheer made them look toward the kitchen to see Bonnie appear with Ciara in her arms. "Down Bon-Bon," Ciara said, trying to wiggle out of Bonnie's arms.

Bonnie placed her on the floor and the baby happily raced across the room to them. As if she couldn't decide which of the two she wanted, she grabbed hold of one of each of their legs. But it was Pete who she smiled up at. "Up, Da-da." Laughing, he leaned down and picked up her, placing her atop his shoulders.

Myra had thought Pete's smile from earlier was mesmerizing but the one covering his face now was so captivating it nearly took her breath away. To breathe she had to look away. Glancing across the room, she looked at Bonnie, who seemed to be watching her and Pete with considerable interest.

Myra cleared her throat. "Do you need my help with anything, Miss Bonnie?"

Bonnie smiled. "No, I'm almost finished. Besides, now that your tour of the place is over you probably want to unpack."

"Yes, I need to do that."

"Before putting the food away, Bonnie, make sure you leave some out for Myra."

Bonnie lifted a brow and shifted her gaze from Pete to Myra. "Aren't you going with them to the Westmorelands?"

Myra shook her head. "No, I need to unpack and get settled. You're still going back to your place tomorrow, right?"

Bonnie shook her head. "No, I plan on returning to my place tonight."

"Tonight? I thought you were staying until tomorrow evening," Pete said, and Myra could tell he was just as surprised as she was. When Miss Bonnie had given her the tour, she'd said she wouldn't be returning to her place until late tomorrow.

"Yes, that had been my plan, but I got a call that one of my church members is sick. I want to check on her before I leave. Besides, I have no doubt in my mind that Myra is capable of handling things until I return."

Myra appreciated the vote of confidence. "Thanks, Miss Bonnie."

Myra glanced over at Pete at the same moment he looked at her. Their gazes collided and she felt a whoosh of air leave her lungs at the same time she heard him draw in a sharp breath.

Had she imagined it?

He quickly broke eye contact with her and asked Bonnie, "Do you know who won the game?"

Bonnie smiled. "Derringer did call to see if you were

licking your wounds so I guess that means your team lost."

"Yes!" Myra said, clapping her hands. "Go Gators!" She couldn't help but laugh when Pete gave her a not-so-nice glare. "Sore loser, Sheriff Higgins?"

"You win some and you lose some. In the end, my team will win more than lose. I can't say the same for your team."

Myra fought back a grin. "We'll see about that, won't we?"

"Yes, we will." And with Ciara still sitting on his shoulders, he moved toward the hall leading to his bedroom.

Pete placed Ciara in the playpen he had set up in his room. They spent a lot of time in here or in his man cave whenever Bonnie returned home and it was just the two of them. Because his bedroom was so spacious, the playpen didn't take up much of the room, although it was plenty big enough for his niece to enjoy herself.

He shook his head, grinning as he recalled Myra's re-action to hearing her team had won…and his had lost. Most women weren't into football so having someone to watch the games with would be…

He paused in the process of unbuttoning his shirt. What in the world was he thinking? They would not be watching football games together. He could just imag-ine sitting beside her on the sofa, sharing a beer or iced tea. He shook his head. That wouldn't be happening. He had to make sure their relationship remained as it should be. He was the employer and she was the em-ployee. This house was her workplace and taking care of his niece was her job.

With that thought firmly planted in his head, he glanced over at his niece. She was playing with her blocks so he went into the bathroom to strip and shower. It had taken a lot of getting used to having Ciara here with him. He'd had to learn how to dress her, undress her, feed her, entertain her. Hell, he even sang to her before she went to sleep at night. He still thought the hardest thing he'd had to do was change her soiled diapers. It still was and he couldn't wait until she was completely potty trained. He knew Bonnie had been working on that, and Ciara was catching on but wasn't totally there yet. He hoped Bonnie had told Myra to continue the training during the time she would be away.

Myra.

As he stepped into the shower and moved beneath the spray of the water, he admitted she looked good sitting astride a horse. He figured she'd gone to riding school. That was pretty obvious by the graceful way she'd held the reins. Tally, the mare he'd selected for her to ride, had liked her. He could tell. Even Satin had liked her and usually his bad-tempered horse didn't like anyone. But Satin had let Myra touch him without trying to bite her fingers off. Amazing.

He would admit that at one point, when she'd picked up speed as if to get Tally to go faster, he'd panicked, hoping she wouldn't try to race the horse anywhere. All he could think about was Ellen. Granted, a human element had caused her accident. Nevertheless, the memories still managed to invade his mind, causing him concern.

Getting out of the shower, Pete dried off and slid into the clothes he'd taken out to wear to dinner at the

Westmorelands. For years he'd had an open invitation to their chow-downs. However, he'd never made a habit of going because of work hours. And then, when the brothers and cousins began meeting women, falling in love and marrying, he preferred not to constantly be around a bunch of happily married people. Although he was happy for his friends, being around married couples only reminded him of what he would never have. What had been taken from him.

Because Ciara should be around kids sometimes, he'd tried to attend the dinners at least once a month. That way she could play with the Westmoreland babies. There was quite a number of them and nobody seemed to be slowing down. Derringer had told Pete the other day that he and Lucia were having another baby and Riley and his wife, Alpha, had announced baby news, as well. It would be their first. But the biggest news had come from the youngest member of the Westmorelands, Derringer's sister Bailey. She presently lived in Alaska with her husband. Bailey had called the family yesterday to let everyone know that she and her husband, Walker, would be having their first child in late spring.

Pete shook his head, finding it hard to believe that Bailey Westmoreland, former holy terror, was having a baby. Hell, he was still reeling at the thought that she'd settled down and married.

He glanced over at Ciara. She was still playing with her blocks. Then, as if she felt his presence, she glanced over at him and smiled. He smiled back and winked at her. She tried imitating what he'd done and instead she blinked both eyes, then laughed at herself. He couldn't help but throw his head back and laugh, too.

It had taken some getting used to, but he would readily admit that his niece had become the brightest part of his life.

Chapter 4

Myra closed the dresser drawer and glanced around. She had finally finished unpacking and had put all her things away. This bedroom was larger than the master suite of the house she'd been leasing the past few months. The huge window provided a stunning view of the mountains.

Another thing she liked about the room, in addition to its close proximity to Ciara's room, was the huge four-poster bed that reminded her of the one that had been in her parents' home. She sighed wearily. That was another thing she had to do when she returned to Charleston. Reclaim her parents' home. It was hers, but of course Baron felt he had every right to be there.

She had contacted her attorney, who had sent him a certified letter advising him that he needed to vacate the premises by the end of the year and that everything on the inventory sheet better be accounted for. She could just imagine what his reaction would be when he got the letter. Honestly, it wasn't her problem.

She glanced at the clock. A couple of hours had passed since Pete had left for the Westmorelands, taking Ciara with him. He had dressed his niece and bundled her up for the cold weather. He had knocked on Myra's bedroom door to let her know they were leaving. She had placed a kiss on the little girl's cheek and told her she would be there when they returned.

"And you're sure you don't want to go?" he'd asked her.

"Positive," had been her quick response. "I've still got a lot to do here." Truly, she didn't, but the last thing she wanted to do was ride in the same car with Pete Higgins anywhere. Being on a horse beside him had been bad enough.

"Then we'll see you when we get back," he'd said, before heading down the hall and out the door.

He hadn't said when that would be but she knew from attending one of those Westmoreland dinners that they could last for a long time, well into the night if the men decided on a poker game. She recalled Pete saying he would be working tomorrow so chances were, he wouldn't be participating in any card game. And she'd discovered that when it came to his niece, he was very considerate of her needs. He would probably want her sleeping in her own bed at a reasonable hour.

Leaving her bedroom, Myra walked down the hall stopping in front of a bulletin board. Bonnie had explained this board held the numbers of those to call in case of an emergency. There were also photos tacked to the board. One was a group photo. Bonnie had told her the photo had been taken the night Pete had taken custody of Ciara. She recognized members of the Westmorelands that she had met, and Bonnie had pointed out Bane's friends and their wives, as well as Westmorelands from Atlanta, Montana and Texas, and their newfound cousins, the Outlaws from Alaska.

Moving away from the wall, she continued down the long hall until she came to the living area. It made her feel good knowing there were some families, like Pete's and the Westmorelands, where family meant something. It was sad that her brother's greed was the driving force behind everything he did.

Myra had just sat down on the sofa and grabbed the remote when the front door opened. Pete entered the house with a sleeping Ciara in his arms. Myra stood. "You guys are back."

He nodded. "Ciara can't keep her eyes open past eight, which is fine since I need to get in bed, as well. I have to be to work at six."

She moved to take Ciara from him and was surprised when he drew back. "I've got her. On those days when I'm off, I like doing everything for her. I guess you can say it's our uncle and niece time."

"Oh, okay. Just call me if you need me."

"Sure thing." He headed down the hall with a sleeping Ciara in his arms.

He didn't call her and when some time passed, she figured he'd gone to bed himself. Then he reappeared, walking into the living room with his shirt out of his jeans and in his bare feet. She tried not to study his masculine build.

Before she could say anything, he said, "She woke

up when I got her jammies on and got fussy. I ended up rocking her and singing her back to sleep."

An image of Pete, in that rocking chair in Ciara's room, touched Myra even more.

"What did you sing?" she asked, wanting to know.

He chuckled. "Well, it wasn't your typical lullaby, that's for certain. It was a Michael Jackson tune."

"Which one?" When he told her, she asked, "Oh. What made you decide on that one?"

Was she imaging things or was his gaze focused on her mouth? Specifically, her lips. Or did she only think that because her gaze was focused on *his* lips?

He slid into the recliner chair across from the sofa. "Matt was a big Michael Jackson fan. I remember visiting him when Ciara was not even a month old. A part of me was proud of how well he'd perfected the role of daddy."

He paused as if remembering that time. "Every night before putting her to bed, he'd rock her to sleep singing that MJ song. When I asked him why he'd selected that particular song, he said that because of his job in the army, there would be times when he would be gone away from her. Depending on the assignment, it could be for long stretches of time. That song was his way of letting her know that no matter where he went, or how long he'd be gone, she would never be alone because a part of him would always be with her."

Myra fought back tears while imagining Pete's brother conveying his love to his daughter that way. She could tell the memories touched Pete and she appreciated him sharing them with her.

The room was quiet before he said, "Whenever I sing that MJ song to Ciara, it's as if she's remembering Matt singing it to her. She settles down and quickly drifts off to sleep."

Myra didn't say anything. She couldn't with the hard lump she felt in her throat. "I think that's special, Pete," she was finally able to say.

He raised a brow. "Do you?"

Why did he sound unconvinced? "Yes."

"Why? Aren't you the one who told me just the other day that Ciara won't remember her parents?"

She heard the bitterness in his voice. "Yes, but that's just visually. Auditory memory is another story. That's why pregnant women often read to babies who're in their wombs, talk to them, play music to them. Babies can relate to sound. I'm sorry if I gave you the impression Ciara wouldn't remember anything about her parents."

He stood. "No harm done." Then, as if he wanted to not only change the subject, but also to end conversation between them completely, he said, "If I don't have an unusually busy day tomorrow, I should be home by five."

He was so tall that she had to tilt her head back to look at him. "Okay, Pete. Ciara and I will be here waiting."

Too late she realized how that had sounded. "What I meant is that we—"

"I know what you meant, Myra. I'll see you tomorrow. Good night."

"Good night, Pete."

Myra watched him walk out of the room. She practically held her breath until she heard the door close behind him.

"Well, do you believe me now, Sheriff?"

Pete studied the image on the mini video recorder. It wasn't the best quality, but it served the older woman's purpose. For months she'd claimed a ghost was try-ing to scare her out of her home. Of course, since there wasn't any such thing as ghosts, he'd figured the eighty-four-year-old woman was just seeing things. However, when she'd called today, he'd told his deputies he would go visit Ms. Katherine. The last thing he had expected was proof.

"How did you get this?" he asked.

"That boy who cuts my grass, Olson Thomas's teen-age grandson. He set up the recorder for me." She gave him an I-told-you-so smile. "What do you say to that?"

Honestly, Pete didn't know what to say. But he was still certain that no matter what the video showed, there was no such thing as ghosts. "I'm going to need to keep this and have the lab analyze it. In the meantime, I need to take a look around."

"Certainly, Sheriff. And how is that pretty little niece of yours?"

He smiled at the older woman who he'd known all his life. "Ciara is doing fine. Thanks for asking."

"I understand Bonnie had to leave unexpectedly and you have a temporary nanny."

"Yes, that's right."

"Have you noticed just how pretty she is?"

Pete smiled. "I notice just how pretty my niece is every time I see her."

The older woman frowned. "I am not talking about your niece, Sheriff."

He held back a chuckle. "Then I can't imagine who's prettier than my niece."

"What about that woman staying with you?"

He met her gaze. "Oh. You mean my temporary

nanny who's living with me to take care of Ciara?" he asked, feeling the need to establish the facts.

"Yes, that's the one."

He nodded. "You think she's pretty?"

"Yes."

He shrugged. "I hadn't noticed."

Thirty minutes later he left Ms. Katherine's house even more baffled. When he'd seen the video, he'd figured it had been a couple of neighborhood teens. Everyone knew of her claim of seeing ghosts. Now, after walking around her backyard, he wasn't 100 percent sold on that theory. He hadn't seen a single footprint.

When he came to a stop sign, he recalled how Ms. Katherine had tried goading him about Myra. When he'd told Myra people would talk about them living under the same roof, Ms. Katherine had headed that list.

As he turned the corner to head back toward his office, he thought about his live-in nanny. It had been a little over three weeks since Myra had moved into his place and so far, so good. They had established a routine where he pretty much avoided her when he got home from work. He'd also put an end to his drop-in visits at home for lunch.

Myra would have dinner prepared, and he'd been surprised what a good cook she was. Granted she was into cooking healthy foods. Instead of frying chicken, she would bake it, and he was eating more salads and fewer starches. She also served herbal tea in place of sweet iced tea. He'd decided not to complain and now he'd gotten used to it. He left the table with his stomach full. After dinner he would get his niece and take her with him to the man cave. Evidently, Myra thought the basement was off-limits since she never ventured down there. Then around seven, he would return upstairs and give Ciara to Myra to get her ready for bed.

Later he would meet them in Ciara's room where he would rock and sing his niece to sleep. Afterward, he would retire to his own room, shower and go to bed. He made it a point to get up and leave for work before Myra got up the next morning to avoid seeing her.

It did bother him, however, that Myra never sat down and ate dinner with them. When was she eating? Before he got home every day? When he and Ciara retired to the man cave after dinner? After he went to bed? Pete felt he had every right to be annoyed about the distance since Bonnie would share dinner with him and Ciara.

His only problem with their living arrangements so far were those nights when he went to bed but couldn't get to sleep. He would lie awake, staring up at the ceiling, hearing her movements beyond his closed bedroom door. He knew when she would wake up to check on Ciara, or when she needed a drink of water or milk at about three in the morning.

He would lie in bed and remember how she'd looked when he'd gotten home that night, recalling her outfit, regardless of whether it was a dress, skirt and blouse, or a pair of leggings with a pullover sweater. She had the figure for anything she put on her body. She could wear a potato sack and he would still give her a second look. And then there was her hair. Some days she had it pulled up and some days she wore it down. It didn't matter how she wore it, it looked good enough to run his hands through.

She didn't wear makeup when she was home. Honestly, she didn't need it since her skin appeared so smooth and soft without it. And she always wore a smile that seemed to come naturally. His attitude or disposition never seemed to faze her. It was as if she'd made up her mind that he was inconsequential. The reason she was there was to take care of Ciara and she could ignore the rest. Including him.

Especially him.

He was well aware that she went out of her way to avoid him as much as he was trying to avoid her. So far they were doing a pretty good job at it and he should be happy. But instead he had to fight down his desire whenever he saw her. That took a lot of work. More than he wanted to put up with.

Since he was off work most weekends, they had agreed those days would be Myra's days off. Because she had moved into his place, she didn't have a house to check on. Instead she had spent the first two weekends with Leola Miller, an older woman who'd lived next door to her rental and whom she'd befriended.

Telling himself he was being considerate, he refused to go to bed on Sundays until he knew she was back, safely under his roof. Deep down he figured it was more than that. He would be sitting in the living room on the sofa and the moment she walked through the door an emotion he wasn't used to feeling would stir inside him. That first time, she'd been surprised to see him waiting up for her and had told him he didn't need to do that. He'd told her he did and without any further explanation, he'd gone to his bedroom. That second time, she'd known what to expect and had merely thanked him for caring for her safety. Her words of appreciation had broken the ice and before going off to bed he'd inquired about Ms. Miller's health. Although it had lasted less than five minutes, it had been the longest conversation they'd shared since she had moved in.

The Westmorelands had invited them for Thanksgiving dinner. She'd declined, saying she'd made plans that would include the entire weekend. She would be leaving early Thanksgiving morning and wouldn't return until Sunday afternoon.

A part of him had wondered what those plans were and with whom she had them, but because he had no right to ask, he hadn't. But that hadn't kept him from imagining things, like that guy named Wallace coming to town. The thought hadn't sat right with him, but what she did was her business.

Myra smiled when she opened the door to Bella Westmoreland. After a couple of days of snow over Thanksgiving, the sun was now peeking through the clouds. Although it was still cold outside, the temperature was a lot better than what it had been. Myra had enjoyed her girls' trip this past weekend to Breckenridge with Rekka. They hadn't spent time together in ages.

She had reached out to her college friend weeks ago after hearing about her recent breakup. She had been careful to pay only in cash, and Rekka had covered the hotel. Rekka was getting on with her life and seemed to be doing a good job of it. Myra was proud of her friend.

"Come in. I'm glad to see you," Myra said to Bella, widening the door to let her in. "I just put Ciara down for her nap. Come sit by the fireplace."

The one thing she and Bella had in common, being Southern girls, was getting used to the Colorado weather. At least Myra didn't have to get used to it too much since she would be leaving to return to South Carolina next month.

"Thanks," Bella said, peeling off her coat and handing it to Myra.

Myra had heard the story of how Bella had moved here to claim the inheritance her grandfather had left, ended up staying and meeting Jason. Myra thought Jason, and any of the male Westmorelands for that matter, was a good catch. Not only were they handsome, but they were also thoughtful and kind.

She had a feeling Pete would be a good catch, too. He was handsome, but the verdict was still out for thoughtful and kind. At least he exhibited those behaviors to his niece. Bottom line, he ignored Myra most of the time. But then, wasn't she trying to ignore him, as well?

"Would you like a cup of tea?" Myra asked.

"I'd love a cup. Thanks."

"I'll be right back."

Moments later Myra returned with two cups of tea on a serving tray she'd found in one of the cabinets.

"Thanks," Bella said. She took a sip, smiled and said, "This is delicious."

"Thanks. So what brings you out in the cold today?" Myra sked, taking a sip of her own tea.

Bella settled comfortably on the sofa. "Two reasons, actually. First, I wanted to see how you're doing since it's been over three weeks since you started here as nanny."

Myra braced her back against the sofa's cushions. She liked Bella and had from the first. There was a genuine kindness in Bella that was lacking in other people. Myra could see how Jason had fallen in love with her. "So far, so good. I've established a routine for Ciara, which is pretty much the same one Miss Bonnie had. She's such a happy baby and a joy to keep."

"That's good news. I knew you would work out well. The girls just loved it whenever Pete would bring Ciara over for a visit. She is such a happy baby and I'm glad Pete's putting her first."

Myra nodded. "He definitely loves her, that's for sure."

Bella took another sip of her tea and then said, "The other reason I'm here is to tell you about the Westmoreland Foundation Charity Ball next month."

"A charity ball?"

"Yes. The Westmoreland Foundation was established years ago to aid various community causes. The charity ball is one of the ways they do so. I was selected as this year's chairperson. The ball holds special meaning for me since it was the first event I attended in Denver and the one where I met Jason."

Myra was always moved by the sparkle she would see in Bella's eyes whenever she mentioned her husband. It was love, through and through. Myra wondered if there was a man who'd put that same sparkle in her eyes one day. She doubted it. Besides, she had so much to do before the year ended and romance was not on the list.

"I'd love to attend but I'm not sure I'll still be here. When is it?"

"This year it would be New Year's Eve night."

Disappointment settled in Myra. She would be gone by then. "Sorry, I won't be here then."

"Oh." She could see Bella's disappointment, as well. "I wish you could extend your visit. I would love for you to meet some of the other Westmorelands. They all fly in for the event."

Myra wished she could but she couldn't. When she arrived back in Charleston, she would officially be twenty-five and removing Baron and putting Wallace in charge was her priority. "I have business I need to take care of in Charleston during the days following Christmas, but if I finish it in time, I will try and come back."

Bella beamed. "That would be great and I hope you truly will come back. There's nothing like starting the New Year off right."

Myra agreed. "Now I have a request to make of you."

"Sure, what is it?" Bella asked, a smile curving her lips from corner to corner.

"I need to stay here in Denver through Christmas, and not leave until the day after. Miss Bonnie will be returning the week before Christmas and I'll need to find somewhere to live for about week. Will you have any accommodations at your bed-and-breakfast inn?"

"I will definitely hold a place for you, but you're welcome to move in with me and Jason."

Myra shook her head. "I can't possibly do that. A room at your inn would work for me. Just let me know how much it will be."

"Nothing. I don't charge for when the family, friends or business associates of the Westmorelands come visiting."

"I have to pay you something."

Bella shook her head. "No, you don't and we won't discuss it any further. Besides, I doubt you'll be needing a room. There's no way Pete will let you leave here without a place to stay. That's just not Pete."

Myra decided not to disillusion her, but it could very well be Pete. To him she was just a paid employee whose time ended when Bonnie returned. He had no reason to care where she would be living after that. Deciding to change the subject, she asked about the twins.

"The girls are fine and of course they are excited with our news."

Myra lifted a brow. "What news?"

An enthusiastic look shone on Bella's face. "Jason and I are expecting another baby, or babies. Everyone thinks I'm nuts for even wanting twins again."

"Congratulations!" Myra said, leaning in to give Bella a hug. "I am so happy for you."

"Thanks. I'm surprised Pete didn't mention it. We announced at the chow-down Friday night."

It was on the tip of her tongue to say that she and Pete didn't have that kind of relationship. They barely talked. Other than asking her about Ciara's day, he never said anything except casual comments about the weather.

"Well, I am happy for you."

Bella smiled happily. "Thanks. Oh, I almost forgot. There's another reason I stopped by. Pam's acting school is hosting a Wild West festival. They are having a lot of games for the kids and even baby activities. It's for all ages, including adults. Pam is even getting her sister, the one who's a Hollywood actress, to fly in and participate. I think it would be great if you brought Ciara."

Myra knew that Dillon's wife, Pam, used to be a movie star and now she owned an acting school in town. From what she'd heard, Pam also held several social events at her school that benefited the community. The Wild West festival was one of them. "Sounds like fun. When is it?"

"Friday night. We're canceling our regular chow-down, which means all the Westmorelands will be on hand to help. I'm sure Pete will be lending a hand, as well."

If he had planned to do so, he definitely hadn't mentioned it to her. But he truly didn't have to since she was not privy to his personal schedule.

Bella glanced at her watch. "I hate to rush off but I have a couple more stops to make. Thanks for the tea."

"You're welcome," Myra said as she walked Bella to the door. "And thanks for your visit."

Chapter 5

The moment Pete entered his home, Myra came into the room with Ciara walking beside her as she held her hand. When his niece saw him, she said, "Da-da," before racing across the room as fast as her chubby little legs could carry her. He automatically bent to capture her in his arms. His little bundle of joy.

Had it only been six months ago that Ciara had come into his life, changing it forever? Honestly, he could barely remember what he'd done before her. When he came in from work, he would go down to his man cave, but he still did that. Now he had company. He also had home-cooked meals and didn't have to eat dinner alone at McKays, the popular restaurant in town.

After hugging his niece and smelling the sweet apple scent of her hair, he looked over her head at Myra, who was watching them with a tender expression on her face.

Why? He always greeted his niece each day with a hug. Usually Myra would appear from the kitchen carrying Ciara in her arms. On those days he would automatically take her from Myra, giving him the opportunity to smell the woman's honeysuckle scent, as well.

"Hello, Myra," he said, standing to his feet with Ciara in his arms.

"Pete. Are you ready for dinner?"

"Yes. What did you prepare today?" Not that it mattered. After skipping lunch, he was hungry enough to eat a horse.

"I made a meat loaf with green beans, squash, rice and yeast rolls."

Pete nodded. It all sounded good. Why was she still standing across the room? He figured since he was holding Ciara, she had no reason to come closer. He intended to remedy that right now. Crossing the room to her, he handed Ciara back, intentionally leaning in to get a whiff of that honeysuckle scent. "If you don't mind holding her while I wash up?"

"Of course, I don't mind."

He moved away, then turned to her. "I prefer that you eat dinner with me and Ciara every day."

She lifted a brow. "Why?"

"Because I want you to." With that said, Pete moved toward his bedroom.

Because he wanted her to...

Myra watched him leave, not sure what to say. What if she didn't want to? She hadn't thought dining with him every evening was a requirement.

It didn't matter that Bonnie had mentioned she would join him and Ciara for dinner and that it was time she used to bring him up-to-date about anything she felt he needed to know. Myra had been fine telling him everything when she handed Ciara over to him when he got home. They had established a routine. So why was he changing it?

Looking down at Ciara, she said softly, "There are days when I don't understand your uncle, sweetie. If he wanted me to join you guys for dinner, then why didn't he say so that first night?"

Not expecting Ciara to respond, she hugged her and headed for the kitchen. She had already set the table for one, so after placing Ciara in her high chair, she moved around the kitchen to put another place setting on the table. She could hear Ciara practicing some words she'd been teaching her. The little girl was a quick learner and the things she could comprehend always amazed Myra.

Myra knew the moment Pete entered the kitchen. Glancing over at him she saw he'd taken a shower. The top of his head still glistened with water. Ciara, who'd been busy with blocks, began clapping and said, "Da-da back."

He went over to her, lightly pinched one of her cheeks and said, "Yes, Da-da is back."

Myra looked away; otherwise she knew she'd get emotional. Whether Pete knew it or not, what he'd just said was monumental. He was acknowledging that his brother was gone and wouldn't be returning. However, Matt had left him with this special gift and allowing her to call him Da-da was something he could deal with. He would tell Ciara the truth as she got older.

He sat down at the table and so did she, after putting a small plate of food in front of Ciara. Before Bonnie left, she'd told Myra that Ciara was ready to feed herself. Myra had continued to show her the proper way to use a spoon. Although the end result was somewhat messy, Ciara managed to put more in her mouth than on the floor.

They were in the kitchen's eating nook instead of the huge dining room. Bonnie had told her Pete preferred the smaller area since it was normally just him and Ciara and Bonnie. After placing their food on the table it occurred to Myra just how small the area was. Just how cozy.

"Is anything wrong?" he asked, sitting down at the table.

She looked at him. "No. There's nothing wrong." She quickly finished what she was doing and sat down.

Before Pete could reach for anything, she said, "Just a minute, Pete." Then, glancing at Ciara, she said, "Grace, Ciara."

Ciara didn't disappoint. She bowed her little head and said the recitation Myra had been teaching her to say all week. When she finished by saying the "Amen," Ciara lifted her head, smiled and began clapping her hands.

Myra heard Pete chuckle. "Well, I'll be," he said in amazement, glancing over at her. "When did you teach her that?"

Myra was glad he was pleased. "This week. Today I decided to put it to the test. She did good, don't you think?"

He nodded. "Yes, my girl did excellent. Thank you for teaching her that."

"You're welcome."

They began eating in silence and then after a short while he asked her, "How did your day go today, Myra?"

She tried looking down at the food on her plate and not at his face. The last thing she needed was to get mes-

merized by his eyes or turned on by his lips. Both had
the ability to render her senseless when she dwelled on
them for long.

"My day went fine. The usual." After she said that it
occurred to her that he probably didn't know what "the
usual" was. So, she said, "We got up around eight, ate
breakfast, did our classes and—"

"What classes?"

She glanced up and the moment their gazes connected, she felt her muscles tighten as desire warmed her
to the core. It was desire, she recognized it, although she
wasn't used to the reaction. But she knew what it was.
It was there whenever she looked at him. There whenever she lay in her bed at night and thought about him.

At first the desire bothered her and she appreciated
that when she woke up in the mornings, he was gone.
Then she had all day to pull herself together by staying
busy. Then when he walked through that door in the
evenings and she looked at him, her torment would start
all over. Heaven help her. What was there about Sheriff
Peterson Higgins that got to her?

"Myra?"

She blinked upon realizing she'd been sitting there
staring at him. He probably thought she was a nitwit.
"Yes?"

"What classes are you teaching Ciara?"

She swallowed and broke eye contact with him to
glance over at Ciara and smile. The little girl was doing
better with the spoon today. "Her colors and shapes. And
in addition to her saying grace, we learned another song
this week, but we're not ready to share that with you yet."

He seemed amused and the husky-sounding chuckle
caused a frisson of fire to rush up her spine. Eating din-

ner with him wasn't a good idea. Not when he was this close, sitting right there in front of her.

"Okay," he said, smiling broadly. "I'll take your word for it."

His smile did it to her again and she nodded. She couldn't help a smile touching her own lips. "Bella stopped by today."

"She did?"

"Yes. She wanted to tell me about the Westmoreland Charity Ball. She's chairperson this year."

"That's what I heard, and I told Jason we better have something stronger to drink than tea," he said, chuckling again.

Myra grinned, not sure how to take this side of him. This was the longest conversation they'd ever held and he seemed to be in such a good mood. "Tea isn't the only drink Southerners drink, you know."

"You could have fooled me," he said, grinning as well, tilting his head to acknowledge her teacup and the tea in it.

She laughed as she took a sip. Moments later she said, "Bella also told me that she and Jason are having another baby."

Another huge smile spread across Pete's lips, making Myra's heart skip a few beats. She still didn't know how a man's smile could affect her that way.

"Yes, and I'm happy for them. I remember the first time I met Bella. I was a deputy and got called out to her grandfather's ranch on official duty. Someone had thrown a huge rock through her living room window with a note telling her to leave town."

"Did you get the person who threw the rock into her house?"

"Yes, we got them."

"Them?"

"Yes, it was two."

She waited to see if he would fill her in on the rest and when he didn't, she decided to change the subject. It was then that she told him about the Wild West festival. He seemed interested.

"Not sure if I'll be able to attend since I might be working that night, but you should take Ciara. It sounds like a lot of fun."

"I think I will." Bonnie had mentioned that periodically Pete worked nights. Myra couldn't imagine having him home during the day and being underfoot.

She glanced up at him and caught him staring. "What? Is something wrong?"

He shook his head. "No, nothing is wrong." He broke eye contact with her and began eating again.

Drawing in a deep breath, she then asked him the same question he'd asked her. "So, how was your day?"

Pete wasn't sure Myra eating dinner with him and Ciara had been a good idea after all. He could barely eat with her sitting right there. But then, that was why he'd suggested she eat with him. He had wanted her close. He was tired of her conveniently being absent during mealtime when he would sit and wonder where she was and what she was doing.

Although it was pure torture, he liked glancing up from his meal every so often to see her sitting there. She looked pretty today like always, and he hadn't realized until now just how much he liked the sound of her voice. He also liked sitting here sharing a meal with her. Holding conversation. That was when he remembered she'd asked how his day had gone.

"It was pretty busy. First off, I answered a call at Katherine Lattimore's house. She's in her eighties and a retired teacher here in town. She claims she gave up teaching after the likes of Bailey and Bane Westmoreland." He heard the sound of Myra's soft chuckle and it seemed to caress his skin.

"I understand those two cousins used to be a handful while growing up."

"Yes, and whatever you were told, believe it. Derringer, Riley and I were constantly covering up for them to keep them out of trouble. Bailey and Bane, along with the twins—Aiden and Adrian—were the terrible foursome."

"So what was wrong with Ms. Lattimore?"

Pete found himself sharing Ms. Katherine's ghost story and liked how Myra would tilt her head, listening attentively. "So, there you have it. She actually captured a ghost on video. Now it's my job to find out what in the heck is going on."

"How do you intend to do that?"

"Not sure yet," he said. "And by the way, this food is delicious." He truly meant it.

"Thanks."

"Who taught you how to cook?"

She shrugged what he thought was a beautiful pair of shoulders. "In college I assisted at a homeless shelter's soup kitchen for an entire year. Various chefs would volunteer their time and they often held cooking classes. It was fun." Not only had she learned her way around the kitchen, she was also educated on how to eat healthy foods without sacrificing the delicious flavor.

He decided to ask the one question he'd pondered. "How did you become a Gators fan? Did you attend the University of Florida?"

She smiled and he swore he felt the brilliance of it spread to him. "No, I didn't, but Wallace did."

His hand tightened on his glass. He recalled the name on her Facebook page. He also recalled the man it belonged to. "Wallace?"

"Yes, Wallace Blue. He works for my father's company and attended the University of Florida. I went to a small all-girls university in Boston for college. My school didn't have a football team so when I wanted to learn about football, Wallace was eager to teach me."

I just bet he was, Pete thought and wondered where the anger toward a man he didn't know came from. "Do the two of you still date?" A part of him regretted asking the question, but it was too late to take it back.

"Date?" She laughed. "Wallace and I have never dated. We're good friends. He's like another big brother to me."

A part of Pete was glad to hear that.

"What about you, Pete?" she asked. "Why are you a Buckeyes fan? Did you go to Ohio State?"

Her question gave him pause and he stopped eating for a minute. Drawing in a deep breath he glanced over at her and said, "Yes, but just for a year. My dad died and I came home to attend college here. But I traveled back to Ohio whenever I could to see Ellen."

"Ellen?"

He met Myra's gaze across the table. "Yes, Ellen, my fiancée. When we graduated from high school, she and I left Denver to attend Ohio State together."

He waited for the next question. The one that usually

followed whenever people heard he'd once been engaged. People who didn't know him well enough to know the full story of what had happened.

When she didn't ask, he glanced up and saw her eating. "Aren't you going to ask what happened?" He wasn't sure why he'd prompted her. For all he knew she'd already heard the story. Bonnie might have told her.

She looked up at him. "Not unless you want to tell me."

He thought about her response. In the past, people had asked him about it even when he hadn't wanted to tell them. "Ellen was killed two weeks before our wedding day. She was an excellent rider and participated in the Martin Luther King parade every year. That year someone tossed a firecracker near her horse's feet. The animal panicked and threw her."

"I am so sorry, Pete."

"Thanks. So am I."

Silence covered the table and he glanced over at Ciara. He'd just shared a part of his past, but Ciara was his future. Making sure she grew up happy was what he intended to do for the rest of his life.

He also knew something else. This was the first time he had mentioned Ellen's name to anyone without a feeling of deep pain in his heart, without bitter agony settling into his every pore. And without the need to look back and cling to those memories of her.

What could that mean? He needed time to himself to think through some things, possibly resolve issues within himself. Pushing his plate back, he said, "Dinner was great, Myra. Look, I need to go check on a few things and meet with my foreman so I might be a while."

"Okay."

He then left the kitchen, grabbing his Stetson off the rack on his way out the door.

Myra watched Pete leave and released a breath when she heard the sound of the door closing. She felt bad for him and regretted that she had reopened wounds for him. Bonnie had already told her how he'd lost his fiancée, so why had she wanted to hear it from him?

It had been heartbreaking. After twelve years he still hadn't gotten over her death.

She glanced over at Ciara and the mess she'd made. At least she hadn't gotten any food in her hair and hadn't thrown any off her plate. She had eaten every single bite. Myra got up from the table. It was time to clean up the kitchen and then clean up Ciara.

She didn't have time to consider the feelings Pete's story raised.

A couple hours later she was done with both and yet Pete still hadn't returned. His truck was still parked outside, which meant he hadn't left the property, but he could very well have gone off on horseback after meeting with his foreman. Holding Ciara closer to her chest, she moved away from the window. The only thing they could do now was to wait for him to return.

It was getting dark and Pete knew it was time to head Satin back toward home. The ride had done him good since he'd needed to clear his head about a few things.

He had loved Ellen since he'd discovered what love was. They'd been so close and had known what they wanted out of their lives. He'd looked forward to their wedding day as much as she had because he'd seen it as the start of what would be the best days of their lives.

And then all his hopes and dreams, his future, had ended because of someone's cold-bloodedness. It had taken years to stop blaming himself, but there were times when his mind would play the "if only" game.

He closed his eyes and tried to remember their last days together. As time passed it was getting harder and harder to recapture the memories and that bothered him. Then he'd had that dream, the one where she'd come to him as if to free him. He hadn't liked it and he'd fought the meaning behind it.

Until Myra walked into his kitchen.

He hadn't expected the emotions he'd felt that day or since. He hadn't known he was capable of finding another woman as desirable as Ellen. Nor had he known he could dream of Myra while fighting to keep Ellen in his heart. He'd found the attempt exhausting. Did that mean it was time to move on?

What had Bonnie said? That he'd been breathing and not living? He could now say that she'd been right about that. He'd made love to women to release primitive urges and nothing more. However, being around the Westmorelands on Thanksgiving and seeing how happy they were with their spouses had made him wish for things that he had turned his back on. Things that deep down he knew Ellen would want him to have, even without her.

During dinner he and Myra had shared a real conversation over a meal. He had enjoyed talking to her, listening to what she had to say. Looking at her. Noticing how she was looking at him. He figured she had no idea what that look had done to him. How his blood had stirred each and every time he'd caught her staring.

He had desired her from the start, but according to

her he wasn't her type. He was older than the men she normally dated.

Maybe Zane was right and he should take her words as a challenge, especially knowing how she'd been sneaking those looks at him. He smiled as he headed Satin back toward home.

Myra Hollister had no idea that things were about to get interesting in the Higgins household.

Myra glanced at the clock when she heard the sound of Pete returning. He'd been gone for nearly four hours. She had gotten Ciara ready for bed and rocked her to sleep, singing the song Pete usually sang.

Instead of going to bed herself she decided to wait up for him to apologize. It was her fault he'd had to talk about his fiancée. Needing to see him before he went to his bedroom, she walked out of the kitchen.

"Pete?"

He turned and she could tell he was surprised to see her. Even though it was still pretty early, usually after making sure Ciara was tucked in for the night, she would escape to her bedroom and watch television until falling asleep.

"Yes?"

"I want to apologize."

He lifted a brow. "Why? What did you do?"

She nervously licked her lip. "I made you talk about something that brought back painful memories for you."

"You don't have anything to apologize for, Myra."

"I feel like I do."

"Well, you shouldn't. Is Ciara asleep now?"

"Yes."

She could tell from his expression that he regretted

not being there to put his niece to bed. "You missed dessert," she told him.

"Did I?"

"Yes."

"What was it?"

"Peach cobbler."

He nodded. "I love peach cobbler."

"I used those peaches Bonnie told me about in the freezer."

He nodded. "It's not too late. I think I'll have some cobbler now," he said, walking toward her. When he got close, she moved out of his way so as not to block the entrance.

Instead of passing by, he stopped. He stood right in front of her, and the way the lamp shone on them, she could look deep into his eyes.

"I don't bite, you know," he said.

She wasn't so sure about that. She could feel the essence of him in every pore, nerve and pulse. "Yes, I know you don't."

He was still looking at her, not having moved an inch. She was about to tell him good-night when he said, "Come eat some cobbler with me."

Not sure she'd heard him correctly, she said, "You want me to eat some cobbler with you?"

The corners of his mouth edged up, displaying that smile that did crazy things to her. "Yes. If you don't, I might end up eating the entire pan myself. I need you to stop me if I try doing such a thing."

She couldn't hold back a grin. "You love peach cobbler that much?"

"Afraid so. Bonnie didn't warn you?"

"She did mention it was your favorite."

"It's more than my favorite. It's one of those things you can become addicted to if you aren't careful."

She doubted he knew that he was effectively pushing her buttons and making her wonder just what other things he could become addicted to if he wasn't careful. She was standing there imagining a lot of things and when his gaze dropped to her mouth, the hormones in her body seemed to burst to life. "That sounds like a big problem for you, Pete."

"It is, so will you join me in the kitchen to make sure I don't overdo it?"

Myra nervously licked her lips. Things were getting pretty hot here in the living room and she didn't want to think what the temperature might be in the kitchen. Honestly, she should have the good sense to tell him that his eating habits weren't her concern, but that would be a lie. Hadn't she made sure all his meals were healthy ones?

Not that he looked out of shape or anything. If he looked any more in shape, she would go bonkers.

"Since you presented it that way, then I guess I will," she said. Turning, she went to the kitchen, knowing he was following her.

Chapter 6

"That's it, Peterson Higgins—no more. You've had three servings already," Myra said, laughing, as she guarded the pan of peach cobbler on the counter. "I thought you were joking about eating the entire pan."

He stood in front of her, grinning from ear to ear. "You should not have baked it so well. It's delicious."

"Thanks, but flattery won't get you any more peach cobbler tonight. You've had your limit."

He crossed his arms over his chest. "I could have you arrested, you know."

Crossing her arms over her own chest, she tilted her chin and couldn't stop grinning. "On what charge?"

The charge that immediately came to Pete's mind was that she was so darn beautiful. Irresistible. But he figured that was something he could not say. He enjoyed this playful side of her and would admit to enjoying this spirited side of himself, as well.

It had started out with them sitting down and eating the cobbler and him commenting on how good it tasted. That got her to talking and she told him about those weekends she'd spent with Ms. Miller and that one of the things they did was watch old movies and how much she enjoyed it. He tried to remember the last time he'd watched a movie. A new one or an old one.

She snapped her fingers in front of his face to reclaim his attention. "If you have to think that hard about a charge, then that means there isn't one."

"Oh, there's one, all right. How about harboring someone else's property?"

She rolled her eyes at him. "How about it? Do you honestly think you can make that charge stick?"

"Oh, you'll be surprised what all I can do, Myra."

She tilted her head to the side as if to look at him better. "Do tell, Pete."

Her words—those three little words—made a full-blown attack on his senses. He drew in a shaky breath, then touched her chin. She blinked, as if startled by his touch. "How about 'do show,' Myra?"

Pete watched the way the lump formed in her throat and detected her shift in breathing. He could even hear the pounding of her heart. Damn, she smelled good, and she looked good, too. Always did. He'd noticed the leggings and pullover sweater when he'd arrived home earlier. She looked comfortable and sexy as hell.

"I'm not sure what 'do show' means," she said in a voice that was as shaky as his had been.

He tilted her chin up to gaze into her eyes, as well as to study the shape of her exquisite pair of lips. "Then let me demonstrate, Ms. Hollister," he said, lowering his mouth to hers.

The moment he swept his tongue inside her mouth and tasted her, he was a goner. It took every ounce of strength he had to keep the kiss gentle when he wanted to devour her mouth with a hunger he felt all the way in his bones. A part of him wanted to take the kiss deeper, but then another part wanted to savor her taste. Honestly, either worked for him as long as she felt the passion between them.

He had wanted her from the moment he'd set eyes on her, but he'd fought the desire. He could no longer do that. He was a man known to forgo his own needs and desires, but tonight he couldn't. Not when they were out of control. She might deny it, but he could tell from the way she was responding to him that need was driving her just as much as it was driving him.

He heard her moan and the sound sent even more heat spiraling through him. Wrapping his arms around her waist, he pulled her closer, loving the feel of her body pressed against him. It was as if she was melting into him. It had been a long time since he'd tasted this much passion in a woman. He doubted she knew just how potent she was, just how she was driving him to the brink. It was as if he couldn't taste her enough, hold her close enough. He wanted to absorb her into his skin, his entire body, as their tongues tangled.

Knowing if he didn't stop kissing her now he would have her spread out on the counter, he ever so slowly broke off the kiss. But not before swiping another lick across her lips with his tongue. Whispering close to her ear, he said, "Peach cobbler isn't the only thing I could become addicted to, Myra."

Then, taking a step back, he dropped his hands to his

sides and stared at her. She wore passion well. "Don't cook dinner tomorrow. I'm taking you and Ciara out."

"Oh."

He dragged in a deep breath, pulling the luscious scent of her through his nostrils. "I'll check on Ciara before going to bed."

"Okay. Good night."

"Good night, Myra." Pete turned to leave the kitchen and as hard as it was for him to do so, he didn't look back.

Myra somehow made it to a chair and sat down at the table before her legs gave out. She'd been kissed before, but never like this. Never with slow, seductive strokes. He'd taken her mouth in a way that seemed effortless yet unquestionably thorough. And she had accepted the stroking of his tongue with ease, as if she'd known it would spread through her bloodstream. And when he'd finally lifted his mouth from hers, she'd wanted to cry in protest.

Drawing in a ragged breath now, she heard the sound of Ciara's door closing and knew he had left his niece's room. Would he go on to his room like he'd said he would, or would he come back into the kitchen to give her another mind-drugging kiss? Did she want him to? She held her breath, wondering what move he would make, and released it when she heard the sound of his bedroom door opening and then closing. He hadn't just kissed her; Pete had devoured her mouth in a way that still had her head spinning.

Standing, she got busy and covered the rest of the peach cobbler and put it in the refrigerator. She wanted to be in her bedroom with the door closed just in case

Pete did decide to come back. He said he didn't bite, but he did a good job of licking and sucking.

And the kiss had gone on and on. It'd seemed neither of them had wanted it to end. She'd become enamored with his taste. He obviously knew what he was doing, and she'd merely followed his lead while his mouth and tongue coaxed hers into moaning.

Just thinking about it now was increasing the beat of her heart and had erotic awareness curling her stomach. Tonight, she had undergone a sexual revelation, insti-gated by a man she'd initially decided wasn't her type and was older than those she would normally date.

Date? Now, that was a laugh. When was the last time she'd gone out with anyone other than Wallace? And just like she'd told Pete, Wallace was more like a brother to her than Baron ever had been.

Moments later, after tidying up the kitchen, she headed down the hall to her bedroom. Once inside, she leaned against the closed door and touched her lips, still feeling a tingling sensation there.

She had to put Pete and that powerhouse of a kiss out of her mind and move forward on the resolve that it couldn't happen again. No matter how enjoyable it had been. She would get a good night's sleep and hopefully in the morning she would be able to think straight.

"So, how's that new nanny working out for you, Sher-iff?"

Pete rubbed his eyes as he glanced up from the com-puter screen. He'd been rewatching the video Ms. Kath-erine had given him. Although it was a long way from being 4K ultra HD, he could still detect a willowy fea-ture that seemed to be floating around her backyard. He and his men had agreed there was definitely something there; they just didn't know what.

His gaze lit on the man standing in the doorway of his office. Pete and Detective Lewis Tomlin had grown up together in Denver. They had started the police academy at the same time, and then Lewis left to work as an FBI agent for a couple of years. "She's working out just fine, Lewis," he said, leaning back in his chair with the palms of his hands bracing against his neck. "She's doing a great job taking care of Ciara and she's a darn good cook. Thanks for asking."

He knew the questions should end there but wouldn't. Lewis's grandmother was one of Ms. Katherine's cronies, so Pete was sure he'd heard something. It didn't take long to find out what. "I heard she's pretty."

Yes, she was definitely that, Pete thought. She was pretty and tasted like heaven on earth. He'd had to force himself to get that kiss they'd shared out of his mind. He had gone to bed thinking of it, had dreamed sweet dreams reliving it, and had awakened that morning yearning for another.

"You heard right," he said, seeing no reason to lie about it.

"Heidi and I would like to meet her."

Pete frowned. "Why?"

"She's only with you temporarily, right?"

"Yes."

"Well, we hear she has a ton of experience taking care of kids. She might come in handy."

Pete lifted a brow. "You're looking for a nanny?"

Lewis chuckled. "No, but Heidi and I are planning to get away for a few days by ourselves and are looking for someone to keep the kids for us."

"When are you planning this trip for?" Pete asked him.

"The second week in January. We want to head up to Aspen for some skiing."

"Sorry, but she won't be around. She plans to leave sometime around the holidays to return south."

"Well, if she changes her mind let me know."

"I will."

Lewis moved on and Pete thought about their conversation. Specifically, the part about Myra leaving. Why was the thought a downer? He shook his head, deciding not to dwell on that. What he wanted to do was think about that kiss some more, how easily their mouths had fit together.

He had left her a note on the kitchen table this morning with directions to McKays, deciding to give her a little break from being in the kitchen tonight. She deserved it. He'd taken Bonnie out to dinner with him and Ciara plenty of times. No big deal. But deep down he knew it was a big deal. At the end of her stay in Denver he wanted her to reach the conclusion that he was her type and not too old for her to date.

Then what?

He rubbed his hand down his face. He hadn't thought that part through yet. At that moment his cell phone went off and he quickly clicked it on. "Sheriff Higgins."

"Pete, this is Bane. Crystal said you called."

"I did and thanks for getting back to me. I remember you mentioning a while back that Flipper had developed some sort of special high-tech video camera."

"Yes, that's right. You know Flipper—whenever you can keep him out of the water, he's inventing some high-tech gadget or other."

"If possible, I'd like to use it in a case I'm working on. I think it might be helpful."

"Then you're in luck. Flipper and Swan will be here this week. They're coming to town with the baby. I'll tell him to bring it when he comes."

"Thanks, I appreciate it." Pete knew Flipper and his wife recently had a little girl. "And by the way, how're Mac and Teri doing? And all your other SEAL team-mates?"

Because Bane was so close to his teammates, namely Viper, Coop, Mac and Flipper, all the Westmoreland family and their friends had gotten to know the guys pretty well.

"The McRoy household is doing fine. I talked to Mac the other day and he said the twins are climbing all over the place and getting into anything that's not nailed down. I told him to stop whining. He wanted sons and now he has two."

Yes, now Mac had two sons and four daughters. "Well, I'm glad he got what he wanted and I heard the ranch they bought in Texas is pretty damn nice."

He talked to Bane for a few minutes more and before ending the call, he asked about Bane's family. Bane and Crystal were the parents of three-year-old triplets: two sons, Adam and Ace, and a daughter, Clarisse. Adam and Clarisse had been named after Bane's parents.

Turning his attention back to the computer screen, Pete jotted down some notes but again his mind began wandering. He'd never allowed a woman to interfere with his work before. He would push thoughts of Myra to the back of his mind. It wouldn't be easy, but he was determined.

* * *

"Welcome to McKays."

Holding Ciara in her arms, Myra smiled up at the waitress. "Thanks. I'm meeting someone here. Sheriff Pete Higgins," she said, glancing around the restaurant. This was her first time here, but she'd heard it was one of the most popular eating establishments in town.

"He's already here and asked for a high chair for the baby. Please follow me."

"Thanks."

Myra was led to the back and around several couples dining. It seemed a number of them recognized Ciara and smiled to greet her by name. Myra figured Pete must have brought his niece here often for her to be so popular. When they rounded a corner, she saw Pete the moment he saw them. The minute their eyes connected she felt like she was burning from the inside out.

He stood and smiled and she could no longer ignore the deep attraction she had for him. She had awakened that morning giving herself a pep talk. Although she had enjoyed their kiss immensely last night, she knew it couldn't happen again. First of all, she was his employee and living under his roof. The last thing she wanted to indulge in was an affair with her boss. Okay, she would be honest with herself and say she would love to indulge in one, but it wouldn't be right. Besides, the man was older and not her type. But he could kiss the panties off a girl without much effort. And there he stood, looking as handsome as sin and with a body to die for.

"Da-da!"

Ciara stretched her hands out and he took her out of Myra's arms. Myra watched the little girl wrap her arms around his neck tight and kiss him on the cheek. It was obvious she'd missed him. This was the first time Ciara had seen her uncle since dinner yesterday. Myra could tell Pete had missed his niece, as well.

"Hello, Pete."

"Myra. I hope you found this place without any problems."

"I did," she said, sliding into the seat at the booth. "I'm glad you wrote down those directions for the short cut. GPS would have probably had me in the middle of rush hour traffic."

"Yes, it would have. How was your day?"

Myra could tell him she had spent a lot of the day thinking about the kiss and trying to convince herself it was one and done. She'd pretty much succeeded, too. But it was hard sitting across from him and staring at his lips and recalling what they'd done to hers last night.

"It was great. That song I taught Ciara at the beginning of the week, she has it down pat now. But please don't ask her to sing it. She gets loud and stuck on what is obviously her favorite part. I don't think you want to get her started in here."

He laughed, placing Ciara in the high chair. "I'll make sure I wait until we get home."

Her breath wobbled at what he'd said. It was as if they were a couple and he was referring to his house as their home. She tried forcing the thought to the back of her mind, but his smile was mesmerizing her.

At that moment the waitress brought them their menus. Myra broke eye contact to look down at it. "What do you suggest?"

"I would say their meat loaf but yours even tops the one here."

"Thanks, that's a kind thing to say."

"I wouldn't lie to you." He then said, "Since we've taken meat loaf off the list, I suggest their pork chops. For Ciara, I usually order the kids' meal ravioli. She seems to like it."

The waitress took their order and Myra glanced around, noticing how crowded the place was and the number of people staring at them. She glanced back at him and knew he noticed, as well. Before she could say anything, he said, "If you recall, I gave you fair warning."

Yes, he had. Not that it mattered for her, but he was the town's sheriff and happened to be single. People were probably curious as to what was going on in his life. Although Denver was a large city, certain parts were pretty close-knit and it seemed this area was one of those.

That was fine because at that moment the waitress returned with their food.

Pete smiled as Ciara entertained them during the meal. She hadn't burst into any songs, but she was trying to tell him about her shoes. He didn't quite understand what she was saying and Myra had to translate. That meant he got to look into her face without it being so obvious he was doing so.

He had been anxiously watching the entrance to the restaurant and remembered the exact moment she walked in with Ciara. It was something about seeing them together that filled him with a sense of contentment that both surprised and confused him. He had pushed the feeling aside to concentrate on Myra.

She was wearing a long flowing skirt with a pair of leather boots. Her wool sweater made the trendy outfit look sexy as hell. The way her curly hair flowed about

her shoulders with this mussed-up look had lust zipping
up his spine. He no longer felt guilty about wanting her
and accepted that was how it would be. He could no
more deny he found her desirable than he could deny
his masculinity.

And whenever she smiled, he felt his breath wobble
in his throat. He would love to one day take her dancing.
He could imagine holding her close in his arms while
burying his face in the hollow of her throat and drinking in her scent. One he was getting used to.

And just think, he had come close to not hiring her
as Ciara's nanny. She'd been with them for weeks now
and he couldn't help but appreciate how well she took
care of Ciara and his household in Bonnie's absence. He
also appreciated how she'd reminded him he was a man.
A man who'd finally realized he hadn't been living but
merely breathing, like Bonnie had claimed.

He hadn't counted on such a change in his life. He
had thought he was satisfied with things staying the
way they'd been for years. But every time he saw Myra,
spent any time around her, he was well aware of what
she did to him. A part of him felt he should be fighting it. After all, why get worked up over a woman who
would be walking out of his life in a month? She would
be leaving Denver and their paths might never cross
again. There could never be a future with them and a
part of him wasn't sure he wanted one with her or any
woman. The only thing he wanted to concentrate on was
the here and now. And right now, he was fully aware of
Myra Hollister in every pore of his body.

Another thing he was aware of was that seeing them
together had drawn a lot of attention. McKays was one
of the few eating places in town that was locally owned.

The owner, Tony McKay, had been close friends with Pete, Derringer and Riley while growing up and had taken over the running of the restaurant when his old man passed away a few years back.

McKays was a place where locals came to eat and in some cases get wind of the latest gossip. A number of the people in here had known Pete his entire life. They had known his parents and Matt and had encouraged him to run for sheriff. They were also people who'd known Ellen and most, like Bonnie, had told him at one time or another that it was time to find someone and settle down, claiming Ellen would have wanted that for him. In the past, he'd harbored feelings of resentment, thinking they had no idea what Ellen would have wanted. But they'd known Ellen as long as they'd known him. They knew Ellen hadn't had a selfish bone in her body. She'd loved life, embraced it fully.

He could admit now that the Ellen they'd known, and the one he'd known, would have wanted him to move on and live again.

"Evening, Sheriff."

Pete snapped out of his thoughts to stare at the man and woman standing beside his table. "Good evening, Mr. Karl and Mrs. Inez."

He knew they expected him to introduce them to Myra. In fact, he was fairly certain that was the main reason they'd come over to his table. "Not sure if you've met Myra Hollister. Myra is helping me out with Ciara while Bonnie is away visiting her sister."

They exchanged greetings with Myra. "The Fosters were good friends of my grandparents," he told Myra.

"Yes, Thomas Higgins was captain of our football

team back in the day," Karl said about Pete's grandfather. "And I was captain of the basketball team."

"And I bet it was a very good basketball team," Myra
said, smiling, causing the old man to blush.

"Yes, we were pretty good. We won the state titles in
both football and basketball our senior year."

The older couple moved on, but their approach had
somehow broken the ice, and other people trickled over
to their table on their way out for an introduction to
Myra, as well. Since they were not sitting by the exit
door, there was no doubt in Pete's mind that everyone
was making a conscious effort to come by.

"This is certainly a friendly town. For such a large
city, Denver still somehow presents itself with a small-
town atmosphere," Myra said, after what Pete hoped was
the last person to interrupt their meal left.

"Only certain parts of the city," he said, taking a sip
of his coffee. "Where you really get the big-town feel is
downtown and in the newer areas, where a lot of people
don't know each other and prefer it that way."

They were about to order dessert when Pete detected
someone else had approached their table. He glanced up
and saw that Derringer, Zane, Riley and Canyon were
out dining with their wives. Greetings were exchanged.
No introductions were needed since Myra had met everyone at a Westmoreland chow-down a few weeks back.

Zane told Pete that his sister Gemma had called that
day to say she and her husband, Callum, would be coming to town for Christmas after missing Thanksgiving.
Riley then chimed in to add that several of their cousins
living in Alaska, the Outlaws, would be joining them
for Christmas, as well. As much as Pete liked the Westmorelands, he was glad when they'd finally moved on,

dismissing the thought that he just wanted Myra's attention for himself.

"You're off work this weekend, right?"

Myra's question reeled in his thoughts. "Yes."

She nodded. "I'll be going back to Breckenridge this weekend."

Her statement gave him pause. "Joining your girlfriend there again?" he asked, in what he hoped was a casual tone. That night when they'd shared peach cobbler, she'd told him where she'd gone over the Thanksgiving holidays. Unknowingly, she had solved a mystery that had plagued him.

She shook her head. "No."

He thought that was all she planned to say, and then she added, "I planned to go there to get away."

Pete wondered if she was making a conscious effort to be gone the weekends he was off. Those first two weekends she'd spent with Ms. Miller, had that been intentional, as well? "Any reason you're going away for the entire weekend I'm off work?" he decided to ask.

She shrugged before saying, "Bonnie said when you had weekends off, she would use that time to return to her place to check on things. I don't have a place to go, but I want to give you and Ciara some alone time."

That was thoughtful of her but not necessary. "Ciara and I will have that even if you're there. Please don't leave to go somewhere on our account."

"You're sure? I don't want to intrude."

"You won't be." In fact, he wanted her there with him and Ciara. He would question the reason why later. Right now, he just wanted to enjoy her company and he had only another month left to do so.

At that moment the waitress returned with their dessert.

* * *

"Thanks again for dinner, Pete," Myra said, when he opened the door to his home. He'd wanted Ciara to ride with him back home and he had an extra baby car seat in the back of his sheriff's cruiser.

"Did Ciara take a nap today?" he asked.

She glanced over her shoulder at him. "Yes, why do you ask?"

He chuckled. "Because she was a lively one tonight. On the way home I made the mistake of telling her to sing that song you taught her and she kept it going until we got here."

Myra couldn't help but chuckle. "You can't say I didn't warn you. But she is getting sleepy. Just look at her."

They both did and although the little girl was fighting it, it was obvious she could barely keep her eyes open. "I'll get her ready for bed," Myra said, reaching to take Ciara out of Pete's arms. Their bodies brushed and Myra felt her heart skip a beat.

Cuddling Ciara close, as if the little girl could serve as a barrier between her and Pete, she took a step back. "I'll let you know when you can come tuck her in." Faking a yawn, she added, "I had a long day and after I get Ciara ready for you, I'm going straight to bed."

"All right."

Why was she feeling a little disappointed that Pete hadn't talked her out of going on to bed? What had she expected him to say? *Meet me in the kitchen later so I can devour your mouth again?* Maybe he regretted the kiss like she wanted to do. Only problem was, she couldn't.

"Is something wrong, Myra?"

Too late, she realized she'd been standing there staring at him. Namely at his mouth. That very sensuous mouth. He had a look in his eyes that almost made her moan. It was a good thing he wasn't privy to her thoughts. "No, nothing is wrong." Holding Ciara tightly in her arms, she hurried on down the hall.

She had given Ciara her bath and had just finished getting her into her jammies when the bedroom door opened. She drew in a sharp breath. This was the first time Pete had ever come into the room while she was here. Usually, he would wait until he knew she'd finished and had gone to her own room. He stood in the doorway looking way too fine.

"You're just in time. She's all ready for you," Myra said, trying to make it seem as if his unexpected appearance hadn't rattled her.

"Good."

He walked over to the dressing table and smiled down at his niece. Myra had wanted to braid Ciara's hair tonight but the little girl had been too fussy to let her do so. Huge locks of curls covered her little head and she could barely keep her eyes open. But when she saw Pete, she smiled up at him and asked, "Want me sing, Da-da?"

He laughed and then quickly said, "No, Ciara, it's my time to sing to you."

Myra watched as he picked up Ciara and carried her over to the rocking chair and sat down. When he was settled in the chair with his niece cuddled in his arms, he glanced over at her. Their gazes collided and too late she noticed her breathing pattern had changed. She wondered if he'd noticed.

She backed up toward the door. "Ahh, I'll leave the

two of you alone now. Good night." She quickly reached the door.

"Myra?"

She turned around. "Yes?"

"Please meet me in my man cave in half an hour."

She swallowed while he held her gaze hostage. "Is there something we need to talk about?"

"No."

She nervously licked her lips as she felt the heat from his eyes drift over her. Her body automatically responded to each lingering visual caress. "Then why do you need me to come down to your man cave?"

"I want to kiss you again."

At least he was honest and now she needed to be, as well. "I don't think that's a good idea." No use lying and saying she didn't want him to kiss her again, because she did. However, it still wasn't a good idea.

"I don't think so either but my mind isn't being ruled by what's a good idea or what's not a good idea. It's being ruled by the memory of your delicious taste."

Before she could respond, although she really didn't know what to say to that, Ciara reached up and took a hold of his chin to force him to look down at her. "Sing, Da-da."

He smiled down at his niece and before he could look back at her, Myra had quickly left the room and closed the door behind her.

Chapter 7

She isn't here.

Pete tried downplaying the pang of disappointment he felt in the pit of his stomach. Had he honestly thought she would be? He had hoped. There was no way he'd misread the chemistry between them tonight. Chemistry he was certain Myra had read, as well. But just because she read it didn't mean she intended to act on it.

He rubbed a hand down his face as frustration set in. Not toward her but toward himself. They'd only shared one kiss and one dinner date and he expected her to… what? Hell, he'd been thinking like a typical man when what he was dealing with wasn't a typical woman. He was finding that out while watching her interactions with Ciara. She was definitely a lot different from any other woman he'd dated over the years. Mainly the ones who understood their role in his life was just for pleasure, and he made sure his role in their lives was for the same purpose.

But what if Myra wasn't into taking on a casual lover?

Pete didn't want to think of that as a possibility, especially now that he was on board with the idea. Now that he'd accepted the fact that the attraction between them was way too strong. It had been hard sitting across from her and watching her eat their dessert of chocolate à la mode. Every time she licked her spoon was an erection waiting to happen.

A sound made him turn toward the stairs and his breath caught when he saw Myra standing there staring at him.

She had come after all.

Myra had questioned herself with every step she took down the stairs.

Peterson Higgins was way out of her league. He unsettled her. Made her wonder about things between a male and female that she'd never thought about before. With her lack of experience, a part of her wished she was getting a PhD in sex education instead of child psychology. Then she would know how to deal with this. How to deal with him.

Drawing in a deep breath, she paused on the stair. That was when he turned and looked at her. The minute their gazes connected she knew he did more than unsettle her.

She'd never had a weakness when it came to a man before. She could stand her ground with any of them. Being a sister to Baron made such a thing possible as he befriended some of the worst men alive. Men who had no respect for women and thought their only purpose was pleasuring a man.

Yet here she was. She'd come to Pete even when she knew it was not in her best interest to do so.

Myra had enjoyed their kiss last night even as she told herself it couldn't happen again. Yet every time she looked at his mouth, she *wanted* it to happen again.

And again and again.

The look in his eyes was telling. So was the erection pressing against his zipper. She should turn and run as fast as her legs could carry her. But she didn't. Something phenomenal was taking place between them and they had yet to exchange a single word. It was so intense it scared her in one sense but fueled the fire within her in another.

She didn't fully understand what was happening but knew it was something she could no longer deny. She didn't want it or need it but wasn't sure how to stop it.

Her father had always told her never to cower. If there was a problem, then you dealt with it. Therefore, somehow and someway, she was here to deal with the likes of Sheriff Peterson Higgins.

"You came."

The sound of his husky voice broke the silence, intruded on the strong sexual chemistry flowing between them. It did nothing to lessen the intensity. If anything, his voice heightened her awareness of him.

"Yes, I came."

She watched the sudden flare of his eyes. It seemed as if her response had ignited something within him. The very thought had her nerves dancing, and her brain racing. Not being able to handle the sexual excitement curling her stomach any longer, she asked, "So what's next?"

He smiled that slow, sensuous, make-your-panties-wet smile. "We talk first."

She blinked. *Talk?* Had he actually said that? Who wanted to talk at a time like this?

Myra's concentration was on him when he took slow, deliberate steps toward her. She hadn't walked all the way down the stairs and now he was coming toward her and bringing all that heat with him. When he reached the stairs, he extended his hand up to her.

She knew she had two options. Refuse the hand he offered and leave, or take it and go where he led.

What did he have to say?

She already had an idea.

Little did he know, although she was innocent about some things, she knew just how a man's mind worked.

Deciding at that moment which option she would choose, she took Pete's hand.

Pete led Myra over to the sofa, fighting hard to stay in control of his senses and his body.

The moment their hands touched, his pulse had done a double kick in response. But he was determined that they have "the talk." It was basically the same conversation he'd had with every woman since Ellen. However, Myra's would be modified somewhat. How? He wasn't sure yet. All he knew was that it would be different because she was different.

He sat down and placed her in his lap. Her sharp intake of breath signaled her surprise. Good, he had a lot more surprises in store for her.

Pete shifted her to face him at the same moment she nervously licked her lips. If she had any idea what that did to him, she would stop.

"What do you want to talk about, Pete? Although I think I know already."

"Do you?"

"Yes. This is where you tell me all you want is sex, sex and more sex and that you're going to make sure I enjoy it every time. However, what you don't want is me getting confused about anything. You don't want me to get sex mixed up with love. You want me to know that you don't do long-term, just short-term, and that your heart is encased in unbreakable glass."

He didn't say anything because what she'd said was true. That was what he'd intended to say, or at least a version of it. Some other man had given her the this-is-how-it-will-be speech before and she fully expected him to give her the same spiel.

Why did he suddenly feel like a total bastard?

"That's right, isn't it, Pete? That's what your talk will be about."

He stared at her, feeling drawn in by the way she was looking at him, by her scent, by the very essence of everything that was her. He drew in a deep breath knowing there was no need to lie, although at that moment he hated admitting the truth. "Yes, my talk would be similar to what you just said."

She nodded and somehow he could detect her disappointment. Had she expected more? Now that she knew she wasn't getting *more*, would she be willing to settle?

"I'm not into casual sex so I'm going to have to think about it, Pete."

A part of him was glad she wasn't going to rush into anything. He wanted her to be certain because once she gave her consent, he planned on taking her on one hell of a sensuous journey.

"I understand and I want you to think about it and not rush into your decision. However, I want to give you something to mull over while deciding."

"What?"

"This."

And then he captured her mouth with his.

Myra groaned. Pete's mouth devoured hers and she tried fighting the desire he was stoking within her. He was laying it on thick, to the fullest. This kiss was even more powerful than the one last night. Again she followed his lead. When he deepened the pressure, she moaned again. *This is what the girls at college would call one of those bone-melting kisses.*

Moments later, when he pulled his mouth away, all she could do was whisper his name. "Pete." She was convinced that she would be consumed with his taste for days.

Nibbling at her, he used his tongue to lick the corners of her mouth over and over again. "Say my name again," he whispered against her moist lips. "I want to hear you say it again."

"Pete." She didn't hesitate and the moment she said it, his tongue slipped back inside her mouth, claiming hers fully. She was tempted to tell him she'd made up her mind already. She wanted to move forward and didn't want any boundaries between them. She would deal with the consequences later.

Shivers rippled through her. If she were to tell him that now, without fully thinking things through, she would be embarking past a point of no return.

She wanted Pete. For her this was a first because she'd never truly wanted any man. She'd been curious about sex but not curious enough to throw caution to the wind. What she was craving wasn't based on curiosity but on something else altogether.

She was being stripped of her senses with this man and so far all they'd done was share kisses. But then he wasn't just kissing her—he was expertly making love to her mouth.

Somehow she mustered up the strength to rebel against her body's desires. No matter how much she was enjoying being in his arms this way, kissing him, she had to hold on to her sanity and not throw away twenty-four years of self-control for one night of passion that would mean nothing to him.

She was the one to pull away and it was only then that she realized he had maneuvered his hands under her skirt and was softly stroking her inner thigh.

Suddenly, memories of a similar scenario with Rick shot through her mind and she scrambled off Pete's lap, nearly falling to the floor in the process.

"Whoa, you okay?" he asked, when he caught her before she hit the floor.

No, she wasn't okay. She needed to breathe in deep, but more than anything she had to get out of there. Now. He must have seen the anxiety in her features. He tightened his hold on her. "Myra? Are you okay?"

She saw the concerned look on his face and instead of answering, she nodded. Drawing in a deep breath she said, "I'm okay and you can release me now, Pete."

The moment he did so, she took a step back. "I should not have come down here tonight. It was a mistake."

Then, without saying anything else, she rushed up the stairs.

Chapter 8

Pete stood at his kitchen window, drinking coffee while looking out at the expanse of his land. This was something he did every morning before leaving the ranch for work. One day Ciara would inherit Matt's share of this place and he was determined to keep things up and running for when that day came.

As he sipped his coffee, he thought about what had happened in his man cave last night. Myra had wanted him as much as he'd wanted her, he'd been sure of it. But when he'd touched her intimately, she'd bolted. Although she had denied anything was wrong, the look on her face had said otherwise. He'd been in law enforcement long enough to know when someone had had a flashback of something they didn't want to remember.

Had she once been the victim of sexual assault? Had some man tried touching her in the same place he had?

The thought that what he'd done might have conjured up bad memories had hit him in the gut last night and he could still feel the pain.

That was the reason he was still here, an hour later than he normally would be. He knew Ciara would wake up around eight and that Myra would get up earlier than that to start breakfast. He intended to be here when she did. He wanted to apologize for taking liberties he should not have. Everything they'd done had been consensual. The last thing he wanted was to create a hostile work environment. He had never taken advantage of a woman and wouldn't do so now.

"You haven't left for work yet?"

He turned at the sound of Myra's voice and then wished he hadn't. It took everything within him to ignore the shivers rushing through him. No woman should look this beautiful so early in the morning. She was wearing a pair of jeans and a pullover pink sweater. That color made her look feminine as hell and just as sexy. Then there was the way her curly hair hung loose around her shoulders. He doubted she was wearing any makeup and she looked simply radiant just the same.

Regaining control of the situation, he said, "No, I was waiting for you to wake up."

She wrapped her arms around herself in a somewhat nervous stance. "Why?"

He wanted to cross the room and pull her into his arms. He wasn't sure how he could make up for last night, but he would try. "I didn't want to leave before apologizing, for touching you in a place that made you uncomfortable. That was not my intent, Myra."

She didn't say anything. Instead she studied the floor for a minute. Then she raised her head and looked at him. "You didn't make me feel uncomfortable. Just the opposite, Pete. I liked you touching me there."

Relief rushed through him. And something else. Confusion. He again fought the urge to pull her into his arms. "Then can you tell me what last night was about? Why you ran away?"

She began nibbling her lips and he knew she was pondering what to tell him, if anything. "It's not important. At least not anymore."

He stared at her, wanting to accept what she was saying, but the cop in him knew there was more to it. However, if it was something she wanted to put behind her, she had that right.

"Okay," he said, moving past her to pour his unfinished coffee in the sink and rinse out his cup. When he turned back around, he asked, "Did you decide if you're taking Ciara to that festival?"

"Yes, I'm taking her."

He nodded. "I promised Pam I would help out after I got off."

"Okay, then we will see you there."

He nodded and headed for the door. Before grabbing his Stetson off the rack, he turned and walked back over to her and did what he'd wanted to do since first seeing her that morning. He pulled her into his arms, waited one moment to see if she'd lean in or away and then kissed her. He needed this. He wanted this. Her taste empowered him. When he released her mouth, he stared at her swollen lips.

"Was that your way of telling me your proposition of an affair is still out there?" she asked, staring up at him with a pair of gorgeous hazel eyes. Whenever she looked at him that way, he felt like a man doing a balancing act right above a dangerous cliff. One wrong move and he could fall.

He touched her chin. "It's my way of letting you know I am here if you ever need me."

Pete turned and headed for the door. Pausing, he grabbed his Stetson off the rack and then he looked back at her and said, "Yes, I still want an affair with you, Myra."

He then opened the door and left.

Myra touched her lips that were still tingling from Pete's kiss. When she heard the sound of his truck leaving, she moved to the table and sat down. The man was way too nice for his own good. And way too sexy.

After she'd left him last night she'd had a lot to think about because she'd done the very thing she'd sworn she would not do, and that was to allow the likes of Rick Stovers to dominate her thoughts. He wasn't worth it.

She would never forget how at twenty she'd drawn his attention, that of an older man, one twelve years older. He was a successful attorney and had seemed quite taken with her. She was in her last year of college and was home for the holidays. They'd met at a party and had immediately hit it off. He was a perfect gentleman and had wined and dined her, made her feel special.

And then one night, after plying her with a delicious dinner, he'd given her "the talk." At first she'd thought she was ready. She'd been a twenty-year-old virgin and had wanted to experience for herself what the whispers were about. But "the talk" from him had bothered her. Maybe because he had stated what he intended to do so matter-of-factly; it had given her pause.

They'd kissed and his hand had found its way under

her dress. He began getting rough. It was then that she had pushed him away and told him she wanted to leave. He'd got mad and told her she wasn't going anywhere. She owed him for the four weeks he'd wasted his time with her and he intended to have her with her brother's blessings. That was when Rick had told her everything, including Baron's suggestion that he seduce her. When she'd headed for the door, he had tried stopping her. The moment he put his hands on her, she put her self-defense training to good use. By the time she left his apartment he'd been on the floor, clutching his precious jewels and bawling like a baby.

She had gone straight to her brother's home and confronted him. He hadn't denied Rick's allegations and even said he didn't appreciate her making such a big deal about it. He'd further stated that Rick was a man and had needs and if she couldn't give Rick what he wanted, then she needed to get out of the game.

That was when she'd made the decision to leave older men alone.

Until Pete.

All she'd felt with Pete had been tenderness. His touch had been so different from Rick's. And so was the way he looked at her. After a good night's sleep, even his proposition of an affair didn't bother her. He wasn't looking for forever and neither was she. He was obviously still in love with his fiancée and would remain single for the rest of his days.

And although she wasn't interested in settling down now, a time would come when she would want to do so. She loved kids. At twenty-four she had plenty of time to find a man who wanted the same things she would want. Still, Pete's proposition was something she was thinking about.

Myra smiled when she heard Ciara waking up singing the song she'd taught her. As she left the kitchen to head toward Ciara's room, the kiss she'd shared with Pete still had her lips tingling and a part of her warned that if she wasn't careful, Pete could start her heart to tingling, as well.

Pete leaned back in his chair and gazed at the two men sitting across from his desk. Navy SEALs, Bane Westmoreland and his teammate David "Flipper" Holloway definitely looked the part even when out of uniform.

"I appreciate you letting me use this camera, Flipper. Now I'll capture some footage of my own to figure out who's trying to scare Katherine Lattimore."

"Any leads?" Bane asked, while sipping coffee.

"None. To be honest, we all thought the ghosts were in her head until she captured the images. It's obvious someone was in her backyard moving around dressed as a ghost. But when I went to check I couldn't find a single footprint."

"You know why," Bane said, grinning.

Pete frowned. "No, why?"

"Because ghosts don't have feet."

Pete shook his head. Having grown up with the Westmorelands, Pete was used to their penchant for humor when there was none. "You're turning into a comedian, aren't you? Maybe it's time for your commander to send you on another mission."

"Ignore Bane," Flipper said, rolling his eyes. "Seriously though, there has to be a reason for that, other than the wisecrack one Bane just gave. Mind if I take a look at the footage that lady captured, Pete?"

"Not at all."

It didn't take a minute for Pete to load the video into his computer and it took Flipper even less time to reach a conclusion. "That's not a real body moving around in her backyard."

Bane joined the two men at the computer. "Flip's right."

Pete frowned and studied the image. It looked pretty damn real to him. "But how?"

"It's fake," Flipper explained. "Made with a high-powered camera similar to what filmmakers use on set. It's so advanced you can basically code in that lady's address, and any sort of image you want will pop up on the property via satellite."

Pete ran a hand down his face. "Then that image could be coming from anywhere."

"Yes," Bane agreed, "but in order for the satellite to pinpoint the target, there has to be a digital receiver somewhere in Ms. Katherine's backyard. It's probably so tiny you either can't see it or it resembles something you wouldn't detect even if you saw it."

"But I bet the two of you probably could."

Flipper chuckled. "Of course. We're SEALs."

Yes, and Pete couldn't help appreciating that such competent men were protecting this country. "Who would go to the trouble of doing this?" he asked, thinking aloud.

Bane nodded. "An even bigger question is why. Ms. Katherine has lived in that house for years."

"It's not the same house that you and Bailey spray painted orange," Pete said.

Flipper glanced over at Bane. "You and Bailey spray painted some old lady's house?"

Bane shrugged. "One of my childhood pranks."

"Why?" Flipper wanted to know.

Bane smiled. "She was my teacher and wanted to promote me to the next grade. I wanted to hang back another year."

Pete contained his laughter when he saw how Flipper was staring at Bane. "Why would you want to be held back in school?" Flipper asked.

"So I could be in the same grade as Bailey."

Pete chuckled. "Now you see what the city of Denver had to put up with? Bane and Bailey, along with the twins, were holy terrors."

"We learned our lesson, trust me," Bane said. "Dillon made us repaint her entire house and not just the part we'd messed up. Ms. Katherine benefited when she got her entire house repainted." He glanced over at Pete. "So where is she living now?"

"In the house her fourth husband left her."

"The lady's been married four times?" Flipper asked.

"Yes." Pete then glanced over at Bane. "I think she got married again after you left for the military, Bane. She was only married to the guy a few years before he passed away."

"Well, it's my guess that someone is trying to scare her out of that house for a reason, Pete," Flipper said. "And whatever the reason is, they feel it's worth the money. Those kinds of illusions aren't cheap."

Later that day Pete pulled up into the acting school's parking lot an hour later than he'd originally planned. Getting out of his truck, he glanced around. The place was packed, and he knew why. One of Pam's sisters,

Paige Novak, had followed Pam's footsteps and pursued an acting career in Hollywood. It seemed she was making a name for herself. No doubt a lot of the people attending tonight were autograph seekers.

He got pulled into several conversations when he was seen by other people. That was fine because the closer he got to the door, the more his stomach became tied in knots knowing he would be seeing Myra.

He finally reached the door and a group of smiling men stepped out, grinning from ear to ear. He overheard their conversations and they were all muttering about how beautiful Paige Novak was. He thought so, too, but it was his opinion that Myra was even more of a stunner. There was something about the woman that got to him.

"Want a soda pop, Sheriff? It's two dollars."

He glanced down at the young woman. It was Pam's other sister, the youngest, who was working on her PhD at Harvard. "Don't mind if I do, Nadia," he said, fishing a couple of dollars out of the back pocket of his jeans. "I see Pam has you working."

Nadia laughed. "She has everybody working. Even Jillian flew home. She's in a booth dressed as a cowgirl and working the cotton candy machine"

Moments later Pete entered the foyer and could hear sounds coming from other parts of the building. He headed toward the auditorium, passing a number of people who tried getting him to stop and engage in conversation. However, he spoke and kept walking because at the moment he was on a mission to see two certain females. One had already stamped her name all over his heart and the other could…

He paused a moment to draw in a deep breath.

This was the first time since losing Ellen that the

thought of another woman getting close to him, especially to his heart, had ever crossed his mind. He couldn't help but wonder what that could possibly mean.

"How do you enjoy living with the sheriff and being nanny to his niece?"

Myra was convinced that if another person asked her that question, she would scream. So far, this was the sixth time. Pete had been right about some people worrying there was more going on under his roof than met the eye. Regardless of whether or not they were wrong in their assumptions, the bottom line was that she and Pete were adults who could do as they pleased.

"I enjoy taking care of Ciara," was her constant reply. She refused to address whether or not she enjoyed living with the sheriff.

"Evening, Ms. Coffer and Ms. Finley. If you don't mind, I need to borrow Myra for a minute," Lucia West-moreland said, appearing seemingly out of nowhere, and looping her arm with Myra's.

"Of course we don't mind," the ladies chimed simultaneously and then she was whisked off with Lucia, pushing Ciara in her stroller.

She gave Lucia an appreciative smile. "How did you know I needed rescuing?" Myra asked when they were out of earshot of the two women.

"Trust me, those two are the nosiest on this side of town."

Myra nodded. "Pete tried to warn me that if I took the job of nanny and moved in with him there would be talk, but I didn't believe him."

Lucia lifted a brow. "Why didn't you?"

"Well, mainly because this is Denver and I figured this town was more progressive than that."

"It is, for the most part, but like any place else there are those who thrive on gossip. Besides, for years Elnora Finley thought she had a vested interest in Pete. She was convinced Pete would make her daughter Rose a perfect second husband."

"Oh. Whatever happened to the woman's first husband?"

"He was killed in a motorcycle accident a few years back. Elnora felt since both Rose and Pete had lost the people they loved, they would be the perfect match."

Interesting. "Did Pete and Rose ever date?" She hated asking but a part of her wanted to know. Needed to know.

"Not that I know of. In fact, Pete had to pretty much tell Rose and Elnora to back off because he wasn't interested. For years after losing his fiancée he didn't date at all. And he rarely dates now."

Yet here Myra was, contemplating giving in to his proposition. Drawing in a deep breath, she knew it was time to make some decisions. Pete had brought out desires within her that she'd never dealt with before. To deny him would mean denying herself. She no longer wanted to do that.

"Well, look who just walked in."

Myra followed Lucia's gaze across the crowded room and her eyes connected with Pete's. His mouth edged up in a smile and she knew at that moment Peterson Higgins had gotten to her in a big way.

"Um, my magazine is doing a segment on law and order. I wonder if Pete would agree to be on the cover,

posing as a sexy Western lawman. I bet it would definitely increase sales."

Myra knew Lucia was editor-in-chief of a national
women's magazine, *Simply Irresistible*. With her gaze
still locked with Pete's, Myra said, "Yes, I bet so, too."

Pete felt the force of meeting Myra's gaze like a jolt
of sexual energy. Never had any woman consumed so
much of his concentration, his thoughts and his desires.
That included Ellen. When Ellen had died, she'd been
the same age Myra was now. Twenty-four. Now, as a
nearly thirty-seven-year-old man, he was facing an entirely different set of emotions. He was dealing with a
degree of lust he hadn't had at twenty-four.

She looked gorgeous, standing there beside Lucia
dressed in a long flowing cowgirl skirt, Western blouse
and cowhide boots. Her hair flowed around her shoulders beneath a cowgirl hat. At that moment he wished
he could cross the room and kiss her, regardless of the
crowd of people here.

"I hope you're staring at your nanny and not my wife,
Pete."

He didn't even break eye contact with Myra when
he responded to the person who'd come to stand beside
him. "I have two eyes and can check out both of them."

Derringer Westmoreland laughed. "You're crazy,
man."

"You think so."

"At least you better be because if for one minute I
thought you were honestly checking out Lucia, I would
have to end your life."

It was only when Myra's attention was drawn to a
woman who'd approached her and Lucia that Pete looked

over at Derringer. "Need I remind you of what could happen when you threaten a man of the law," he said, opening his bottle of pop to take a swig. He felt hot and needed a drink, even if the contents weren't as strong as he'd like.

Derringer chuckled. "That badge won't matter any to me. Besides, it won't be the first time you and I have battled it out."

Pete smiled, remembering that time in fifth grade. "Oh, yeah, and then when we got home, your momma gave us another ass-whipping."

"Only because Zane told on us. What we should do is go find him and beat the crap out of him. I don't care if it was close to thirty years ago. We can even get Riley to help us since he was the victim of Zane's snitching a few times, as well."

Pete glanced back over to where Myra stood, still talking. "Let's do it another night," Pete said. "I need to go rescue Myra from Ida."

"Okay, but just so you know, now you have me wondering about something."

Pete lifted a brow. "What?"

"Who's going to rescue Myra from you?"

Instead of addressing Derringer's comment, Pete moved across the room toward Myra.

Although the woman standing in front of her was steadily chatting, Myra was aware of Pete crossing the room toward her. His heat called out to her, encompassed her. She thought about what Lucia had said about him being on the cover of a magazine. She could envision him dressed as he was now, in jeans, a Western shirt,

Stetson and boots. The rugged cowboy type had never appealed to her before. Now, thanks to Pete, it did.

"Evening, ladies."

Before either Myra or the woman could return the greeting, Ciara let out a huge "Da-da." Myra watched the grin spread across Pete's face when he leaned down to take his niece out of the stroller. Once she was in his arms, Ciara planted a huge kiss on her uncle's cheek, nearly knocking his Stetson off in the process.

"My hat, too, Da-da," she then said, pointing to the miniature cowgirl hat on her head.

"I see. It's pretty."

"Me pretty, too."

Pete laughed. "You certainly are."

"Evening, Sheriff," Ms. Ida said. "I was just telling your nanny that if she needed more work after Bonnie comes back that I know a family on the other side of town who could use her services."

Had the woman said that? Myra wondered. She couldn't recall anything they'd discussed since becoming aware of Pete's approach. "I appreciate you looking out for me, Ms. Ida, but I'll be returning to Charleston not long after Miss Bonnie returns."

The woman looked disappointed. "Oh, how sad."

Myra wondered what would be sad about her leaving Denver. Before she could ponder that any further, Pete said, "If you don't mind, Ms. Ida, I need to borrow Myra for a moment." He took her arm and steered her off.

"Oh, of course."

Myra didn't say anything as she walked beside Pete, who carried Ciara. There was no need to tell him he could place Ciara back in her stroller since it was apparent he wanted to carry her around.

"I thought I'd better save you from Ida. She's known to be long-winded."

"She seems to be a nice lady."

"Yes, she is. Just talkative."

They didn't say anything for a while, satisfied to let Ciara take center stage as she sat atop Pete's shoulders, pointing out a number of things that caught her attention. "She's alert—that's good."

Myra chuckled. "She won't be for long. She missed her nap today."

"Have you guys eaten yet?" he asked her.

"Yes, we got here early and Pam fed all the helpers before the door opened."

He lifted a brow. "You're a helper?"

"I was. Ciara and I volunteered to take the first hour of face painting."

Pete grinned. "Let's be honest. You did the face painting and Ciara watched."

"She was my little helper. And by the way, I like your look."

He raised a brow. He had nice brows and his lashes were nice, as well. "And what look is that?"

"One of a notorious cowboy." He hadn't left home dressed that way this morning so he must have changed clothes at the office.

He chuckled. "A notorious cowboy? Evidently, you missed seeing this," he said, pointing to his badge. "This makes me a lawman."

As they continued to walk around, stopping at various booths, Myra was not only aware of the man by her side but that several people were staring at them…like they'd done that night at McKays. Pete was a very observant man and she figured he was noticing, as well.

"I could kiss you and really give them something to talk about," he whispered close to her ear.

She jerked her gaze up at him and saw the devilish twinkle in his eyes. He was joking, right? "I wouldn't suggest you do that," she said, biting back a smile. "How was your day?" she asked, switching their conversation to a safer topic. The last thing she needed was for the thought of them kissing to dominate her mind. It didn't take much to recall last night when she'd sat in his lap while he'd kissed her into sweet oblivion.

"Busy but hopefully productive. I think we might have a break in the case of Ms. Katherine's ghost."

"Really? How?" she asked him.

They continued walking while he told her. "There's something else I did a lot of today," he said while placing Ciara back into her stroller.

"Oh, what?" Myra asked him. She studied the broadness of his back as he bent down to the stroller. He had nice shoulders bulging beneath his Western shirt. Why were her palms suddenly aching to rub over them?

When he straightened, he glanced over at her. "I thought about you a lot today, and do you know what I mostly thought about?"

She wished she had the strength not to ask, but she was powerless while staring into the darkness of his eyes. "No, what did you mostly think about?"

"How it would feel making love to you."

She started them walking again, mainly to keep herself from shivering all over. She was glad they were in a somewhat secluded section of the auditorium. No one had heard what he'd said, she was sure of it. But she had heard him, loud and clear, and his words had glided over her body like molten liquid. It was as if she could feel his body's heat and his body's lust. At that moment breathing became difficult.

She knew what all this meant. It was time for her to walk on the sensuous side and be the passionate woman she believed she could be. But only with this man.

Glancing around to make sure they were still pretty much alone, she leaned in close to him and said, "Then maybe it's time for you to find out how it feels, Pete."

Chapter 9

Pete drove home following close behind Myra's vehicle, while images of kissing her again and making love to her all through the night aroused him in ways he'd never been aroused before. It had been hard to remain at the school and work the booth Pam had talked him into doing, handing out fake badges and telling kids about the importance of obeying laws. As soon as his time was up, he'd found Myra and Ciara and escorted them toward the parking lot so they could leave.

He doubted she had a clue what her words had done to him, but she would soon find out. What she'd said had pushed him to the edge. Yet he was determined not to pounce on her the moment they reached his ranch. Besides, she needed to get Ciara ready for bed and he would sing his niece to sleep. After all that, the night would belong to him and Myra.

He released a sigh when they reached the marker to his land. When had the drive from the acting school to his place become never ending? He slowed his pace, giving Myra time to maneuver her car along the long, winding driveway. His heart began pounding the closer he got to the house and when she parked her car, he pulled in beside her.

He got out of his truck and approached her car to open the back passenger door and take a sleeping Ciara from the car seat. Holding tight to his niece he wordlessly followed Myra up the walkway to the front door. After unlocking the door, she stepped aside when he carried Ciara to her room. Myra followed and after placing his niece on the dressing table, he stepped back.

"I'll be in the kitchen," he whispered, then left them alone. They might have eaten earlier, but he hadn't and he was hungry. Luckily for him, Pam had prepared him a to-go plate of ribs, corn on the cob, baked beans and coleslaw. He just needed to go back out to the truck to get it.

He had just finished the meal when the sound of Myra's voice came over the intercom. "Ciara is ready for bed now."

When he arrived in his niece's room it was to find her standing in the crib, barely able to keep her eyes open. She was getting older and it would soon be time to put her in a kiddy bed. He wasn't ready for the change and a part of him wished she could stay a baby forever. A baby who would always wait for her uncle to tuck her in and sing her a lullaby.

Closing the door behind him he noticed Myra had left. Was she somewhere having second thoughts about them sharing a bed tonight? Pete hoped not. He'd barely handled the buildup and couldn't imagine dealing with a letdown.

Taking Ciara into his arms, he moved to the rocker, and for the next few minutes he sang her to sleep, enjoying this time, their time, together. He had placed her in her bed when he noticed the note that had been slid under the door. A part of him was almost too nervous about what it might say to pick it up, but he picked it up anyway. Was it a note from Myra calling off their plans for tonight?

Drawing in a deep breath, he opened the sheet of paper and read the words.

Mr. Lawman, please meet me in the man cave. Myra.

Myra glanced around the room. She'd had to work fast to arrange things in here just right. While going through the pantry the other day she had found a box of candles, probably meant to be used in case of a power outage. However, tonight she intended to put them to a different use.

She'd grabbed a blanket off her bed to place in front of the fireplace, where a bottle of wine sat, along with two wineglasses. She'd even grabbed several pillows off the sofa upstairs.

The lights were dimmed and soft country music played—the theme of Pam's Wild West festival. Myra's goal was for them to continue in that vein and have their own Wild West night. She'd never done anything like this before; never deliberately set out to seduce a man. She should be the last person on earth to entertain thoughts of seducing a man—an older one at that—after what she'd gone through with Rick. But at least she had enough sense to know Pete wasn't anything like Rick.

Both were older, good-looking men, but when it came to class, Rick had somehow missed the boat. Whatever foolishness some women had told him over the years had gone to his head and stayed there.

With Rick it had been about conquering. But Myra believed with Pete it would be about pleasuring. The two men were as different as night and day. She was experiencing emotions and desires with Pete that she honestly hadn't thought she was capable of feeling. That was one of the reasons she'd initially gravitated to older men— because none of the guys her age ever made her desire or crave anything.

Last night Pete had not only been gentle, but he'd offered her a proposition and hadn't tried forcing it on her. He'd left the decision up to her and tonight she would let him know she intended to take him up on it. Literally. With her lack of experience, that might be an impossible feat, but she was energized and ready to try.

Pete Higgins had tempted her enough. He aroused her even when he didn't realize he was doing so, just by being him.

She glanced down at herself. She had changed out of her long skirt and blouse and put on another cowgirl outfit. This was one she'd seen while shopping in Breckenridge. Although at the time she hadn't a clue where she would wear it, it had been way too cute to pass up.

It was a black rhinestone-adorned minidress with an attached petticoat. What she'd liked most was the metal-and-rhinestone horseshoe belt buckle that came with it. The outfit was so short on her that it barely hit midthigh, and the way the lapels were turned back showed a generous amount of cleavage.

It was simply scandalous. Myra smiled thinking how

much she loved it. She couldn't wait to see Pete's expression when he saw her in it. Feeling a little nervous, she pushed her hair back from her neck and began pacing to the rhythm of the country music. A few beats later she stopped when she heard the door closing on the main floor. She glanced toward the staircase.

Swallowing, she watched as Pete descended the stairs with his eyes glued to her. He had the note she'd written in his hand. He was here and all those things she'd thought she would be brave enough to do and say to him suddenly left her. Drawing in a deep breath, she tried willing them back.

He moved away from the stairs toward her while sliding the note into the back pocket of his jeans. She could tell by the way he was smiling while his gaze roamed over her outfit that he liked what she was wearing. The heated look in his eyes was enough to make her back up a few steps.

"Going somewhere?" he asked, coming to a stop in front of her.

Pete looked like the sexiest man alive and now it was her turn to roam her gaze over him. She'd seen him when he first entered Pam's acting school, but now she was really getting her fill. The only thing missing was the Stetson he'd been wearing. He'd removed it when he'd entered the house, but she was still wearing her cowgirl hat.

She nervously licked her lips. "No, I'm not going anywhere. You came."

His chuckle was throaty and she was convinced the sound made the tips of her nipples harden. "Did you honestly think I wouldn't?"

At the moment, she couldn't think at all. She wanted

to run her hands all over him, trace her tongue across his lips and—

"You want to dance, Myra?"

His question caught her off guard, but she quickly recovered, or at least tried to. She had invited him to this party, so she needed to take ownership of it. But still, she appreciated that he was being patient with her.

"Yes, I want to dance."

He opened his arms and she went into them. She wasn't sure what song was playing. At the moment the only thing that mattered was she was here and so was he. Their bodies were pressed close together and his arms were wrapped around her as they swayed to the slow beat. She felt him. All of him. Especially his erection poking her middle. That was a sign that he wanted her and she knew without a doubt that she wanted him, as well.

She looked up at him and the arousal in his gaze nearly made her weak in the knees. He then smiled that same smile that always whacked her senses. Swallowing, she said, "I hope you don't mind me taking over your man cave."

"No, it looks good. You look good. I love your outfit. It's definitely an eye-catcher. I'm glad you didn't wear it to the Wild West show tonight. Otherwise, I would have had to hurt somebody."

His words heightened the beat of her pulse. "You mean you would have arrested them, right?"

"No, I would have hurt them first and arrested them later."

That made her smile because it hinted at a possessive nature she wasn't used to him demonstrating. And when he tightened his arms around her, she felt a throbbing sensation near his middle. Suddenly, he stopped dancing and stared at her. The silence in the room wasn't helping. The air between them seemed to thicken with sexual energy.

And then he leaned in and kissed her. He wrapped his arms around her even more tightly as his mouth took hers with a hunger that she felt in every part of her body. They'd kissed before, a few times, so why did it feel like every time their mouths joined there was some kind of awakening in her body? His kisses could arouse her, make her desire things that simply astounded her. She was feeling the full impact of Pete's kiss and she couldn't help but moan her pleasure over and over again.

Pete finally released Myra's mouth on a low, throaty groan. Then, sweeping her off her feet, he carried her over to the blanket in front of the fireplace. Never had he known such a responsive woman and he loved hearing every moan she made.

And he loved touching her, probably way too much. He couldn't recall ever wanting a woman with this much intensity…and that included Ellen.

With Ellen he'd had the desires of a young buck feeling his way around. Now he was a man with a different type of sexual hunger. He wanted to do more than just seduce Myra, more than merely satisfy primitive urges. He wanted to embark on emotions he'd long ago laid to rest. Miraculously, Myra was enticing him to reconnect. He'd tried ignoring her and had failed. She was not a woman a man could ignore, at least not for long or in some cases, not at all.

Getting on his knees, he joined her on the blanket and then stretched out beside her. He didn't want to rush her, was determined to make tonight as pleasurable for her as he knew it would be for him. After tonight she wouldn't remember any other before him. Why that was important to him he wasn't sure. All he knew was that it was.

He kissed her again and when he finally released her mouth, he whispered, "If I ever do anything that makes you uncomfortable, I want you to let me know. Okay?"

She stared at him through glazed hazel eyes and slowly nodded. For him it was important that she not only know that but believe it. The cop in him knew there had been more to her actions last night than she'd shared with him. He hoped in time she would share it all. For now, he'd resolved that whatever bad experiences she might have had, he would replace them with good ones.

"I'm wearing too many clothes," she whispered.

He smiled. Was that her way of letting him know she wanted to get naked? If so, he had no problem obliging her. "Then let me remove them."

Sitting up, he gently pulled her to face him. The flickering blaze from the fireplace was dancing all over her, making him burn even hotter for her. She was so beautiful and he loved looking at her. And this outfit he was about to take off her had been hot. When he'd come down the stairs and seen her, his erection had nearly doubled in size. She didn't look like your ordinary cowgirl— she looked like a cowgirl out of every man's fantasy.

"Let's start here," he said, removing her hat and placing it aside. He loved the way her hair looked all tumbled around her shoulders. Then he reached down for her feet so he could remove her boots and socks. She had pretty feet and her toes were painted a bright red. It occurred to him that he'd never paid much attention to a woman's feet before, just their legs. And tonight, with this outfit, she was showing a lot of hers and they were gorgeous.

"Did I tell you how much I like your outfit?"

Her chuckle was soft and sexy. "Yes, you told me."

"As much as I like it, now it's time to take it off."

She used the tip of her finger to trace along the collar of his shirt. "Do I get to take your outfit off of you?"

"Yes. I wouldn't want it any other way."

His words seemed to please her and he knew what would please him was kissing her while undressing her. So he proceeded to do just that. By the time he had her down to her bra and panties, her lips were swollen. What it was about her mouth that made him want to devour it, he wasn't sure. All he knew was that he did.

"Sexy," he said, running his fingers along the black lace of her matching bra and panties. He was careful not to touch her inner thigh, remembering what happened last night. But then he remembered what she'd told him this morning.

That she liked him touching her there.

"Now for this," he said, releasing the clasp of her bra and easing the straps from her shoulders. His breath caught when the twin mounds were freed from confinement. Her breasts were perfect. His erection doubled in size. Leaning toward her, he lowered his head and eased a nipple between his lips.

Myra was convinced Pete was trying to drive her mad. What man sucked a woman's breasts this way? With enough suction that she could feel the tips hardening in his mouth. With enough pressure that it triggered sensations between her legs. She closed her eyes and cupped the back of his head, to hold him there. She cried out in protest when he pulled his mouth away, but he moved to the other nipple. She sighed out her pleasure over and over again.

When he finally released her breasts, he stared at her as his fingers eased toward her inner thighs. Tentative at first, as if to gauge her reaction. She knew why. To ease his mind, she whispered, "Like I told you, I love the feel of you touching me anywhere."

He smiled. "In that case, now for these," he said, inching his fingers beneath the black lace of her panties. In a movement that was swifter than anything she'd ever witnessed before, he lifted her hips just enough to eased the panties down her legs.

This was the very first time any man had seen her naked and she wasn't sure how she was supposed to handle such a thing. The blatant heat, the fire and desire she saw in his eyes made any awkwardness she might have felt nonexistent. Instead, she felt empowered.

"Now for *your* clothes," she whispered, reaching for his shirt.

She held his gaze while working free the buttons, not thinking about how many there were but about what she would find when she had them all undone. Then he licked his lips. She didn't have a clue as to why.

Myra only licked her lips when she was nervous about something and she couldn't see him being nervous about anything. It must have had another meaning altogether. He did it again and the motion did something to her, made her nipples harden even more.

Evidently he saw the look on her face. "You know what that means, right?"

She wasn't ready to let him know about her lack of

experience. He would discover that soon enough. So for now, she lied and said, "Yes."

"Just making sure."

She had reached the last button and removed his shirt from a pair of masculine shoulders. She gazed at his stomach and flat chest and, giving in to temptation, she stroked her hand up and down his chest.

"Sweetheart, if you knew what your touch does to me, you wouldn't do that."

His words nearly undid her already capsized senses. "I'll be able to handle whatever that might be, Pete."

Instead of saying anything, he gave her a long, drugging kiss that had her whimpering. When he released her mouth, he eased her to her feet. "Now for my jeans. Do you want me to take over from here?"

She met his gaze and smiled. "I want to finish, but you can certainly help."

He nodded and ran his fingers across her nipples. "Just let me know when you need me to jump in."

She nodded. There was a first time for everything and it was her first time undressing a man.

Removing the huge belt buckle was easy. Undoing his zipper against a massive erection was another matter.

"Jump in," she finally said.

"No problem."

Not only did he unzip his pants for her, but he inched them past his waist so all she had to do was tug them down his legs so he could step out of them. That left him completely naked except for a sexy pair of black briefs. Hmm, Mr. Lawman had a downright sexy streak.

"One piece of clothing to go," she heard him say.

And she could just imagine what would happen when that last piece was gone. She reached out and gently tugged the briefs down a pair of masculine thighs to uncover what he was packing.

Lordy.

She looked at him and swallowed deeply. Before she could say anything, he said throatily, "I'll take over from here. Time for you to enjoy."

Pete couldn't help it when his gaze shifted down to Myra's womanly core. She was beautiful and he wanted to kiss her there. He *needed* to kiss her there. Brand her. Claim her. Possess her. His erection throbbed at the thought of doing all three.

He fought back a groan at the thought of kissing her all over, especially there. Without saying anything, he gently eased her back down on the blanket and kissed her mouth with a hunger he felt all through his body.

He moved from her mouth and kissed around her face and neck, eagerly making his way down south, kissing every area he traveled.

"Pete…"

He knew why she had moaned his name. It was as if his tongue had a mind all its own and was licking her everywhere, loving the taste and texture of her. When he'd reached the area between her legs, she grabbed his shoulders as if to stop him from going further. He remembered what he'd told her from the beginning. If he ever did anything that made her uncomfortable, to let him know.

Pete lifted his mouth from her stomach to stare up at her. "Has a man ever gone down on you before, Myra?"

She nervously licked her lips. "No."

He nodded and then, wanting to assure her that her lack of experience in that particular area was fine with him, he said, "Then I am happy to introduce you to the wonder of it all. Is that okay?"

"Yes."

He then lowered his mouth back to her stomach to pick up where he'd left off. He licked her, loving the taste of her skin. He kissed below her navel and continued moving lower.

He felt her tense and looked back up at her to make sure she was okay. "We're good?"

She nodded, a tentative smile on her lips. "No, *you're* good. I don't think you know how you're making me feel, Pete."

He wanted to tell her that she hadn't felt anything yet, but decided he could show her better than tell her. He lowered his head and gently nudged her thighs apart. Her feminine scent was intoxicating. She moaned his name the moment he slid his tongue inside her.

Not wanting to wake Ciara, Myra fought back a scream of pleasure. And when his tongue began moving inside her with intense strokes, she fought back another scream while thrashing on the blanket. He finally used his hands to grip her thighs and hold her still. What on earth was his mouth doing to her? She wanted him to stop, but knew if he stopped she would die. Never had she experienced anything like this. All kinds of sensations were plummeting through her all at once.

And when his tongue went deeper and the strokes became more intense, she did release a scream. Her body was hit with what she knew had to be an orgasm. Her very first. Ever. She closed her eyes as she felt like she was undergoing some sort of out-of-body experience with Pete's tongue still planted deep inside her.

Then suddenly another orgasm hit, this one stronger than the last. She felt the intensity of it in every bone. Her body bucked several times beneath his mouth, but he held tight to her hips, refusing to remove his tongue.

When the tremors slowly subsided, she felt Pete move away and she slowly opened her eyes. He was sliding on a condom. Then he came back and straddled her body.

"You're ready for me now, baby," he said as he eased into her.

She knew now was the time to tell him that not only had no man ever gone down on her before him, but none had gone inside of her before either. Moments later, when his body suddenly went still and he stared down at her, she knew it was too late. He'd figured things out for himself.

Before he could ask her anything, she placed her arms around his neck to force his mouth down to hers. Before their lips touched, she whispered, "We're good?"

Instead of answering he pushed more into her tight womanly core until it seemed he couldn't go any farther. He went still again, as if giving her time to adjust to the pressure of his engorged erection planted deep inside her.

Then he began moving, slow at first and then with more intensity. More vigor. It wasn't long before his thrusts became long, hard and deep and she unwrapped her arms from his neck to grab hold of his shoulders. It was as if he was riding her the way he would ride Satin and she could feel his every moment.

Suddenly her body was hit with tingling sensations all over again, with more intensity. And this time she wasn't alone. Pete threw his head back and let out a deep, guttural growl as his body bucked several times. They reached orgasmic pleasure together. She held on to him and he held on to her.

When the last of the tremors had passed through their bodies, he eased down beside her. Entwining their legs, he pulled her into his arms. The last thing she remembered before sleep claimed her was the feel of him softly caressing her stomach and whispering, "No, sweetheart. *You're* good."

Pete stopped the alarm before it could go off. The last thing he wanted was to wake the woman sleeping naked beside him. It had been one hell of a night. He'd wanted to be gentle, after he'd learned it was her first time, but she hadn't let him. She'd deliberately brought out the lusty beast in him.

He found it amazing that at twenty-four she hadn't shared a bed with a man until last night. Until him. He'd had the honor of introducing her to pleasure and she'd told him so many times how much she had enjoyed it.

After that first time, he'd carried her upstairs where he joined her in a hot, sudsy tub bath. Then he'd toweled her dry and carried her to his bed. When she complained about them not drinking any of the wine, he'd gone back down to the man cave to snuff out the candles and grab the wine bottles and glasses. They'd sipped wine in bed, then made love all over again before dozing off to sleep.

She was the one who'd awakened him at two in the morning telling him it was her turn to do the licking. He wouldn't let her, simply because having her mouth on him would have killed him and he wasn't ready to die yet. In the end they'd made love again. And from the looks of it, she was sleeping peacefully now, and he figured she was just as satisfied as he was.

He wished he could stay in bed with her all day, but he had a job to go to and she had Ciara to take care of. However, there would be tonight and he was looking forward to coming home to her. Their days of ignoring each other were done.

Pete forced himself to remember that whatever they were sharing was short-term. She would be leaving Denver in a few weeks. He knew it and accepted it. The only thing they had was the present and he intended to take advantage of the time they had left. He refused to dwell on the fact that Myra Hollister was definitely everything a man could want in a woman.

She was everything he not only wanted but also what he needed.

"Good morning, lawman."

He shifted in bed and smiled over at her. "Good morning. I didn't mean to wake you."

"You didn't. I'm too wound up to sleep long after last night."

"Because of last night you should be exhausted."

She chuckled. "I'm not. Are you? Being an old man and all."

He leaned toward her. "But you enjoyed this old man last night, right?"

"Immensely. I can't describe exactly how I feel, Pete."

Myra decided not to even try. All she knew was what they'd shared had been a game changer for her. She knew it and felt assured Pete knew it, as well. Just like they both knew this affair would end when Miss Bonnie returned. She tried not to let the thought bother her. He had his life here and she had hers someplace else.

She had entertained the thought of returning to Denver for the Westmoreland Charity Ball on New Year's Eve, but now she wasn't sure that was a good idea. What she should do was enjoy what they were sharing now, and when it was time for her to move on, to do so without looking back. Without coming back.

In the meantime…

"Pete?"

"Yes, sweetheart?"

She wondered if he knew what the endearment did to her. "Do you know what I'd like?"

From the look in his eyes she knew he had an idea. "No, what would you like?"

"For you to leave me with something to think about all day until you return."

The smile that appeared on his face was priceless. "That can definitely be arranged."

He then pulled her into his arms.

Chapter 10

"So, there you have it, Pete," Detective Lewis Tomlin was saying.

"Carl Knight, who is serving time in prison for armed robbery, claims he buried his loot in Ms. Katherine's backyard underneath that storage shed while he was hiding out from the Feds. It's my guess that he shared that information with a fellow inmate who passed it to someone on the outside who's trying to scare her into selling the house."

Pete nodded. "Did you question Ms. Katherine about anyone trying to buy her house in the last year?"

"Yes," Lewis said, "she did say that someone had shown up twice inquiring if she wanted to sell and both times she told them she didn't. Said he was a nice man and that he gave her his business card in case she changed her mind."

"Knowing Ms. Katherine, I bet she still had that card."

"Yes. We put a trace on it and the name is connected to a trust. But I'm on it. Hopefully in a week I'll have the name of the person that trust belongs to."

Pete leaned forward in his chair. "Okay, and since we're talking about money missing from a bank robbery, at some point we'll need to get the FBI involved."

When Lewis left his office, Pete leaned back in his chair. When would people learn that crime didn't pay? He knew Lewis wouldn't leave any stones unturned. But if whoever owned that trust couldn't scare off Ms. Katherine, then what? He didn't feel good about this entire thing.

He pressed a button on his desk phone. When his administrative assistant came on the line, he said, "Monica, find deputies Anderson and Sims. I want to see them."

"Okay, Sheriff."

He would instruct them to drive by Ms. Katherine's home more frequently, especially at night. They were squad leaders and would make sure it was done. Standing, he walked over to the window and looked out. He would never tire of this view of the mountains.

Glancing at his watch, it seemed the day was dragging by. It wasn't even lunchtime yet. He shook his head. He'd never been a clock-watcher when it came to his job, but now there were two special females waiting for him. Namely, Ciara Higgins and Myra Hollister.

It was hard to believe it had been almost two weeks since the night he and Myra first made love. Things had certainly changed since then. They now shared the same bed every night, and his day would start with them making love every morning. She also joined him for breakfast, usually preparing him pancakes…made of wheat of course…and turkey bacon and sausage. Her kind of food was beginning to grow on him, and he did feel healthier.

What he enjoyed most was at night, after they'd put Ciara to bed, when over dessert he would share with Myra how his day had gone. It felt nice having someone to come home to and share details with. Then they would go down to his man cave and watch a movie or football. When they retired for bed, it was together. He enjoyed sleeping with her at night and waking up with her in his arms every morning.

They spent their time talking about several subjects. However, the one thing they never talked about was the time when she would be leaving. He'd heard from Jason that Myra had approached Bella about staying at the inn after Bonnie came back. He intended to tell Myra she didn't have to do that. He certainly had enough room at his ranch.

Bottom line, he wasn't ready for her to leave and doubted he ever would be. However, he had to face the fact she *was* leaving. Therefore, he would do the only thing he could, which was to make every moment count.

He turned at the sound of his phone and then moved to click it on. "Sheriff Higgins."

"Pete, this is Pam."

He smiled as he settled into the chair behind his desk. "Hey, Pam, what can I do for you?"

"Dillon's birthday is coming up and he doesn't want us to make a fuss since a lot of the family will be here for the Westmoreland Charity Ball. But I wanted to at least prepare a special meal for this Friday's chow-down. I'd love for you to make it, and please bring Myra and Ciara. I appreciated Myra's help at the Wild West show."

"Ciara and I will be there and I will let Myra know the invitation extends to her, as well."

"Okay, thanks."

He hoped Myra would attend with him. It'd be another moment to cherish.

"So, how are things going with that nanny gig?" Wallace asked Myra, after she'd put the casserole in the oven and sat down at the kitchen table to call him.

She'd just put Ciara down for her nap after feeding her lunch. From where Myra sat, she could see the Christmas tree in the living room. She would never forget the day they'd gotten it. And because this would be Ciara's first Christmas with Pete, and he'd never thought of having a tree before, that had meant shopping for ornaments, as well. The two of them, with a little help from Ciara, had decorated it. Myra would never forget the look of happiness on the little girl's face when Pete had switched on the lights for the first time. Even now, whenever they lit the tree, Ciara would sit in front of it and stare at the blinking lights.

"Myra?"

Wallace had asked her a question that she had yet to answer. "It's going great. Ciara is wonderful."

"And Ciara's uncle?"

She wondered why Wallace would ask her about Pete. She wasn't sure who knew that her and Pete's relationship had changed. They seldom went out. They now had a reason to stay in. She certainly hadn't breathed a word about anything to Wallace.

"Why would you ask me about her uncle?"

He paused and then said, "Well, you did say that early

on he hadn't wanted to hire you because he thought you were too young."

She couldn't help but smile at the memory. A lot had certainly changed since then. "Well, once I began working here and he saw how competent I was, his opinion changed."

"I knew it would. I figured you would eventually win him over."

Myra had news for Wallace. Pete had won her over, as well.

She had fallen in love with him.

That fact couldn't be disputed even though she wished otherwise. But she lived with the evidence every day—when she looked forward to him coming home, when he found her in the kitchen, when he would pull her into his arms with a kiss...

"You don't have long now."

Wallace's words pulled her back into the present. "I don't have long for what?"

"To work for the guy. Won't the regular nanny be back in two weeks?"

Yes, Miss Bonnie would be back and Pete wouldn't need Myra anymore. She and Pete never talked about her leaving because it was a foregone conclusion that she would be. She needed to go to Charleston and claim the company back and then turn it over to Wallace. But what then?

Pete was very much aware of when her last day would be. He hadn't shown any inclination that he'd want to see her again after she left. She doubted he knew she planned to remain in Denver until the day after Christmas. If he knew, would he invite her to spend Christmas with him and Ciara?

She'd known she had to leave, but she had fallen in love with him anyway.

On top of that, his heart still belonged to a dead woman.

"Myra?"

Again she'd left one of Wallace's questions hanging. "Yes, Miss Bonnie will be back in two weeks." Then, deciding to change the subject, she said, "How are things going at the office?"

"So far, okay, but I have a feeling Baron and his friends are up to something. I don't know what, but it's not good. They have been whispering a lot amongst themselves."

"They're probably trying to come up with a plan for stopping me from reclaiming the company. I talked to Lloyd the other day and he assures me there is nothing they can do. All I have to do is show up."

Lloyd Kirkland had been the company attorney for years and one of her father's close friends. He'd been appalled at how Baron had managed to manipulate the stockholders into putting him in charge and replacing Wallace.

"According to Irene, they still think you're out of the country. Baron has hired someone to find you."

Irene was one of the department heads and, like Lloyd, had worked for the company for years. She was loyal to Wallace and tried keeping him abreast of what Baron was up to.

"Let them try. I covered my tracks well. They will see me when it's time for them to see me."

When she ended the call with Wallace, Myra decided to grab a nap for herself while Ciara slept. She and Pete made love every night before they went to sleep and in the mornings when they woke up. She wasn't used to such a vigorous routine.

She smiled when she thought about all they'd done together since making love that first time. Once he'd gotten over the fact that she was inexperienced, it was as if he intended to give her all the training she needed. She couldn't keep up with all the positions they'd tried and the rooms where they'd made love. Her favorite spot still remained on a blanket in front of the fireplace.

Myra walked out of the kitchen the same time the front door opened and Pete walked in. "Pete! I didn't know you were coming home for lunch. Had I known, I would have made—"

"I didn't come home for lunch," he said, tossing his Stetson on the rack with perfect aim, all while walking toward her.

"Oh?"

"I came home for you."

The combination of what he'd said and how he'd said it caused the pulse at the base of her throat to throb. And she could only stare as he walked toward her, the epitome of masculinity.

When he came to a stop in front of her, he placed his hands at her waist and a surge of longing ripped through her.

"So what do you have to say to that, Myra Hollister?"

She started to speak and felt her breath wobble. So, instead of saying anything, she leaned up on her tiptoes and pressed her mouth against his. That was another thing she was in training for. Kissing 101. She took her time brushing her lips over his full and sexy ones. And then she used her tongue to lick the curve of his mouth and lower to his jawline.

Myra heard the way he was breathing and decided to exert a little pressure with her mouth and tongue. She was convinced that she hadn't been properly kissed until Pete. She continued to let her lips roam over his while teasingly licking, sucking and nibbling, loving how he let her do her thing while he fought for control. The hands holding her at the waist tightened as she greedily sucked his lower lip.

It didn't take long for Pete to grow impatient with her playing around with his mouth. Suddenly he crushed his mouth to hers. His hands plunged into her hair, as if to pull her head even closer so he could consume her.

Then, with the same intensity, he released her mouth, only to sweep her into his arms and head toward the bedroom.

Chapter 11

"So are you going to tell her?"

Pete lifted a brow at Derringer. They'd been standing on the other side of the room watching Dillon cut his birthday cake while the women were busy setting out plates. "Tell who what?"

Derringer rolled his eyes. "Myra Hollister. Are you going to tell her how you feel about her?"

Pete crossed his arms over his chest. "And just how do I feel about her?"

Derringer shook his head. "If you have to ask me, then you're in worse shape than I thought. You love her. I can see that."

"Can you?" Pete asked, before taking a sip of his punch.

"Sure can, and I hope you tell her before she leaves town."

Pete didn't say anything as he glanced across the

room to where Myra stood holding Ciara while smiling and talking to Bella, Lucia and Bane's wife, Crystal. She fit in well with them, the wives of the men he considered good friends. And Derringer was right.

He had fallen in love with her, even though he knew doing so had been a mistake.

They could have no future. She had a life beyond Denver, although he hadn't a clue what she intended to do with it other than leave here. It was something they never talked about, a subject he avoided because the idea of her leaving was something he tried not to think about. But he didn't have much time left with her so he had to think about it whether he wanted to or not.

What could he offer her? He tried to ignore the voice that said: *You have your love to offer.*

"Well?"

Derringer reclaimed his wayward thoughts. "Well, what?"

"Are you going to stop her from leaving?"

Stop her from leaving?

"Not without a warrant," he said, trying to bring a little lightheartedness into the conversation.

Derringer wasn't having it. "Don't be a smart-ass, Pete. Are you or are you not going to tell her you love her to stop her from leaving?"

"No, I'm not. I might desire Myra but my duty is to my niece."

"Then I think you are making a huge mistake."

Although Myra was contributing to the conversation with the ladies around her, she was conscious of Pete's eyes on her. She was tempted to return his stare but she didn't for fear that he would look into her very soul.

And see her love. Feel her love. Discover the thing she didn't want exposed.

"So, Myra, you and Pete share the same birthday?"

Megan Westmoreland's question reclaimed her immediate attention. Did they? She'd had no reason to ever ask when his birthday was. "If we do, I didn't know it."

"Pete is also a Christmas baby," Lucia said, grinning. "That's the one thing I remember about his parents while growing up. They would come into Dad's paint store around the holidays. Mr. Higgins was good with his hands and every holiday he would make something for Pete. Since Pete was a Christmas baby, he wanted to make a special birthday gift for him so he wouldn't feel cheated out of a birthday celebration."

Myra took a sip of her punch, remembering her parents did the same thing for her birthday. They always made it special. This would be her first without them. "If I was going to be around, I would bake him a cake, but I'm leaving the day after Christmas."

"You're still leaving?" Bella asked, surprised.

"Yes, I'm still leaving." Myra could see the confused looks on the women's faces. "Why do you ask?"

"We thought… We were hoping that something was going on between you and Pete," Megan said, hesitating before getting it out there.

Myra knew it would be a waste of time to lie to the three women. Besides, women who were in love would recognize that same emotion in another woman and there was no denying that she had fallen in love with Pete.

"Yes, something is going on, but not what you think," she said softly, feeling the impact of the words she'd spoken. She knew they understood her meaning.

"I think you might be wrong," Megan said gently.

"I've known Pete all my life. He's been best friends with Derringer and Riley forever. I remember Dad would often tell him that if he continued to hang around with them as much as he did he would begin to look like a Westmoreland," she said, chuckling. "There were times people thought he *was* a Westmoreland because he would go on a lot of family trips with us."

She took a sip of her punch and added, "I know how hard he took Ellen's death and how he shut himself off because of it. But over the past month I've seen him come to life. He began thawing out when Ciara got here, but now he's back to being the Pete we all know and love. I think you might be underestimating his feelings for you, Myra."

Megan's words remained on Myra's mind all through the ride home from Dillon's party. They were like a seed in her heart that she wanted to bloom. Was she underestimating his feelings for her? Could there really be more between them than sex?

And what if there was? She would still have to leave to return to Charleston and handle that business with the company. It would be a smooth transition if Baron didn't try making things difficult. Yet she couldn't see him agreeing to leave without a fuss. Either way, she would love nothing more than to have it settled and be done with it so she could return to Pete and Ciara—if he truly cared for her like the Westmoreland ladies thought.

On top of that, Myra couldn't ignore the call she'd gotten from Wallace two days ago. Baron had run into one of his old college girlfriends and she'd mentioned seeing Myra in Breckenridge, Colorado, around Thanksgiving. That meant there was a good chance Baron would be moving his search to that area. Wallace felt she should tell Pete what was going on. She disagreed. Baron was her problem and the last thing she intended to do was get Pete involved.

"You're quiet. Is everything all right, Myra?"

She blinked, realizing they had reached Pete's ranch. Forcing a smile, she looked over at him. "I just have a lot on my mind. Miss Bonnie will be returning next week."

"But that doesn't mean you have to move out. Derringer mentioned you intended to stay at Bella's inn for a week before leaving town."

"Yes, those are my plans. I do have to move out, Pete." Surely he didn't think she could stay here and continue their relationship with Miss Bonnie in the house?

As if he read her thoughts he said, "We're adults, Myra. We shouldn't have to sneak around. Besides, I'm too old for that sort of thing."

"This is coming from a man who didn't want to hire me because of possible talk?" she asked, frowning.

"And you're the one who said you didn't care what people might say or think about you living with me."

She rolled her eyes. "We're not talking about people, Pete. We're talking about Miss Bonnie."

"I know. But you don't have to worry about Bonnie. I got a call from her today and she asked if she could remain with her sister an additional week. I think she might feel guilty about leaving her alone for the holidays. I told her I would talk to you to see if you could remain another week. Would you?"

Undisguised happiness swelled inside of Myra. That meant she would have an extra week to spend with Pete and Ciara. That would make leaving even harder, but she would take it and deal with the consequences later.

Drawing in a deep breath, she said, "Yes, I'll remain for an additional week."

Pete woke up the next morning and glanced over at the clock. Although it was Saturday, he usually would get out of bed early anyway since it was his day to take care of Ciara. Myra was still entitled to two days off even though she never really took them anymore. She seemed content to spend her off days hanging out at the ranch with him and Ciara and he didn't have any problem when she did. Regardless, he didn't want to take advantage of her time in case she had something else to do.

But then he had made sure she would be free this weekend for an entirely different reason.

He glanced at the empty spot in his bed wondering how Myra had gotten up without waking him.

He hadn't told her yet, but he'd asked Charity Maples to babysit Ciara for him tonight because he planned to take Myra out on a date. Two days ago, he'd made reservations at Barnacles for dinner and figured they could take in a movie afterward.

Pete chuckled. He wasn't as slow as Derringer thought. Although the timing wasn't right to tell her how he felt about her. Chances were, she didn't feel the same way, and there was no way he could stop her from leaving. What he *could* do was give her a reason to come back. He no longer felt he had to chose between duty and desire. He could have both.

Getting out of bed he quickly went into the bathroom and washed up, brushed his teeth and shaved. A short while later he was walking out of his bedroom and headed toward the kitchen where the sound of voices could be heard. Namely, Myra and Ciara. They were both singing…or trying to sing.

He couldn't help the smile he felt touch his lips. Myra had made his house a home and he wasn't sure how he and Ciara would handle her absence. Bonnie taking an additional week had postponed the inevitable but for how long?

At least Myra would be here on Christmas Day, since she was leaving the day after. He had assured her he could handle things for a day until Bonnie got back.

Walking into the kitchen, he said, "Good morning."

Two pairs of feminine eyes glanced over his way. He would give anything for them to keep that look of happiness in their gazes when they saw him.

"Da-da," Ciara said, reaching out her arms to him.

He headed toward her, but not before stopping in front of Myra to place a lingering kiss on her lips. "I didn't hear you leave the bed this morning."

She gave him a mischievous grin. "I guess one of us was exhausted for some reason, Mr. Lawman."

He leaned in close to her ear and said, "I guess I should be thankful you aren't calling me Mr. Old Man."

She threw her head back and laughed. "I must admit I am finding it hard to believe that you're letting this young woman get the best of you."

He smiled. "Only because I'm exhausted from getting the best of you."

Now he was the one to throw his head back to laugh; he had effectively put her at a loss for words. And while he had her in that condition, he figured it would be a good time to tell her about his plans.

"By the way," he said, after taking Ciara out of the high chair. "I hired a babysitter for Ciara tonight."

Myra looked at him dumbfounded. "A babysitter? Why?"

He knew he had to be careful how he answered. "Because I want to show my appreciation for all you've done for me and Ciara while Bonnie has been gone. I want to thank you."

"You don't have to thank me, Pete. Besides, are you okay with a sitter keeping Ciara? She won't stay with just anybody."

He studied Myra's features and wondered if she'd gotten upset with what he'd said. For some reason she sounded annoyed.

"I do need to show you how much I appreciate what you've done and as far as a sitter goes, Charity is seventeen and the daughter of one of my deputies. She's kept Ciara a number of times for me in the past. She's a responsible teen and she and Ciara get along just fine. There's no need for you to worry about anything."

Myra knew she sounded pretty ungrateful and that wasn't how she wanted to come off. Taking her to dinner was truly a nice gesture on his part. Just because she was in love with him didn't mean she should expect him to feel the same way about her.

"Then after dinner we would take in a movie."

She stared at him. Dinner and movie? Did he not know those things constituted a date?

That was probably the last thing he wanted but those were his plans, not hers. He would figure out the mistake he'd made when he ran into people who knew him and recognized her as the nanny, and noted the two of

them were out and about without Ciara. She would be
leaving after next week. He would be the one left here
to deal with talk because he'd sent out the wrong message in trying to show his appreciation.

She wished she could tell him that she didn't want his
appreciation but his love, but that was out of the question. She had to take care of her family business, and
his heart was still taken.

"Do you not want to go to dinner with me?"

She wanted to go. She valued him showing his appreciation. She'd get over her feelings.

He had explained his intentions from the beginning.
He had not been looking for a lasting relationship. It was
only about sex. It wasn't like he hadn't told her because
he had, and she'd accepted his terms.

"Yes, I'd love to go out to dinner with you, Pete,"
she said.

And just like he wanted to show his appreciation to
her, she could certainly show hers to him, in her own
special way.

It wasn't too late when they returned home. Charity
told them what a great little girl Ciara had been, before
leaving in her own car.

"I like her," Myra said about Charity, when Pete
joined her in Ciara's room. They both stood over the
little girl's bed just watching her sleep. Pete knew his
niece had captured Myra's heart the same way she'd
captured his. Even if Myra didn't care about seeing him
again after leaving Denver, she would be tempted to return to see Ciara.

"Want to join me for a cup of coffee, lawman?" Myra
said, smiling.

He smiled back. "I don't mind if I do, cowgirl."

Because he had such a wide hallway, they managed to walk down the hall side by side while holding hands, which was something they'd done at the movies. Dinner had been great and the movie had been entertaining, as well. They'd run into a number of people he knew, most of them his age, and they hadn't found it newsworthy that he was out on date with his niece's nanny. In fact, when he had introduced her to them, he'd introduced Myra as a good friend.

He sat down at the table while she got the coffee going. He liked watching her move around his kitchen, loved the movements of her hips and the sway of her hair around her shoulders. When she turned around, catching him staring, she smiled.

"I enjoyed dinner and the movie, Pete. Thanks for taking me."

"I'm glad you did and you're welcome." He wanted to suggest that they do it again, but he didn't want to bring up the fact that she was leaving soon.

She placed his cup of coffee in front of him and then joined him at the table with hers.

Finally, he decided to ask, "Are you looking forward to returning to Charleston?" She didn't answer right away. Could it be that she would miss him and Ciara? He knew they would miss her.

"Yes, I'm looking forward to returning home."

He didn't say anything as he sipped his coffee, wondering how he was going to let her leave when the time came. "You'll be leaving Denver before the coldest part of our winter."

"I won't miss that."

Because he had to know, he asked, "Will you miss me?"

She met his gaze and held it for a long moment. "Most definitely. I'm going to miss you, Pete."

A surge of passionate energy passed between them and they placed their coffee cups down at the same time. Who got up from their seat first, Pete wasn't sure. Nor did it matter. All he knew was that Myra was in his arms and he was kissing her in a way he hoped let her know he would also miss her. Miss kissing her. Miss making love to her. Miss seeing her. Miss talking to her. He would miss her in ways he couldn't even imagine right now.

Their tongues tangled with a desperation and hunger he'd never experienced, never with such urgency as this. The cause might have been knowing they were racing against time. Soon they would have to say their goodbyes. Now, though, they were succumbing to unbridled passion.

Suddenly, he swept her off her feet into his arms. He'd intended to make it to his bedroom, but he only made it to the dining room before he knew he had to have her now. "I need you now, baby. I can't wait."

After placing her back on her feet, Pete yanked his shirt from his pants and proceeded to take it off while watching her remove her own clothes. It didn't matter to him that this was the first time he'd ever stripped naked in his dining room. He knew before it was all said and done, he would be doing a hell of a lot more in this dining room.

She was back in his arms and he was kissing her again with a fervor he felt in every part of his body, especially in his throbbing erection. He broke off the kiss, needing to touch and taste her everywhere. He needed to feel his hands glide over her breasts, enjoying how her nipples hardened beneath his fingers.

He needed to know if she was ready for him, so he lowered his hands to the area between her legs. She moaned when he touched her there, and he eased his finger inside of her. Yes, she was ready for him.

Lifting her up, he placed her on the dining room table and wrapped her legs around his neck. Then, nudging her thighs apart, he thrust into her, going as deep as he could go. And when he was satisfied he couldn't go any further, he held tight to her hips and began moving in and out of her. He was filled with a greed that went beyond anything he'd ever experienced before. It was as if he'd become insatiable, but only for her.

With this position he not only felt her but he could look at her, see the play of emotions on her face caused by his every thrust. He loved watching her expressions and knowing he was the cause. As if she needed to see his emotions as well, she used her inner muscles, as if trying to milk every single thing out of him.

It was then that he grasped he wasn't wearing a condom. That realization must have shown in his expression, because she whispered, "I'm on birth control and I'm safe."

"And I'm safe, too," he said, continuing to pump hard into her.

When he felt her begin to shudder, he leaned in and captured her mouth as the same orgasm that struck her hit him, as well. His body bucked and then bucked again as he poured into her, the first time he'd done such a thing with any woman.

But he was doing it with her. The woman he loved with every part of his being. The woman who didn't have a clue what she meant to him. He wanted her to have it all. He kept thrusting until there was nothing left to give.

It was only then that he released her mouth and slumped down on her. Burying his face between the most gorgeous pair of breasts, and the tastiest.

At that moment Pete knew the hardest thing he would ever have to do would come on the day he would have to let her go.

Chapter 12

Pete tossed the pencil on his desk, leaned back in his chair and placed the palms of his hands at the back of his neck. He'd been doing that all morning, in the middle of reading or writing a report. That was when thoughts of Myra would flash through his mind.

It had been almost a week since their date on Saturday night, when he'd taken her to dinner and a movie and then they'd later made love on his dining room table. He still smiled at the memory and he had new admiration for that table and its sturdiness.

He tried not to think about how time seemed to be quickly going by. Christmas was next week. And he'd fallen deeper and deeper in love with Myra. He tried showing her every time they made love without saying the words. A couple of times during the throes of passion the words nearly slipped out anyway. She still hadn't de-

cided if she would return for the Westmoreland Charity
Ball on New Year's Eve.

Although she'd never said she felt anything for him,
whenever they made love he swore he could feel her
emotion. A part of him wanted to believe a woman like
Myra could not share with him what she'd shared, holding back nothing, if she didn't care. Or was it mere wish-
ful thinking on his part?

He would soon find out because he planned on telling
her how he felt tonight. He couldn't kiss her again, hold
her in his arms and make love to her again, without her
knowing that he loved her. She might think it was just
sex for him, but it was time she discovered it was a lot
more. Then he would convince her that if she gave him
a chance, she could love him, too.

At least he was praying that she could.

He looked up at the knock on the door. "Come in."

Lewis came in smiling, looking pleased with himself, and Pete figured he should. A week ago, Lewis had
traced that trust to a corporation in New York, and a few
days later an arrest had been made. Yesterday, the FBI
had brought in equipment to scan the perimeter of Ms.
Katherine's backyard and they'd uncovered the loot that
had been hidden there. The recovery had made national
news. Because of all the long hours Lewis had put in
trying to solve the case, Pete had given him extra days
off. He would be leaving tomorrow to take his family
to visit his wife's parents in Boulder.

"Your first day off and you couldn't resist coming
here anyway?"

Lewis dropped down in the chair in front of Pete's
desk. "I needed to wrap up a few things before leaving.
How are you going to handle things without me?"

Pete chuckled. "I'll manage."

At that moment the intercom on Pete's desk went off. "Yes, Monica?"

"Ms. Katherine is on the line and she says it's important that she talk to you."

Pete glanced over at Lewis and raised a brow as he said, "Okay, put her through."

When the connection was made, Pete placed the call on speaker so Lewis could listen in on the conversation since he was the one who'd worked on her case. "Ms. Katherine, don't tell me you're seeing more ghosts," Pete said jokingly.

"Of course not, Peterson, but there's something strange going on."

"Strange how?" he asked, reclining back in his chair.

"I met with Lucille and Alma today. We're knitting holiday hats for the babies at the hospital. And they told me a well-dressed man was going around their neighborhood asking questions."

Pete lifted a brow. Lucille's and Alma's homes were at least a good four to five miles from where Ms. Katherine lived. "What kind of questions?"

"They were about your nanny."

Pete sat up straight in his chair and frowned. "My nanny?"

"Yes. Ms. Hollister. The man knew her name and even had a picture of her and everything. Said he was looking for her, but didn't tell them why. Of course Lucille and Alma didn't tell him anything. They told me about it and I told them I would pass the information on to you to tell Ms. Hollister. The man didn't look dangerous, but you can't take any chances these days. You don't think he's an ex-husband, do you?"

"No," Pete said, his frown deepening. "Myra has never been married." He was damn well certain of that. "Thanks for telling me. I'll pass the information on to Myra. If the man comes back, tell Ms. Alma and Ms. Lucille to let me know. Did the man say how he could be reached?"

"No, he didn't tell them anything, which is another reason they found the man odd."

Pete found that odd, as well. "I appreciate the information. Goodbye, Ms. Katherine." He then clicked off the phone.

"Who would be looking for your nanny?" Lewis asked Pete.

Pete stood. "I don't know but I intend to find out. Enjoy your time off."

Lewis nodded, standing, as well. "Is there anything you need me to do? I can delay my trip another day if—"

"No," Pete said, pushing his chair to his desk. "There's no need for you to do that. I was going home for lunch anyway, so that gives me a chance to ask Myra about it."

Twenty minutes later, Pete was pulling into his driveway. On the way home, all kinds of scenarios ran through his mind. It could very well be an insurance agent since her parents had been killed a few months ago. But why would an insurance man be going around showing her picture? Sounded to Pete like a process server or bounty hunter, which didn't make sense. She would have told him if she was in some kind of trouble. Wouldn't she?

Then there was another possibility. She was being stalked…like Ellen had been. She'd told Bonnie she'd come to Denver because of her parents' deaths and that she needed to get away. What if there was more to that story? His hand tightened on the steering wheel, not wanting to go there, but his mind was trying to do that very thing. Now he was getting damn paranoid and there was no reason for that. But the thought of not knowing was driving him crazy.

He started to call out to her the minute he opened the door, but caught himself. If Ciara was taking a nap he didn't want to wake her. He went into the kitchen and found it empty, but something was baking in the oven. He left the kitchen to head down the hall the exact moment Myra was walking out of Ciara's room.

She saw him and threw her hand to her chest and took a deep breath. "Pete! You scared me. I thought you said you weren't coming home for lunch."

He tried reining in all those rampant emotions hitting him at once. "Do you know why a man is going around town looking for you, Myra?"

Breaking eye contact with Pete, Myra took a slow, deep breath as she stared down at the floor. She should have known Baron wouldn't give up on trying to find her. She should have taken heed of Wallace's warning.

"Myra? I asked you a question."

She snapped her head up and met Pete's gaze. She didn't like his tone. He sounded angry. What did he have to be upset about? It wasn't him with the issue of a ruthless brother. "Yes, I know why he's here. Now, if you will excuse me, I need to check on dinner." She brushed by him to walk to the kitchen.

"Wait just a damn minute!" he said, grabbing hold of her wrist.

She jerked her hand from him. "Pete, what is wrong with you? Please lower your voice or you'll wake Ciara.

I just put her down for her nap." She then turned toward the kitchen and he followed.

Myra still didn't understand what he was upset about. She should be the angry one. All her calculated plans to make Baron believe she was out of the country had gotten blown to bits because one of his ex-girlfriends had seen Myra that day in Breckenridge. Well, she had news for her brother and that witch of a mother of his. She would not hide out like a criminal anymore.

Entering the kitchen, she walked over to the oven to check on the baked chicken, very much aware of Pete moving behind her. When she turned around, he was standing in the middle of the kitchen with a fierce frown on his face and his arms crossed over his chest. "You owe me an explanation, Myra."

A part of her knew she did. She was living in his house and taking care of his niece. If someone was going around town looking for her, he should be told why. "Yes, I do owe you an explanation and I will give you one, Pete, but you have no reason to be angry about it. You and Ciara were never in any danger."

He frowned. "Danger? What in the world are you involved in?"

She disliked his accusations even more. "I am not involved in anything and I resent you thinking that. Maybe we shouldn't have this conversation after all—it's not like I have to confide in you. I'm leaving soon, and all we've been sharing is a relationship that's not going anywhere."

She watched him grit his teeth and his neck seemed to expand while he fought for control. He looked like a great specimen of furious masculinity with his tight thighs and heaving chest. She had never seen him this angry before.

He took a couple of steps toward her and pointed at her. "You think that's all it's been, Myra? Nothing but a relationship that's not going anywhere?"

His question surprised her and she lifted her chin and met his intense glare. "What else am I supposed to think, Pete?"

He stiffened. She watched his already tight muscles appear to tighten even more. Then she said, "I clearly recall your proposition. So yes, all we've shared is a relationship to nowhere and I'm fine with that. If I hadn't been, I would not have slept with you." And she didn't regret any of the times she had.

He took a closer step to her. "Don't try changing the subject. I want to know why some man is looking for you."

Myra rolled her eyes. "Change the subject? You're the one who wanted me to explain what I meant by *relationship*, as if you didn't already know."

"Answer my question, Myra," he said in a tone that indicated his patience was running thin.

In a way, she didn't want to tell him. She didn't want to explain how a brother could treat his sibling this way, especially when Pete and his brother had shared such a close and loving relationship. He had suffered a loss when Matt had died and now he was caring for his brother's daughter, giving her everything he knew his brother would want her to have. Especially love. All Myra's brother felt toward her was loathing.

"Myra!"

She jumped. "Will you stop screaming?"

"I am not screaming," he said, lowering his voice somewhat. "Now answer my question."

Moving away from the stove, she walked over to the table to sit down in a chair. She needed to sit. Just the thought that Baron had tracked her here was too much to take in at the moment. She glanced at Pete. He was still standing in the same spot. Still angry. Drawing in a deep breath, she said, "The man was sent by someone to find me. The reason I came to Denver was to hide out and I thought I'd done a good job of leading the person to believe I was out of the country somewhere, so he would have no reason to look for me here."

"He?" Pete all but roared. "You're being stalked? By whom?" Before she could respond he said, "Some men are crazy. They *want*. Nothing else matters. They will do anything to have you and if you turn them away, they will hurt you because the sick bastards have demented minds."

Stalker? Maybe he assumed that because he was a law enforcement officer. Drawing in a deep breath, she said, "I wasn't being stalked, Pete. I was being tracked. It was imperative to Baron that I not return to Charleston to cause problems, which is why that man is looking for me."

"Baron? Who the hell is Baron? An ex-boyfriend? A guy who doesn't understand the meaning of no?"

None of the above...

She still heard the anger in his voice but now it wasn't directed at her, but rather the man he was inquiring about. She truly didn't want to tell him any more than she had already.

Why did he want the identity of the person involved? She knew the answer. It wasn't because he cared about her, but because he was a cop. A sheriff. It was his job to know details.

Myra met his intense stare. "Baron Hollister is my brother."

Pete was certain he'd heard her wrong. Did she say her brother?

As if she read the confusion in his features, she said, "Yes, my brother. I told you we had the same father but different mothers. His mother, Charlene, was my dad's first wife. They were married only four years and divorced when Baron was only two."

Pete came to the table to sit down opposite her. "Are you saying your brother is stopping you from returning home?"

With a sigh, she nodded. "Yes and no. He's never told me per se but he's sent his warnings through others. I know Baron and how ruthless he can be and decided not to take chances. I needed to leave Charleston anyway and grieve after losing my parents. I chose not to tell him where I was going because I knew he would have someone watch me and let him know when I was on my way back home. Not knowing my location upset him and he's been looking for me."

The thought that she knew someone was out there looking for her and hadn't told him anything about it had Pete boiling in rage. "I think you need to start at the beginning."

He listened as Myra told him everything and the more he heard, the angrier he got. As far as he was concerned, Baron Hollister was a fool. Myra had allowed him to get away with it when she could have reported his threats. She should have told someone. She should have told him.

She had been living under his roof and sleeping in his bed, yet she hadn't trusted him enough to confide what her brother was doing to her. Just like Ellen hadn't confided in him about the stalker's threats.

While listening to Myra, that day twelve years ago came back to him. Ellen had told her best friend about the threats but not him. In the end, the man had taken her life. Pete recalled sitting in this very kitchen while listening to Sheriff Harper tell him that Ellen's death hadn't been an accident but an intentional, malicious act. The man had been arrested and, after being told his purchase of the firecrackers had been captured on a video camera inside Paul Markam's feed store, he'd confessed.

Suddenly, those memories became unbearable, almost suffocating to the point where Pete couldn't breathe. He needed to get out of there. Standing quickly and without saying a word, he crossed the room and walked out the back door.

His mind was filled with memories of Ellen's death as well as all the things Myra had just told him. All the things that, like Ellen, Myra *hadn't* told him.

Within minutes he had Satin saddled and was riding off, no particular destination in mind. He had to get away and think. So he kept riding.

In his lifetime he had fallen in love with two women, and neither had trusted him enough to tell him what was happening in their lives, even though he could have helped. He would not have let them face anything alone. He would have taken care of them. He would have been there for them.

It wasn't long before he'd come to the edge of his property, which connected to Gemma Lake. In the distance, across the way, he saw all the wild horses running loose on Westmoreland land. Bringing Satin to a stop, he dismounted and sat on a huge tree stump and gazed at both the lake and the horses. The water indicated calmness while the horses displayed just the opposite. He could feel their untamed energy. Pretty much like the energy flowing through him now. Untamed and unmanageable.

He had to come to terms with the fact that life was sometimes unpredictable. Unruly. Undisciplined. That was one of the reasons why he'd wanted to become a lawman. To battle the bad guys. To bring order. Then after Ellen's death, he'd been even more determined to do so.

Now, twelve years later, he'd fallen in love again. When Myra had walked into his life, he hadn't been ready for her and had tried to fight what he'd felt. But it seemed fate had decreed she was to be a part of his life, for better or for worse.

He had accepted weeks ago that he loved her, but could he accept her not telling him when her life was in possible danger?

Yes, he could accept it because he loved her, mistakes and all. More than anything, he needed to let her know his feelings for her went beyond the bed they shared every night. He needed her to know that he was there to help fight her battles, whatever they were, and that she wasn't alone. She would never be alone because she would always have him and Ciara.

It was time to let her know that.

"Any reason you're sitting here staring into space, Pete?"

He turned at the sound of Riley Westmoreland's voice. "No reason. What are you doing out here and

not at the office?" Although Riley might enjoy the out-
doors, he worked in an office setting in the Westmoreland family-owned Blue Ridge Management Company.
Most of the time he was in a business suit instead of
Western wear.

Riley chuckled. "I decided to play hooky today. Everyone needs to do that every once in a while."

Before Pete could respond, his cell phone rang and he
saw it was Lewis. "Hold that thought a sec," he said to
Riley before clicking on his phone. "Any reason you're
calling me? Need I remind you again that you were given
time off?"

"Hey, consider it the former FBI agent in me, but
I couldn't leave town until I checked out something.
Namely, why someone was in town looking for your
nanny. I decided to investigate and you won't believe
what I found out."

Pete listened to what Lewis was saying and a frown
covered his features. "I'm on my way."

He looked over at Riley. "I need to get back to town
immediately and I'm closer to your place than I am to
mine. Can you give me a ride? I'll get one of my men to
bring me back home later."

"Sure."

Pete got on his horse and, like in the old days, he and
Riley raced across the meadows to where Riley lived, a
few minutes away on one hundred acres of land he called
Riley's Station. Minutes later and they were in Riley's
car and on their way into town.

"Hey, we traded one type of horsepower for another,"
Riley said jokingly, as he drove his two-seater sports car
down the interstate. When Pete didn't respond to his jest,

he said, "I hope what's going on at police headquarters is not too bad."

"Nothing I can't handle."

"Figured as much," Riley said. "So what had you sitting on that stump and looking into space?"

Pete decided to be honest with the man who for years had been one of his best friends. "Women and their secrets."

Riley chuckled. "They all have them. Alpha reminds me of that often."

Alpha was Riley's wife. The one who'd turned the once womanizer into a one-woman man. The one who'd made Riley burn his playa card and decide he wanted marriage instead.

Pete glanced over at Riley. "But when it's a case of their life being threatened…"

"You know what I think, Pete?"

He truly didn't want to know because the last thing he wanted was a Riley Westmoreland lecture, especially after that phone call he'd gotten from Lewis. "What?"

"At some point you need to stop blaming yourself for Ellen's death. Yes, maybe things might have turned out differently had she told you she was being harassed by that guy, but things could have taken another turn, and I think she knew it and tried to avoid it."

Pete lifted a brow. "What other turn?"

"You had just gotten accepted into the police academy and were still in training. Had she told you, being the hothead that you still were at the time, you would have gone after that guy and whipped his ass. Of course you would have told me and Derringer about it. Then we would have whipped his ass right along with you and all three of us would have gotten into trouble."

"Yes, but at least Ellen would still be alive."

"We won't ever know that for certain, Pete. There's no telling how he would have retaliated. Personally, I think he would have gone after the both of you. If you recall, Sheriff Harper also found that box of explosives in his house. Harper figured the bastard planned on blowing up the church the day of your wedding."

Pete always thought that as well, especially when the address of the church was found on a slip of paper in a drawer in the man's apartment. But although the man admitted to throwing the firecracker, he wouldn't confess to anything he had planned with the explosives.

"I've watched you with Myra, Pete. Don't you think it's time to admit how you feel about her?"

"You're late, Ry. I have admitted it to myself."

"But not to her?"

Pete shook his head. "No."

A frown touched Riley's face. "You haven't told her?"

Pete drew in a deep breath. "No, I haven't told her."

"Damn, man. What are you waiting on?"

Pete didn't say anything. He'd planned to tell her tonight and now he knew those plans hadn't changed.

Myra stood at the kitchen window and looked out. Pete had been gone for a while now. Where was he? His truck was parked outside, which meant he hadn't gone back to work. Wherever he'd gone it was on horseback and it was now getting dark.

Ciara had awakened from her nap and Myra had played with her while listening for Pete. Maybe he'd found what she'd told him so repulsive that he'd left. What she needed to tell him was what she'd been trying to tell him all along. It wasn't his problem. It was hers and she would deal with Baron when she would have the upper hand. Not a minute before.

She fed Ciara dinner and then played with her some more before giving her a bath. Pete still hadn't returned. She knew he could take care of himself but that didn't stop her from worrying and caring. She loved him and couldn't help being concerned.

"Da-da."

She glanced over at Ciara, who was standing in her crib. The little girl knew this was usually the time of day when her uncle would come in and rock her to sleep while singing her a lullaby. After a while, sleep took over her and Ciara slumped down in the bed and dozed off.

Myra had taken her own bath and was in her bed when she heard the sound of Pete returning. Footsteps passed her bedroom door headed for his bedroom. Then she heard him come out of his room and walk back down the hall. He knocked on her door.

Pulling up in bed, she switched on the lamp on the nightstand and after pushing her hair away from her neck, she said, "Come in."

He opened the door and stood in the doorway looking handsome while staring at her. "Why aren't you in my bed?"

In his bed?

Myra frowned. Did he not see things weren't the same now? Why was he acting like they were? Before she realized what he was about to do, he entered the room and swept her into his arms.

"What do you think you're doing, Pete?"

"Taking you to my bedroom where you belong."

Where she belonged?

"But you don't want me there now."

"Don't know what gave you that idea," he said, leaving her bedroom and heading to his. He closed his door with the heel of his boot before placing her in the center of the bed. "We need to talk."

"You left when we were talking."

Sitting on the edge of the bed he rubbed his hand down his face. "I know and I apologize for that."

"I know what I told you repulsed you. I know it's hard to believe one sibling can harbor that much dislike for another one."

He reached out and took her hand. "You didn't repulse me and it's not hard to believe. As a police officer I've seen and heard things even more far-fetched."

"Then why did you leave like that?"

He drew in a deep breath. "Because listening to what you were saying reminded me of Ellen and how she died. At that moment, I was feeling like I'd let the both of you down."

"Ellen? Your fiancée?"

"Yes."

"I don't understand. Why would you feel that way? Your fiancée died in a horse accident."

He shook his head. "It wasn't an accident but an intentional act by a guy she'd rebuffed for weeks." He shared what had happened with Ellen.

"Oh, no!" Myra tightened her hand on his. "I am so sorry, Pete."

He didn't say anything for a minute and then he continued, "The hardest thing for me to accept was that she hadn't told me anything about him. I had no idea her life had been threatened. That someone had targeted her. I felt as if I'd let her down in that she didn't come to me. I now know why she did it. Mainly because she didn't want me to get into any trouble. But still, as the woman I loved, I felt I should have known to protect her."

Pete paused again. "Do you have any idea how I felt listening to you telling me about your brother? About how you've been hiding here, trying to keep a low profile so he wouldn't find out where you were?"

"It's not the same, Pete."

He'd loved Ellen, but he didn't love her. He might feel responsible for her since she was living in his house, but still, it wasn't the same. Besides, Baron wouldn't hurt her that way. He was ruthless, true, but he mainly wanted to scare her into staying away. He wouldn't physically harm her.

"And why isn't it the same, Myra?"

Why did he need her to spell it out for him? Okay, if she had to, then she would. "First of all, Ellen was your fiancée, the woman you loved. Second, she was murdered. Baron might be ruthless but he isn't violent. The reason I was in hiding was because I didn't want to be bothered with him until I was good and ready, which would have been after my birthday. The only reason Baron is looking for me is because he wants to know where I am at all times."

Pete shook his head. "No, it's a little more serious than that, Myra."

She lifted a brow. "What do you mean?"

"One of my detectives picked up that guy who'd been looking for you. Under interrogation, he revealed the plan your brother had in store for you."

"Plan? What plan?"

"It seems that one of his associates convinced Baron that he could keep the company beyond your twenty-fifth birthday if you signed everything over to him."

She shook her head. "I would not have done that."

"He intended to force you to do it."

"How? By blackmailing me with a video that he was going to get Rick to film? One of me in a compromising position? As if I'd let Rick get within ten feet of me again. Baron's wife, Cleo, overheard him making those plans with his friends and told me about them. That's when I left Charleston."

Pete lifted a brow. "Who's Rick?"

She released a deep breath. "My one mistake in life. He was older, worldly, a guy I thought I could fall in love with. He got rough with me and I didn't like it. When I tried to leave, he told me the only reason he was wasting his time with me was because my brother had encouraged him to seduce me."

Myra saw the way Pete's jaw tightened. "So that's why you had this thing against older men?"

"Yes. All Baron's friends were older and undesirable. And that's why I freaked out the night in your man cave when you inched your hand under my skirt. It reminded me of Rick." She paused and then asked, "So how was Baron supposed to get me to sign everything over to him, Pete?"

Pete didn't say anything for a minute, and then he said, "By having you kidnapped and taken to some private island in the Caribbean that's owned by someone his mother knows. They would have drugged you up enough to make you do anything. Even say you were happy there and never intended to return to the States."

Myra stared at Pete. "You're kidding, right?"

"No, I wish I was. The guy we picked up, a friend of your brother's, doesn't relish any time in jail and has provided enough proof for us to bring in the FBI on attempted kidnapping charges. So far, the Feds have validated much of his claim, including the exchange of money, text conversations and where the island is located."

She shook her head, not wanting to believe that. "But that is ludicrous."

"Greed will make some people do unbelievable things, Myra."

She fought back tears at the thought that Baron would go that far. "I guess I was wrong about him." A tear she couldn't hold back fell down her cheek.

Pete reached up and gently swiped it off. "You were wrong about something else you said."

Mentally, she wasn't sure she could take much more. "What?"

"That the situation with you and the one with Ellen are different because I loved her. Well, I love you, too, Myra."

She blinked. "What did you say?"

"I said that I love you and as the woman I love, I would have done whatever I could to protect you. Now that I know what's going on, I am doing that. Your brother will not get away with anything."

She swallowed as she stared into his eyes. "You love me?"

"Yes, with all my heart. I honestly think I fell halfway in love with you the first time I saw you. That day you walked into my kitchen. I got pushed the rest of the way when I saw how you interacted with Ciara and what a great job you were doing taking care of her. Taking care of me."

"Oh, Pete, I love you, too. I truly do."

He pulled her into his arms and kissed her thoroughly.

When he finally released her mouth, he held her close. So close she could feel his heart beat against hers.

"I can't imagine my life without you and didn't want to tell you how I felt for fear you weren't feeling the same way. But I had made up my mind to tell you tonight regardless and take my chances. Then I got the call about that man in town asking questions about you."

He paused and then said, "I want a life with you. I want me, you, Ciara and any kids we have together to be a family. Will you marry me, Myra?"

Happiness exploded within her and, swiping at her tears, she said, "Yes! I will marry you, Pete."

He pulled her back into his arms and held her, and at that moment she knew how it felt to love someone and feel their love in return. When he pulled back to look at her, she smiled up at him. "I love you so much, Pete."

"And I love you, too." He then pulled her back into his arms for another kiss.

Epilogue

"You look absolutely beautiful, Myra."

Myra smiled at the man who held her in his arms while they danced at the Westmoreland Charity Ball.

Last night, in this same ballroom, she and Pete had exchanged vows to become husband and wife. It had turned out to be the perfect plan since most of his friends had already arrived in town for the ball. Miss Bonnie had returned to town, as well. Wallace was the one who'd given her away. He and Pete had hit it off the moment they'd met. She and Pete would leave tomorrow on their honeymoon, a week in Honolulu. That was the longest they wanted to be away from Ciara.

"Thank you, and I think you look rather handsome yourself."

He grinned at the compliment. "Are you happy?" he asked her.

"Immensely. Especially since that matter with my company has been resolved."

The situation involving Baron had been more serious than Myra had known. It seemed the FBI already had Baron, Charlene and his cohorts under their radar. Baron's friend, the one he'd sent to grab her in Denver, had taken a plea deal. The man's confession and evidence had resulted in the arrests of Baron, Charlene and several of Baron's friends. The FBI had uncovered a number of their extortion schemes. It was also discovered that the island where they'd intended to take Myra was known as a depot for human trafficking.

Pete had accompanied her back to Charleston where she claimed total control of her company and then turned the head job over to Wallace, just like her father had wanted. Christmas morning had been wonderful, waking up to celebrate their birthdays together. Miss Bonnie had baked a huge chocolate cake for them. Later that day they had joined the Westmorelands for dinner at Dillon and Pam's home.

"That woman is absolutely gorgeous," she said, looking over Pete's shoulder.

"Who?"

"Garth Outlaw's date."

He chuckled. "Regan isn't actually his date. They've known each other for years. She took over as his pilot when her father retired. I understand he'd been the Outlaws' personal pilot for over forty years. And by the way, I happen to think you're absolutely gorgeous, as well."

She looked at him and smiled. "Thanks, sweetheart." She then returned her attention back to the couple. Like them, Regan and Garth were on the dance floor. "That might be the case, but I still think they look good together. And I can't get over how much Garth looks like Riley."

Pete chuckled. "I know. Anyone who thinks the Westmorelands and Outlaws aren't related just has to look at those two. Same thing with Dillon and Dare Westmoreland from Atlanta. Those are some strong Westmoreland genes."

Myra had to agree. And regardless of what Pete said about Garth and his pilot, she could detect a romance brewing between those two, even if they couldn't detect it themselves. She gazed back into her husband's eyes and at that moment she knew that he was her joy and her happiness.

She had loved being the sheriff's nanny and now she looked forward to forever being the sheriff's wife.

* * * * *

USA TODAY bestselling author **Jules Bennett** has published over sixty books and never tires of writing happy endings. Writing strong heroines and alpha heroes is Jules's favorite way to spend her workdays. Jules hosts weekly contests on her Facebook fan page and loves chatting with readers on Twitter, Facebook and via email through her website. Stay up-to-date by signing up for her newsletter at julesbennett.com.

Books by Jules Bennett

Harlequin Desire

The Rancher's Heirs

Twin Secrets
Claimed by the Rancher
Taming the Texan
A Texan for Christmas

Lockwood Lightning

An Unexpected Scandal
Scandalous Reunion
Scandalous Engagement

Texas Cattleman's Club: Rags to Riches

Tempted by the Boss

Visit the Author Profile page
at Harlequin.com for more titles.

SINGLE MAN MEETS SINGLE MOM

Jules Bennett

To Jill, Amy and Inez. I love you three more than the frozen yogurt we devour. Thanks for the road trip and all the laughs. May we have many, many more!

Chapter 1

Oomph!

Out of nowhere, Ian Shaffer had his arms full of woman. Curvy, petite woman. A mass of silky red hair half covered her face, and as she shoved the wayward strands back to look up, Ian was met with the most intriguing set of blue eyes he'd ever seen.

"You okay?" he asked, in no hurry to let her down.

He'd taken one step into the stables at Stony Ridge Acres and this beauty had literally fallen into his arms. Talk about perfect timing.

The delicate hand against his shoulder pushed gently, but he didn't budge. How could he, when all those curves felt perfect against his body and she was still trembling?

He may not know much about the horse industry, but women… Yeah, he knew women really well.

"Thank you for catching me."

Her low, husky voice washed over him, making him even more thankful he'd come to this movie set to see to his client's needs in person…and to hopefully sign another actress to his growing roster of A-listers.

Most agents didn't visit movie sets as regularly as he did, but he sure as hell wasn't missing the opportunity to keep Max Ford happy and allow prospective client Lily Beaumont to witness just what a kick-ass, hands-on agent he was. Given his young age, the fact that he was known as a shark in the industry happened to be good for business.

Ian glanced to the ladder that stretched up into the loft of the spacious stables. His eyes narrowed in on the rung that hung vertically, the culprit of the lady's fall.

"Looks like your ladder needs repairing," he told her, looking back to those big, expressive blue eyes.

"I've been meaning to fix it," she told him, studying his face, his mouth. "You know, you can let me down now."

Yeah, he was probably freaking her out by keeping her in his clutches. But that didn't stop him from easing her down slowly, allowing her body to glide against his.

Hey, he may be there to concentrate on work, but that didn't mean he couldn't enjoy the samplings of a tempting woman when an opportunity presented itself.

Keeping his hand on her arm, Ian allowed his gaze to sweep down her body. He justified the touch by telling himself he was looking for signs of injury, but in all honesty, he simply wanted to get a better look. If this was what they called taking in the local scenery, then sign him up.

"Are you hurt anywhere?" he asked.

"Just my pride." Stepping back, forcing his hand to

fall away, she brushed her fingers down her button-up plaid shirt. "I'm Cassie Barrington. And you are?"

He held out his hand. "Ian Shaffer. I'm Max Ford's agent."

And if all went well, he'd be signing Max's costar Lily, too. There was no way he'd let her go to his rival agency without one hell of a fight first. And then maybe his very unimpressed father would see that Ian had become a success. He was a top agent in L.A. and not just hanging out at parties with women for a living. He'd become a powerful man in the industry.

Though the parties and women were a nice added bonus, Ian enjoyed stepping away from the glamour to be on set with his clients. And it was that extra touch that made him so successful. Between forging connections with producers and getting to know the writers and actors better, he could place his clients in the roles best suited to them.

The role Max was playing was perfect for him. The top actor was portraying the dynamic Damon Barrington, famous horse owner and former jockey. And for Ian, escaping L.A.'s hustle and bustle to spend time on a prestigious Virginia horse farm was a nice change of pace.

"Oh, Max mentioned you'd be coming. Sorry for falling on you." Her brows drew together as she gave him a quick assessment. "I didn't hurt you, did I?"

Ian shoved his hands into his pockets, offering her a smile. She could assess him anytime she wanted. "Not at all," he assured her. "I rather enjoyed the greeting."

Her chin tilted just enough to show defiance. "I don't make a habit of being clumsy...or throwing myself at men."

"That a fact?" he asked, trying not to laugh. "Such a shame."

"Do you make a habit of hitting on women?" she asked.

Unable to resist the gauntlet she'd thrown before him, Ian took a step forward, pleased when her eyes widened and she had to tip her head up to hold his gaze.

"Actually, no. But I'm making an exception in your case."

"Aren't I lucky?" Her tone told him she felt anything but. "Max should be in his trailer. His name is on the outside, and I believe another trailer was recently brought in for you."

Apparently she was in a hurry for him to be on his way—which only made him want to stay longer. Finding someone who didn't care about his Hollywood status, someone who wasn't impressed with his power and money, was a refreshing change. The fact that someone was curvy, wore jeans as though they were made to mold those curves and had expressive baby blues was the icing on the proverbial cake.

"So you're the trainer and your sister is the famous jockey?" he asked, crossing his arms over his chest.

The warm late-spring sun beat against his back as it came through the wide doors of the stable. Summer blockbuster season was just around the corner and, hopefully, once the film wrapped and he'd signed Lily, his agency would still be on top. His ex-partner-turned-rival would no longer be an issue.

He'd started working for an agency right out of college, thanks to a referral from a professor he'd impressed, but some lucky breaks and smart business sense had had him quickly moving to open his own. Unfortunately, he'd taken on a partner who had stabbed him in the back and secretly wooed most of their clients in the hopes they'd work exclusively with him in a new venture.

For the sake of his pride, he had to win Lily over and get her under contract. But how could his mind be on business with this voluptuous distraction before him?

"You've done your homework," she commented. "I'm impressed you know about me and my sister and our different roles."

"I do my research. You could say I'm pretty hands-on as an agent."

"Apparently you're hands-on with everything."

Oh, that was such a loaded statement—one he wouldn't mind exploring if he had the time. His eyes held hers as he closed the gap between them. The pulse at the base of her throat quickened and her breath caught as she stared, unblinking, at him.

Damn work responsibilities. But surely a little flirting, hell, even a fling, would make this an even more riveting trip.

"Everything," he whispered. "Let me know if you ever want an experience."

When her gaze dropped to his mouth again, Ian resisted the urge to grab her, to taste her. There would be plenty of time for…anything she was willing to give. Besides, wasn't the chase half the fun?

"I think you know where my trailer is."

And because he'd probably crossed some sort of moral, ethical boundary, Ian turned and walked from the barn, leaving her with her mouth open.

Well, this was already the most exciting movie set he'd ever visited and he hadn't even seen his client yet.

* * *

Cassie tightened her grip on MacDuff's lead line. He was still new, still skittish, but she was working with him every single day and he was showing improvement. Every now and then he'd let her father, Damon Barrington, ride him, but he had a touch that every horse seemed to love.

At least MacDuff had quit trying to run from her. Now, if she could just get him to understand her silent commands that he had to mimic her pace and direction when they walked.

Her work with MacDuff and the other horses was just one of the many issues that had ended her marriage. Derek had wanted her to stop spending so much time with the "strays" she brought in. He'd insisted she stop trying to save every animal, especially when she'd become pregnant.

Cassie would never stop trying to save animals... especially since she hadn't been able to save her marriage. Her husband had obviously loved women and liquor more than her and their baby. His loss, but the pain still cut deep.

She focused on the line, holding it tight and trying to keep up with the routine because she was running a tad behind now.

Of course, she'd been thrown off her game already this morning after falling into the arms of that handsome, bedroom-eyed stranger. For a split second she'd wanted to revel in the strength with which he held her, but then reality had slapped her in the face, reminding her that she'd fallen for a smooth talker once. Married him, had his child and hadn't seen him since.

Well, except when he'd shown up for the divorce

proceedings, mistress in tow. As if that busty bleach blonde would ever play stepmom to Cassie's precious baby. Hell. No.

Cassie swore she'd never let another man play her for a fool again, and she sure as hell wouldn't get swept away by another pretty smile and sultry touch.

Unfortunately, when she'd fallen into Ian's arms, she'd forgotten all about that speech she'd given herself when her husband had left. How could she have a coherent thought when such strong arms were holding her flush against a taut body? No woman would blame her for the lapse in judgment.

But no more. Cassie had her daughter to consider now.

With sweet Emily just turning one, Cassie knew she'd definitely gotten the best part of her marriage, and if Derek didn't want to see their baby, he was the one missing out.

So, no more sexy men who thought they were God's magnificent gift to this world. Although Cassie had to admit, even if just to herself, that her insides had tingled at Ian's touch. He'd been so strong, had smelled so… manly and had looked in her eyes as if she truly was a beautiful, desirable woman.

She hadn't felt anything but frumpy and still a bit pudgy since having Emily. The extra weight that refused to go away coupled with her husband leaving her for another woman were damaging blows to her self-esteem. Yet, Ian had held her with ease, which wasn't helping her ignore the potency of the mesmerizing man.

Getting swept away by another handsome man with sultry eyes and a powerful presence wouldn't do her any good. She had to concentrate on helping her sister, Tessa, win her way to the Triple Crown. They'd worked side by side nearly their entire lives, always with the dream of being Triple Crown winners like their father. And here they were, about to make history, and Cassie couldn't be more excited.

When Cassie had been too far along with her pregnancy, her father had stepped up to train Tessa. This racing dynasty truly was a family affair.

One race down, two to go.

The fact that the Barrington estate had been turned into a film set was icing on the cake. A script surrounding her father's legacy, legendary racing and past winning streak had piqued the interest of Hollywood A-listers, and, suddenly, the horse farm was all abuzz with lighting, sound guys, extras and security.

Cassie actually loved seeing her father's life played out by Max Ford, the handsome, newly married actor. And playing the role of her late mother was beautiful Southern belle and it-girl Lily Beaumont. So far the two were doing an amazing job, and Cassie couldn't wait to see the final product.

To cap off the racing season, Cassie was moving full throttle toward opening her own riding school for handicapped children. Since having her own child, Cassie wanted to slow down, and she'd always had a soft spot for kids anyway…something she'd thought she and her ex had in common.

Launching the school would be one more step in the healing process. So now she just needed to keep saving up—she wouldn't dream of asking her father or anyone else for money—to get it off the ground.

"Daydreaming?"

Keeping a firm grip on the lead line, Cassie glanced over her shoulder to see Tessa moving toward her in

slow, cautious steps. MacDuff really did get treated with
kid gloves by everyone until he learned they were his
friends.

"Maybe just a little," Cassie admitted, gently pulling
MacDuff into a soft trot. "Give me just a few minutes
and we'll get to work."

Tessa shoved her hands into the pockets of her jeans.
"I'd rather hear what has my big sister so distracted this
morning."

Cassie rolled her eyes at Tessa's smirk and quirked
brow. She led MacDuff forward a few steps, stopped
and moved back a few steps, pleased when the stallion
kept up with her exact number and didn't try to fight her.

He was learning. Finally.

"I'm always amazed at how broken they seem to be,"
Tessa said softly. "You have this patience and gentle-
ness. It's almost as if they know you're determined to
help them."

"That's because I am." Cassie reached up to
MacDuff's neck, offering him praise. "He's just misun-
derstood and nobody wanted to work properly with him."

"He was abused."

Cassie swallowed as she led MacDuff back to the stables. The thought of someone beating him because he
hadn't had the right training sickened her. She'd known
he'd been abused on some level, simply because of how
he'd arrived all wide-eyed and nervous and then threw
Tessa the first time she'd mounted him. But the second
any horse, rescued or not, stepped onto Stony Ridge
Acres, they were treated like royalty. No matter their
heritage. Yes, they bred prizewinning horses and bought
from a long lineage of winners, but it wasn't always
about the win.... It was about the love and care of the

animal. And since Stony Ridge was a massive farm, they could take in those strays Cassie had a soft spot for.

She'd always loved watching the trainers her father had for his horses. Years ago, female trainers had been frowned upon, but her father had insisted women were more gentle and less competitive by nature than men, thus producing better-tempered horses—and winners.

"You didn't happen to see a certain new hunk on the set this morning, did you?" Tessa asked as she pulled out the tack box and helped to brush MacDuff.

Cassie eyed her sister over the horse's back. "Aren't you engaged?"

"I'm not dead, Cass." Tessa brushed in large circular strokes. "I'll take your lack of answering to mean you did see him."

Saw him, fell into his arms, got lost in those sexy eyes that could make a woman forget she'd been burned… and maybe reveled in that powerful hold a tad too long.

"Even you have to admit he's one attractive man," Tessa went on.

"I can admit that, yes." Cassie switched from the currycomb to the dandy brush. "I may have had an incident this morning involving that loose rung on the ladder to the loft and Mr. Shaffer."

Tessa stepped around MacDuff's head, dropped the brush into the tack box and crossed her arms over her chest. "Okay, spill it. You know his name and you said 'incident.' I want all the details."

Cassie laughed. "It's no big deal, Tess. I fell off the ladder. Ian happened to be there, and he caught me."

"Oh, so we've gone from Mr. Shaffer to Ian."

"He's Max's agent and apparently visits his clients' film sets. We exchanged names," Cassie defended herself. "Seemed like the thing to do since he was holding me."

"I love where this story is going." Tessa all but beamed as she clasped her hands together.

Laughing, Cassie tossed her brush aside, as well. "No story. That was pretty much it."

"Honey, you haven't even mentioned a man's name since *you know who* left and—" Tessa held up a hand when Cassie tried to intervene "—your face seemed to brighten up a bit when you said his name."

"It did not," Cassie protested.

Tessa's smile softened. "If you want to argue, that's fine. But he's hot, you finally showed a spark of life about a man and I'm clinging to hope that you haven't given up on finding love. Or, for heaven's sake, at least allowing yourself a fling."

Cassie rolled her eyes and patted MacDuff's side. "Just because this romance business is working for you doesn't mean it will for me. I tried that once—it didn't last. Besides, I have no time for love or even a date between training with you and Emily."

"There's always time. And, romance aside, have a good time. A little romp with a sexy stranger might be just what you need," Tessa said with a naughty smile. "Aren't you the one who forced me to take a few days off last month? You have to make time for yourself."

Cassie had conspired with Tessa's now fiancé, producer Grant Carter, to whisk Tessa away during her training and the filming of the movie. Grant had wanted to get Tessa far from the limelight, the stress and the demands of their busy schedules, and Cassie had been all too happy to help because her sister needed a break.

Tess had found the right man, but Cassie seriously

doubted there was a "right man" for her. All she required was someone who loved her and didn't mind her smelling like horses more often than not, someone who would offer stability in her life, make her feel desirable and love her daughter. Was that too tall of an order?

"I'm not looking for a fling," Cassie insisted, even though she'd pretty much already envisioned a steamy affair with Ian.

Tessa raised a brow. "Maybe a fling is looking for you."

"I just met the man. I'm sure he's not going to be around me that much anyway, so there's very little chance of seduction. Sorry to burst your bubble."

"Maybe you should show Ian around the estate," Tessa suggested as she went to grab a blanket and saddle for her racing horse, Don Pedro.

Cassie sighed, closing the gate to MacDuff's stall. "I don't want to show him around. Max is his client—he can do it."

"Max is going to be busy filming the scene with Lily down by the pond. I want to make sure we're there to see that taping."

Cassie smiled and nodded in agreement. She loved watching the two actors get into character, loved watching her father's reaction to reliving his life through the eyes of a director, and there was no way she'd miss such a monumental scene. This was the scene where Max would propose to Lily. The replay of such a special moment in her parents' lives was something she had to witness.

"I'll make sure we're done here about the time shooting starts," Cassie assured her sister. "All the more reason I don't have time to show Ian around."

"Now, that's a shame."

Cassie and Tessa both turned to see the man in question. And just like with their earlier encounter, the mere sight of him caused a flutter to fill her belly. Of course, now she couldn't blame the sensation on the scare from the fall…only the scare from the enticing man.

"I'd like to have a look around the grounds if you have time," he said, looking directly into her eyes, seeming to not even notice Tessa.

Cassie settled her hands on her hips, cursing herself when his gaze followed her movements. Great, now she'd drawn his attention to her hips…not an area a woman wanted a man looking.

"I thought you went to see Max," Cassie said, refusing to acknowledge his request.

"I saw him for a brief moment to let him know I was here. He actually was talking with Grant and Lily."

Cassie cast a glance at her sister, whose face had split into a very wide grin. *Darn her.*

With a gracefulness that would've pleased their late mother, Tessa turned, extended her hand and smiled. "I'm Tessa Barrington, Cassie's sister. We're so glad to have you here at the farm."

Ian shook Tessa's hand as the two exchanged pleasantries. He finally settled his gaze back on Cassie. Did those eyes have some magical power? Seriously, why did she have to feel a jolt every single time he looked at her?

"Go ahead and show Ian around, Cassie. I'm fine here."

If Cassie could've reached out and strangled her sister with the lead line she so would have, but then Ian would be a witness.

"It will have to be tomorrow or later this evening."

No, she wasn't too busy right now, but she wouldn't allow Mr. Hollywood Hotshot to hold any control over her. "I'll come find you when I'm ready."

"Well, I'm going to walk Don Pedro out," Tessa said. "It was a pleasure to meet you, Ian. Cass, I'll see you later."

Great, now they were alone. Cassie would definitely kill her sister for that little stunt.

Ian stepped closer, and Cassie held her ground. This was her property and no matter how charming, how sexy and how...

Damn, he smelled good. She lost all train of thought; Ian's masculine scent was enough to render her mind blank. How long had it been since she'd been with a man, felt his touch?

Too long. So why did this man with an inflated ego turn her on? Could she not attract the right kind of guy just once?

"I can wait till tomorrow," he told her. His eyes searched her face as a hint of a smile played around his lips. "I'm a pretty patient man."

Placing a hand on his chest to stop him may have been a mistake. A jolt of awareness tingled up her arm. The strength, the chiseled pecs beneath her palm... Yeah, she was very aware of the sexiness that encompassed Ian Shaffer.

"I appreciate the fact you're taking the time to use your charm on me, but I'm too busy for games. Besides, I'm pretty sure I'm a lot older than you."

Ian shrugged. "Age hadn't entered my mind."

Cassie laughed. "I'm pretty sure I know what entered your mind."

He stepped forward again, giving her no choice but to

back up until the gate to a stall stopped her. Ian put one hand on either side of her head, blocking her.

"Then I'm sure you're aware I find you attractive." His eyes dropped to her mouth, then traveled back up. "I can't wait for that tour, Cassie."

He pushed off the stall and walked out of the stable. When was the last time a man had caught her attention, inspired her sexual desire so fast? The danger of falling into lust scared her to death.

But she had to be realistic. There was nothing special about her. And if she did allow herself to act on these very new, very powerful emotions, she highly doubted he'd remember her name in a few months.

No way could she succumb to his charms.

Chapter 2

Cassie's parents had been married nearly twenty years when her mother was killed suddenly in a car accident. She'd always admired the love her parents had for each other, always wanted a marriage like that for herself.

Unfortunately, a happy, loving marriage wasn't in the cards for her. And hindsight was a harsh slap in the face because Cassie realized she'd probably married Derek too quickly.

She'd craved the love her parents had had and thought for sure Derek—the Barringtons' onetime groom—had the same outlook on marriage.... As in, it was long-term and between only two people.

How could she trust her feelings for a man again? Cassie swiped the tear from her cheek as she headed back toward the stable. The sun was slowly sinking behind the hills surrounding the estate. Spring was gradually turning into summer, giving the evenings just a bit more light.

The day's filming was complete and the scene she'd just witnessed had left her raw and hopeful all at the same time.

Max Ford and Lily Beaumont had beautifully reenacted Cassie's parents' proposal. Cassie had heard stories, had seen pictures of her parents' early love. But to witness that moment in person… Cassie had no words for how precious the experience had been.

She'd stood with Tessa off to the side, and even with the directors and producers stopping and starting and rearranging in the middle of the scene, the moment had captured her heart.

Added to that, each time she'd glanced at Ian, his gaze had been on hers. He hadn't even bothered trying to hide the heat that lurked in those dark, heavy-lidded eyes. Thankfully, at one point he'd slid on his aviator shades, but his dominating presence still captured her attention…and her hormones.

There went those lustful emotions again. She couldn't afford to get swept away by a sexy body and killer smile. Lust was the evil that had overtaken her once before and look where that had gotten her. Oh, she didn't regret her marriage because she had Emily, but the pain from the rejection and having her love blatantly thrown back in her face was humiliating. Who wanted to be rejected?

Cassie reached the stable, intending to work with MacDuff again, but her eyes moved up to the rung of the ladder that still hung vertically.

She'd meant to mention the problem to Nash, the new groom, but between the emotional shoot and a certain hot agent plaguing her mind, she'd simply forgotten. Besides, he'd been so busy today cleaning out all the stalls, she really hated to add to his list.

Her father took pride in his stables, always making sure everything looked pristine and perfect. Cassie would bite the bullet and fix the ladder herself. At least working on something would keep her mind off Ian... hopefully. Her tendency to fix things and have everything in her life make sense would have to be satisfied with just this piece of wood for now. The Ian issue—and she feared he was fast becoming an issue—would have to wait.

She grabbed the hammer and several long nails from the toolbox in the equipment room. She shoved the nails in her back pocket and held on to the hammer as she climbed the ladder that stretched to the loft of the stable.

The setting sun cast a soft glow into the structure. Horses neighed, stomped hooves and rustled in their stalls. The sounds, the smells—none of it ever got old. Cassie loved her life here and she looked forward to bringing her daughter up in such a beautiful, serene environment.

During her four years of marriage, she'd been away from the estate. Even though she and Derek had lived only ten minutes away, it just wasn't the same as being on the grounds. Cassie loved living in the cottage, being with the horses and knowing her family was all right here helping with her emotional recovery.

With her tears mostly dry, Cassie sniffed. Crying had never been her thing. Anger fit more into her life, especially since she'd been abandoned only two months after giving birth. Tears hadn't brought her cheating husband back, not that she'd wanted him after the fact, and tears certainly weren't helping her raise her daughter or move on like the strong mother she needed to be.

Halfway up the ladder, she eyed the broken rung, then carefully slid it back into place. Widening her stance as far as she could to balance her body while holding the hammer, she reached around into her back pocket for a nail.

"I can help you with that."

Cassie glanced over her shoulder to see Ian at the base of the ladder, his watchful gaze raking over her body. *Great.* She had red-rimmed eyes and a red-tipped nose, she was sure. She was not a pretty crier. She always got the snot-running, red-splotchy-face and puffy-eyes look.

Cassie slid a nail out and turned back around to place it against the wood. "I've got it, but thanks."

She knew he hadn't left, but Cassie didn't say anything else as she worked quickly and repaired the rung. With a hefty tug on the wood, she made sure it was securely in place before she started her descent. Just as she'd gotten to the last rung, Ian moved his hard body against hers, trapping her between the ladder and a most impressive chest. Her body was perfectly aligned with his, causing ripples of heat to slide through her. They were both fully dressed, but the sensations spiraling through her had never occurred before, even when she'd been completely naked with her ex.

Yeah, she was doomed where this sexy stranger was concerned.

Cassie swallowed, closed her eyes. Ian made her aware of just how feminine she was. When was the last time she'd felt desirable? Was it so wrong to want a man to find her attractive? After being married to someone who kept looking elsewhere for his desires to be fulfilled, Cassie knew she was probably grasping at any attention at this point.

She also knew she didn't care—not when his body was so hard, so perfectly perfect against hers. Not when his soft, warm breath tickled the side of her neck, and not when his masculine aroma enveloped her.

"What are you doing here?" she whispered.

Ian slid his arms up to align with hers, his hands covering hers on the wood. "I saw you walking this way. You looked upset."

No. He didn't care. He couldn't. Not this soon and not about her. Sexual desires were clouding his mind… and hers, too, apparently, because she was enjoying the heat of his body a little too much.

What man would follow a woman into a stable just because she looked upset? No. He'd followed her for one reason and one reason only. A reason she certainly didn't think she was ready for.

"I'm fine," she lied.

Ian nuzzled her hair. Oh…when he did that she forgot all arguments about why being attracted to someone so full of himself was wrong. Her mind completely voided out any pep talks she'd given in regard to steering clear of lustful feelings and attractive charmers.

"You're a very beautiful woman, Cassie." His soft voice slid over her body, reinforcing those tremors that were becoming the norm where he was concerned. "I tried to ignore this pull I have toward you, but it was damn hard when I saw you during the shoot. How do you do that to a guy?"

Um…she had no clue. Power over men had certainly never been something she'd mastered. If it had, she'd still be married.

"Ian, we just met and…"

He used one hand and slid the hammer from her grasp, letting it fall to the concrete floor with a loud thud.

"And I'm older than you," she continued. "I'm thirty-four. You can't even be thirty."

With an arm around her waist, he hauled her off the ladder and spun her around until she faced him—their mouths inches apart.

"I'm twenty-nine, and I assure you I'm old enough to not only know what I want, but to act on it."

His mouth came down on hers, hard, fast, hungry. Cassie didn't have time to think or refuse because her body was already melting into his.

The passion pouring from him stirred her desire even more as she gripped his thick biceps. Giving in to just a few seconds of bliss wouldn't hurt.

And when Ian's mouth traveled from her mouth down the column of her throat, Cassie tipped her head back as her breath caught. What was he doing to her? A full-on body attack. His mouth may be in one spot, but Cassie could feel every inch of her body tingling and wanting more.

Wait…this wasn't right. She couldn't do this.

Pushing him away, Cassie slid her hand up over the exposed skin peeking out of her shirt…the skin his mouth had just explored.

"Ian, I can't… We can't…" Words were useless because her mind was telling her one thing and her body was telling her another. "I just met you."

"You're attracted to me."

She couldn't deny the statement. "That doesn't mean I should act on it. I don't just go around kissing strangers."

"After you learned my name this morning, I was no longer a stranger."

Those dark eyes held her gaze. Even without a word the man exuded power, control. Derek had been so laid-back, so uncaring about everything that this was quite a change.

And Cassie would be lying if she didn't admit the fact that Ian was the polar opposite of her ex turned her on even more.

"You're only here for a short time," she went on, crossing her arms over her chest. "We can't just…you know."

"Have sex?" he asked, quirking a brow.

Oh, mercy. The words were now out, hovering in the air, and from the smirk on his face, she was the only one feeling awkward at this moment.

"Yes, that." *Dear Lord.* It wasn't as if she hadn't had sex before; she'd had a baby, for crying out loud. But she couldn't discuss something like that with him. Now she felt foolish and juvenile. "Acting on sexual attraction isn't something I normally do."

That was an understatement, considering she'd had sex with one man and that had been her husband. What if she did throw caution to the wind? What if she had some sordid affair?

Seriously? Was she contemplating that? She was a mother—a mother to a little girl. What kind of example was she?

"You're thinking too hard." Ian started to step forward, but he stopped when Cassie held up a hand.

"Don't. I can't think when you're touching me."

"I'll take that as a compliment."

Cassie rolled her eyes. "You would."

"See? You know me already."

One of them had to think rationally. Apparently it would be her. She maneuvered around him toward the opening of the stable.

"You're going to have to keep your hands and your mouth to yourself."

Those tempting lips curved into a smile. "You're no fun."

"I don't have time for fun, Ian."

And more than likely he was the proverbial good time back in L.A. She could easily see him hopping from one party to the next, beautiful women draped over his arm, falling into his bed.

Cassie flicked the main switch to light up the pathways between the stalls. The brightness from the antique horseshoe-style chandeliers put a screeching halt to any romantic ambience that had been lurking in the darkening stable.

When she turned back around, Ian had his hands on his narrow hips, his focus still locked on her. There was a hunger in his eyes she'd never seen from any man before.

Without a word, he closed the gap between them. Cassie's heart had just started to settle, but now it picked back up again. She should've known better than to think the intense moment would pass.

Ian framed her face with his hands and brought his mouth to within a fraction of an inch of hers. "A woman who kisses, who responds to my touch without hesitation, has pent-up passion that needs to be released."

His lips barely brushed hers. "Come find me when you're ready."

Ian walked around her, leaving her still surrounded

by that masculine scent, his arousing words and the tingling from his touch still on her lips.

 She'd known the man twelve hours. There was no way she could handle him being on the grounds for two more months. She was a woman—a woman with needs.

 And a part of her wondered just what would happen if she allowed herself to put those needs first for once.

Chapter 3

Two days had passed since she'd been up close and personal with Ian, but Cassie was more than aware of his quiet, yet dominating, presence on the estate. She'd seen him from a distance as he talked with Max. She'd found out she'd just missed him on the set of one scene she'd gone to watch, but she refused to admit she was wondering about his schedule, about when she'd see him again. Feel his body against hers.

She refused to fall for another man who set her hormones into overdrive, so where did that leave her? Considering a fling?

Groaning, she made her way from the stables to the main house. The sun was making its descent behind the mountains and Emily was at her weekly sleepover with Tessa and Grant. After witnessing the shooting of the engagement scene over the past couple of days, Cassie was feeling more and more nostalgic.

She missed her mother with each passing day; seeing Rose's life depicted in the film had Cassie wanting to feel closer to her. And with Emily away for the night, this was the perfect opportunity to reminisce and head up to the attic, where all her mother's things were stored.

Rose's unexpected death had shaken up the family in ways they'd never even imagined. As teen girls, Tessa and Cassie had really taken it hard, but they'd all been there for each other, forming an even stronger bond. But Cassie still ached for her mother's sweet smile, her encouraging words and her patient guidance.

Because right now she truly wanted a mother's advice. Ian had her completely tied in knots. When he'd left her in the stables two days ago, Cassie had never felt so torn, so conflicted in her life. And he hadn't approached her since. What was up with that? Had he changed his mind? Had he decided she wasn't worth the trouble?

Why was she even worried about this anyway? No doubt Ian was used to those flawless women who had been surgically perfected. More than likely Cassie's extra pounds and shapelier curves were not what Ian was looking for in a…fling? What was he doing exactly with his flirting? Where had he expected this to go?

Never mind. He'd thrown out the word *sex* like nothing. Cassie knew exactly where he was headed with his flirting.

Leaving the attic door propped open, Cassie headed up the narrow wooden staircase. At the top she flicked on the small light that was so soft, it really only set off a glow on one wall. But that was the wall where her mother's boxes were stacked.

In the silence of the evening, Cassie was all alone

with her thoughts, her memories. She pulled the lid off the first bin and choked back tears.

How could anyone's life, especially that of her beautiful, loving, vivacious mother, be condensed to a few boxes? All the memories, all the smiles, all the comfort Rose Barrington had offered to the world…all gone. Only tangible items remained stored neatly in plastic bins.

Cassie couldn't help but smile. Her very organized mother wouldn't have had it any other way.

After going through pictures from her parents' simple, elegant wedding day, Cassie knew the wedding dress was around. Tessa actually planned on wearing it for her upcoming vows, and Cassie couldn't wait to see her baby sister in their mother's gown. Just that image was enough to have her tearing up again.

This film was certainly wreaking havoc on her emotions, that was for sure.

Cassie kept searching through storage bins, looking for a box or a folded garment bag. Would the crew need to duplicate that dress for the wedding scene? More than likely they'd already researched pictures to find inspiration for the costumes, just as they had for the settings.

Cassie had been itching for a chance to look through the old photos again herself.

Moving from the bins, Cassie went and looked inside the narrow antique wardrobe, where she discovered a white garment bag. Slowly unzipping, so as not to tear the precious material inside, Cassie peeled back the bag and pulled out the classy gown she'd been hunting for.

The dress had been preserved so that the cream-colored material was still perfect. Tessa would be just as beautiful a bride as their mother had been.

Cassie had thought about wearing it for her own wedding, but her ex had insisted on getting married at the courthouse. She should've known then that he wasn't the one. Not that there was anything wrong with a small civil ceremony, but Derek had known she'd always wanted a wedding in the small church where her parents had married. She'd wanted the lacy gown, the rice in her hair as they ran to their awaiting car…the special wedding night.

None of those young-girl dreams had come true.

Unable to resist, Cassie stripped from her jeans, boots, button-up and bra and pulled on the strapless floor-length dress. A straight cut with lace overlay may be simple to some, but the design was perfect to Cassie.

Smoothing a hand down the snug bodice, Cassie went to the antique mirror in the corner. If she fell in love one day—real love this time—maybe she could wear it. Wouldn't that be a beautiful tradition? Rose, Tessa and Cassie all wearing the same gown. Perhaps if the material held up and the gown was well preserved again, little Emily would one day walk down the aisle wearing the dress her grandmother had.

If it weren't for baby weight, the frock would fit perfectly. Unfortunately, right now her boobs threatened to spill out the top and lace was definitely not a forgiving material, so her curves were very…prominent.

Behind her, the attic door clicked. Cassie turned, her hand to her beating heart as footsteps sounded up the stairs. No time to cover up all her goods, so she kept her hand in place over her generous cleavage.

"Hello?" she called.

Ian rounded the landing and froze. He took in her state of dress—or undress, really—of course zeroing in on where her hand had settled.

So much for her evening of reminiscing. Could fate be any more mocking? Dangling this sexy stranger in her face when she knew full well that nothing could or should happen?

"What are you doing?" she asked, keeping her hand in place and trying to remain calm. Kind of hard when she was on display and just the sight of the man had her heart accelerating.

"I wanted to apologize for the other day," he told her, coming up the last couple of steps. "I never force myself on a woman, and I didn't want you to have that impression of me. But if I'm going to be here any length of time, and I am, we need to clear the air."

Clear the air? Cassie sighed and prayed because she had a sinking feeling they may be there for a while.

"Well, now's the perfect time because if that door latched all the way, we're locked in here."

Ian drew his brows together. "Locked in?"

"The door locks from the outside. That's why I had left it standing open."

Pulling up the hem of the dress with one hand and trying to keep the bodice up with the other, she moved around him down the steps and tugged on the handle. She leaned her forehead against the door and groaned.

"I didn't know," he murmured behind her.

Cassie turned and looked up the steps to see Ian looking menacing and dangerous—in that sexy way only he could—standing at the top. His muscles filled out his long-sleeved T, those wide shoulders stretching the material, and his dark jeans fit his narrow hips beautifully.

She knew firsthand exactly how that body felt against hers. Knew just how well he could kiss a woman into forgetting her morals.

In a house this size, with only her father living here and his bedroom on the first floor, no one would hear them yell until morning, when they could open the small window and catch someone's attention.

Risking another full-body glance at Ian, Cassie knew she was in big, big trouble. Her attraction to him was the strongest she'd ever felt toward a man. But it wasn't so much the level of heat between them that scared her; it was the quick onset of it. It felt as if she had no control over her own reaction. She'd been helplessly drawn to this intriguing man. How could she trust her emotions right now? He was honestly the first man to find her desirable since her ex. Was he just a sexy diversion or were her feelings more in-depth than that?

Earlier tonight she'd flirted with the idea of a fling, but now the reality of being trapped with Ian made her heart flutter and nerves dance in her belly.

Her gaze met his. Crackling tension vibrated between them in the soft glow and the silence.

And Cassie had all night to decide what to do with all her attraction and the hungry look in Ian's eyes…

Ian stared down at Cassie, struck by those creamy exposed shoulders, that poured-on, vintage-style wedding gown molded to her sweet curves. From his vantage point, he could see even more of her very exposed breasts and most impressive cleavage—even though she was trying her hardest to keep gravity from taking over the top of that dress.

Mercy. Being straight in front of her had been torture, but this angle offered a much more interesting, gut-clenching view. Not that he was complaining.

Being stuck in an attic with Cassie would be no hardship because he'd caught a glimpse of the passion she held beneath her vulnerability. And there wasn't a doubt in his mind that her war with herself stemmed from some past hurt.

Cassie attempted to cross her arms over her breasts, which only tortured him further, because she failed to cover the goods and actually ended up offering him an even more enticing view. Was she doing this as punishment?

"Text Max and have him come to the main house and ring the doorbell. Dad won't be in bed yet."

Ian shook his head. "Sorry. I only came over to apologize to you, so I left my phone in my trailer to charge."

Groaning, Cassie tipped her head back against the door and closed her eyes. "This isn't happening to me," she muttered. "This cannot be happening."

Ian had to smile. Of all the scenarios he'd envisioned on his short walk from his trailer to the main house, he hadn't once thought of being stuck for hours with someone so sexy, so unexpected, and wearing a wedding dress to boot.

This couldn't have been scripted any worse…or better, depending on the point of view.

Cassie lifted the dress and stomped back up the steps, her shoulder slamming into him as she stormed by.

"Wipe that smirk off your face, Ian. Nothing about this is comical."

"Can't you call someone with your phone?" he asked, turning to face her.

Cassie propped her hands on her hips. "No. I came up here to be alone, to think."

Damn, she was even sexier when she was angry. But getting too wrapped up with Cassie Barrington was a dangerous move. She wasn't a fling type of girl and he'd pushed too hard in the stables. Had she given in to his blatant advances, he knew she would've regretted it later.

He needed to do the right thing and keep his hands off her. He was here for two main purposes: keep Max happy and sign Lily so she didn't go to his rival. Period.

But his hormones didn't get the memo, because the more he was around Cassie, the more alluring and sexy she became. Of course, now that he'd seen a sample, he had to admit, he wanted to see more. That dress... Yeah, she looked like a 1950s pinup. Sexy as hell, with all the right curves and none of that stick-thin, anorexic nonsense, and she was even hotter with a slight flush from anger.

For the past two days he'd seen her working with her sister, training the horses and driving him unbelievably mad with the way her lush body filled out a pair of jeans. He'd seriously had to get his damn hormones in check and then approach her with a much-needed apology for his Neanderthal tendencies.

But now that he was here, those hormones were front and center once again, overriding all common sense and rational thoughts.

"How did you know I was up here?" she asked. "I figured all the crew was either in their trailers or back at the hotel."

"I ran into Grant on my way to your cottage. He told me you were here. As I was coming in the back door, your cook, Linda, was going out for the night and she said you mentioned coming to the attic."

"You came all this way just to apologize? I'm sure you would've seen me tomorrow."

Ian shrugged, shoving his hands into his pockets.

"True, but I knew too many people would be around tomorrow. I assumed you wouldn't want to discuss this in front of an audience. Besides, I think we need to address this spark between us and figure out what to do with it since I'll be here several weeks."

Cassie threw her hands in the air. "Could you at least turn around so I can put my clothes back on?"

His eyes traveled down her body, darting to the pile of clothes behind her, zeroing in on the leopard-print bra lying on top.

"Sure," he said, trying to get the visual of her in that leopard bra out of his mind before he went insane.

Fate may have landed him up here with the sassy, sexy Ms. Barrington, and fate also provided a window directly in front of him, where he was afforded a glorious view of Cassie's reflection as she changed. Of course, that made him a bit of a jerk, but no man with air in his lungs would look away from that enticing view. This evening just kept getting better and better.

Cassie would probably die before she asked for help with the zipper, so he didn't offer. And she didn't have any trouble. As the dress slid down her body, Ian's knees nearly buckled.

Lush didn't even begin to describe her. Her full breasts, rounded belly and the slight flare of her hips were a lethal combination.

"As I was saying," he went on, cursing his voice when it cracked like that of an adolescent. "I realize that neither of us was prepared for the instant physical attraction—"

"You're delusional," she muttered as she tugged her jeans up over her hips and matching bikini panties.

"But just because I find you sexy as hell doesn't mean I can't control myself."

Her hands froze on her back as she fastened her bra. Apparently his words had struck a chord. She glanced up and caught his gaze in the reflection. Busted.

"Seriously?" she asked with a half laugh. "Why did you even turn around?"

"I didn't know the window was there." That was the truth.

"And you weren't going to say anything?"

Ian spun around—no point in being subtle now. "I'm a guy. What do you think?"

Rolling her eyes, Cassie shrugged into her shirt and buttoned it up with jerky, hurried motions.

Fighting the urge to cross the room and undress her again, Ian slid his hands into his pockets and met her gaze.

"You are stunning," he told her, suddenly feeling the need to drive that point home. "I'm not sure why that statement caught you off guard."

Most women in Hollywood would pause at such a comment, try to deny it in order to hear more pretty words in a vain attempt to boost their own egos, but Ian knew Cassie was different. She truly didn't believe she was beautiful, and he had a feeling all that insecurity circled back to whatever the basis was for her vulnerability.

Damn, he didn't have time to delve into distressed damsels. But there was a desire in him, something primal, almost possessive that made him want to dig deeper, to uncover more of Cassie Barrington. And not just physically.

That revelation alone scared the hell out of him.

"I don't need to be charmed, Ian." She propped her

hands on her hips. "We're stuck up here and lying or try-ing to make me want you isn't going to work."

"I don't lie, Cassie." When she quirked a brow, he merely shrugged. "I find you sexy. Any man would be insane or blind not to."

Cassie shook her head. After zipping the dress into a white garment bag, she headed over to a storage box and popped off the lid. She flopped down on the floor, crossing her legs and offering him the view of her back.

He waited for her to say something, but she seemed to have dismissed him or was so wrapped up in the mem-ories of the photos she was pulling out, she just didn't care that he was there.

"You ever look at a picture and remember that mo-ment so well, you can actually feel it?" she asked, her soft voice carrying across the room.

Ian took that as his invitation to join her. He closed the distance between them, taking a seat directly beside her. Cassie held a picture. A young girl, he presumed it was her, sat atop a horse, and a dark-haired beauty, who he assumed was her mother, held the lead line.

"That was my first horse," she told him, her eyes still on the picture. "I'd always ridden with Dad and helped him around the stables, but this one was all mine. I'd picked him out at auction and Mom and Dad told me I had to care for him all by myself."

Ian looked at the image of a young Cassie. "How old were you?"

"Eight. But I knew as soon as I saw him that I'd want him. He was skittish and shied away from the men, but when I approached him, against my father's advice, he came right to me and actually nuzzled my neck."

Ian listened to her, refusing to let himself fall into

her sea of emotions. He'd noticed her and Tessa holding hands at the shoot, tears swimming in both of their eyes.

"I've never ridden a horse," he admitted.

Cassie dropped the picture back into the bin and turned to stare at him. "Seriously? We'll have to rectify that while you're here."

Ian laughed. "I wasn't asking for an invitation. Just stating a fact."

She turned a bit more to face him, her thigh rubbing against his. Did she have a clue that she was playing with fire? She may be older than him, but something told him she wasn't necessarily more experienced.

Arrogance had him believing they weren't on a level playing field. He had plenty he wanted to show her.

"I love teaching people how to ride," she went on, oblivious to his thoughts. "It's such an exhilarating experience."

Cassie's wide smile lit up her entire face. The room had a soft glow from the single-bulb sconce on the wall and Ian could resist those full lips for only so long... especially now that he knew exactly how they tasted.

Without warning, he slid his hands through her hair and captured her lips. She opened freely, just like when they'd been in the stables.

Ian tipped her head, taking the kiss deeper. He wanted more, so much more. He wanted to feel her hands on him as he explored her mouth, relishing her taste, but she didn't touch him. Maybe she did know how to play this age-old game of catch and release.

Easing back, Ian took in her swollen lips, her heavy lids and flushed cheeks and smiled. "Actually, *that's* an exhilarating experience."

And God help them both because between the inter-

lude in the stables and that kiss, he had the whole night
to think about how this sexual chemistry would play out.

The real question was: Could he make it all night
without finding out?

Chapter 4

Cassie jumped to her feet, instantly feeling the chill without Ian's powerful touch. The man was beyond potent and he damn well knew it.

"You seriously think because we're locked in here and we kissed a few times that I'll just have sex with you?" Cassie ran a shaky hand through her hair, cursing her nerves for overtaking her as fast as those heated kisses had. "I don't know what lifestyle you lead in L.A., but that's not how I work."

Ian stared up at her, desire still lurking in those dark-as-sin eyes. "Are you denying you were just as involved in those kisses as I was?"

"You had your hands all over me," she threw back. "Just because I like kissing doesn't mean I always use it as a stepping-stone for sex. I technically just met you, for crying out loud. I don't know anything about you."

Moving as slowly as a panther hunting its prey, Ian came to his feet and crossed to her. "You know how quick you respond to my touch, you know how your heartbeat quickens when you wonder what my next move will be and you know you're fighting this pull between us."

Cassie raised a brow, trying for her best bored look. "That has nothing to do with Ian Shaffer. That's all chemistry."

"So you don't deny you want me?" he asked with a smirk.

Crossing her arms and taking a step back, Cassie narrowed her eyes. "Drop the ego down a notch. You just proved how very little we know about each other. You may sleep with virtual strangers, but I don't."

Ian laughed, throwing his arms in the air. "Okay. What do you want to know?"

"Are you married?"

Shock slid over his face. "Hell no. Never plan to be."

Commitment issues? Lovely. Hadn't she just gotten out of a relationship with a man of the same nature?

On the other hand, Ian wasn't cheating on a wife back in California. That was at least one mark in his favor. Okay, the toe-curling kisses were major positive points in his favor, but she'd never confess that out loud. And she wasn't actually looking to jump back into another relationship anyway.

"No girlfriend?" she asked.

"Would I be all over you if I did?"

Cassie shrugged. "Some guys wouldn't care."

That heated gaze glided over her and was just as effective as a lover's touch. Her body trembled.

"I'm not like a lot of other guys."

He was powerful, sexy and wanted in her pants. Yeah, he was just like some guys.

With a sigh, Cassie laughed. "I can't believe this," she muttered more to herself than to Ian. "I'm actually playing twenty questions because I want to have sex."

"Sweetheart, I don't care a bit to answer a hundred questions if you're considering sex."

Lord have mercy, it was hot up there. Not just because of the ridiculous way her body responded to this charmer, but literally. The heat in the attic was stifling.

Cassie unbuttoned the top two buttons of her shirt, exposing her cleavage area, but she needed air. She rolled her sleeves up and caught Ian's eyes taking in her actions.

"Don't get excited there, hotshot. I'm just trying to cool off."

Sweat trickled between her shoulder blades and she so wished she'd at least pulled her hair up earlier. There had to be something up here. As she started to look around in boxes for a rubber band of any type, she tried not to think of Ian and if he had sweat on the taut muscles beneath his shirt.

Okay, that mental blocker was broken because all she could see was glistening bronzed skin. And while she hadn't seen him without a shirt, she had a very good imagination.

"Can I help you find something?" he asked.

Throwing a glance over her shoulder, she caught his smirk as he crossed his arms over his chest. "I just need something to pull my hair up. I'm sweating."

There, that should douse his oversexed status a little. What man found a sweaty woman attractive? And she was pretty sure her wavy red hair was starting to look like Bozo the Clown's after a motorcycle ride…sans helmet. She lifted the flap off a box in the far corner and shuffled things around in her hunt.

"So, why is an agent needed on a film set?" she asked, truly wondering but also wanting to keep his mind on work—which was what he should be doing anyway.

"Max is one of my top clients." Ian unbuttoned his shirt halfway. "I often visit my clients on set to make sure they're taken care of. And with this being a very impressive script and plot, I knew I had to be here. I've actually blocked off a good bit of time to spend at Stony Ridge."

And wasn't that just the news she needed to hear? Mr. Tall, Dark and Tempting would be spending "a good bit of time" here. Just what her very inactive sexual life needed…temptation.

"Yes," she shouted as she grabbed a rubber band off a stack of school papers from her primary days.

"Max is a great guy, from what I've seen." After pulling her hair into a knot on top of her head, she turned to Ian. "He and Lily are doing an amazing job, too. Lily seems like a sweetheart."

Nodding his agreement, Ian rested a hip against an old dresser. "She's rare in the industry. L.A. hasn't jaded her or sucked the goodness out of her. She had a rough patch with a scandal at the start of her career, but she's overcome it. She's a rare gem."

"And I'm sure you've tried to get her into bed."

Rich laughter filled the space. The fact he was mocking her only ticked Cassie off more. But, if she were honest, she was ticked at herself for wanting him.

"I've never slept with Lily," he told her, a grin still spread across his handsome face. "I've never even tried to. I'm actually hoping to sign her to my agency. I respect my clients and they respect me. This business is too risky and too exposed for anything like that to remain a secret. There are no secrets in Hollywood."

"Is that all that's stopped you? The fact that people could find out?"

Ian straightened to his full height and took a step toward her. *Great.* She'd awoken the sex beast again.

"What stopped me," he said as he took slow steps toward her, "was the fact that, yes, she's beautiful, but I'm not attracted to her. Added to that, I want a professional relationship with her, not a sexual one. If I want a woman in my bed, she won't be on my client list. Plain and simple."

He'd come close enough that Cassie had to tip her head back. Thankfully, he hadn't touched her. Too much more touching—or, heaven forbid, kissing—and she feared her self-control would be totally shot.

Cassie swiped a hand over her damp neck. "Is everything a business strategy with you?"

"Not at all. Right now, I'm not thinking anything about business."

The way his eyes held hers, as if she was the only person that mattered right now, made her wonder...

She may be naive and she was certainly still recovering from Derek walking out on her, but what would a fling hurt? Tessa had even verbally expressed Cassie's thoughts on the matter. She'd married for "love," or so she'd thought. Hell, she'd even saved herself for marriage and look how that had turned out.

"I promise I won't ravage you if you'd like to take something off," he told her with a naughty grin. "I'm sure your shirt will be long enough to cover things if you need to get out of those jeans. If not, I've seen naked women before."

Yeah? Well, not *this* naked woman, and with that last bit of baby weight still hanging on for dear life, she most definitely wasn't comfortable enough with her body to flaunt it. Even if she did indulge in a fling with the sexy agent—and she couldn't believe she was seriously considering such a thing—she wasn't going to make the catch so easy for him. What fun would that be?

Deciding to teach him a lesson, Cassie reached up and patted the side of his face. "You're so sweet to sacrifice yourself that way."

Cassie knew her mother had a box of old clothes up here. Perhaps something could be used to cool her off and make Ian squirm just a bit more.

As she went toward the area with the clothing boxes, she opted to keep Ian talking.

"So, tell me more about Lily." Cassie pulled the lid off an oblong box and nearly wept with relief at the colorful summer dresses inside. "She's very striking and has a strong resemblance to my mother."

"When this film came across my desk, I knew I wanted Max to try for it and I was sincerely hoping they paired him with Lily. This role was made for her. She's already got that Southern-belle charm your mother had, according to everyone on set. Lily has the sweet little twang in her voice like all of you Barringtons do."

Cassie turned, clutching a simple strapless cotton dress to her chest. "I do not have a twang."

Ian quirked a brow. "It's actually even more prominent when you get ticked. Very cute and sexy."

Rolling her eyes, Cassie turned back to the box and

placed the lid back on. "I'm going to change. Could you try not to stare at me through the reflection again?"

Ian shrugged one broad shoulder. "I promise."

Cassie waited for him to turn around or move, but he just sat there smiling. Damn that man. Now that she'd reminded him he'd seen her pretty much naked, Cassie had no doubt she'd just thrown gasoline on the fire.

"Aren't you going to turn around?" she finally asked.

"Oh, when you just said not to look at you through the reflection, I assumed you wanted to let me in on the full viewing."

"I didn't want to let you into this room…let alone treat you to a viewing."

Cassie resisted the urge to kiss that smirk off his face. He knew he was getting to her, and she wondered just how much longer she'd deny it to herself.

"I'll move, then," she told him, stomping to the other end of the attic behind a tall stack of boxes. "And don't you follow me."

"Wouldn't dream of it." He chuckled. "But you're just putting off the inevitable, you know."

She quickly wrestled out of her clothes and yanked the strapless dress up over her heated body. Her bare arms and legs cooled instantly.

"I'm not putting anything off," she informed him as she came back around the boxes. "I know your type, Ian. Sex shouldn't just be a way to pass the time. It should mean something, and the couple should have feelings for each other."

"Oh, I feel something for you. And I plan on making you feel something, too."

Why did her body have to respond to him? And why did she always have to be so goody-goody all the time?

She didn't even have the ability to make him squirm. No wonder her husband had left her for another woman.

"I'm not sure what put that look on your face, but I hope it wasn't me."

Cassie drew her attention back to Ian, who had now moved in closer and was very much in her personal space. His dark eyes stared at her mouth and Cassie really tried to remember why she was putting up such a fight.

Had her husband ever looked at her like this? As though he was so turned on that all that mattered was the two of them? Had he ever made her tingle like this or feel so feminine and sexy?

No to all the above.

Cassie swallowed. If she was really going to do this, she needed to be in control. She'd been dominated enough in her marriage and right now she wanted something totally different. She wanted sex and she wanted Ian.

Mustering up all her courage, Cassie looked up at him with a wide smile and said, "Strip."

Chapter 5

It wasn't often Ian was shocked—he did live in Hollywood, after all. But that one word that had just slid from Cassie's lips truly took his breath and left him utterly speechless.

"Excuse me?"

Raising a brow, she crossed her arms as if she dared him to refuse. "I said strip. You want this, fine. But on my terms."

"I don't do sex with rules."

Cassie shrugged. "I don't do flings, but here we both are, stepping outside of our comfort zones."

Damn, she was hot. He never would've guessed the shy, quiet sister had this vixen streak. Of course, she admitted she was stepping outside her comfort zone, so perhaps this was all new territory. He had to hand it to her—she was doing a spectacular job. But he couldn't let her have all the control.

Reaching behind his neck, Ian fisted his shirt and tugged it off, flinging it to the side. Hands on his hips, he offered a grin.

"Now you."

Cassie laughed. "You're not done yet."

"No, but I'm ahead of you." He met her gaze, the silent challenge thrown down between them. "I'm waiting."

Even though her eyes never left his, he didn't miss the way her hands shook as she reached beneath the dress and pulled her panties down her bare legs.

Just that simple piece of silk lying discarded at her feet had his pulse racing, his body responding.

She quirked a brow again, as if waiting for him to proceed.

Without hesitation he toed off his shoes and ripped off his socks. "Looks like you're down to only one garment now," he told her, taking in the strapless dress she'd donned.

And it was about to get a whole hell of a lot hotter in here.

She eyed the lamp across the room and started for it.

"No," he told her. "Leave it on."

Glancing over her shoulder, she met his stare. "Trust me when I say you'll want that off."

"And why is that?"

Turning fully to face him, she pointed to her body. "In case you haven't noticed, I'm not one of those Hollywood types who starve themselves for the sake of being ultrathin."

Crossing the narrow space between them, Ian ran both his hands up her bare arms and tucked his fingers in the elastic of the top of the dress, causing her arms to fall to her side.

"Oh, I've noticed." He yanked the dress down until it puddled at her feet, leaving her bare to him. "And that's precisely why I want that light on."

Her body trembled beneath his. No way did he want her questioning her gorgeous curves or the fact that he wanted the hell out of her.

Without a word he shucked off his pants and boxer briefs and tossed them aside.

Her eyes drank him in, causing the same effect as if she'd touched his entire body with her bare hands. Dying to touch her, to run his fingers along her curves, Ian snaked his arms around her waist and tugged her against him.

"As much as I want to explore that sexy body of yours, I'm hanging on by a thread here," he admitted as his mouth slammed down onto hers.

Cassie wrapped her arms around his neck. Their damp bodies molded together from torso to thigh, and she felt so perfect against him.

Perfect? No, she couldn't be perfect for him. Perfect for right now, which was all either of them was after.

They were simply taking advantage of the moment… of the sexual attraction that had enveloped them since she'd literally fallen into his arms only a few days ago.

Ian gripped her waist and lifted her.

"Ian, don't—"

"Shh," he whispered against her mouth. "I've got you."

Her lips curved into a smile. "What about a condom? Do you have that, too?"

Condom, yes. They needed a condom. His mind had

been on the subtle moans escaping from her lips and getting those curves beneath his hands.

He eased her down his body and went to his jeans, where he pulled a condom from his wallet and in record time had it on.

When he turned back to her, he fully expected her to have her arms wrapped around her waist, maybe even be biting her lip out of nerves. But what he saw was a secure woman, hands on her hips, head tilted and a naughty grin on her face.

"Your confidence is sexy," he told her as he came back to her.

"You make me feel sexy."

Yeah, she wasn't a Hollywood size zero. Cassie Barrington was more old-school Hollywood starlet. She was a natural, stunning, vibrant woman, and now that she'd agreed to leave the light on, he could fully appreciate the beauty she was.

And when she reached for him and nearly wrapped herself around him as she claimed his mouth, her sexy status soared even higher.

Damn, he wasn't going to make it through this night.

Ian backed her against the wall and lifted her once again. This time her legs went around his waist and he had no control. None. The second he'd shucked that dress off her he'd been holding on by that proverbial thin thread.

Ian took her, causing her body to bow back, and her head tilted, eyes closed as she groaned once again.

As their hips moved together, Ian took the opportunity to kiss his way across her shoulders and the column of her throat before taking her face between her palms and claiming her mouth.

Sweat slick between them, the air around them grew even hotter as Cassie gripped his bare shoulders. Her nails bit into his skin; her heels dug into his back.

He wouldn't have it any other way.

She tore her mouth from his. "Ian, I—"

Yeah, he knew. He was right there with her as her body stilled, trembled. Following her over the edge, watching her face as she succumbed to the passion was one of the most erotic moments of his life.

Her body slid down his and he was pretty sure she would've collapsed to the floor had he not been leaning against her. He needed to lean into her or he'd be a puddle, too.

And the night had just begun.

Cassie slid back into her dress, ignoring the panties. Why bother with modesty at this point?

She may not live in Hollywood, but she'd put on one hell of an acting display. Ian thought her confident? She'd played along simply because she secretly wanted to be that wanton, take-charge woman, that woman who claimed what she wanted. And if he thought she was so comfortable with her body in this situation, then who was she to tell him different?

She'd been meek in her marriage, not a sex goddess in any way. But the way Ian had looked at her, touched her, was nothing like she'd ever experienced.

How could a man she'd known only a handful of days provide so much self-assurance? He'd awakened something within her she hadn't even known existed.

Cassie was certainly not used to one-night stands or flings, but she couldn't regret what had just happened. A virtual stranger had just given her one of the greatest gifts…self-esteem. Not too long ago she'd thought she'd never have that back, but right now, with her body still tingling from his talented hands and lips, Cassie knew without a doubt that she was better than the husband who had left her for another woman.

She'd just scooped up her discarded panties from the floor when Ian placed his hands around her waist and tugged her back against his bare chest.

"How's that age thing now?" he asked, nipping her ear. "Any complaints about how young I am?"

Laughing, Cassie shook her head. "You certainly know what you're doing."

His lips trailed over her neck. "I'm not done, either."

Oh, mercy. Her entire body shivered as she let her head fall back against his shoulder, enjoying the kisses he sprinkled across her heated skin.

"I'm not sure why you put this dress back on," he told her between kisses. "It's so hot in here and all."

Yes, yes, it is.

Cassie turned in his arms, noticing he was still completely naked. Those ripped muscles beneath taut, tanned skin begged for her touch.

"I didn't get to appreciate all of this a moment ago, before you attacked me," she told him, trailing her fingertips along his biceps and across his pecs.

"Appreciate me all you want," he told her with a crooked grin. "But let it be known, I didn't attack. You ordered me to strip, so I believe you started this."

Cassie playfully smacked his chest. "Who started what? You were the one who propositioned me in the stables."

"How's a man supposed to react when a sexy woman falls into his arms?"

"Yes, naturally that's what most people would do," she said, rolling her eyes.

Ian reached down, cupped her backside and widened his sexy smile. "I'm glad this little incident happened with the lock."

Cassie had to admit she was, too. There was no way she would've been able to focus on work with all her emotions fluttering around inside her. Now hopefully she wouldn't have to worry about this overwhelming physical attraction to Ian. They'd had sex, gotten it out of their systems and could move on.

His body stirred against hers. Okay, maybe they hadn't gotten it out of their systems.

"We still have hours before anyone will find us." He started backing her up again. "I have so many ideas to fill the time."

The backs of Cassie's thighs hit the edge of an old table. Ian wasted no time hoisting her up onto the smooth wooden surface.

"Do you have more condoms?" she asked.

His heavy-lidded gaze combined with that Cheshire-cat smile had her quivering before he even spoke.

"I may be out of condoms, but not out of ways to pleasure you."

And when he proceeded to show her, Cassie was suddenly in no hurry for daylight to come.

Chapter 6

Unable to sleep for appreciating the feel of this sexy woman tangled all around him on the old chaise, Ian smoothed a hand down Cassie's bare back. Trailing down the dip in her waist, up over the curve of her hip had his body stirring again.

What on earth was he doing? Sex was one thing, but to lie awake most of the night rehashing it over and over in his head like some lovesick fool was, well…for fools. Not that he was any expert on relationships.

His mother was gearing up to divorce husband number four, no doubt with number five waiting in the wings, and his father… Ian sighed. His father probably wasn't even capable of love. Ian hadn't spoken to his father in years and rarely talked with his mother. He had nothing to say to either and it was obvious both of his parents were battling their own issues that didn't include him.

It shouldn't come as a surprise that Ian didn't do relationships.

He was great at his job, however, and what he wanted was to take his client roster to the next level. Lily Beaumont was the key.

Yet here he was, getting involved with Cassie Barrington. And, yes, they'd just had sex, but during the moments in between their intimacy, he'd gotten a brief glimpse of a playful, confident woman and he couldn't deny he liked what he saw.

The sound of a car door jarred him from his thoughts. He eased out from beneath Cassie's warm, lush body and moved over to the small window that faced the side of the house.

Tessa and Grant had arrived. He didn't know if he wanted to call for their attention or crawl back over to Cassie and give her a proper good-morning wake-up.

But their night was over, and he had responsibilities. He honestly had no clue how she'd react once she woke up. Would she regret what they'd done? Would she want more and expect some sort of relationship?

Ian gave the window a tug and it rose slowly with a groan.

"Hey," he yelled down. "Up here."

Tessa and Grant both looked around and Ian eased his arm out to wave. "We're locked in the attic," he called.

"Ian?" Grant shouted. "What on earth? We'll be right up."

Of course, now it dawned on him that both he and Cassie were as naked as the day they were born, and he turned around to see her already getting up. Shame that he hadn't ignored the rescue party and gone with his original idea of waking her, especially now that she was covering that made-for-sex body.

"Was that Tessa and Grant?" she asked, tugging on her jeans from the previous day.

"Uh-huh." He pulled on his own clothes, trying to keep his eyes off her as she wrestled into her bra.

Several moments later, the door below creaked open and Ian rushed over to the top of the stairs to see Tessa.

"We'll be right down," he told her, hoping to save Cassie some time to finish dressing.

He didn't know if she wanted it public knowledge that they'd slept together. This was all her call. He was much more comfortable with a fling than he figured she was. Plus this was her home, her family, and the last thing he wanted to do was put her in an awkward position.

"Who's up there with you?" Tessa asked, her brows drawn together.

"Your sister."

Tessa smiled. "Really? Well, we'll meet you all down in the kitchen. Take your time."

Once she walked away, Ian glanced up to Cassie, who was wearing a lovely shade of red over her neck and face.

"I tried," he defended, holding out his hands. "But I'd say your sister knows."

Cassie nodded. "That's okay. Tessa won't say anything."

Okay, maybe he hadn't wanted a relationship, but her statement hit a nerve. Seconds ago he'd thought he was fine with a fling and she wasn't, but perhaps he'd had that scenario backward.

"Is that what we're going to do? Keep this quiet?"

Smoothing her tousled hair away from her face, Cassie eyed him from across the room and sighed. "I don't know. This is all new to me. Can we just go downstairs and talk later?"

The voice of reason had him nodding. He didn't want to analyze what had happened too much. They both needed to concentrate on their jobs. After all, he had a mission and she was in the middle of the biggest racing season of her life.

Cassie started to ease by him when he stepped in front of her, blocking her exit. Her eyes went wide, then dropped to his mouth. Why was he doing this?

Quit stalling and let her go.

But he needed one more taste before their night officially came to an end.

He shoved his hands into her hair, tilting her head as he closed the distance between them. "Before you go," he whispered as his mouth slid across hers.

She melted into him as she returned the kiss. Her hands gripped his wrists as he held on to her. As much as Ian wanted her naked once again, he knew that was not an option.

Easing back, he smiled when her eyes took a moment to open. He released her, and, without a word, she walked by him and down the stairs.

And like some nostalgic sap, he glanced around the attic and smiled. This was definitely his favorite place on the estate.

Ian met up with Cassie in the kitchen. As soon as he entered the open room, he took in several things at once.

Tessa and Grant were seated at the bar, where Linda was serving cinnamon rolls. Both Tessa and Grant were eyeing Ian with knowing grins on their faces.

But it was Cassie, yet again, who captured his attention.

The woman he'd spent the night with was currently squatting down in front of a little girl with soft blond curls. The little girl looked nothing like Cassie, but the interaction didn't lie. The way she clung to Cassie, Cassie's sweet smile and laughter as she kissed her—it all had a sickening feeling settling deep in his gut.

"And who's this?" he asked, hoping it was Linda's grandchild or something because he knew Tessa and Grant had no children.

Coming to her feet with the little girl wrapped in her arms, Cassie still wore that vibrant smile as she turned to face him. "This is my daughter, Emily."

All eyes were on Ian. Granted, they were watching him because of the unspoken fact that he and Cassie had spent the night together, but they couldn't know the turmoil that flooded him. Cassie had a child and hadn't told him.

Not that they'd played the getting-to-know-you game before they'd shed their clothes, but wasn't that something that would come up?

Cassie's smile faded as Ian remained silent. Her protective hands held Emily close to her chest.

"Why don't you have some breakfast?" Linda asked, breaking the silence.

His eyes darted to her, then back to Cassie, who still watched him with a questioning look. Tessa and Grant had yet to move as they also took in the unfolding scene.

"I have things to do," he said as he walked by Cassie, ignoring the hurt in her eyes, and out the back door.

He couldn't stay in there another second. Rage filled him at the idea that Cassie had kept such a vital part of her life a secret. Was she the mother who pawned her kid off on other people so she could go have a good time? She'd been so confident, so eager to please him last night. Perhaps he was just the latest in a long line of men she threaded into her web.

No, he hadn't wanted anything beyond sex. And he sure as hell didn't want to discover that the woman he'd spent the night with was manipulative and selfish, looking for attention…just like his mother.

Humiliation flooded her.

The look of utter shock layered with anger had consumed Ian when she'd announced Emily was her daughter.

"Cass?"

Swallowing the hurt, Cassie turned to see her sister watching her. Because this awkward moment didn't need any more fuel added to the fire, Cassie smiled.

"Thanks for watching her last night," Cassie said as she held Emily with one arm and grabbed the overnight bag off the counter. "I need to go change and then I'll meet you at the stables."

"Cassie." Tessa slid from the stool and crossed to her. "Don't do this."

"Do what?"

Blue eyes stared back at her and Cassie wanted nothing more than to sit and cry, but feeling sorry for herself wouldn't accomplish anything. She'd tried that when Derek had left her.

"I just want to go feed Emily and change." Cassie blinked back the burn of tears. "I'll meet you in an hour."

"Leave Emily here," Linda said. "I'm keeping her today anyway. Do what you need to do. I'll make sure she's fed."

As much as Cassie wanted to keep Emily with her,

she knew it was silly. She'd just have to put her in her crib with toys while she grabbed a shower.

"All right," she conceded, dropping the bag back onto the counter and easing Emily into the wooden high chair next to the wide granite island. "Thanks, guys."

Barely keeping it together, she started for the door. When Tessa called her name again, Cassie raised a hand and waved her off. She just wanted to be alone for a minute, to compose herself.

How could she be so naive? Of course some big-city bachelor would be turned off by kids, but to act so repulsed by the fact made her flat-out angry.

She'd sworn when Derek had left she wouldn't allow herself to get hurt again. So, what did she do? Sleep with the first man who showed her any kind of affection.

Seriously, she thought she had more self-respect than that.

More angry at herself now, Cassie marched across the Barrington estate to her cottage next to the stables. Swatting at her damp cheeks, she squinted against the bright early-morning sun.

And because of the light in her eyes she didn't see Ian until she was in the shadow of her house. There he stood, resting against one of the porch posts as if he belonged there.

"Don't you have a client who needs your attention?" she asked, not stopping as she brushed past him and slid her key from her pocket to let herself in.

When she tried to close the door behind her, Ian's muscular arm shot out and his hand gripped the edge.

Those dark eyes leveled hers as she reined in her tears. No way would she let him see just how upset she truly was.

Tension crackled between them as Ian stood on the threshold, making no move to come in or leave.

"What do you want?" she asked.

"I want to know why you didn't tell me you had a daughter."

"Do you have kids?" she retorted.

He blinked. "No."

"Why didn't you tell me you didn't?"

"It never came up."

She threw her arms out. "Exactly. We didn't discuss too much personal stuff before…"

Shaking her head, Cassie looked up to the ceiling and sighed. "Just go. I made a mistake—it's over."

When her front door slammed, she jumped.

"I don't like being played." Ian fisted his hands on his narrow hips.

"This is my life, Ian." She gestured toward the Pack 'n Play in the corner and the toys in a basket next to the sofa. "I'm a mom. I'm not apologizing for it, and you won't make me feel bad."

When he continued to stare, muscle ticking in his jaw, Cassie tried her hardest not to wilt under his powerful presence. His gray T-shirt stretched over taut muscles, and she instantly recalled him taking her against the wall.

"Look, you're going to be here for a while," she said, reality sinking in. "I'm going to be here for the most part except during races. We're going to see each other."

His eyes roamed over her as if he were recalling last night, too. A shiver crept through her, but she remained still, waiting on his response.

"I wish you were different," he told her, his voice low.

Stunned, Cassie crossed her arms. "What?"

Cursing, Ian turned for the door. "Nothing. You're right," he said, gripping the handle and glancing over his shoulder. "We have to see each other, so why make this harder than necessary? Last night was a mistake, so let's just forget it happened."

He walked out the door and Cassie resisted the urge to throw something. For a second, when he'd said he wished she were different, she'd seen a sliver of vulnerability in his eyes. But he'd quickly masked it with his cruel, hurtful words. *Fine.* She didn't need anybody, especially someone who acted as if her child was a burden. Emily came first in her life. Period.

And no man, not her ex-husband and certainly not this sexy stranger, would make her feel ashamed.

Cassie turned toward her bedroom and cursed her body. She hated Ian Shaffer for his words, his actions, but her body still tingled from everything he'd done to her last night. How could someone so passionate and gentle turn into someone so hurtful?

Something about Emily had triggered such a dramatic turnaround. Unfortunately, Cassie didn't have the time or the energy to care. Whatever issues Ian had didn't concern her.

Now she just had to figure out how to see him on a daily basis and block out the fact he'd made her so alive, so confident for a brief time. Because now she didn't feel confident at all. She wished she could have a do-over of last night.

This time she'd keep her clothes on.

Chapter 7

Ian may have had the best sexual experience of his life last night, but any desire he felt for Cassie was quickly squelched when he'd discovered her with a baby. A baby, for crying out loud.

It wasn't that he didn't like children. Kids were innocent in life, innocent in the actions of adults. How could he not love them? He just didn't see any in his future. And Cassie having a child certainly wasn't a problem in and of itself.

No, the issue had been when he'd seen her holding her child and he'd instantly flashed back to his mother, who would drag him from sitter to sitter while she went out at night.

But he wouldn't blame his past for his present problems. His body seemed to forget how angry he was and continued to betray him. Cassie was still sexy as hell and he'd forever be replaying just how hot their encounter had been.

But now that he knew she had a daughter, messing around on a whim was definitely out. He wasn't cut out for the long term, and he refused to be the lover floating in and out of a kid's life the way his mother's lovers had floated through his.

Shaking off the unpleasant memories seeing Cassie with her baby had inspired, Ian approached Max Ford. His client had recently married his high school sweetheart and the couple had adopted a little girl. Ian couldn't be happier for the guy, but he wanted no part in the happily-ever-after myth himself.

"Hey," Max greeted him as he headed toward the makeup trailer. "Coming in with me?"

"Yeah."

Ian fell into step behind Max. The actor tugged on the narrow door and gestured for Ian to enter first. After climbing the three metal steps, Ian entered the cool trailer and nodded a greeting to the makeup artist.

Max closed the door behind him and exchanged pleasantries with the young lady. Ian took a seat on the small sofa across from the workstation and waited until the two finished their discussion of the day's events.

"You're working out in the stables and field today?" Ian asked. "I saw the script. Looked like the scene with you and Lily when the first horses were brought onto the estate after the wedding."

Max nodded as the makeup artist swiped over his face with a sponge full of foundation. "Yeah. It's a short scene. This afternoon and evening we'll be shooting some of the wedding scenes at the small church in town."

Ian settled deeper into the sofa, resting an arm across the back of the cushion. "Everything going okay so far?"

"Great," Max told him. "Raine is planning on joining me in a few days. She was excited I was shooting on the East Coast."

Ian knew Max and Raine had been through hell after years apart before finally finding their way back to each other in Max's hometown of Lenox, Massachusetts. Ian couldn't imagine trying to juggle a family while working in this crazy industry, let alone from across the country. Speaking of crazy, Ian never thought Hollywood heartthrob Max Ford would settle down, much less on some goat and chicken farm in New England, but to each his own and all that. Love apparently made you do some strange things.

"You talking to Lily soon?" Max asked.

Max had been one of Ian's first clients. They'd both taken a chance on each other, the risk had paid off and here they were, at the top of their games. They had no secrets and oftentimes their relationship was more like friends than business associates.

"Yeah. Hoping to get a few more minutes with her today."

The makeup artist reached for a brush and started stroking a shadow across Max's lids. Yeah, Ian would much rather stay on this side of the industry...the side where his face stayed makeup-free.

"I'll keep you posted," Ian said, not wanting to get too detailed since there were other ears in the room. "I plan on being on set for the next several weeks, so hopefully something will come from that."

Something positive. There was no way Ian wanted his ex-partner to get his clutches on Lily. Not to mention

Ian was selfish and now that Lily was between agents, he wanted her because she was one of the top Hollywood leading ladies.

Added to that, she was the rare celebrity who hadn't been jaded or swayed by the limelight. Lily was the real deal who made a point to keep her nose out of trouble.

Any agent's dream client.

"I've discussed some things with her," Max stated. "She's interested in hearing your terms and ideas, so hopefully she makes the right decision."

Ian was counting on it. Lily was smart enough to know the industry. After all, she'd just left her agent, who'd been a bit shady with her career. She'd put a stop to that immediately.

Ian could only hope she saw the hands-on way he worked and how invested he was as an agent. Visiting movie sets was his favorite job perk. Getting out of a stuffy office and being on location was always the highlight. Plus he wanted to make sure his clients were comfortable and there were no glitches.

"I'll be around if you need me." Ian came to his feet and moved toward the trailer door, pulling his phone from his pocket to check his emails. "I plan on being at both scenes today."

"Sounds good. I assume you've met all the Barringtons?" Max asked as the makeup artist ran the powder brush over his neck.

Ian swallowed. "Yeah. I've met them."

Met them, slept with one and still felt the stirrings from the continuous play of memories.

"They're one impressive family," Max went on, oblivious to the turmoil within Ian. "Damon is an amazing man with all of his accomplishments, but I swear, Cassie and Tessa are a force to be reckoned with."

Ian bit the inside of his cheek to avoid commenting on one of those "forces." The image of her in that body-hugging dress still made his knees weak, his heart quicken.

"That's why this movie is going to kick ass," Ian said, circling back to work, where his mind needed to stay. "Everyone loves a story like this, and having it on the big screen with two of Hollywood's top stars will only make it pull in that much more at the box office."

"I hope you're right."

Ian was confident this movie would be one of the biggest for both Max and Lily. Hollywood's heartthrob and sweetheart playing a married couple in a true story? It was a guaranteed slam dunk for everybody.

Which reminded him, he needed to check his emails and hopefully line up another client's role.

"I'll see you in a bit," Ian said as he exited the trailer.

He refused to glance toward Cassie's cottage. He wasn't some love-struck teen who'd slept with a woman and now wondered what she was doing every waking minute.

Okay, so he did wonder what she was doing, but love had absolutely nothing to do with it. His hormones were stuck in overdrive and they would just have to stay there because he refused to see her in any type of personal atmosphere again.

Even flings warranted a certain type of honesty, and getting involved, in any manner, with a woman who reminded him of the past he'd outrun was simply not an option.

A flash of movement from the field in the distance caught his eye. He headed toward the white fence stretching over the Barrington estate. As he neared, his gut tightened.

Cassie sat atop a chestnut-colored horse flying through the open field. Her hair danced unrestrained in the wind behind her and the breeze carried her rich laughter straight to him…and his body responded…work and emails instantly forgotten.

Ian stood frozen and admired the beauty. From behind her came Tessa on her own horse, but Ian's gaze was riveted on Cassie. He hadn't heard that deep laugh. She all but screamed sex with that throaty sound, her curves bouncing in the saddle, hair a wild mass of deep crimson curls.

Her carefree attitude would've been such a turn-on, but in the back of his mind he couldn't forget where he came from. From a father who had standards so high nobody could reach them and a mother who spent her time entertaining boyfriends and husbands, leaving a young Ian a distant second in her life.

He never wanted to go back to that emotional place again.

"You've got an audience."

Breathless and smiling, Cassie turned to her sister as Tessa came to a stop beside her. This felt good, to get out and not worry about training or anything else for a few minutes. Just getting back to their roots and racing was something she and her sister didn't do nearly often enough.

"Who's the audience?" Cassie asked, fully expecting to see some of the film crew. The cameramen and lighting people seemed to be all over the estate, moving things around, making the place their own for the sake of the film. The Hollywood scene was definitely a far cry from the usual relaxed atmosphere of Stony Ridge.

A sense of pride welled deep within her at the fact that Hollywood loved her family's story as much as she did. Horses, racing and family... That was what it meant to be a Barrington, and they excelled at it all because they worked hard and loved harder.

"Your agent," Tessa replied, nodding back toward the fence line. "I saw him stop when you raced by. He hasn't moved."

Cassie risked a glance and, sure enough, Ian stood turned in her direction. He was just far enough away that she couldn't make out his facial expression...not that she cared. But damn, why did he have to be a jumbled mess? He'd wanted her with such passion last night, had made her feel so special and wanted. How dare he pull such emotions out of her when she was still trying to piece the shards of her heart back together after her divorce?

Today when he'd seen Emily, he'd become detached, angry and not at all the same man she'd been with last night. His silence had hurt her, had made the night before instantly ugly.

And after coming home, she'd checked her phone and found a missed call from Derek. Seriously? After months of no contact whatsoever, now he decided to call? Cassie had deleted the message without listening. She didn't care what he had to say, and, after her emotional morning with Ian, she wasn't in the mood.

"He's not my anything." Cassie turned back toward Tessa, turning her back on Ian and willing him to go away.

"He was something to you last night."

Squinting against the sun, Cassie shrugged. "He was my temporary mistake. Nothing more."

Leaning across the gap between the horses, Tessa slid her hand over Cassie's. "I'm not judging at all. I just want you to know people aren't perfect. We all make rash decisions, and beating yourself up won't change what happened."

Cassie knew Tessa would be the last person to judge her, but that didn't stop the embarrassment from settling in her gut.

"I just hate that I gave in to the first man to show me any attention since being divorced," Cassie explained, gripping the reins.

Tessa's warm smile spread across her face. "Honey, Ian is a very attractive man, you're a beautiful woman and you all were locked in an attic all night. Instant attraction is hard to ignore, especially when you have nothing else to focus on."

"Self-control is a beautiful thing," Cassie murmured. "Too bad I didn't have any."

Laughing, Tessa squeezed Cassie's hand before pulling back. "Yeah, well, I didn't have any where Grant was concerned, either, and look how well it worked out for us."

Cassie's eyes darted down to the impressive diamond band surrounding Tessa's ring finger. Grant had gotten a flat band because of Tessa's riding career; he knew she wouldn't want to work with anything too bulky.

And that proved just how beautiful a relationship her sister and Grant had. The man knew Tessa inside and out, loved her and her career. He'd even overcome his own personal demons to be with her.

Cassie couldn't be happier for the two of them, but her situation was different.

"I'm pretty sure my attic rendezvous will not be leading to any proposals," Cassie joked. She had to joke with Tessa, otherwise she'd cry, and she refused to let this experience pull her down and make her feel guilty for having needs. "Besides, I think seeing Emily was like a bucket of cold water in Ian's face. I won't be with anybody who can't accept that I'm a package deal."

"I saw Ian's face when he found out Emily was yours," Tessa said, shoving her hair behind her ear. "He was definitely caught off guard, but the man wasn't unaffected by whatever happened between the two of you or he wouldn't have just stopped to watch you ride by. He may be torn, but he's still interested. You can't blame him for being shocked you're a mother."

Yeah, well, Ian's interest more than likely consisted of getting in her pants again...which she wouldn't allow.

But the memory of last night still played through her mind. His touch had been perfect. His words had seduced her until she'd forgotten about anything else but the moment they were locked in.

No matter how her body craved to be touched by his talented hands again, Cassie knew she deserved better than the way she'd been treated afterward.

So if Ian wanted her, that was his problem and he'd have to deal with it. She had enough on her plate without worrying about some big-time Hollywood agent who was only looking for only a fling.

She had a racing season to finish and a school for handicapped children to get started.

Her soon-to-be brother-in-law, Grant, had a paralyzed sister who used to ride, and her story had inspired Cassie on so many levels. Even though they hadn't met yet, just her story alone was enough to drive Cassie to want more for the next chapter of life. And what better way to teach her daughter to give back and love and care for others? Instilling love in young children made all the difference. She and Tessa were evidence of that.

Throwing a glance over her shoulder, Cassie had mixed emotions when she saw Ian was nowhere in sight. On one hand, she was glad he'd moved on. On the other, she kind of liked knowing she'd left some sort of impression on him.

No matter how things were now, for a time last night, she'd been in a sexy man's arms and that man had been attentive and giving and had made her feel more self-worth than ever.

Having regrets at this point was kind of in vain.

Besides, no matter what common sense played through her mind, she couldn't deny the physical pull she still felt toward Ian. And she was positive she hadn't seen the last of him.

Chapter 8

After shooting wrapped for the day, Ian headed toward the stables to see if Lily was in there. He hadn't seen her for two days, and Max had mentioned he'd seen her heading that way. Ian hadn't had a chance to speak with her yet. The chaos of filming and so many people around had gotten in the way. Other than the usual small talk, he'd not been able to catch her alone.

Hopefully he could find her and perhaps they could arrange for a time to sit down and talk.

The sun was just at the edge of the horizon, casting a vibrant orange glow across the sky. The air had turned warmer as spring approached summer. Soon they'd be off to the Preakness Stakes, where Tessa would try to win the second race on her way toward the coveted Triple Crown.

The entire crew was riding the high of the shoot as

well as getting sucked into the excitement of cheering the Barrington girls on toward victory. He had no doubt Tessa and Cassie were a jumble of anticipation and nerves.

Ian shoved his hands into his pockets as he approached the stables. He wasn't letting his mind wander to Cassie, because if he thought of her, he'd think of her sweet curves, her tempting smile and the fact he still wanted her.

Before he could travel too far down that path of mixed emotions, Ian rounded the corner of the open stable door and froze.

Lily was in the stable all right. But she wasn't alone. The groom, Ian believed his name was Nash, had his back to Lily, and Lily's hand rested on his shoulder, a look of concern marring her beautiful face.

She whispered something Ian couldn't make out and Nash's head dropped at the same time Lily's arms slid around his waist and she rested her forehead on his back. The intimate, private moment shocked Ian and he really had no clue what he'd walked in on.

The old-fashioned lanterns suspended from the ceiling cast a perfect glow on them and Ian quickly stepped out of the stable before he could be spotted…or interrupt whatever was happening.

He had a feeling whatever was going on between the groom and the star of the film was on the down low… especially since an affair had nearly cost Grant Carter his job when he'd been sneaking to see Tessa.

But that had all worked out and the two were headed down the aisle in the near future.

Their secret would be safe with him. For one, he wanted Lily to trust him and sign with his agency. And for another, why stir up trouble? Ian couldn't help but laugh. He and Cassie were pretty far-fetched in terms of the possibility of getting together, but look where they were now after a heated night in the attic.

Heading back toward his on-site trailer, Ian stopped when a scream cut through the evening. It was loud enough to have him trying to figure out where the sound was coming from.

He heard it again and moved toward the row of cottages settled beyond the main house. The grounds were deserted now since the entire crew had left for the hotel in town. Only a handful of people were staying on the property in trailers like the one Max had requested for him. The scream split through the air once more and Ian quickly found the culprit.

Just behind Cassie's cottage there was a small patio area and suspended from the pergola was a child's swing.

Cassie pushed her daughter, and each time the child went high, she let out a squeal. Ian's heart dropped at the sight. He didn't recall ever having that one-on-one playful time with either of his parents. Perhaps when he'd been a toddler, but he doubted it, considering they weren't affectionate when he'd been old enough to recall.

The sweet little girl with blond curls blowing in the breeze giggled and kicked her feet when Cassie grabbed the back of the plastic seat on the swing and held it back.

"Hold on," Cassie warned. "Here comes the biggest push of all."

When she let go of the swing, Cassie laughed right along with her daughter and Ian found himself rooted to his spot at the edge of her concrete patio.

The man in him watched, admiring Cassie's laid-back style, with her hair in a ponytail and wearing leggings and an oversize T-shirt that slid off one delicate, creamy shoulder. Her feet were bare and her face was void of any makeup, which was how he'd seen her since he'd arrived. Everything about her screamed country girl.

While the man in him watched, the lost little boy in him turned his attention to Emily. He took in all the delight from the sweet girl still clutching the rope holding up her swing and wondered where her father was. Did the man even know he had a child? Did Cassie have any contact with him?

All the questions forming in his head were absolutely none of his business, yet he couldn't help but want to know more.

Ian's gaze traveled from Emily back to Cassie…and he found her looking right back at him with those impressive blue eyes.

"What are you doing here?" she asked, giving the swing another light push.

Ian tried not to focus on the fact that her shirt had slipped in the front, giving him a glimpse of the swell of her breast.

"I heard screaming." He stepped onto the concrete pad, cursing himself for being drawn in even more. "I wasn't sure who it was."

Cassie's eyes held his for a second before she turned her attention back to the swing. She held on to the ropes, thus bringing Emily's fun to a screeching halt.

The little girl twisted in her seat to look back at Cassie. Cassie went to the front of the swing, unfastened the safety harness and lifted Emily out.

"We were just heading in for dinner," Cassie said, propping Emily up on her hip.

Damn if her tilted, defiant chin didn't make him want

to stay longer. Why torture himself? He wanted her physically, nothing more. Yet he found himself being pulled ever so slowly toward her.

"Don't go in just because of me."

Emily stared at him with bright, expressive blue eyes like her mother's. Her hand reached toward him and he couldn't stop himself from reaching back. The moment he looked into those little baby blues something unidentifiable slid over his heart.

Emily's tiny hand encircled his finger as a smile spread across her baby face. That innocent gesture touched so many places in him: the child who'd craved attention, the teen who'd needed guidance and the adult who still secretly wished he had a parent who gave a damn without being judgmental.

Ian didn't miss the way Cassie tensed at the sight of Emily holding on to his finger, but he wasn't pulling back. How could he deny such an innocent little girl human touch? She was smiling, happy and had no clue the turmoil that surrounded her right now.

"Don't you have a client you should tend to?" Cassie asked, her meaning that he was not welcome all too clear.

"I already talked with Max after the shooting wrapped and we came back here." The crew had taken a few shots of the wedding scene in town. "I didn't see you at the church earlier."

Cassie reached up, smoothing away blond curls from Emily's forehead. "I was there. I stayed in the back with Tessa. We didn't want to get in the way."

"What did you think of the shoot?"

Why was he still here talking to her? Why didn't he just leave? He had calls to return, emails to answer, contracts to look over.

Besides the fact a little cherublike toddler had his finger in a vise grip, he could walk away. Cassie had made it clear she didn't like him, and he certainly wasn't looking for a woman with a child.

Yet here he stood, talking to her and eagerly awaiting her answer.

"It was perfect," she said, a soft smile dancing across her lips. "Lily looked exactly like the pictures I've always seen of my mother on that day. My father teared up, so I know Lily and Max hit that scene beautifully."

Ian wiggled his finger, making Emily giggle as she tugged on him. He took a step forward, now being drawn in by two intriguing ladies.

"I think the fans will fall in love with this film," he told Cassie as his eyes settled on hers. "And your family."

The pulse at the base of her throat quickened and Ian couldn't help but smile. Good to know she wasn't so unaffected. What they'd shared the other night was nothing short of amazing. No matter what transpired afterward, he couldn't deny that had been the most intense night of his life.

Damn it. Cassie and her innocent daughter were the exact picture of the commitment he could never make.

So how could he be drawn to this woman?

"I just want my father to be happy with the end result," she told him. "I want people to see what a hard worker he is and that everything didn't get handed to him."

Ian couldn't help but admire her for wanting people to see the other side of Damon Barrington. The man was a phenomenon, and Ian had no doubt whatsoever that this film would be a mega blockbuster.

Emily let go of his finger and started patting her

mother's cheeks. Instantly Ian missed the innocent touch, but he stepped back and shoved his hands into his pockets.

"Was there something else you wanted?" she asked.

Clearing his throat, Ian shoved pride aside and nodded. "Actually, yeah. I'm sorry for how I handled the other morning."

Cassie's brows rose as she reached up to try to pull Emily's hands from her face. "I never expected you to apologize."

He hadn't expected it, either, but he couldn't deny the fact he'd been a jerk. If he'd learned anything from growing up, it was to know when to apologize. He'd never seen his parents say they were sorry to each other, and he'd always wondered if such a simple gesture would have made a difference.

"I can admit when I make a mistake," he informed her.

Those bright eyes darted down as she sighed. "This is a first for me."

"What's that?"

Glancing back up, she shook her head. "Nothing. I appreciate you apologizing. Since you're going to be here awhile, I really don't want tension. Between you working and me training, I just can't handle more stress."

Ian noticed the soft lines between her brows, the dark circles beneath her eyes. This single mother was worn-out and he'd added to her worry because she hadn't wanted any awkwardness between them.

"Who helps you with Emily?"

Great, now he was asking questions before he could fully process them. He needed a filter on his mouth and he needed to mind his own business. The last thing he wanted was to worry about Cassie and her daughter. He certainly wasn't applying for the position of caregiver.

"My family." Her chin tilted as she held his gaze, unblinking. "Why?"

Yeah, why indeed? Why was this his concern? They'd slept together one night after days of intense sexual tension and now he was all up in her personal space…a space that hit too close to home and touched his heart way too deeply.

He pushed aside the unwanted emotions. He would be here only a short time. Even if his past hadn't mixed him all up, he still couldn't get too involved with Cassie Barrington.

Besides, she had her hands full and they'd definitely done a complete one-eighty since they'd spent the night together. That night had been full of passion and surrender. Now Cassie had erected walls, thanks to him, and the only thing he saw in her eyes was exhaustion.

"I'll let you get in to dinner," he told her, not answering her question. "See you tomorrow."

When he turned away, Cassie called his name. He glanced over his shoulder and found two sets of beautiful blue eyes staring at him.

"We're not having much, but you're welcome to join us."

The olive branch had been extended and he wondered if this was her manners and upbringing talking or if she truly wanted him to stay.

"I'd be a fool to turn down dinner with two pretty ladies," he told her, turning back to face her. "Are you sure?"

With a shaky nod, Cassie smiled. "I'm sure."

Well, hell. Looked as if he was getting in deeper after

all. But he followed her through the back door like the lost man that he was.

They could be friends, he thought. Friends ate dinner together; friends apologized when they were wrong. That was where they were at now because Cassie and her little girl deserved a commitment, a family life—things he couldn't offer.

As Cassie slid Emily into her high chair, Ian watched her delicate skin as her shoulder peeked from her shirt once again. Anything he was feeling right now went way beyond friendship and ventured down the path at warp speed toward carnal desire.

Chapter 9

Cassie had no clue what had prompted her to invite Ian inside. She wasn't weak. She didn't need a man and had been just fine on her own for the better part of a year now. But something about Ian kept pulling her toward him, as if some invisible force tugged on her heart.

And when Emily had reached for him, Cassie had waited to see his reaction. Thankfully, he'd played right along. She'd barely noticed his hesitation and hard swallow, but he hadn't disappointed Emily. Maybe kids weren't the issue with him; perhaps he was just upset because she hadn't said anything. But really, when would that conversation have occurred? When she had fallen into his arms that first day or when she'd told him to strip in the attic?

The image of him doing just that flooded her mind. Cassie was thankful her back was to him as she turned on the oven.

"Hope you like grilled cheese and French fries." Cassie reached into the narrow cabinet beside the oven and pulled out a cookie sheet.

"Considering I was going to probably have microwave popcorn back in my trailer, grilled cheese and fries sounds gourmet."

Her phone vibrated on the counter next to the stove. She saw Derek's name flash across the screen. No and no. If he was so determined to talk to her, he knew where she was.

Right where he'd left her months ago. Pompous jerk.

As she busied herself getting the meager dinner ready for the other man who was driving her out of her mind in a totally different way, she mentally cursed. Ian was probably used to fine dining, glamorous parties and beautiful women wearing slinky dresses and dripping in diamonds. Unfortunately, tonight he was getting a single mother throwing together cheese sandwiches while wearing an old, oversize T-shirt to hide her extra weight.

More than likely he'd said yes because he felt sorry for her. Regardless, he was in her house now. Surprisingly he'd pulled up a kitchen chair next to the high chair and was feeding puff snacks to Emily.

The sight had Cassie blinking back tears. Emily's father should be doing that. He should be here having dinner with them, as a family. He should've stuck it out and kept his pants zipped.

But he'd decided a wife and a baby were too much of a commitment and put a damper on his lifestyle.

In the back of her mind, Cassie knew she was better off without him. Any man that didn't put his family first was a coward. Not suitable material for a husband or father to her child.

But the reality of being rejected still hurt. Cassie could honestly say she'd gotten over her love, but the betrayal… That was something she would probably never recover from. Because he'd not just left her; he'd left a precious, innocent baby behind without even attempting to fight for what he'd created.

Being rejected by Ian was just another blow to her already battered self-esteem.

"You okay?"

Cassie jerked back to the moment and realized two things. One, Ian was staring at her, his brows drawn together, and two, she'd worn a hole in the bread from being too aggressive applying the butter.

Laughing, Cassie tossed the torn bread onto the counter and grabbed another piece from the bag. "Yeah. My mind was elsewhere for a minute."

"Were you angry with that slice of bread?" he asked with a teasing grin.

"I may have had a little aggression I needed to take out." Cassie couldn't help but laugh again. "You're pretty good with her. Do you have nieces or nephews?"

Ian shook his head. "I'm an only child. But there was a set I visited not too long ago that had a baby about Emily's age. He was the cutest little guy and instantly wanted me over anyone else. I guess kids just like me."

Great. Now he had a soft spot for kids. Wasn't that the exact opposite of the image he'd portrayed the other morning when seeing Emily for the first time?

Ian Shaffer had many facets and she hated that she wanted to figure out who the real Ian was deep down inside.

Dinner was ready in no time, and thankfully, the silence wasn't too awkward. Eating and caring for a baby helped fill the void of conversation. When they were done, Ian went to clear the table and Cassie stopped him.

"I'll get it," she told him, picking up her own plate. "It's not that much."

"You cooked. The least I could do is help clean." He picked up his plate and took it to the sink. "Besides, if you cook more often, I'll gladly clean up after."

Cassie froze in the midst of lifting Emily from her high chair. "You want to come back for dinner?" she asked.

"I wouldn't say no if you asked."

Cassie settled Emily on her hip and turned to Ian, who was putting the pitcher of tea into the refrigerator. Okay, now she knew this wasn't pity. He obviously wanted to spend time with her. But why? Did he think she'd be that easy to get into bed again? Of course he did. She'd barely known his name when she'd shed her clothes for him. What man wouldn't get the impression she was easy?

Cassie turned and went into the living room, placed Emily in her Pack 'n Play and handed her her favorite stuffed horse. Footsteps shuffled over the carpet behind her and Cassie swallowed, knowing she'd have to be up front with Ian.

"Listen," she said as she straightened and faced the man who stood only a few feet away. "I have a feeling you think I'm somebody that I'm not."

Crossing his arms over his wide chest, Ian tilted his head and leveled those dark eyes right on her. "And what do you believe I think of you?"

Well, now she felt stupid. Why did he make this sound like a challenge? And why was she getting all heated over the fact he was standing in her living room? No man had been there other than her father and her soon-to-be brother-in-law. She'd moved into the guest cottage on the estate after Derek had left her so she could be closer to the family for support with Emily.

So seeing such a big, powerful man in her house was a little…arousing. Which just negated the whole point she was trying to make. Yeah, she was a juxtaposition of nerves and emotions.

"I think because we slept together you think I'm eager to do it again." She rested her hands on her hips, willing them to stop shaking. She had to be strong, no matter her physical attraction to Ian. "I'm really not the aggressive, confident woman who was locked in that attic."

Ian's gaze roamed down her body, traveled back up and landed on her mouth as he stepped forward. "You look like the same woman to me," he said, closing the gap between them. "What makes you think you're so different from the woman I spent the night with?"

She couldn't think with him this close, the way his eyes studied her, the woodsy scent of his cologne, the way she felt his body when he wasn't even touching her.

"Well, I…" She smoothed her hair back behind her ears and tipped her head to look him in the eye. "I'm afraid you think that I look for a good time and that I'm easy."

A ghost of a smile flirted around those full lips of his. "I rushed to judgment. I don't think you're easy, Cassie. Sexy, intriguing and confident, but not easy."

Sighing, she shook her head. "I'm anything but confident."

Now his hands came up, framed her face and sent an insane amount of electrical charges coursing through her. As much as she wanted his touch, she couldn't allow herself to crave such things. Hadn't she learned her lesson? Physical attraction and sexual chemistry did not make for a solid base for family, and, right now, all she could focus on was her family. Between Emily and the race with her sister, Cassie had no time for anything else.

But, oh, how she loved the feel of those strong, warm palms covering her face, fingertips slipping into her hair.

"You were amazing and strong in the attic," he told her. He placed a finger over her lips when she tried to speak. "You may not be like that all the time, but you were then. And that tells me that the real you came out that night. You had no reason to put on a front with me and you were comfortable being yourself. Your passion and ability to control the situation was the biggest turn-on I've ever experienced."

Cassie wanted to tell him he was wrong, that she wasn't the powerful, confident woman he thought she was.

But she couldn't say a word when he leaned in just a bit more, tickling his lips across hers so slowly that Cassie feared she'd have to clutch on to his thick biceps to stay upright.

She didn't reach up, though. Didn't encourage Ian in tormenting her any further.

But when his mouth opened over hers so gently, coaxing hers open, as well, Cassie didn't stop him. Still not reaching for him, she allowed him to claim her. His hands still gripped her face, his body pressed perfectly against hers and she flashed back instantly to when they'd had nothing between them. He'd felt so strong, so powerful.

More than anything to do with his looks or his

charming words, he made her feel more alive than she'd ever felt.

Ian's lips nipped at hers once, twice, before he lifted his head and looked her straight in the eyes.

The muscle ticked in his jaw as he slowly lowered his hands from her face and stepped back. "No, Cassie. Nothing about you or this situation is easy."

Without another word, he turned and walked through her house and out the back door. Cassie gripped the edge of the sofa and let out a sigh. She had no clue what had just happened, but something beyond desire lurked in Ian's dark eyes. The way he'd looked at her, as if he was wrestling his own personal demon...

Cassie shook her head. This was not her problem. Sleeping with the man had brought up so many complications—the main reason she never did flings.

Was that why she kept feeling this pull? Because sex just wasn't sex to her? For her to sleep with someone meant she had some sort of deeper bond than just lust. How could she not feel attached to the man who made her feel this alive?

Glancing down to sweet Emily, who was chewing on her stuffed horse, Cassie rested her hip against the couch. This baby was her world and no way would she be that mother who needed to cling to men or have a revolving door of them.

Better to get her head on straight and forget just how much Mr. Hollywood Agent affected her mind.

Trouble was, she was seriously afraid he'd already affected her heart.

Chapter 10

"My girls ready for next week?"

Cassie slid the saddle off Don Pedro and threw a glance over her shoulder to her father. Damon Barrington stalked through the stables that he not only owned, but at one time had spent nearly every waking hour in.

Even though the Barringtons' planned to retire from the scene after this racing season, Damon still wasn't ready to sell the prizewinning horses. He'd had generous offers, including one from his biggest rival in the industry, Jake Mason, but so far no deal had been made. Cassie highly doubted her father would ever sell to Jake. The two had been competitors for years and had never gotten along on the track…or off it.

"We're as ready as we'll ever be," Tessa said as she started brushing down the Thoroughbred. "My time is even better than before. I'm pretty confident about the Preakness."

Damon smiled, slipping his hands into the pockets of his worn jeans. The man may be a millionaire and near royalty in the horse industry because of his Triple Crown win nearly two decades ago, but he still was down-to-earth and very much involved in his daughters' careers.

"I know you'll do the Barrington name proud, Tess." He reached up and stroked the horse's mane as Cassie slid in beside her father.

"What are you doing down here?" Cassie asked. "Thought you'd be keeping your eye on the film crew."

Damon patted the horse and reached over to wrap an arm around Cassie's shoulders. A wide grin spread across his tanned, aged face. His bright blue eyes landed on hers.

"The lighting guys are reworking the living room right now," he explained. "The scene they shot the other day wasn't quite what they wanted. They're shooting a small portion again this afternoon."

This whole new world of filming was so foreign to her, but the process was rather fascinating. "I plan on heading into town and picking up some feed later," she told him. "I guess I'll miss watching that."

And more than likely miss seeing Ian again—which was probably for the best. She needed space after that simple dinner and arousing kiss last night. He hadn't been by the stables and she hadn't seen him around the grounds, so he was probably working...which was what she needed to concentrate on.

"I thought I'd take Emily with me and maybe run her by that new toy store in town," Cassie went on. "She's learning to walk now and maybe I can find her something she can hold on to and push around to strengthen her little legs."

Damon laughed. "Once she starts walking, she'll be all over this place."

Cassie smiled. "I can't wait to see how she looks in a saddle."

Tessa came around Don Pedro and started brushing his other side. "Why don't you take her for a ride now? I'm sure she'd love it and it's such a nice day out. We're done for a while anyway."

The idea was tempting. "I still need to get feed, though."

"I'll send Nash to get it," Damon spoke up. "He won't mind."

Cassie leaned her head against her father's strong shoulder. "Thanks, Dad."

Patting her arm, Damon placed a kiss on top of her head. "Anytime. Now go get my granddaughter and start training her right."

Excited for Emily's first ride, Cassie nearly sprinted to the main house and through the back door to the kitchen, where Linda was washing dishes.

"Hey, Linda." Cassie glanced over the island to see Emily in her Pack 'n Play clapping her hands and gibbering to her animals. "I'm going to take Emily off your hands for a bit."

"Oh, she's no trouble at all." Linda rinsed a pan and set it in the drainer before drying her hands and turning. "I actually just sat her in there. We've been watching the action in the living room. She likes all the lights."

Cassie scooped up her girl and kissed her cheek. "I'm sure she does. She'd probably like to crawl all over and knock them down."

Laughing, Linda crossed to the double ovens in the wall and peeked inside the top one. "I'm sure she would, but I held on tight. The cranberry muffins are almost done if you'd like one."

Yeah, she'd love about six warm, gooey muffins dripping with butter, but she'd resist for the sake of her backside.

"Maybe later. I'm taking Emily for her first ride."

A wide smile blossomed across Linda's face. "Oh, how fun. She's going to love it."

"I hope so," Cassie said. "I'll be back in a bit."

When Cassie stepped back into the barn, Tessa had already saddled up Oliver, the oldest, most gentle horse in the stables. Cassie absolutely couldn't wait to see Emily's excitement as she took her first horseback ride.

"He's all ready for you," Tessa exclaimed, reaching for Emily.

Cassie mounted the horse and lifted Emily from Tessa's arms. Settling her daughter in front of her and wrapping an arm around her waist, Cassie reached for the rein and smiled down to Tessa.

"Get a few pics of us when we're in the field, would you?"

Tessa slid her hand into her pocket and held up her phone. "I'm set. You guys look so cute up there," she said, still grinning. "My niece already looks like a pro."

Cassie tugged on the line and steered Oliver out of the barn and into the field. The warm late-spring sunshine beat down on them and Cassie couldn't help but smile when Emily clapped her hands and squealed as the horse started a light trot.

"This is fun, isn't it, sweetie?" Cassie asked. "When

you get big, Mommy will buy you your own horse and he will be your best friend."

Cassie didn't know how long they were riding, and she didn't really care. Memories were being made, and even though Emily wouldn't recall this day at all, Cassie would cherish it forever. She thought of her own mother and held Emily a little tighter. Her mom lived in her heart and there was an attic full of pictures and mementos to remember her by.

Turning Oliver to head back toward the front fields, Cassie swallowed as new memories overtook her. That attic wasn't just a room to store boxes and old furniture. Now the attic was a place where she'd given herself to a man…a dangerous man. He made her feel too much, want too much.

And what was with him wanting to eat dinner with her and Emily? Not that she minded, but having him in her house just once was enough to have her envisioning so much more than just a friendly encounter.

She had to admit, at least to herself, that Ian intrigued her. And if she was going that far, she also had to admit that every part of her wished he weren't just passing through. She missed the company of a man…and not just sex. She missed the conversation, the spark of excitement in harmless flirting… Okay, fine, she missed the sex, too.

But it really was so much more than that. There was a special connection, a certain bond that strengthened after being intimate. At least there was for her. Perhaps that was why she couldn't dismiss what had happened between her and Ian so easily.

As she neared the stables, she caught sight of Ian walking toward the main house with the beautiful Lily

Beaumont at his side. The gorgeous actress was laughing and Cassie had to ignore the sliver of jealousy that shot through her. Ian wasn't hers by any means, no matter what she may wish for.

And Lily was a very sweet woman, from what Cassie had experienced on the set. As Cassie watched the two head toward the front door, she couldn't help but get a swift kick back into reality. Ian and Lily were from the same world. They were near the same age, for crying out loud.

In comparison, Cassie was just a worn-out single mom. Squeezing Emily tight and placing a kiss on her little mop of curls, Cassie knew she wouldn't wish to be anything else. Being the solid foundation for Emily was the most important job of her life, and for now, all her daughter's needs had to come first. One day, Cassie vowed, she'd take time for herself and perhaps find love.

"I'm actually considering your offer and one other," Lily stated.

Ian rested his hand on the knob of the front door. "You don't have to tell me the other agency. I already know."

And damn if he'd lose this starlet to his rival. They'd ruin her and not give a damn about reputation, only the bottom line, which was money to them.

"It's not a decision I'm going to make overnight." Lily lifted her hand to shield her eyes from the afternoon sun. "I am glad you're on set, though, because that will give us more of a chance to discuss terms and what I'm looking for in an agency."

Good. That sounded as though she was interested in him. "I'm ready to talk anytime you are."

A bright smile spread across her face. "Well, right

now I'm needed for a scene, but perhaps we could have lunch or dinner one day while we're both here?"

Returning her smile, Ian nodded and opened the door for her, gesturing her in. "Let me know when you're not filming and we'll make that happen."

Nodding her thanks, Lily headed into the house. Ian wasn't sticking around for the short scene retake. He had other pressing matters to attend to. Like the beauty he'd seen out in the field moments ago. With red hair blazing past her shoulders and a heart-clenching smile on her face, Cassie had captured his attention instantly. So what else was new? The woman managed to turn him inside out without even being near. More times than not she consumed his thoughts, but when he'd seen her taking her daughter on a horseback ride, Ian had to admit that the sight had damn near stopped him in his tracks.

Emily's sweet squeals of delight, the loving expression on Cassie's face... The combination had shifted something in Ian's heart, something he wasn't quite ready to identify.

But he did know one thing. He'd been wrong. He was wrong about Cassie in thinking she was just like his mother. His mother never would've taken the time to have precious moments with him like the ones he'd seen with Cassie and Emily. His mother had been too busy on her quest for love and Mr. Right.

Ian ran a hand over his hair and sighed. He'd turned out just fine, no thanks to Mom and Dad, but getting involved with a woman and an innocent child was a hazardous mistake that would leave all parties vulnerable and in a risky position. What did he know about children or how to care for them?

And why was he even thinking this way? He was

leaving in a few weeks. No matter his attraction and growing interest in Cassie Barrington, he couldn't afford to get personally involved.

Hours later, after he'd drafted a contract he hoped would entice Lily Beaumont into signing with his agency, Ian found himself leaving his trailer and heading toward Cassie's cottage.

Night had settled over the grounds and all was quiet. No bustling crew or noisy conversation. Max's wife and baby had shown up earlier in the evening, so they were probably holed up in his trailer for family time. And the producer's and director's families had arrived the day before. Bronson Dane and Anthony Price were at the top 1 percent of the film industry and still made time for their growing families.

Everyone had a family, a connection and the promise of love.

Ignoring the pang of envy he didn't want to feel, Ian stepped up onto Cassie's porch, which was illuminated with a lantern-style light on either side of the door. As soon as he knocked, he glanced down to his watch. Damn, maybe it was too late to be making a social call.

The door swung open and Ian took in the sight of Cassie wearing a long T-shirt and her hair down, curling around her shoulders. Long legs left uncovered tempted him to linger, but he brought his eyes back up to her surprised face.

"I'm sorry," he said, shoving his hands into his pockets. "I just realized how late it was."

"Oh, um…it's fine." She rested her hand on the edge of the oak door and tilted her head. "Is everything okay?"

Nodding, Ian suddenly felt like an idiot. "Yeah, I was

working and lost track of time. Then I started walking and ended up here."

A sweet smile lit up her features. "Come on in," she told him, opening the door and stepping aside. "I just put Emily to bed, so this is fine."

He stepped inside and inhaled a scent of something sweet. "Is that cookies I smell?"

Cassie shut the door and turned to face him. "I thought I'd make some goodies for the wives who arrived. This way they can stock their trailers with snacks. I already made a batch of caramel corn."

His heart flipped in his chest. He hated the fact he kept going back to his mother, but he honestly couldn't recall a time when his mother had baked anything or even reached out to others by doing a kind act.

A shrink would have a field day in his head with all his Mommy and Daddy issues. *Jeez.* And here he'd thought once he'd left for L.A. he'd left all of those years behind.

"They will really appreciate that," he told her.

Shrugging, Cassie maneuvered around him and grabbed a small blanket from the couch and started folding it. "I'm no Linda, but I do enjoy baking when I have the time."

She laid the folded blanket across the back of the couch and looked back at him. He couldn't stop his eyes from traveling over her again. How could he help the fact he found her sexier than any woman he'd ever met? She probably wouldn't believe him if he told her that her curves were enticing, her low maintenance a refreshing change.

Cassie tugged on the hem of her shirt. "I should probably go change."

"No." He held up his hand to stop her. "This is your house—you should be comfortable. Besides, I've seen it all."

Her eyes flared with remembrance and passion as Ian closed the space between them and looked down at her mouth. "I've tasted it all, too, if you recall."

With a shaky nod, she said, "I remember."

The pulse at the base of her throat increased and Ian ran a hand over his face as he took a step back. "I swear, I didn't come here for this."

Cassie's bright blue eyes darted away. "I understand."

"No, you don't." Great, now she thought he was rejecting her. "It's not that I don't want you, Cassie. That's the furthest from the truth."

Shoving her hair back from her shoulders, Cassie shook her head. "Ian, it's okay. You don't have to make excuses. I'm a big girl. I can handle the truth. Besides, we're past this awkward stage, right?"

"Yeah," he agreed because right now he was feeling anything but awkward. Excited and aroused, but not awkward. "I don't know what possessed me to show up at your door this late, but…"

Cassie produced that punch-to-the-gut smile. "You can stop by anytime."

How did she do that? Instantly make him feel welcome, wanted…needed. There was so much more to Cassie Barrington than he'd first perceived. There were sides to the confident vixen, the single mother and the overworked trainer he had yet to discover.

Cassie was giving, loving and patient. He'd known instantly that she was special, but maybe he just hadn't realized how special. This woman embodied everything he hadn't known he'd been looking for.

"Why are you looking at me like that?" she asked, brows drawn together, smile all but gone.

Ian took a step toward her. He'd been mentally dancing around her for days and now he was physically doing it as he made up his mind on how to approach her.

"Because I just realized that all of your layers are starting to reveal themselves, one at a time." He slid his fingertips up her arms and back down, relishing the goose bumps he produced with such a simple touch. "I didn't want to see all of that before. I wanted you to be unattainable. I wanted you to be all wrong and someone I could easily forget."

Those vibrant eyes remained locked on his as her breath caught.

"But there's no way I could ever forget you, Cassie. Or us."

He didn't give her time to object. He claimed her lips and instantly she responded—opening her mouth to him, wrapping her arms around his neck and plunging her fingers into his hair.

Ian knew he wasn't leaving anytime soon. He also knew her T-shirt had to go.

Chapter 11

Cassie had no idea what she was doing. Okay, she knew what she was doing and who she was doing it with, but hadn't she just had a mental talk with herself about the hazards of getting wrapped up in Ian's seductive ways? Hadn't she told herself she'd already been burned once and was still recovering?

But the way his mouth captured hers, the way he held her as if she were the rarest of gems, Cassie couldn't help but take pleasure in the fact that Ian pulled out a passion in her that she'd never known existed.

When Ian's hands gripped the hem of her T-shirt and tugged up, she eased back and in an instant the unwanted garment was up and over her head, flung to the side without a care.

Dark-as-sin eyes raked over her body, which was now bare of everything except a pair of red lacy panties. The old Cassie wanted to shield herself with her hands, but the way Ian visually sampled her gave her the confidence of a goddess.

"I could look at you forever," he said, his voice husky.

Forever. The word hovered in the air, but Cassie knew he was speaking only from lust, not in the happily-ever-after term.

Ian pulled his own shirt off and Cassie reached out, quickly unfastening his pants. In no time he was reaching for her, wearing only a smile.

"Tell me you know this is more than sex," he muttered against her lips. "I want you to know that to me, this is so much more."

Tears pricked the backs of her eyes as she nodded. The lump in her throat left her speechless. She really didn't know what label he wanted to put on this relationship, but right now, she couldn't think beyond the fact that Ian's hands were sliding into her panties and gliding them down her shaky legs.

Cassie wrapped her arms around his broad shoulders and kicked aside the flimsy material. Ian's hands cupped her bottom as he guided her backward.

"Tell me where your room is," he muttered against her lips.

"Last door on the right."

He kissed her on the throat, across the swells of her breasts, all the while keeping his hands firmly gripped on her backside as he maneuvered her down the hallway and into her room.

A small bedside lamp gave the room a soft glow. Ian gently shut the door behind him and looked her right in the eyes. There was an underlying vulnerability looking back at her, and Cassie knew what he was thinking.

"I've never had a man in this room," she told him. "And there's no other man I want here."

As if the dam had broken, Ian reached for her, capturing her lips once again and lifting her by the waist.

When she locked her legs around his hips and they tumbled onto the bed, Ian broke free of her lips and kissed a path down to her breasts. Leaning back, Cassie gripped his hair as he tasted her.

"Ian," she panted. "I don't have any protection."

His dark gaze lifted to hers. "I didn't bring any. I hadn't planned on ending up here."

Biting her lip, Cassie said, "I'm on birth control and I'm clean. I've only been with my ex-husband and you."

Ian's hands slid up to cup her face as he kissed her lips. "I've never been without protection and I know I'm clean, too."

She smiled. "Then why are we still talking?"

Cassie moved her hands to his waist. Before she could say another word, Ian slid into her. Closing her eyes, Cassie let out a soft groan as he began to move above her.

"Look at me," he demanded in that low tone. "I want you to see me and only me."

As if any other man could take his place? But as she stared into his eyes, she saw so much more than lust, than sex and passion. This man was falling for her. He may not even recognize the emotion himself, but it was there, plain as day, looking back at her.

When his pace increased, Cassie gripped his shoulders and arched her back. "Ian...I..."

Eyes still locked on to her, he clenched the muscle in his jaw. "Go ahead, baby."

Her body trembled with her release, but she refused

to close her eyes. She wanted him to see just how affected she was by his touch...his love.

When his arms stiffened and his body quivered against hers, Cassie held on, swallowing back the tears that clogged her throat.

One thing was very certain. The night in the attic may have been all about lust, but this moment right here in her bed, Cassie had gone and fallen in love with Ian Shaffer.

"I have to be on set early," Ian whispered into her ear.

Pulling himself away from the warm bed they'd spent the night in, Ian quickly gathered his clothes and dressed. Cassie eased up onto one elbow, and the sheet slipped down to stop just at the slope of her breasts. All that creamy exposed skin had him clenching his jaw and reliving what had just transpired hours before between those sheets.

"How early?" she asked, her voice thick with sleep.

"I'd like to see Max before he starts."

Okay, so the lie rolled easily off his tongue, but he couldn't stay. He couldn't remain in her bed, smelling her sweet scent, playing house in her little cottage, with her innocent baby sleeping in the next room.

What did he know about family or children...or whatever emotion was stirring within him? His career had always taken precedence over any social life or any feelings. With his parents' example of the epitome of failed marriages and love, he knew he wanted something completely different for his own life, so perfecting his career was the path he'd chosen.

How could he put his career, his agency and the impending addition of Lily to his client roster in jeopardy simply because he'd become entangled with Cassie Barrington? She was the poster child for commitment, and an instant family was something he couldn't get wrapped up in.

Cassie was a beautiful, intriguing complication. His eyes darted to the bed, where she studied him with a hint of desire layered with curiosity.

"Everything okay?" she asked.

Nodding, he shoved his feet into his shoes. "Of course. I'll lock the door behind me."

Unable to avoid temptation completely, Ian crossed the room, leaned down and kissed her lips. Just as her hand came up to his stubbled jaw, he pulled away and left her alone.

He stepped onto the front porch, closed the door behind him and leaned against it to catch his breath. The easy way Cassie welcomed him into her bed—and into her life with Emily—terrified him. Last night she'd accepted him without question and she'd given him everything she had…including love. He'd seen it in her eyes, but even more worrisome was what she may have seen reflected in his.

Because in those moments, when they were one and her bright blue eyes sought his, Ian had found himself completely and utterly lost. He wanted so much, but fear of everything he'd ever known regarding love and family made him question his emotions and his intentions.

Damn it. His intentions? What the hell was this? He wasn't the kind of man who had dreams of driving a minivan or heading up a household. He was a top Hollywood agent and if he didn't get his head on straight, he could lose one of the most important clients he'd ever had the chance of snagging.

Shaking his head, Ian pushed off the door and forced himself to walk toward his trailer. Twenty-nine years old and doing the walk of shame? *Classy, Shaffer. Real classy.*

Darkness and early-morning fog settled low over the estate. He shoved his hands into his pockets and decided he needed to shower and change before seeing Max... especially considering he was wearing the same clothes as yesterday.

He hadn't totally lied when he'd left Cassie's bed. He would talk to Max, but it wasn't dire and they could always talk later. Yet he worried if he stayed, he'd give Cassie false hope.

Okay, he worried he'd give himself false hope, too, because being with her was like nothing he'd ever experienced before and he wanted to hold on to those moments.

But the reality was, he was passing through.

Ian took his time getting ready for the day, answered a few emails and jotted down notes for calls he needed to make later in the week. He hated to admit he was shaken up by this newfound flood of emotions, but he had to come to grips with the fact that whatever he was feeling for Cassie Barrington was most definitely not going away.... It was only getting stronger.

By the time he exited his trailer, he had a plan of action, and today would be all about work and focusing on the big picture and his agency.

Crew members were gathered around the entrance of the stables, and off to the side were Max and Lily, holding their scripts and chatting. Ian headed in their direction, eager to get the day started.

"Morning," he greeted them as he approached.

Max nodded. "Came by your trailer last night to discuss something. Have a late night?"

The smile on Max's face was devilish—and all-knowing.

"What did you need?" Ian asked, dodging the question.

With a shrug, Max shook his head. "It can wait. I'm going to talk to Bronson before we start filming. Excuse me."

Ian figured Max left so Ian could chat with Lily. *Good boy.*

"I glanced over today's filming schedule." Ian stepped in front of Lily to shade her face from the sun. "Looks like after three today you guys are free."

Lily smiled. "We are indeed. Are you available to talk then?"

He'd be available anytime she wanted if it meant persuading her to sign with him. "I am. Would you like to stay here or go out to grab something for dinner?"

"I say go out," she replied. "Hopefully we can talk privately without everyone around."

Before he could respond, Lily's gaze darted from his to a spot over his left shoulder. A smile like he'd never seen before lit up her face and Ian couldn't help but glance around to see who she was connecting with.

Nash.

More confirmation that this Hollywood starlet and the groom on the Barrington estate had something going on.

Ian only hoped whatever was happening with the two of them was kept quiet and didn't interfere with filming or hinder her judgment in signing with him.

"Going out is fine," he told her.

Blinking, she focused back on him. "I'm sorry. What?"

Yeah, definitely something going on there.

"I said we could go out for a bite to eat. I can come by your trailer about five. Does that work?"

"Of course," she replied with a nod. "I'll see you then."

As she walked away, Ian turned and caught Nash still staring as Lily entered the stable. Nash had the look of a man totally and utterly smitten and Ian couldn't help but feel a twinge of remorse for the guy. Nash and Lily were worlds apart.

Exactly like Ian and Cassie.

What a mess. A complicated, passion-induced mess.

Ian stood to the side as lighting and people were set in place to prepare for filming. Bronson was talking with Max, and Lily's hair was being smoothed one last time. Grant and Anthony were adjusting the bales of hay at the end of the aisle.

Ian wasn't sure what Cassie's plans were for the day, but he intended to keep his distance for now. He needed to figure out exactly how to handle this situation because the last thing she needed was more heartache. And he, who knew nothing about real intimacy, would most certainly break her heart if he wasn't careful.

Damon Barrington settled in beside him and whispered, "Their chemistry on set is amazing."

Ian watched Max and Lily embrace in the middle of the aisle, horses' heads popping out over their stalls. The set was utterly quiet except for Lily's staged tears as she clung to Max. The couple was the perfect image of a younger Damon and Rose Barrington, according to the pictures Ian had seen.

As soon as Anthony yelled, "Cut!" the couple broke apart and Lily dabbed at her damp cheeks.

Damon glanced around. "I can't believe my girls aren't down here. You haven't seen Cassie or Tessa, have you?"

Ian shook his head. "I haven't."

No need to tell Cassie's father that just a few hours ago Ian had slipped from her bed. Best not bring that up.

"I'm sure they'll be along shortly." Damon looked over at Ian and grinned. "My girls haven't let too many scenes slip by. They've enjoyed this process."

"And you?" Ian asked. "Have you enjoyed the Hollywood invasion?"

Nodding, Damon crossed his arms over his chest. "It's not what I thought it would be. The scenes vary in length and everything is shot out of order. But I'm very interested in seeing how they piece this all together."

Ian liked Damon, appreciated the way the man had taken charge of his life, made something of it and encouraged his children to do the same. And when his wife had passed, the man had taken over the roles of both parents and loved his children to the point where both women were now two of the most amazing people he'd met.

Ian had never received encouragement from his father and couldn't help but wonder what his life would've been like had his father been more hands-on.

Shrugging off years that couldn't be changed, Ian excused himself from Damon. If Cassie was going to come watch the filming, he needed to be elsewhere.

Because he had no doubt that if he hung around and

had to look Cassie in the eye in front of all these people, there would be no hiding the fact that he'd developed some serious feelings for her.

Chapter 12

Who was he kidding? There was no way he could stay away from Cassie. All during the business dinner with Lily, his mind had been on Cassie and what she was doing.

By the end of the night he'd nearly driven himself crazy with curiosity about what Cassie and Emily had done all day. Added to that, Lily hadn't signed with him. Not yet. She'd looked over his proposed contract and agreed with most of it, but she'd also said she needed to look over one other contract before deciding.

He was still in the running, but he'd rather have this deal signed and completed so he could move on to other deals waiting in the wings...not so he could focus on the woman who had his head spinning and his gut tied in knots.

After walking Lily to her trailer, Ian crossed the estate toward the two cottages. Only one of Cassie's outdoor lights was on and she was on her porch switching out the bulb in the other.

"Hey," he greeted her as he stepped onto the top step. "Need help?"

"I can manage just fine."

As she stood on her tiptoes and reached, her red tank top slid up over her torso, exposing a tantalizing band of flesh.

"I can get that so you don't have to stretch so far," he told her.

She quickly changed out the bulb and turned to face him, tapping the dead bulb against her palm. "I've been doing things on my own for a while now. Besides, I won't be anybody's second choice. I figured you were smart enough to know that."

"I'm sorry?"

Somehow he was not on the same page as her and she was mad at someone. From the daggers she was throwing him, he'd done something to upset her. Considering he hadn't sneaked out of her bed that morning without saying goodbye, he really had no clue what was going on.

"Forget it." She shook her head and opened her front door, then turned before he could enter. "I'm pretty tired, but thanks for stopping by."

Oh, hell no. He wasn't going to just let her be mad and not tell him what was going on. More than that, did she really believe he'd just leave her when she was this upset?

His hand smacked against the door as she tried to close it. "I'm coming in."

Cassie stepped back and let him pass. Emily sat in her

Pack 'n Play and chattered with a stuffed horse, oblivious to the world around her.

"I need to get Emily ready for bed." Cassie maneuvered around him and picked up Emily. "I may be a while."

Code for "I'm going to take my time and let you worry." That was fine; he had no intention of going anywhere.

If Cassie was gearing up for a fight, he was ready. Seeing her pain, masked by anger, had a vise gripping his heart, and he cared too much about her to just brush her feelings aside.

Ian glanced around the somewhat tidy living area and started picking up toys before he thought better of it. He tossed them into the Pack 'n Play; then he folded the throw and laid it on the back of the sofa, neatened the pillows and took a plate and cup into the kitchen and placed them in the dishwasher.

By the time he'd taken a seat on the couch, he found himself smiling. Where had this little domestic streak come from? He hadn't even thought twice about helping Cassie, and not just because she was angry. He found himself wanting to do things to make her life easier.

Ian had no clue what had happened with her life before he'd come along, but he knew she was divorced and assumed the ex had done a number on her.

Well, Ian intended to stick this out, at least for as long as he was here. He would make her smile again, because she deserved nothing less.

Cassie wasn't jealous. Just because she'd heard Ian and Lily had had dinner didn't mean a thing. Really.

But that green-eyed monster reared its ugly head and

reminded Cassie that she'd fallen for a cheating man once before.

On the other hand, what hold did she have over Ian? He wasn't staying and he'd never confessed his undying love to her. But she'd seen his eyes last night, she'd seen how he looked at her, and she'd experienced lovemaking like she never had before. How could he deny that they'd formed an unspoken bond?

Cassie quickly dried off Emily and got her dressed in her footed bunny pajamas. After giving her a bottle and rocking her gently, Cassie began to sing.

This was the time of night she enjoyed most. Just her and her precious baby girl. Cassie might sing off-key, she might even get an occasional word wrong, but Emily didn't care. She just reached her little hands up and patted Cassie's hand or touched her lips.

They had a nightly ritual and just because Ian was out in her living room didn't mean she would change her routine. Before Emily fell asleep in her arms, Cassie laid her in her crib, giving her a soft kiss on her forehead, then left the room.

Cassie took a moment to straighten her tank and smooth her hair over her shoulders before she started down the hallway. As she entered the living room, she noticed that Ian was reclined on her sofa, head tilted back, eyes closed, with his hands laced across his abdomen. He'd picked up the toys and neatly piled them in the Pack 'n Play in the corner.

No. She didn't want that unwelcome tumble of her heart where this man was concerned. She couldn't risk everything again on the chance that he could love her the way she loved him.

Tears pricked her eyes as she fully confessed just how much she did love this man. But he could never know.

Her feet shuffled over the hardwood floors, and Ian lifted his lids, his gaze seeking hers.

"Thank you for picking up," she told him, still standing because she intended to show him out the door.

Shifting to fully sit up, Ian patted the cushion beside him. "Come here, Cassie."

She didn't like being told what to do, but she wasn't going to act like a teenager who pouted over a boy, either.

She was a big girl, but that didn't exempt her from a broken heart.

Taking a seat on the opposite end of the couch, she gripped her hands in her lap. "What do you want, Ian? I don't have time for games."

His eyes locked on to hers. "I don't play games, Cassie, and I have no idea what you're so upset about."

Of course he didn't. Neither had her ex when he'd cheated.

She eased back against the arm of the sofa and returned his stare. "Do you know why I'm divorced?"

Ian shook his head and slid his arm along the back of the couch as if to reach for her.

"My husband got tired of me," she told him, tamping down the sliver of hurt and betrayal that threatened to make her vulnerable. Never again. "The whole marriage-baby thing was cramping his style. Apparently he'd been cheating on me for most of our marriage and I was too naive and dumb to realize it. You see, I assumed that when we took our vows they meant something to him."

"Cassie—"

"No," she said, holding up her hand. "I'm not finished. After Emily was born, Derek left. She was barely two months old. He left me a note and was just…gone. It seems the sexy wife he once knew was no longer there for him, so, in turn, his cheating and the divorce were my fault. I know now that he was a coward and I'm glad he's gone because I never want Emily to see me settle for someone who treats me like I'm not worth everything.

"I want my daughter to see a worthy example of how love should be," she went on, cursing her eyes for misting up. "I want her to see that love does exist. My parents had it, and I will find it. But I won't be played for a fool while I wait for love to come into my life."

Ian swallowed, his eyes never leaving hers as he scooted closer. He wasn't stupid; he could put the pieces together and know she'd assumed the worst about his dinner meeting with Lily.

"I didn't play you for a fool, Cassie." His tone was light as he settled his hand over both of hers, which were still clasped together in her lap. "I have never lied to a woman and I've never pretended to be something I wasn't."

With a deep sigh, Cassie shook her head. "Forget I said anything. I mean, it's not like we're committed to each other," she said as she got to her feet.

But Ian jumped right up with her and gripped her shoulders before she could turn from him.

"Do you seriously think for one second that I believe you're so laid-back about the idea of me seeing you and another woman?" he demanded. "I had a business meeting with Lily. I told you I've wanted to sign her to my agency for months. She's the main reason I came to the set and why I'm staying so long."

Cassie's eyes widened, but he didn't give her a chance

to speak. He needed her to know she didn't come in second…and she should never have to.

"I spent the entire evening trying to win her over,
outlining every detail of the contract and all the perks
of having me as her agent." Ian loosened his grip as he
stepped closer to Cassie and slid his hands up to frame
her face. "But the entire evening, I was thinking of you.
Wondering what you were doing, how long it would be
until I could see you again."

Her shoulders relaxed and her face softened as she
kept those stunning baby blues locked on his. The hope
he saw in her eyes nearly melted him on the spot. He
knew she wanted to trust. He knew she'd been burned
once and he completely understood that need, the yearning for that solid foundation.

"I'm sorry," she whispered. Cassie's lids lowered as
she shook her head before she raised her gaze to his once
more. "I don't want to be that woman. I seriously have
no hold on you, Ian. You've promised me nothing and I
don't expect you to check in."

Ian kissed her gently, then rested his forehead against
hers. A soft shudder rippled through her and Ian wanted
nothing more than to reassure her everything would be
all right.

But how could he, when he knew he wasn't staying?
How could they move forward with emotions overtaking them both?

"I hate what he did to me," she whispered, reaching
up to clasp his wrists as he continued to cup her face. "I
hate that I've turned bitter. That's not who I want to be."

Ian eased back and tipped her face up to his. "That's
not who you are. You're not bitter. You're cautious and

nobody blames you. You not only have yourself to think of—you have Emily, too."

Cassie's sweet smile never failed to squeeze his heart, and Ian had no clue how a man could leave behind a wife and child. Ian wouldn't mind getting ahold of Cassie's ex. He obviously was no man, but a coward. Selfishly, Ian was glad Derek was out of the picture. If the man could throw away his family so easily, he wasn't worthy.

"What's that look for?" she asked. "You're very intense all of a sudden."

He had to be honest because she was worth everything he had inside him.

"Where is this going?" he asked. "I care about you, Cassie. More than I thought I would, and I think we need to discuss what's happening between us."

A soft laugh escaped her. "You sound like a woman."

Ian smiled with a shrug. "I assure you I've never said this to anyone else, but I don't want you getting hurt."

Cassie nodded and a shield came over her eyes as if she was already steeling herself. "Honestly, I don't know. I care for you, too. I question myself because I'm still so scarred from the divorce and I told myself I wouldn't get involved again. Yet, here we are and I can't stop myself."

Her inner battle shouldn't make him happy, but he couldn't help but admit he liked the fact she had no control over her feelings for him…. At least he wasn't in this boat of emotions alone.

"I don't want you to be the rebound guy," she murmured. "But I'm so afraid of how you make me feel."

Stroking her silky skin, wanting to kiss her trembling lips, Ian asked, "How do I make you feel?"

He shouldn't have asked. Cassie pursed her lips together as if contemplating her response, and Ian worried he'd put her on the spot. But he had to know. This mattered too much. *She* mattered too much.

"Like I'm special."

She couldn't have zeroed in on a better word that would hit him straight in the heart. *Special.* She was special to him on so many levels. She was special because he'd never felt more alive than he did with her. He'd never let his career come second to anything before her, and he sure as hell had never thought, with his family issues, that he'd be falling for a woman with a child.

Cassie inspired him to be a better person, to want to care for others and put his needs last.

But most of all he understood that need to feel special. He'd craved it his entire life, and until this very moment, he hadn't realized that was what he'd been missing.

"You make me feel special, too." Before now he never would've felt comfortable opening up, showing how vulnerable he was on the inside. "I don't want to be the rebound guy, either."

Her eyes widened as she tried to blink back the moisture. "So what does that mean?"

Hell if he knew. Suddenly he wanted it all—his career, the Hollywood lifestyle, Cassie and Emily. Cassie had him rethinking what family could be.

There was that other part of him that was absolutely terrified and wanted to hightail it back to Hollywood. But for now, he would relish their time together until he could come to grips with this mess of emotions.

"It means for now, you're mine." He kissed the corners of her mouth. "It means you are more to me than any other woman has ever been." He kissed her directly on the mouth, coaxing her lips apart before murmuring,

"It means I'm taking you to bed to show you just how much you mean to me."

Only wanting to keep her smiling, keep her happy for as long as he was here, Ian slid his arms around her waist and pulled her body flush against his own.

When Cassie's fingers slid up around his neck and threaded into his hair, Ian claimed her mouth and lifted her off the ground. She wrapped her legs around his waist and he carried her toward the bedroom, where he fully intended to make good on his promise.

Chapter 13

The day couldn't be more perfect. God had painted a beautiful setting with the sun high in the sky and the temperature an ideal sixty degrees. The stage was set for Tessa to win the Preakness and take the second step toward the Triple Crown.

But no matter the weather, the thrill that always slid through Cassie at each race had to do with the stomp of the hooves in the stalls as the horses eagerly awaited their shining moment, the thick aroma of straw, the colorful silks adorning each horse, the tangible excitement of the jockeys as they shared last-minute talks with their trainers.

Which was exactly what Cassie and Tessa had just finished doing. Cassie had the utmost confidence that this race would go in their favor, but strange things always happened and they both knew better than to get cocky—especially at this point.

The first third of the Triple Crown was theirs, but this was a new day, a new race and a whole other level of adrenaline rushes.

Cassie followed behind as Tessa rode Don Pedro from the stables through the paddock and entered the track. No matter the outcome, Cassie was proud of her sister, of what they'd accomplished in their years together.

Soon their racing season would come to an end and Cassie would move on with her goal of opening a riding camp for handicapped children. Training a Triple Crown winner would put her in high demand in the horse-breeding world, but she hoped to use that reputation as a launching point for her school.

And beyond the school worries, her father was getting offers from his most heated rival, Jake Mason, to buy the prizewinning horses. Their season wasn't even over yet, for heaven's sake.

But those thoughts would have to wait until after the competition.

As would her thoughts of a certain Hollywood agent who had stayed behind on the estate to get some work done without distractions. The majority of the film crew had accompanied the Barringtons to Baltimore, Maryland, but today they were spectators, enjoying the race. They'd gotten many great shots from Louisville a couple of weeks ago, so now they were able to relax…somewhat. Cassie knew they were still taking still shots for the ad campaign, but not as many as at the derby.

As Tessa rode onto the track, Cassie couldn't help but smile. There was so much to be thankful for right now in her life. One chapter of her career was coming to an end. Another was going to begin in a few months.

Her daughter was happy and healthy and nearing her first birthday.

And, delicious icing on the cake, Ian Shaffer had entered her life. For how long she didn't know. But she did know that, for now, they were together and he had admitted his feelings were strong. But did that mean he'd want to try something long distance? Or would he stay around a little longer after the film was finished?

So many questions and none of them would be answered today. She needed to concentrate and be there for Tessa. All else could wait until this race was over.

In no time the horses were in their places and Cassie felt her father's presence beside her. His arm snaked around her waist, the silent support a welcome comfort. Each race had nerves balling up in her stomach, but nothing could be done now. The training for the Preakness was complete and now they waited for the fastest, most exciting moment in sports.

Cassie glanced toward the grandstands, and the colorful array of hats and suits had her smile widening. Excitement settled heavily over the track as everyone's gaze was drawn to the starting gate.

"You're trembling," her father whispered into her ear.

Cassie let out a shaky laugh. "I think that's you."

His arm tightened around her waist as a robust chuckle escaped. "I believe you're right, my dear."

The gun sounded and Cassie had no time for nerves. She couldn't keep her eyes off the places switching, the colored numbers on the board swapping out as horses passed each other and inched toward the lead.

Don Pedro was in forth. Cassie fisted her hands so tight, her short nails bit into her palms.

"Come on. Come on," she muttered.

Tessa eased past third and into second on the last turn.

The announcer's tone raised in excitement as Tessa inched even farther toward the head of the race. Cassie wanted to close her eyes to pray, but she couldn't take her gaze off the board.

Just as the first two horses headed to the finish line, Cassie started jumping up and down. Excitement, fear, nerves... They all had her unable to stand still.

And when the announcer blared that the winner was Don Pedro by a nose, Cassie jumped even higher, wrapped her arms around her father's neck and squealed like a little girl.

"We did it," he yelled, embracing her. "My girls did it!"

Damon jerked back, gripped her hand and tugged her toward the winner's circle, where Tessa met them. Her radiant smile, the mass of people surrounding her and the flash of cameras all announced there was a new winner.

Grant was right there in the throng of people, his grin so wide there was no way to hide the pride beaming off him.

Cassie's heart lurched. She loved that Tessa had found the man of her dreams, couldn't be happier for the couple. But, for the first time, Cassie was not the first one Tessa turned to after a race.

And that was not jealousy talking.... Cassie loved seeing Tessa and Grant so happy, and sharing Tessa's affection was fine. It was the fact that Cassie still felt empty when monumental things happened. Whom did she turn to to celebrate or for a shoulder to cry on?

Tessa turned her head, caught Cassie's eye and

winked down at her. Returning the wink, Cassie smiled to hide her sad thoughts.

Soon reporters were thrusting microphones in her face, as well. Very few ever won the Triple Crown, and a team of females was practically unheard of. History was definitely in the making.

The Barrington sisters had done it again, and with only one more race to go to round out the season and secure the coveted Triple Crown, Cassie knew she needed to focus now more than ever on training for the Belmont.

Which meant keeping her heart shielded from Ian, because if he penetrated too much more, she feared she'd never be able to recover if it all fell apart.

They were gone for days, weeks.

Okay, maybe it wasn't weeks, but Ian felt as if he hadn't seen Cassie forever. Which told him he was going to be in trouble when it came time for him to head back to L.A.

She'd arrived home late last night and he'd known she'd be tired, so he had stayed away to let her rest and spend time with Emily. But knowing she was so close was hard.

As he headed toward the stables just as the sun peeked overtop the hilltops, Ian wanted to spend some time with her. He'd actually ached for her while she'd been away. Like most of the nation, he'd watched with eyes glued to the television during the Preakness and he'd jumped out of his seat and cheered when Don Pedro crossed the finish line for the win.

The familiar smell of hay greeted him before he even hit the entrance. As soon as he crossed the threshold, Ian spotted Nash cleaning out a stall.

"Morning," Ian greeted him.

Nash nodded a good-morning and continued raking old hay. "Cassie isn't here yet," he said without looking up.

Ian grinned. Apparently he and Cassie weren't very discreet…not that they'd tried to be, but they also hadn't been blatant about their relationship, either.

"Hey, Ian."

He turned to see Tessa striding into the stables, all smiles with her hair pulled back.

"Congrats on the win." Ian couldn't help but offer a quick hug with a pat on her back. "That was one intense race."

Tessa laughed. "You should've seen it from my point of view."

Her eyes darted to Nash, then back to Ian. "What brings you out this early?"

Ian shrugged, sliding his hands into his pockets. "Just looking for Cassie."

Tessa's grin went into that all-knowing mode as she quirked a brow. "She actually was up most of the night with Emily. Poor baby is teething and nobody is getting any sleep."

"But Cassie has to be exhausted. You just got back late last night," he argued, realizing he was stating nothing new to Tessa.

Shrugging, Tessa sighed. "I know. I offered to take Emily for the night, but Cassie wouldn't hear of it."

Probably because the last time Cassie had been without her child, she had been locked in the attic with him.

"She's spreading herself too thin," Ian muttered.

Nash walked around them and pulled a bale of hay from the stack against the wall, then moved back into the stall. Ian shifted closer to the doorway to get out of the quiet groom's way.

"Follow me," Tessa said with a nod.

Intrigued, Ian fell into step behind the famous jockey. She stopped just outside the stables, but away from where Nash could overhear.

"This isn't where you tell me if I hurt your sister you'll kill me, is it?" he asked with a smile.

Tessa laughed and shook her head, eyes sparkling with amusement. "You're smart enough to know that goes without saying. I wanted to discuss something else, actually."

"And what's that?"

"Did Cassie ever tell you about the little getaway she and Grant came up with for me? Grant felt I was pushing myself too hard, never taking time for myself to regroup and recharge."

Ian grinned. "Must run in the family."

"Yeah, we Barringtons are all made of the same stubborn stuff."

Ian had no doubt the almighty Damon Barrington had instilled all his work ethic into his girls and that hard work and determination were paying off in spades.

"I'd like to return the favor," Tessa went on. "Are you up for taking a few days away from here?"

Was he? Did he want to leave Lily when they were still negotiating a contract? He didn't mind leaving Max. The actor could handle anything and Ian was very confident with their working relationship.

It was Lily that worried him. But he couldn't be in her face all the time. He'd spoken with her a few times since their dinner meeting. She'd promised a decision once she realized which agency would offer her the most and which one she'd feel most at home with.

He had to believe she'd see that his company was hands down the front-runner.

And a few days away with Cassie? He had deals and meetings to get back to, but after days without her, how could he not want to jump at that chance?

"Should I take that smile to mean you're going to take me up on this offer?"

Ian nodded. "I think I will. What did you have in mind?"

Chapter 14

How long could a baby be angry and how many teeth would be popping through?

Cassie had just collapsed onto the couch for the first time all day when someone knocked on her door. She threw a glance to Emily, who was playing on the floor and crawling from toy to toy...content for now.

Stepping over plush toys and blankets, Cassie opened the door and froze. Ian stood on her porch looking as handsome as ever, sporting aviator sunglasses and a navy T-shirt pulled taut across his wide shoulders and tucked into dark jeans.

She didn't need to look down at her own outfit to know she was just a step above homeless chic with her mismatched lounge pants with margarita glasses on them and her oversize T-shirt with a giant smiley face in the middle.

And her hair? She'd pulled it up into a ponytail for bed and hadn't touched it since. Half was falling around her face; the other half was in a nest on the side of her head.

Yeah, she exuded sex appeal.

"Um…are you going to invite me in?"

Cassie shoved a clump of hair behind her ear. "Are you sure you want to come in? Emily is teething. She's cranky more often than not since last night, and I'm… well…"

Ian closed the gap between them, laying a gentle kiss on her lips. "Beautiful."

Okay, there was no way she couldn't melt at that sweet declaration even if he was just trying to score points. He'd succeeded.

When he stepped into the house, Cassie stepped back and closed the door behind him. Emily grabbed hold of the couch cushion and pulled herself to her feet, throwing an innocent smile over her shoulder to Ian.

Cassie laughed. "Seriously? She smiles for you and I've had screaming for over twelve hours?"

"What can I say? I'm irresistible."

No denying that. Cassie still wasn't used to his powerful presence in her home, but she was growing to love it more and more each time he came for a visit.

"Hey, sweetheart," he said, squatting down beside Emily. "Did you have your mommy up last night?"

Emily let go of the couch to clap her hands and immediately fell down onto her diaper-covered butt. She giggled and looked up at Ian to see his reaction.

Cassie waited, too. She couldn't help but want to know how Ian would be around Emily. He hadn't spent too much time with her, considering he stopped by at night and he'd gone straight to Cassie's bed.

Reaching forward, Ian slid his big hands beneath Emily's delicate arms and lifted her as he came to his full height.

Cassie couldn't deny the lurch of her heart at the sight of this powerful man holding her precious baby. Was there a sexier sight than this? Not in Cassie's opinion.

"I know we talked on the phone, but congratulations." A smile lit up his already handsome face. "I'm so happy for you and Tessa."

Cassie still couldn't believe it herself. Of course they'd trained to win, but what trainer and jockey didn't? The fact they were that much closer to winning that coveted Triple Crown still seemed surreal.

"I'm still recovering from all the celebrating we did in Baltimore," she told him. "I've never been so happy in all my life. Well, except for when Emily was born."

"I have a surprise for you," Ian told her as Emily reached up and grabbed his nose.

Cassie went to reach for Emily, but Ian stepped back. "She's fine," he told her. "I love having my nose held so my voice can sound a little more like a chipmunk when I ask a sexy woman to go away with me for a few days."

Shocked at his invitation, Cassie shook her head, trying to make sense of it. "Go away with you?"

Ian nodded as Emily reached up on his head and tugged his glasses off. Immediately they went to her mouth.

"She's still fine," Ian told Cassie as he dodged her again. "They're sunglasses. She can chew on them all she wants."

"They'll have drool on them."

Ian's eyes darted to the lenses, but he just sighed. "Oh, well. So, what do you say? You up for getting away for a few days?"

Oh, how Cassie would love to get away. To not worry or train or do anything but be with Ian because their time together was coming to an end and she was certainly not ready to let go.

"Ian, going away with you sounds amazing, but I can't."

Ian glanced at Emily. "She's going to use you as an excuse, isn't she?"

Cassie laughed. "Actually, yes. But she's not an excuse. I mean, I can't ask anyone to keep her for days, especially with her teething and upset."

Bringing his gaze back to Cassie, Ian crossed the space between them until he stood so close she could see the flecks of amber in his dark eyes.

"I'm not asking you to hand her off to anybody. I want to take you both away."

Cassie stared back at him, sure she'd heard him wrong. He wanted to take her and a baby? A cranky baby?

"But…but…are you sure?"

Ian dipped his head and gently kissed her before easing back and giving her that heart-melting grin. "I wouldn't have asked if I wasn't sure."

A million things ran through her mind. Could she actually take off and be with Ian for a few days? Did he honestly know what he was asking? Because she really didn't think he knew how difficult playing house could be.

"Stop thinking so hard." He shifted Emily to his other

side and reached out to cup the side of Cassie's face. "Do you want to go?"

Cassie nodded. "Of course I do. It's just—"

"Yes, you want to go. That's what I need to hear. Everything else is taken care of."

Intrigued, Cassie raised her brows. "Oh, is it?"

A corner of Ian's mouth quirked into a devilish half smile. "Absolutely. How about I come back and get you in an hour. Just pack simple clothing and whatever Emily can't live without. I'll be back to help you finish up and then we'll go."

"Where are we going?" she asked.

Handing Emily back to Cassie, Ian shrugged. "I guess you'll find out when we get there."

She tried to get the sunglasses away from Emily and noticed slobber bubbles along the lenses. Ian waved a hand and laughed.

"No, really, keep them," he said as he headed toward the door. "She apparently gets more use out of them than I did."

Cassie was still laughing after he'd closed the door behind him. A getaway with Ian and Emily? How could she not want to jump at this chance?

And how could she not read more into it? Was Ian silently telling her he wanted more? Or was he getting in all the time he could before he said his final goodbye?

Ian didn't know if he was making a mistake or if he was finally taking a leap of faith by bringing Cassie and Emily to his beachfront home. They'd flown from the East Coast to the West and he'd questioned himself the entire way.

Tessa had suggested he take Cassie to Grant's mountain home for a getaway, but Ian wanted Cassie on his turf. Deep down inside he wanted her to see how he lived, see part of his world.

And he wanted to find out how well she fit into his home. Would she feel out of place or would she enjoy the breathtaking views from his bedroom, which overlooked the Pacific Ocean?

Surprisingly, Emily was wonderful on the plane ride, thanks to the pain reliever aiding in her teething process. As Ian maneuvered his car—it had been waiting for him at the airport—into his drive, he risked a glance over to Cassie. He wanted to see her initial reaction.

And he wasn't disappointed. Her eyes widened at the two-story white beach house with the porch stretching across the first floor and the balcony wrapping around the house on the second. He'd had that same reaction when his Realtor had shown him the property a few years ago. Love at first sight.

"Ian, this is gorgeous," she exclaimed. "I can't believe you managed to get a beach house on such short notice."

He hadn't told her he was bringing her to his home. He'd wanted to surprise her, and he was afraid if he told her, then she'd back out.

As he pulled into the garage and killed the engine, Ian turned to face her. "Actually, this is my house."

Cassie gasped, jerking her head toward him. "Your house? Why didn't you tell me we were coming to your house?"

He honestly didn't have an excuse unless he wanted to delve way down and dig up the commitment issues he still faced. His fear of having her reject his plan, his fear of how fast they'd progressed and his fear of where the hell all of this would lead had kept him silent.

"I can't believe you live on the beach," she said, still smiling. "You must love it here."

Yeah, he did, but for the first time in his life, he suddenly found himself loving another location, as well. Who knew he'd fall in love with a horse farm on the other side of the country?

While Cassie got Emily out of the car, Ian took all the luggage into the house. He put his and Cassie's in the master bedroom and took Emily's bag into the room across the hall.

Thankfully, he'd called ahead and had his housekeeper pick up a few items and set them up in the makeshift nursery. Since she was a new grandmother, she knew exactly what a baby would need. And judging from the looks of the room, she'd gone all out.

Ian chuckled. The woman was a saint and deserved a raise…as always.

"Ian, this house is—"

He turned around to see Cassie in the doorway, Emily on her hip, eyes wide, mouth open.

"I had a little help getting the place ready," he informed her, moving aside so she could enter. "I hope you don't mind that I had my housekeeper get Emily some things to make her comfortable while you guys are here."

Cassie's gaze roamed around the room, pausing on the crib in the corner. "I don't know what to say," she whispered as her eyes sought his. "This is… Thank you."

Warmth spread through him. Cassie was absolutely speechless over a package of diapers, a bed and some toys. Cost hadn't even factored into his plan; Emily's comfort and easing Cassie's mind even a little had been his top priorities.

Before he could respond, Emily started fussing.

Cassie kissed her forehead and patted her back. "It's okay, baby. You're all right."

The low cries turned into a full-fledged wail and a sense of helplessness overtook him. Yes, he could buy anything for her, but what did he know about consoling a child or what to do when they were hurting or sick?

With a soft smile, Cassie looked back to him. "Sorry. I'm sure this isn't the getaway you'd hoped for."

Ian returned her smile and reached out to slide his hand over Emily's back. "The only expectation I had was spending time with both of you. She can't help that she's teething."

Her eyes studied him for a moment before she said, "I don't know what I did to deserve you, Ian."

"You deserve everything you've ever wanted."

He wanted to say more, he wanted to do more and give more to her, but they were both in uncharted territory, and taking things slow was the best approach. God knew they hadn't started out slow. Working backward might not have been the most conventional approach, but it was all they had to work with.

"Can you get in the side of her diaper bag and get out the Tylenol?" she asked.

While Cassie got Emily settled with pain medication and started to sing to her, Ian watched from the doorway. Had his father ever felt this way about him? Had the man wanted to be hands-on? Because Ian desperately found himself wanting to be more in not just Cassie's life, but Emily's, as well. He didn't have the first clue about caring for children, but he wanted to learn.

How could he ever be what they needed?

But how could he ever let either of them go?

Chapter 15

Thankfully, after a round of medicine and a short nap, Emily was back to her happy self. Cassie put on her bathing suit, wrapping a sheer sarong around her waist, then put Emily into her suit, as well.

Why waste time indoors when there was a beach and rolling waves just steps away?

"You ready to play in the ocean?" Cassie asked Emily as she carried her toward the back door. "You're going to love it, baby girl."

The open-concept living room and kitchen spread across the entire back of the house, and two sets of French doors led out onto the patio. Cassie stepped out into the warm sunshine and stopped.

At the edge of the water, Ian stood with his back to her wearing black trunks and flaunting his excellent muscle tone. The fabric clinging to the back of his well-toned thighs, his slicked-back hair and the water droplets glistening on his tanned shoulders and back indicated he'd already tested the waters.

The man was sinful. He tempted her in ways she never thought possible, made her want things that could never be. They couldn't be more opposite, yet they'd somehow found each other. And they'd grown so close since their encounter in the attic.

The night of the lock-in had been filled with nothing but lust and desire. Now, though, Cassie was wrestling with so many more emotions. At the top of her list was one she'd futilely guarded her heart against...love.

She completely loved this man who had brought her to his home, shown her his piece of the world. But the clincher was when he'd assumed Emily would accompany them. He knew Cassie and Emily were a package deal, and he'd embraced the fact and still welcomed them.

How could she not fall hard for this intriguing man? He was nothing like her ex, nothing like any man she'd ever known, really. And that was what made him so special.

Emily started clapping and pointing toward Ian. Cassie laughed. "Yeah, we're going, baby."

Sand shifted beneath her toes as she made her way toward the man who'd taught her heart to trust again. Just the sight of him had her anticipating their night alone after Emily went to bed.

It wasn't as if she hadn't seen or touched him all over, but still, his sexiness never got old.

Emily squealed and Ian turned to face her. His gaze traveled over her modest suit and Cassie tamped down that inner demon that tried to tell her that her extra baby weight was hideous. Ian never, ever made her feel less than beautiful, so that inner voice could just shut the hell up.

"You look good in a suit, Cass."

His low voice, combined with that heavy-lidded gaze, had her insides doing an amazing little dance number.

"I was thinking the same thing about you," she told him with a grin.

"Mom, Mom, Mom," Emily squealed again, clapping her little hands and staring out at the water.

"Can I?" Ian asked, reaching for Emily.

Handing Emily over, Cassie watched as Ian stepped into the water. Slowly, he waded in deeper, all the while taking his hand and cupping water to splash up onto her little pudgy legs. Emily's laughter, her arms around Ian's neck and seeing Ian bounce around in the water like a complete goofball had Cassie laughing herself.

This getaway was exactly what she needed. Coming off the win at the Preakness and rolling right into a special weekend had Cassie realizing that her life was pretty near perfect right now. For this moment, she would relish the fact that Ian had to care for her on some deep level…possibly even love her. If he only had feelings of lust, he wouldn't have brought her to his home, wouldn't have invited a teething, sometimes cranky kid, and he certainly wouldn't be playing in the water with Emily like a proud daddy.

Cassie hated to place all her hope, all her heart, on one man…but how could she not, when he'd captured her heart the instant they'd been intimate in that attic?

Not wanting to miss out on a single moment, Cassie jumped into the ocean, reached beneath the water and pinched Ian on the butt.

The grin he threw over his shoulder at her told her she was in for a fun night.

Rocking a now peaceful baby had Ian truly wishing for so much. He'd convinced Cassie that he could put Emily to bed. He figured the little one was so tired from the day of playing in the ocean and taking a stroller ride around his neighborhood that she'd fall fast asleep.

She'd been fussy at first and Cassie had shown Ian how to rub some numbing ointment onto Emily's gums. He'd given Emily a bottle, even burped her, and rocked her until her sweet breath evened out.

He glanced down to the puckered lips, the pink cheeks from the sun—even though they'd slathered her with sunscreen—and smiled. Was it any wonder Cassie worked herself to death? How could a parent not want to sacrifice herself to make such an innocent child happy?

Cassie worked so hard with her sister, worked harder in the stables caring for horses, and she busted her butt to make a secure life and happy home for Emily…all without a husband.

Oh, she'd be ticked if she knew he worried about her not having someone in her life to help her. Granted, she had her father, Tessa and Linda, but whom did she have at night? Who helped her at home?

God help him, but Ian wanted to be that man. The weight of a sleeping baby in his arms, the sweet smell of her skin after her bath and the thought that this innocent child had complete and total trust in him were truly humbling.

Once he knew she was asleep, Ian eased from the rocking chair and laid Emily into the new crib, complete with pink-and-white-striped sheets. When he stood up, she stirred a little, but she settled right in.

A sigh of relief escaped Ian. He'd mastered numerous multimillion-dollar movie deals, he rubbed elbows with A-list actors and he'd managed to start his own agency at the age of twenty-four. But putting a child to sleep all by himself felt like quite an accomplishment.

He glanced at the monitor beside the crib and made sure it was on before he stepped out into the hall and quietly shut the door behind him.

He barely managed not to jump when he noticed Cassie across the hall, leaning against the doorway to his bedroom.

"You did it," she said with a wide smile. "I'm impressed."

All thoughts fled his mind as he took in the muted glow that surrounded her from the small lamp in his room. Her long red curls slid around her shoulders, lying against the stark white silk robe she wore—and what she wasn't wearing beneath. The V in the front plunged so deep, the swells of her breasts begged for his touch.

"I like your pajamas," he told her, crossing the hallway and immediately going to the belt on her robe. "Reminds me of something…"

Cassie lifted her arms to wrap around his neck. "What's that?"

"The fact I haven't seen you naked in several days."

She shifted, allowing the material to slide from her shoulders and puddle at her feet. Ian's hands roamed over the soft, lush curves he'd come to love and crave.

"You feel so good," he groaned as he trailed his lips from her jawline down the smooth column of her neck. "So perfect."

When she trembled beneath his touch, Ian cupped her behind and pulled her flush against his body. Nothing had ever felt so right. Every time Cassie was in his arms, contentment settled deeper and deeper into his heart.

She undressed him rapidly, matching his own frenzy. Ian had brought other women to his home. Not many, but a few. Yet he knew the second he laid Cassie beneath him and looked down into her blue eyes…he never wanted another woman in this bed.

He knew she wasn't asleep. The full moon shone through the wide expanse of windows across the room from the king-size bed and directly across their tangled bodies.

Cassie's breathing wasn't even and he'd felt the soft flutter of her lashes against his arm. Whatever thoughts consumed her mind, they were keeping her awake.

More than likely they were the same things that had him awake hours after they'd made love…twice.

Ian trailed his fingertips over her hip, down into the dip of her waist and back again. Goose bumps prickled beneath his touch.

"Talk to me," she whispered in the darkened room.

Words that had frightened him on more than one occasion after sex. But this was so different from any other time. First, Cassie was like no other woman. Second, what had just happened between them was so far beyond sex. And third, he actually didn't cringe as the words hovered in the air between them.

Moreover, he *wanted* to talk to her. He wanted her to know about his past, his life and what had brought him to this point…and why the thought of commitment scared the hell out of him.

Part of him truly wanted to try for her. Never before had he even considered permanent anything in his life, let alone a woman and a child. Cassie changed everything for him, because she was starting to *be* everything for him.

Of course, there was that devil on his shoulder that kept telling him he couldn't just try out playing house with this woman. She was genuine, with real feelings and a heart of gold that she had to protect. If he attempted to try for a long-term spot in her life and things didn't work out, he would never be able to forgive himself.

"My childhood wasn't quite as rosy and enjoyable as yours." The words tumbled out before he thought better of opening up about the past he hated to even think about. "My father was a military man. Things had to be perfect, and not just perfect, but done five minutes ago. When he was home on leave, if I had a chore, I had better get to it the second he told me or I would face punishment."

Cassie gasped next to him. "He hit you?"

Ian stared up at the darkened ceiling as he continued to trail his fingertips over her lush, naked curves. "On occasion. But it wasn't a beating. He was old-school and a hand to my backside wasn't unheard of. But then he came home less and less because he and my mother divorced. That's when she started bringing her male friends into the house."

Ian recalled how weird it felt having a strange man at the breakfast table when he woke up, but eventually he didn't question his mother…and he didn't ask the names of the men. Would it matter? They'd be gone when she finished with them anyway.

"My mom is currently in the middle of her fourth divorce and I've no doubt number five is waiting in the wings absolutely convinced he's the one."

Cassie's arm tightened around his abdomen. "I'm sorry. I can't imagine."

Her warm breath tickled his chest, but Ian wouldn't have it any other way. He loved the feel of her tucked perfectly against him, her hair falling over his shoulder, the flutter of her lashes against his side.

"Don't be sorry," he told her. "There are kids way worse off than I was. But I always wished I had parents who loved each other, who loved me. A family was everything to me when I was younger, but I wanted the impossible."

A drop of moisture slid down his side. Ian shifted his body, folding Cassie closer as he half loomed over her.

"Don't cry for me." In the pale moonlight, her eyes glistened. Had anyone ever cried for him before? "I'm fine, Cassie. I guess I just wanted you to know what I came from."

Soft fingertips came up to trail down his cheek. Her thumb caressed his bottom lip, and his body responded instantly.

"I'm crying for the little boy who needed love and attention," she whispered. "And I'm crying for the man who fits so perfectly into my family, I'm terrified of how we'll get along without him."

Her declaration was a punch to his gut. The fact that they'd never mentioned his leaving after the film wrapped hung heavy in the air between them. And knowing she not only worried about his absence, but she'd cried over it had him hating himself on so many levels.

"I don't want to hurt you," he murmured as he slid his lips across hers. "That's the last thing I'd ever want."

Adjusting her body so she could frame his face with her hands, Cassie looked up at him with those damn misty eyes and smiled. "I know. I went into this with my eyes wide-open. For right now, though, you're mine and I don't want to think about tomorrow, Ian. I don't want to worry about that void that will inevitably come when you're gone."

Her hips tilted against his. "I just want you. Here. Now."

As he kissed her lips he had a hard time reining in his own emotions, because Cassie was dead-on about one thing.... There would most definitely be a void— the one he would feel without her by his side.

Chapter 16

Cassie reached across the bed, only to encounter cool sheets. Quickly she sat up, clutching the material to her chest and glancing to the nightstand clock.

How on earth had she slept until nine? Between having a career set around a working horse farm and being a single mother, sleeping in was a foreign concept and a luxury she simply couldn't afford.

Another reality hit her hard as she jerked to look at the baby monitor on the dresser across the room. The red light wasn't on, which meant at some point the device had been turned off. Throwing the covers aside, Cassie grabbed the first available article of clothing—which happened to be Ian's T-shirt—and pulled the soft cotton over her head. She inhaled the embedded masculine scent of Ian as she darted across the hall.

The nursery was empty. Giggling erupted from downstairs, so Cassie turned and headed toward the sweet sound. At the base of the steps, Cassie froze as she stared into the living room. Ian stood behind Emily, her little hands held high, clutching on to his as he helped her walk across the open space. He'd pushed the coffee table against one wall, leaving the dark hardwood floor completely open.

Emily squealed as she waddled through the area, and Cassie, who still stood unnoticed, had to bite her lip to control the trembling and wash of emotions that instantly consumed her.

Ian Shaffer had officially stolen her heart, and there was no way she could go back to her life before she'd ever met him. The man had opened his home to her and her daughter. He wasn't just interested in having her in his bed. Granted, that was how they'd started out, but over a brief period of time they'd grown together and meshed in such a way that had Cassie hopeful and wishing. Dare she set her sights so high and dream for things that once seemed unattainable?

"Mamamama," Emily cried when she saw Cassie in the doorway.

Cassie stepped toward her daughter and squatted down. "Hey, sweet pea. Are you making Ian work this morning?"

Emily's precious two-toothed grin melted her heart. When she glanced up to meet Ian's gaze, her breath literally caught. He still clung to Emily's fingers and he'd been hunched over so he could accommodate her height, but he just looked so at peace and happy.

"What time did she get up?"

Ian shrugged. "Maybe around seven."

Cassie straightened. "Why didn't you get me up?"

Scooping Emily into his arms, Ian smiled. "Because you needed to sleep, so I turned the monitor off and got her out of the crib. She's been changed and fed—probably not how you'd do it, but it's done nonetheless."

Cassie was utterly speechless. The man had taken such care of her daughter all so Cassie could sleep in. He'd been watching and loving over Emily...over another man's baby, and all without a care or second thought. And now he stood holding her as if the act were the most natural thing in the world.

"Don't look at me like that," he told her. Emily turned her head into Ian's shoulder and his wide, tanned hand patted her tiny back. "I wanted to help and I knew you'd refuse if you even thought she was awake. Besides, I kind of wanted to see how Emily and I would get along. I'm pretty sure she loves me."

Cassie couldn't help but laugh. "I'm sure she does love you. She knows a good thing when she sees it."

Ian's eyes widened, and the muscle in his jaw moved as if he were hiding his words deep within. Had she said too much? At this point, with time against them, Cassie truly believed she couldn't hold back. She needed to be up front and honest.

"I'm not saying that to make you uncomfortable," she informed him, crossing her arms over her chest. "But you have to know this is so much more than physical for me, Ian."

Those dark eyes studied her a second before he nodded. "I'd be lying if I said this was all sexual for me. You and Emily..."

He shook his head as his words died on his lips. Cassie wanted him to go on, but she knew the internal battle he waged with himself and she didn't want to push him. He'd opened up to her last night, bared his soul, and she knew what he'd shared hadn't come easy for him.

Placing a hand on his arm, Cassie smiled. "We don't need to define anything right now," she assured him. "I just wanted you to know this thing between us—it matters so much to me."

With Emily lying against one shoulder, Ian pulled Cassie to his other side and wrapped an arm around her. "Everything in my arms right now matters more to me than I ever thought possible," he told her with a kiss to the top of her head.

Before she could completely melt into a puddle at his feet over his raw, heartfelt words, Ian's hand slid down her side and cupped her bottom beneath his T-shirt.

"This shirt never looked this sexy on me," he growled into her ear. "So unless you want to end up back in bed, you better go get some clothes on."

Shivers of arousal swept through her. Would she ever get enough of him? More so, would he get enough of her?

Tipping her head back, she stared up into his eyes. Desire and, dare she say, love stared back at her. No, she didn't think they'd get enough of each other, which meant whatever they were building wouldn't come crumbling down when he left Virginia after the film was done shooting. But how they would manage was a whole other hurdle to jump.

Extracting herself from his side, Cassie pulled Emily from his arms. "How about we spend the day on the beach?" she suggested.

Emily's little hand went into Cassie's hair, and she started winding the strands around her baby fingers.

"You in a suit?" Ian's gaze raked over her once more. "I'd never say no to that."

With this being their last day of complete relaxation, Cassie wanted to live for the moment, this day, and not worry about what obstacles they faced tomorrow or even next week. She was completely in love with Ian. He wasn't a rebound; he wasn't a filler or a stepping-stone until the next chapter of her life.

Ian Shaffer *was* the next chapter of her life.

Chapter 17

"I just need someone who's good with advertising," Cassie muttered as she stared down at the new plans for her riding school for handicapped children.

"How about that hunky agent you're shacking up with?"

Cassie threw a glare across the room at her sister. Tessa silently volleyed back a wicked grin.

"We're not shacking up." Not technically, anyway. "And that's not his job."

"Maybe not," Tessa replied, coming to her feet. "But he'd know more about it than we would, and I guarantee he'd do anything to help you."

More than likely, but Cassie wasn't going to ask. Venturing into personal favors would imply something… something they'd yet to identify in their relationship.

Yes, they'd admitted they had strong feelings for each

other, but after the giant leap into intimacy, they'd pulled back the emotional roller coaster and examined where they were going.

And they still didn't know.

Cassie spoon-fed another bite of squash and rice to Emily. Right now she needed to focus on the final race of the season, getting her school properly advertised and caring for her daughter. Ian, unfortunately, would have to fall in line behind all of that and she highly doubted he would want to. What man would? He deserved more than waiting on her leftover time.

"You're scowling." Tessa came to stand beside the high chair and leaned against the wall. "What's really bothering you?"

Sisters. They always knew when to dig deeper and pull the truth from the depths of hell just to make you say the words aloud.

"Ian is out to dinner with Lily."

A quirk of a smile danced around Tessa's mouth. "You're jealous? Honey, the man is absolutely crazy about you. All you'd have to do is see how he looks at you when you aren't paying attention."

The idea that he studied her enough to show emotion on his face for others to see made her way more thrilled than she should be. She wanted to tell him she'd fallen for him—she wanted to tell everybody. But there was that annoying little voice that kept telling her this was too good to be true and that she needed to come back to reality before she ended up hurt.

"He's not like Derek," Tessa informed her as if she were reading her mind. "Ian may be younger, but he's all man and he's only got eyes for you."

Cassie smiled with a nod and scooped up the last bite,

shoving it into Emily's waiting mouth. "I know. There's just that thread of doubt that gets to me, and I know it's not Ian's fault. He can't help the mess that is my life."

Laying a hand over Cassie's arm, Tessa squeezed. "Your life is beautiful. You have a precious baby, an awesome career and the best sister anyone could ever ask for. What more could a girl want?"

To be loved. The words remained in her head, in her heart.

"So where's your guy tonight?" Cassie asked, wiping off the orange, messy mouth, hoping to unearth her daughter. "You two aren't normally separated for more than an hour at a time."

With a smile that could only be equated to love, Tessa positively beamed. "He's going over some things with Bronson and Anthony. I'm pretty sure Dad weaseled his way into that meeting, as well."

Cassie scooped Emily from the high chair and settled her on her hip. "I've no doubt Dad is weighing in with his opinion. I need to give her a bath. You sticking around?"

Shaking her head, Tessa sighed and started across the living room. "I think I'll head home and make some dinner. It's not often I get to cook for Grant, and he's worked so hard lately. He needs to relax."

Cassie squeezed her eyes shut. "I don't want to hear about you two relaxing. Just a simple no would've answered my question."

With a naughty laugh, Tessa grabbed her keys from the entry table and waved. "See you tomorrow."

Once Cassie was alone, she couldn't help that her thoughts drifted to Ian, to the days they'd spent at his home in L.A. and to the fact he'd taken such good care of her sweet Emily.

Yes, the man may be five years her junior, but so what? Her ex-husband had been two years older and look how well that had turned out. Cassie couldn't hang a single argument on age, not when Ian went above and beyond to show her just what type of man he was.

After Emily was bathed and dressed in her light-weight sleeper, Cassie set some toys on a blanket and let her daughter have some playtime before bed. Settling on the couch, curling her legs to the side, Cassie rested her elbow on the arm of the sofa and watched Emily smack soft yellow and red cubes together, making them jingle.

Exhaustion consumed her, but how could she not be tired? Her plate was not only full—it was overflowing. Physically, mentally, she was drained. Her head was actually pounding so fiercely her eyes ached. Maybe she could just lay her head on the arm of the couch while Emily played for a bit longer.

Adjusting her arm beneath her head, Cassie closed her eyes, hoping to chase away the dull throb.

After the flash of panic in seeing Cassie slumped over the arm of the couch and Emily holding herself up against the edge of the couch by her mama, Ian realized Cassie had merely fallen asleep.

"Hey, sweetie," he said softly when Emily smiled up at him, flashing her two little baby teeth. "Your mama is pretty tired. Why don't we let her sleep?"

Ian scooped Emily up, set her in her Pack 'n Play across the room and made sure she had her favorite stuffed horse. He had to ignore her slight protesting as he crossed back and gently lifted Cassie into his arms. Murmuring something, she tilted her head against his chest and let out a deep sigh. She was exhausted and apparently couldn't even keep her eyes open. It was so unlike her to fall asleep with Emily still up and not confined to one area.

A small bedside lamp sent a soft glow through her bedroom. After gently laying her down, he pulled the folded blanket from the foot of the bed and draped it over her curled form. Smoothing her hair from her face, Ian frowned and leaned in closer to rest his palm across her forehead.

She wasn't burning up, but she wasn't far from it. Careful not to wake her, he peeled the throw back off her to hopefully get her fever down. Her cheeks were pink and the dark circles beneath her eyes were telltale signs of an illness settling in. He had a feeling Cassie would only be angry to know she was getting sick.

He went into her adjoining bath, got a cool cloth and brought it back out, carefully laying it across her forehead. She stirred and her lids fluttered open as she tried to focus.

"Ian?"

"Shh." He curled a hand over her shoulder to get her to remain down. "It's all right. You need to rest."

"Emily…" Cassie's eyes closed for a moment before she looked back up at him. "I don't feel very well."

"I know, baby. I'm not going anywhere and Emily is fine. Just rest."

He had no clue if she heard him; her eyes were closed and her soft, even breathing had resumed.

The woman worked herself too hard. Not that he could judge. After all, he hadn't grown to be one of Hollywood's most sought-out agents at such a young age by playing assistant and errand boy. No, he'd done grunt work, made his career his since he'd left home determined to prove to his free-spirited mother and domineering father that he could manage on his own and succeed way above anything they'd ever dreamed.

And he'd done just that.

But now that he looked down at Cassie resting peacefully, he couldn't help but wonder if there wasn't more in store for him. Work was satisfying on so many levels, but it didn't keep his bed warm, didn't look to him for support and compassion and sure as hell didn't make his heart swell to the point of bursting.

Cassie and Emily, on the other hand…

After clicking off the bedside lamp, he went straight to the hall bath to wash his hands. If Cassie was contagious, he didn't want to get her daughter sick. Granted, the child had been with her mother all evening, but still. Weren't people supposed to wash their hands before dealing with kids?

Yeah, he had a lot to learn. As he lathered up and rinsed, he glanced across the open floor plan to Emily, who had long since forgotten she was angry with being confined. Ian dried his hands on a plaid towel and smiled. Definitely had a lot to learn about little people.

And suddenly it hit him that he actually wanted to do just that. Who knew that when he came out here to sway Lily into signing with his agency that he'd completely get sidetracked by a beauty who literally fell into his arms?

After getting a bottle ready—thank God he'd had those alone days with Cassie and Emily in California so he knew a bit more about Emily's care—Ian set it on the end table and went to retrieve one happy baby.

"Are you always in a good mood?" he asked as he lifted her from the baby prison. "Your mama isn't feeling good, so it's just you and me."

Emily patted his face and smiled. "Dadadada."

Ian froze. *Oh, no. No, no, no.* As if a vise was being tightened around his chest, Ian's breath left him.

"No, baby. Ian."

Emily patted his cheek again. "Dadada."

Okay, he had to put his own issues aside at the thought of someone calling him Daddy because this poor girl honestly didn't know her daddy. She didn't remember the man who was supposed to be here for her and her mother.

Ian held her closer, silently wanting to reassure her that she was not alone. But was he also silently telling himself that he'd be here beyond the rough night right now? Would he be here after the film wrapped up?

Since he was alone with his thoughts he might as well admit to himself that being with Cassie and Emily for the long term was something he wanted and, dare he say…ached for?

As he settled into the corner of the couch with Emily, he slid the bottle between her little puckered lips and smiled as those expressive blue eyes looked back up at him. Eyes like her mother's. Both ladies had him wrapped around their fingers.

Emily drifted off to sleep about the time the bottle was empty. He set it back on the table and shifted her gently up onto his shoulder. If she spit up on his dress shirt, so be it. He hadn't taken the time to change after his dinner meeting with Lily. She was pretty confident she'd be signing with his agency.

And the fact this was the first time he'd thought of that monumental career development since he'd come in and discovered Cassie ill should tell him exactly how quickly his priorities had changed where the Barrington females were concerned.

Once Emily had fallen asleep, he figured it was okay for him to rest on the couch with her. He carefully got up and turned off the lights in the living room, leaving on only the small light over the stove in the kitchen. Pulling the throw off the back of the sofa with one hand and holding Emily firmly with the other, Ian toed off his shoes and laid the little girl against the back of the sofa before he eased down onto his side beside her. Not the most comfortable of positions, but he was so tired he could've slept standing up, and there was no way he'd leave Cassie alone with the baby tonight.

Resting with the baby on a couch was probably some sort of Parenting 101 no-no, but since he'd taken no crash courses in this gig, he was totally winging it.

The next thing he knew someone was ringing the doorbell. Ian jerked up, taking in the sunlight streaming in through the windows. It was Sunday and the crew was taking the day off. Was someone looking for him? The doorbell chimed again and Emily's eyes popped open, too.

Ian picked her up and raked a hand over his hair as he padded to the door. The last thing he needed was for someone to ring that bell again and wake Cassie. Apparently they'd all slept uneventfully through the night.

As he flicked the lock, Ian glanced out the sidelight, frowning when he didn't recognize the stranger on the porch.

Easing the door open slightly, Ian met the other man's gaze. "Can I help you?"

The stranger's eyes went from Emily back to Ian before the muscle in his jaw jumped. "Who the hell are you, and where is Cassie?"

Shocked at the immediate anger, Ian instantly felt defensive. "I should be asking you who you are, considering you're on the outside."

Narrowed eyes pierced Ian. "I'm Cassie's husband. I'll ask again. Who the hell are you?"

Husband. Ian didn't miss the fact the prick left out the "ex" part.

"I'm her lover," Ian said, mentally high-fiving himself for wiping that smug look off the man's face.

Chapter 18

Cassie held on to the side of her head, which was still pounding, but now she had a new problem.

Frozen at the end of her hallway, she had full view of Ian holding Emily and the front door wide-open with Derek standing on the other side looking beyond pissed. This was the dead-last thing she wanted to deal with in her life, particularly at this moment.

"Derek, what are you doing here?" she asked, slowly crossing the room, praying she didn't collapse.

"Go back to bed, honey." Ian turned to her, his face softening as he took in what she knew was impressive bed head. "Emily is fine and he can come back later."

"Don't tell my wife what to do," Derek practically shouted as he shouldered his way past Ian and into the living room.

"She's not your wife." Ian's eyes narrowed. When

Emily started to fidget, Ian patted her back and murmured something to her. "I need to feed her and change her diaper."

Derek's gaze darted from Ian to Cassie and back to Ian. "What the hell is this? You move in your lover to shack up? Never took you for a whore."

Cassie didn't think she could feel worse. She was wrong. But before she could defend herself, Ian had turned back, clenching the muscle in his jaw.

"Apologize," Ian said in a low, threatening tone.

Cassie had no doubt if Ian hadn't been holding the baby, he would've been across the room in an instant.

"This has nothing to do with you," Derek shot back. "Why don't you give me my daughter and get out."

No matter how awful Cassie felt, she raised her hand to silence Ian and moved closer to Derek. Too bad whatever bug she'd picked up couldn't be fast-acting or she'd so exhale all over him.

"You relinquished any right you had when you walked out on us." Cassie laid a hand on the back of the couch for support. She'd be a little more intimidating if she wasn't freezing and ready to fall onto her face. "You can't just barge into my house and try to take control. I don't know why you're here, but I don't really care."

Cassie felt Ian's hard body behind her, his strong hand settled around her waist. The man offered support both physically and emotionally with one simple, selfless touch. And the sea of differences between the two men in this room was evident without so much as a spoken word.

Ian had watched her with care, concern and, yes, even love. Derek stood glaring, judging and hating. When he'd first walked out she would've done anything to get her family back, but now that he was here, she loathed the sight of him.

"I'm here to see my wife and daughter," Derek told her.

"I'm not your wife," Cassie fired back. "And if you want to see Emily, you can contact your attorney and he can call mine. You can't just charge in here after being gone for nearly a year and expect me to just let you see her. Did you think she'd be comfortable with you?"

"She seems fine with him." Derek nodded his chin in Ian's direction.

"That's because she knows who I am," Ian stated from behind her. "Now, Cassie has asked you to leave. She's not feeling good and my patience has just about run out. Leave now or I'll escort you out personally, then notify the crew's security to take you off the estate property."

Derek looked as if he wanted to say more, but Ian stepped around Cassie, keeping his arm wrapped around her waist. He said nothing and kept his gaze on Derek until Derek stepped back toward the front door.

"I plan on seeing my daughter," Derek threatened. "And my wife. I'll go through my lawyer, but I will be getting my family back."

He slammed the door, leaving the echoing sound to fill the silence. Cassie hadn't seen Derek in so long, she had no idea how to feel, how to react. She didn't feel like battling him.

And had he threatened to take Emily? Was that what he'd implied?

Cassie sank onto the back of the couch and wrapped her arms around her waist. Maybe she should have listened to those voice mails.

"Go back to bed, Cass. Don't think about him—just go rest for now."

Cassie looked up at Ian, still holding Emily. The image just seemed so...right. The three of them *felt* right. They'd all been random puzzle pieces and when they'd come together they'd instantly clicked into place without question.

Shoving her wayward hair behind her ears, Cassie shook her head. "I can't rest, Ian. He just made a veiled threat to take Emily. He can't do that, right? I mean, what judge would let him have my baby after he walked out on us?"

Tears pricked her eyes. She couldn't fathom sharing custody of her baby. Emily belonged here.

"She doesn't even know him," Cassie murmured, thinking aloud. "There's no way he could take her. Emily would be terrified."

Ian rested a hand on her shoulder and held on to Emily with his other strong arm. "You're jumping the gun here. He didn't say he was going to ask for custody. I honestly think those were just hollow words. He wants to scare you because he's angry I was here. I guarantee had you been alone, his attitude would've been completely different. One look at me, especially holding his daughter, and he was instantly on the defensive."

Emily started to reach for Cassie, but Ian shifted his arm away. "Go on back to rest. I'll feed her breakfast and then I'll check on you to see if you feel like eating. You're exhausted and working too hard."

Cassie raised a brow. "Working too hard? Are you the pot or the kettle?"

Laughing, Ian shrugged. "Does it matter?"

Cassie pushed away from the couch and sighed.

"Thanks, Ian. Really. I don't know what I would've done without you here last night."

After a light kiss across her forehead, Ian looked into her eyes. "There's nowhere else I would've rather been."

As Cassie got back into bed, she knew Ian wasn't just saying pretty words to try to win her over. The man was full of surprises, and she found herself falling harder with each passing revelation.

And now here she was, 100 percent in love with a man who lived on the other side of the country, who would be leaving in a couple of weeks to go back to his life. And, of all the rotten timing, her ex had decided to show up now.

Cassie curled into her pillow and fisted her hands beside her face as the tears threatened to fall. Somehow this would all work out. She had faith, she had hope and, for the first time in her life, she had love. All of that had to count for something…didn't it?

Once Cassie had gotten a little food in her, she seemed even more tired, so Ian insisted on taking Emily for a few hours and then checking back. There was no way he could leave her alone with a baby, but he still had work to do.

Single parents worked while caring for their babies all the time, right? Shouldn't be too hard to send some emails and make a few phone calls.

After fighting with the straps on the stroller and narrowly missing pinching Emily's soft skin in the buckle, he finally had her secured and ready to go. Diaper bag over his shoulder, Ian set out across the estate, pushing Emily toward his trailer.

Bright purple flats covered her feet as she kicked her

little legs the entire way. Ian knew he was smiling like an idiot, but how could he not? Emily was an absolute doll and she was such a sweet kid. He was actually looking forward to spending time with her.

Max Ford and his wife, Raine, were just stepping out of their trailer as he passed by. Max held their little girl, Abby, who was almost two now.

"Look at this," Max said with a wide grin. "You seeing how the family life fits you?"

Ian didn't mind the question. Actually, he kind of warmed at the idea of it. "Cassie isn't feeling too great, so I told her I'd take Emily for the day."

Max's daughter pointed down to Emily. "Baby."

Laughing, Raine took the little girl and squatted down to the stroller to see Emily. "Her name is Emily," Raine explained.

"You're pretty serious about Cassie," Max said in a softer tone. "Happened pretty quick."

Ian shook his head and raked a hand over his hair, which was probably still sporting a messy look after sleeping on the sofa all night. "Yeah, it did. But I can't help it, man. I didn't see this coming."

"You plan on staying after the film is done?" Max asked.

Ian watched the interaction between the two little girls and Raine and his heart swelled. "I honestly don't know," Ian said, looking back to Max. "How hard was it for you with the transition?"

Max's gaze drifted to his family, and a genuine smile, not what he used for the cameras or his on-screen love interests, but the one that Ian had seen directed only at Raine, transformed his face. "When you want something so bad you'd die without it, there's no transition. It's the easiest and best decision I've ever made."

Yeah, that was kind of where Ian's mind was going. Having Cassie and Emily in his life made him feel things on a level he hadn't even known existed inside him.

Ian said his goodbyes to Max and his family and stepped inside his trailer. After settling Emily on a pink fuzzy blanket from her house, Ian placed her favorite toys all around her. Standing back to admire his feat of babysitting, he went to boot up his laptop, grabbed his phone and sat at the small kitchenette. Thankfully, the trailer was all open and small, so Emily couldn't leave his sight.

After answering a few emails, Ian glanced at the little girl, who was chewing on one toy and pounding the other one against the side of her rainbow-striped leggings. So far so good.

As he dialed one of his clients, rising star Brandon Crowe, who was on his way to Texas for filming, Ian scrolled back through his emails, deleting the junk so he could wade through and find things that actually needed his attention.

"Hello."

"Brandon, glad I caught you." Ian closed out his email and opened the document with his client's name on it to make notes. "You arrive in Houston yet?"

"About an hour ago. I'm ready for a beer, my hotel room and about five days of sleep. In that order."

Ian chuckled. His client had been filming all over with a tight schedule; the crew had literally been running from one location to another.

"What's up?" Brandon asked.

"I know your mind is on overload right now, but I

need to discuss the next script. I have a film that will be set in Alaska and the producer has specifically asked for you. I'd like to send this script to you and see what you think."

Brandon sighed. "Sure. Did you look it over?"

"Yeah. I think this character would be a perfect fit for you. I can see why they want you for the role."

"Who's the producer?" Brandon asked.

Ian told him more specifics and turned to see Emily… only she wasn't there. Panic rushed through him as he jerked to his feet, sending his chair toppling to the floor behind him.

"Emily," he called, glancing around the very tiny area.

"Excuse me?"

Ian glanced at the phone. For a second he'd forgotten about the call. "I need to call you back. The baby is gone."

"Baby?"

Ian disconnected the call and tossed his phone on the table. Stepping over the toys and blanket, Ian crossed to the other end of the trailer. He peeked into the tiny bathroom: no Emily.

"Emily," he called. "Sweetheart?"

In the small bedroom, Ian saw bright rainbow material sticking out from the side of the bed. He rounded the bed. Emily sat on her bottom, still chewing her favorite stuffed horse. Of course, when she saw him she looked up and gave that heart-melting smile.

"You're rotten," he told her. "Your mom is not going to let you come play with me anymore if you give me a heart attack."

He scooped her up and was rewarded with a wet, sloppy horse to the side of the face. *Nice.*

The next hour went about as stellar as the first, and by the end of hour two, Ian knew he was an amateur and needed reinforcements. There was just no way he could do this on his own.

How the hell did Cassie manage? Not only manage, but still put up the front of keeping it together and succeeding at each job: mother, sister, daughter, trainer. She did it all.

Of course, now she was home, in bed, flat-out exhausted and literally making herself sick.

As Ian gathered up all Emily's things, she started crying. The crying turned into a wail in about 2.5 seconds, so Ian figured she was hungry. Wrong. He changed her diaper. Still not happy.

He picked up the bag and Emily, stepped outside and strapped her into the stroller. Perhaps a walk around the estate would help.

Keeping toward the back of the main house, Ian quickly realized this also wasn't making her very happy. That was it. Reinforcements were past due.

He made his way to the back door, unfastened the very angry Emily and carried her into the house, where—*thank you, God*—Linda greeted him with a smile and some heavenly aroma that could only be her cinnamon rolls.

"I've done something wrong," Ian yelled over Emily's tantrum. "We were fine." A slight lie. "But then she started screaming. She's not hungry. She has a clean diaper. We took a walk. I don't know what to do."

Linda wiped her hand on a plaid towel and tossed it onto the granite counter before circling the island and holding her hands out for Emily. The baby eagerly went to the middle-aged woman and Ian nearly wept with gratitude that someone else surely knew what they were doing.

"She probably needs a nap," Linda told him as she jostled and tried to calm Emily.

Ian laughed and pushed a hand through his hair. "After all of that, I need one, too."

Smiling, Linda patted Emily's back. "You say you fed her?"

Ian nodded. "She took a bottle. I have some jar food, but Cassie said to save that for a bit later."

"If she's had her bottle, then her little belly is full and she's ready to rest. I'll just take her into the master bedroom. Damon has a crib set up in there for when Cassie is over here."

Ian sank to the bar stool, rested his elbow on the island and held his head in his hands. Good grief, being in charge of one tiny little being was the hardest job he'd ever had…and he'd had the job only a few hours.

Hands down, parenting was not for wimps.

A slither of guilt crept through him. Had he been too hard on his parents all those years? His free-spirited mother who was always seeking attention and his by-the-book father who could never be pleased…were they just struggling at this whole parenting thing, too?

Ian didn't have the answers and he couldn't go back in time and analyze each and every moment. The most pressing matter right now was the fact that he was in love with Cassie and her sweet baby, and the ex had just stepped back into the picture.

Great freakin' timing.

But Ian needed to wait, to let Cassie deal with this

matter in her own way. He wasn't stepping aside, not by any means. He'd offer support any way she wanted it, but this was her past to handle, and with a baby involved, Ian had a bad feeling things were about to get worse before they could get better.

Chapter 19

Cassie jerked when the loud knock on her door pulled her out of her sleep. Glancing to the clock on the bedside table, she realized she'd slept most of the day. Damn, she'd never slept that much.

Throwing off the covers and coming to her feet, Cassie was thrilled when she didn't sway and within moments knew she was feeling better. Perhaps her body was just telling her she needed to slow it down every now and then. The pounding on her door continued and Cassie rolled her eyes. There wasn't a doubt in her mind who stood on the other side of the door. Ian wouldn't pound on her door. He'd knock or just come on in, and so would her father and Tessa.

And that left only one rude, unwanted guest.

Shuffling down the hall, probably looking even more stellar than earlier today when Derek had stopped by,

Cassie actually laughed. Was he really here to plead for his family back when she looked like death and after he'd left her for some young, hot bimbo? Oh, the irony was not lost on her.

Cassie took her time flipping the lock on the knob and opening the door. Sure enough, Derek stood there, clutching a newspaper. Disapproval settled in his eyes.

"Funny," she told him, leaning against the edge of the door. "That's the same look you wore when you left me. What do you want now?"

He slapped the paper to her chest and pushed past her to enter.

"Come on in," she muttered, holding on to the paper and closing the door. "I thought I told you to have your lawyer contact mine."

Derek scanned the living area, then stretched his neck to see down the hall. "Where's Emily?"

"With Ian." Crossing her arms, crinkling the paper, Cassie sighed. "What do you want, Derek?"

"First of all, I don't want my daughter with a stranger."

Hysterical laughter bubbled out before she could even try to control it. "Seriously? If anyone is a stranger to her, it's you. We've already established what you think of Ian, so state your reason for this unwanted visit or that threat of calling security will become a fast reality."

He pointed toward the paper. "Apparently you haven't seen today's local paper. Maybe your pretty boy is a stranger to you, as well."

Cassie unfolded the paper. She'd play his game if it meant he'd leave sooner.

Her eyes settled on the picture of Lily and Ian. Cassie had known they were having a business meeting the evening before, she'd known they were discussing a major career move for both of them, but she hadn't known the media would spin the story into something…romantic.

Her eyes landed on the headline: Hollywood Starlet on Location Still Finds Time for Romance.

The way their two heads were angled together in the grainy picture did imply something more than a business meeting. The intimate table for two complete with bouquet and candles also added to the ambience of love.

Cassie glanced back up to Derek. "What about it?"

She would not give her ex the satisfaction of letting it get to her, of coming between something she and Ian had built and worked hard at.

"Looks like your boy toy has someone else on the side." Derek smirked. "Is this really what you've moved on to?"

"Why are you here?" she demanded. "What do you want from me?"

"If you'd answered my calls or texts you'd know I want my family back. I had no idea you opted to replace me with such a younger man."

Cassie smacked the paper down on the table beside the door. "Don't you dare judge me. You left me, remember? And if we're casting stones, I'll remind you that when you left, you moved on with a much younger woman with boobs as her only major asset."

Fired up and more than geared for a fight, Cassie advanced on him. "You're just upset because Ian is a real man. He cares about me, about Emily. My looks don't matter, my size doesn't matter and he's taken to Emily like she is his own, which is a hell of a lot more than you ever did for either of us."

Derek clenched his jaw as he loomed over her and held her gaze. "I just want you to know that this man, this kid, really, will get bored with the family life. He'll move on, and then where will you be? I'm man enough to admit I was wrong and that I'm willing to try again."

She hated that she felt a small tug, hated that for months she'd prayed for this moment. But she loved Ian. How could she deny herself the man she felt she'd been waiting for her whole life?

But on the other hand, how could she deny her daughter the bond of her parents raising her in the same house?

Cassie shook her head, refusing to listen to the conflicting voices in her head. She needed to think, needed to be alone.

"I waited for months for you to come back," she told him, hoping her words would make him squirm, make him feel the heavy dose of guilt he was due. "I cried myself to sleep when I thought of Emily not knowing her father. But you know what? After the tears were spent, I realized that Emily was better off. Both of us were, actually. Neither of us needed a man in our life who didn't put us first. We needed a man who would love us, put our needs above his own selfish ones and be there for us no matter what."

When he opened his mouth, Cassie raised a hand to silence him. "I would've given you the same in return. I married you thinking we were both in love, but I was wrong. You didn't love me, because if you did, you wouldn't have found it so easy to leave me."

"I'm back, though." He reached out, touched her face. "I want my family back, my wife back. I know I made a mistake, but you can't tell me you're ready to throw everything away."

When the door opened behind her, Cassie didn't have

to turn to know Ian stood just at the threshold. She closed her eyes and sighed.

"Actually," she whispered. "You already threw it all away."

Derek's eyes darted from hers to just over her shoulder before he dropped his hands. "You can keep the paper. Maybe it will give you something to think about."

She didn't move as he skirted around her. When the door shut once again, Cassie turned slowly to see Ian, hands on his hips. Even with the space between them, Cassie saw so many emotions dancing in his eyes: confusion, hurt, love.

"Where's Emily?" she asked, hoping to keep the conversation on safer ground.

"I actually just left her with Linda. She's taking a nap."

Cassie nodded, worry lacing through her. "What you just saw was—"

"I know what I saw," he murmured. "I know he wants you back. He'd be a fool not to. It's just—"

Ian glanced down, smoothing a hand over the back of his neck, then froze when his gaze landed on the paper. Slowly he picked it up, skimming the front page.

Cassie waited, wondering how he would react.

When he muttered a curse and slammed the paper down, Cassie jumped.

"Tell me this wasn't Derek's defense," Ian begged. "He surely wasn't using me as his battle to win you back."

Shrugging, Cassie crossed her arms around her waist. "It's a pretty damning photograph."

Closing the spacious gap between them, Ian stood within a breath of her and tipped her chin up so she looked him in the eyes. "The media is known for spinning stories to create the best reaction from viewers. It's how they stay in business."

Cassie nodded. "I'm aware of that."

Ian studied her for a moment before he plunged his fingers through her disheveled hair and claimed her lips. The passion, desire and fury all poured from him, and Cassie had to grip his biceps to hold on for the ride.

He attacked her mouth, a man on a mission of proving something, of taking what was his and damning the consequences.

When he pulled away, Ian rested his forehead against hers. "Tell me you believe that I could kiss you like that and have feelings for another woman. Tell me that you don't trust me and all we have here is built on lies. Because if that's the case, I'll leave right now and never come back."

Cassie's throat tightened as she continued to clutch his arms. "I don't believe that, Ian. I know you wouldn't lie to me. You've shown me what a real man is, how a real man treats a lady."

Taking a deep breath, she finally stepped back, away from his hold. "But I also know that this is something I'm going to have to deal with if we're together. The media spinning stories, always being in the limelight."

"I'm an agent, Cassie. Nobody cares about me. If I had been out alone, nobody would've known who I was."

Cassie smiled. "But you were out with the breathtaking Lily Beaumont. All of your clients are famous, Ian. There will be other times, other photos."

Shaking her head, she walked around and finally sank onto the sofa. Ian joined her but didn't touch her. She hated this wedge that had settled between them…

a wedge that had formed only once Derek had entered the picture.

"I want to be with you, Cassie," he told her. "As in beyond the movie, beyond next month or even next year. I want to see where this can go, but if the idea of my work will hold you back, maybe we both need to reevaluate what we're doing."

Tears pricked her eyes as she turned to face him fully. "You want to be with me?"

Reaching out to swipe the pad of his thumb across her cheek to clear the rogue tear, Ian smiled. "Yes. I know it's crazy and we've only known each other a short time, but I do want to be with you."

"Is this because my ex is back? Are you feeling threatened?"

Shaking his head, Ian took her shoulders and squeezed. "This has nothing to do with Derek. His appearance is just bad timing, that's all. I can't deny myself the fact that being with you has made me a better person. Finding myself wrapped around yours and Emily's lives makes me want more for myself. I never thought about a family before, but I want to see where this will lead and how we can make it work."

Hope filled Cassie as she threw her arms around Ian's neck and sniffed. "I know I'm a hot mess right now," she told him. "I have no idea how I was lucky enough to get you, but I want to see where we go, too. I'm just sorry you'll have to deal with Derek." Cassie eased back and wiped her cheeks. "He's Emily's father, and even though he abandoned us, I can't deny him if he wants to see her."

"What if he wants custody? Did he mention that again?"

"No. I hope he was just trying to scare me, like you said."

Smoothing her hair behind her ear, Ian smiled and settled his palm against her cheek. "No matter what, I'm here for you. Okay?"

For the first time in a long time, Cassie knew there was something to be hopeful about, something more than her career and Emily to fight for. And that was the love of a good man.

Ian was right. Damn if Derek's visit hadn't come at the worst possible time. Not only was the estate covered in film crew and actors, but Ian had settled so perfectly into her life and now the Belmont Stakes was upon them.

The final of the three most prestigious races in the horse world. There was no way Cassie could possibly think of Derek and his threats right now...and yet he had left her with a doozy last night.

He'd called her and issued an ultimatum—either she take him back and give their marriage another go or he would go to his lawyer with a plea to get full custody. Of course, she doubted he could, but the threat was there, and even if he didn't get full, there was always a chance he could get shared. And then where would she be?

Cassie sank down onto the bed in her hotel room and rested her head in her hands. Crying would be of no use, but she so wished she could cut loose and absolutely throw a fit. Being an adult flat-out sucked sometimes.

The adjoining door to the bedroom next to hers creaked open and Cassie glanced up to see Tessa standing in the doorway wearing a gray tank top and black yoga pants.

"I know you're not in a good spot, and as much as I

think you could use a drink, that won't help us any in tomorrow's race." Tessa held up a shiny gold bag. "But I do have chocolates and I'm willing to share."

Cassie attempted a smile. "Are they at least rum balls?"

Laughing, Tessa crossed the room and sank onto the bed, bumping Cassie's hip. "Sorry. Just decadent white-chocolate truffles. You ready to talk about Derek being back and wreaking havoc? Because it's been all I could do not to say something to you, but I figured you'd tell me on your own."

Cassie took the bag and dug out a chocolate. No, the sweetness wouldn't cure all, but it would certainly take the edge off her rage.

"I was hoping if I ignored the fact he was in town he'd just go away," Cassie said as she bit into the chocolate.

"How's that working?"

"Not well. How did you find out anyway? He's only been in town two days."

Tessa reached into the bag and pulled out a piece for herself. "Ian and Max were discussing the problem, and I may have eavesdropped on their conversation."

Swallowing the bite and reaching for another truffle, Cassie shifted on the bed to face her sister, settling the bag between them. "I planned on telling you. I was just trying to focus on Ian, make sure Emily was all settled with Linda before we left and praying Derek didn't try to get back onto Stony Ridge while we were gone. I've got security keeping an eye out for him."

"Can you legally do that?" Tessa asked.

Shrugging, Cassie smoothed her hair back and tugged the rubber band from her wrist to secure the knotty mess. "I have no clue. But if he's trespassing on the property, that's all the guards need to know to have him escorted off. If he wants to play the poor-father card, I doubt he'll have a leg to stand on."

"After the race tomorrow, go on home." Tessa reached in the bag and offered Cassie another chocolate, but Cassie wasn't in the mood anymore. "Nash and I will make sure everything is handled and taken care of. Take the truck Nash brought, and he and I can take the trailer and other truck."

Cassie bit her lip when tears threatened. "I don't want him to ruin this, Tessa. We've worked too hard, come too far, and we're both retiring after this season. I can't let him destroy our dreams of going out on top."

Reaching between them to take Cassie's hand, Tessa smiled. "Derek won't destroy anything. You won't give him that power. He's a jerk and he'll probably be gone when we get back because you weren't falling all over yourself to take him back when he appeared on your doorstep."

"He's threatening to file for custody," Cassie whispered.

Tessa let out a string of words that would've made their mother's face turn red. "He's an ass, Cassie. No judge will let him take Emily."

"What about joint custody?"

With a shrug, Tessa shook her head. "Honestly, I don't know, but the man has been gone almost a year, so I would certainly hope no judge would allow someone so restless to help raise a child."

Cassie had the same thoughts, but life and the legal system weren't always fair.

Flinging herself onto the bed, Cassie crossed her arms over her head. "I just never thought I'd be in this situation, you know? I mean, I married Derek thinking we'd be together forever. Then when we had Emily I really thought my family was complete and we were happy. Derek leaving was a bomb I hadn't expected, but now that he's back, I don't want him. I feel nothing but anger and resentment."

Tessa lay on her back next to Cassie and sighed. "You know, between me, Dad, Grant, Linda and Ian, Derek doesn't stand a chance. There's no way we'd let him just take Emily without a fight. If the man wants to play daddy, he'll have to actually stick around and prove he can man up."

"I agree," Cassie told her, lacing her fingers behind her head and staring up at the ceiling. "I won't deny my daughter the chance of knowing her father if I truly believe he won't desert her in a year just when she's getting used to him. I will do everything in my power to protect her heart from him."

And wasn't that just the saddest statement? Protecting a little girl's heart from her own father. But Derek had given her little choice.

"So, you want to tell me what you and Ian are doing?" Tessa asked. "Because I'm pretty sure the two of you are much more than a fling."

Cassie laughed. "Yeah, we're definitely much more than a fling."

"Who knew when you got locked in that attic the man of your dreams would come to your rescue?"

"Technically he didn't rescue me," Cassie clarified.

Tessa glanced over, patted Cassie's leg and smiled. "Oh, honey. He's rescued you—you just might not see it yet."

She was right. Ian had come along at a time in her life

when the last thing she'd wanted was a man. But he'd shown her love, shown her daughter love. He'd shown her what true intimacy was all about. When she'd been sick he hadn't thought twice about taking Emily, even though he knew next to nothing about babies.

He made Cassie's life better.

There was no way that she could not fight for what they had. Maybe she should look into a riding school in California. With her income and her knowledge, she technically could start it anywhere.

She had to deal with Derek first; then she would figure out how being far away from her family would work.

Tessa's brows lifted. "I know that look," she said. "You're plotting something. Share or I'll take my chocolates back to my room."

"Just thinking of the future," Cassie replied with a smile. "Thinking of my school. I've already started putting the wheels in motion for Stony Ridge, but who's to say that's where it has to be?"

Tessa hugged her. "I was so afraid this is what you'd do. Damn, I'm going to miss you if you move."

"Don't go tearing up on me," Cassie ordered. "Ian hasn't asked me, but if he did, I can't say that I would tell him no. On the other hand, Grant has a home out in L.A., too, so I'm sure you'd spend time out there."

"It wouldn't be the same." Tessa sniffed, blinked back tears. "But I want you happy and this is truly the happiest I've seen you in your entire life. I'll support any decision you make."

Cassie reached out, grabbed Tessa's hand and settled in with the fact she'd move heaven and earth to be with Ian. And now she couldn't wait to get home to tell him just that.

Chapter 20

Ian had a wonderful surprise planned for Cassie. He couldn't wait for her to get home.

Not only had Tessa and Cassie taken the Belmont Stakes and the coveted Triple Crown, but Cassie was on her way back and Ian had to get the stage set. They had so much to celebrate.

Very few had ever taken home the Triple Crown title, and Tessa was the first female jockey to own the honor. The Barrington sisters had officially made history and Ian was so proud he'd been able to witness a small portion of their success. He hated he wasn't there in person, though.

Ian had opted to stay behind for two reasons. So they could both concentrate on their own work without distractions and to see if he could handle being without her.

He couldn't.

After a perfect morning in which Lily officially signed with his agency, he was now in town hitting up the quaint little florist, about to buy an exorbitant amount of flowers in a variety of colors and styles. He wanted her cottage to be drowning in bouquets for the evening he had planned. Not only because he had high hopes about their future, but because she deserved to be placed on a pedestal after such a milestone win.

He may have also had Linda's help in the matter of planning.

The days they'd been apart had been a smack of reality to the face. He didn't want to be without her, without Emily. He was ready to make a family with them.

He also realized that love and marriage—and fatherhood—weren't scary at all once you found the person who totally completed you.

This family had instantly been so welcoming, so loving, and Ian couldn't be happier. From Linda to sweet Emily, he was so overwhelmed by how easily they accepted him. And now Cassie was about to get the surprise of her life.

As Ian rounded the building that housed the flower shop, he smacked into someone…Derek. *Great.*

"You're still in town?" Ian asked, eyeing the man clutching a massive bouquet of roses.

Derek shielded his eyes from the warm afternoon sun. "I'm not leaving until I get what I want."

Becoming more irritated by the moment, and a tad amused, Ian crossed his arms over his chest. "That will be a while, considering what you want is mine."

"Yours? My family is not your property," Derek clarified.

"They're also not your family. Not anymore. Cassie made her choice."

"Did she? Because the Cassie I know loves family." Derek adjusted the flowers to his other hand and shifted beneath the awning of the flower shop to shield himself from the sun. "It means more to her than anything. Do you think she'd honestly choose some young guy who she just met over the father of her child? Because I can assure you, she'll put Emily's needs ahead of her own."

There was a ring of truth to Derek's words, but there was also no way Ian would show any emotion or allow this guy to step into the life he was trying to build.

"Don't blame me or Cassie because you realized too late that you made a mistake," Ian said, propping his hands on his hips and resisting the urge to take those flowers, throw them on the ground and crush them. "Cassie and I have something, and there's no way you're going to come charging in like you belong. You missed your chance."

Derek smiled. "I didn't miss anything. You see, no matter how much you hate me, I am Emily's father. She will want to know me and I will make damn sure my lawyer does everything he can to get my baby girl in my life. Now, if Cassie wants to come, too, that's her decision, but I'll fight dirty to get what I want. Considering the fact that you are a Hollywood playboy, combined with the perfectly timed image in the paper, I don't see how I can't use that against Cassie. Obviously she's eager to get any man's attention—"

All control snapped as Ian fisted Derek's shirt and slammed him against the old brick building. Petals flew everywhere as the bouquet also smacked against the wall.

"Listen here, you little prick." It was all Ian could do not to pummel the jerk. "I will not be bullied into giving up what I want, and Cassie will not be blackmailed, either. If you want to see your daughter, then go through your attorney the proper way, but don't you dare use your own child as a pawn. Only a sick ass would do that."

Stepping back, Ian jerked the bouquet from Derek's hand and threw it down on the sidewalk. He'd held back long enough and Ian knew full well whom that arrangement was meant for.

Ian issued one final warning through gritted teeth. "Stay away from me and mine."

As he walked away, he didn't go into the flower store as originally intended. He had some thinking to do.

No, he wouldn't be intimidated by some jerk who thought he could blackmail his way back into Cassie's life, but if Ian's presence was going to cause issues with custody of Emily, Ian knew he had a difficult decision to make.

As he headed back to his sporty rental car, the small box in his pocket felt heavier than ever.

Cassie had never been so eager to return from a race, especially one as important as this one.

They'd done it. The Barrington women had conquered the racing world and brought home the Triple Crown. Cassie was pretty sure she'd be smiling in her sleep for years to come. She and Tessa had worked so hard, prayed even harder, and all their endless hours and years of training had paid off.

But beyond the joy of the racing season coming to an amazing end, Cassie couldn't wait to celebrate with

Emily and Ian and wanted to get Derek taken care of so he would leave her alone once and for all.

Because she'd gotten home later than intended, Linda had stayed in the cottage and put Emily to bed. Now Cassie was alone, her baby sleeping down the hall and unpacked bags still just inside the door where she'd dropped them.

She had to see Ian now. Too many days had passed since she'd seen him, touched him. Each day she was away from him she realized just how much she truly loved him.

A gentle tap on her front door had her jerking around. The glow of the porch light illuminated Ian's frame through the frosted glass. She'd know that build anywhere and a shiver of excitement crept over her at the thought of seeing him again. She hadn't realized she could miss someone so much.

But the second she flung the door open, ready to launch into his strong hold, she froze. Something was wrong. He wasn't smiling, wasn't even reaching for her. Actually, his hands were shoved in his pockets.

"What's wrong?" she asked, clutching the door frame.

Ian said nothing as his gaze moved over her. Something flashed through his eyes as he settled back on her face…regret?

"Ian?"

He stepped over the threshold, paused within a breath of her and then scooted around her. After closing the door behind her, she leaned against it, unsure of what to say or how to act.

Her eyes locked on to Ian's as silence quickly became the third party present. Moments ago she'd had nothing but hope filling her heart. Now fear had laid a heavy blanket over that hope.

"This is so much harder than I thought it would be," he whispered, his eyes glistening. "I had tonight planned so different."

"You're scaring me, Ian."

Wrapping her arms around her waist, Cassie rubbed her hands up and down her bare arms to ward off the chill.

"I love you, Cassie. I've never said that to another human being, not even my own parents." Ian stepped closer but didn't touch her. "Tonight I thought I would tell you I loved you, show you that I can't live without you and Emily, but I've thought about it all evening and came to the hardest decision of my life."

Cassie wasn't a fool. She knew exactly what he was going to say. "How dare you," she whispered through tears clogging her throat. "You tell me you love me a breath before you're about to break things off? Because that's what this is, right?"

Ian ran a hand over his face. "Damn it, Cassie. I'm letting you go to make things easier. I can't keep you in my life, knowing I could be the one thing that stands between you and keeping custody of your daughter."

Realization quickly dawned on Cassie. "You bastard. You let Derek get to you, didn't you? I never took you for a coward, Ian."

"I'm not a coward, and if Emily weren't in the picture I would stay and fight for you…and I'd win. But Emily deserves a chance to know her father, and I can't stand the thought of you sharing custody or possibly losing because Derek is going to fight dirty. He said it himself. This way, with me gone, maybe you two can come to some sort of peaceful middle ground."

Torn between hurt, love and anger, Cassie tried to rein in her emotions. "You're leaving me because you're afraid. I understand that you didn't have a great childhood, which makes me respect you all the more for stepping up and loving Emily the way you have. But don't you dare leave now when things get tough. I thought you were more of a man than that."

He jerked as if she'd slapped him. "Trust me, Cass. In the long run, this is the best for Emily."

"What about me?" she cried. "I love my daughter and her needs will always come first, but you say you love me. So what about that? What about us?"

The glistening in his eyes intensified a second before a tear slid down his cheek. He didn't make a move to swipe it away and Cassie couldn't stop staring at the wet track.

Her heart literally ached for the man who was trying to be strong and, in his own way, do the right thing. But damn it, she wanted more and she thought she'd found it with him.

As she stepped forward, Ian took a step back. And that lone action severed any thread of hope she had been holding on to.

"I'm barely hanging on here," he whispered. "You can't touch me. I have to be strong for both of us. Just think about what I said. You'll know that I'm right. There's no other way if you want to keep Emily. Derek won't play fair, and if I'm in your life, he'll use that against you."

He took in a deep, shuddering breath. "I want to be part of your life, Cass. I want to be part of Emily's. But it's because I want so much to be a part of your family that I must protect you both, and unfortunately, that means I need to step aside."

Cassie hated the emotions whirling about inside her. So much love for this man and so much hatred toward another. Damn Ian for being noble.

"If you're not staying to fight for me and with me, then leave." Blinking back tears and clenching her fists at her side to keep from wrapping her arms around him, Cassie held his gaze. "You've done what you came to do, so go."

Ian slid a hand from his pocket, clutched something and reached out to place it on the end table by the sofa. "What I came to do was quite the opposite," he told her as he took a step toward her. "But I want you to have that and remember that I do love you, Cassie. No matter what you think right now. I'll always love you."

Without touching her, without even a kiss goodbye, Ian stepped around her and quietly walked out of her life. Drawing in a shaky breath, she took a step toward the end table and saw a blue box. Her heart in her throat, Cassie reached for the box. Her hands shook because she knew exactly what would be beneath that velvety lid.

Lifting the lid with a slow creak, Cassie gasped. Three square-cut stones nestled perfectly in a pewter band had tears spilling down both cheeks. Cassie's hand came to her mouth to hold back the sob that threatened to escape.

Ian had put all of their birthstones in the ring…a ring he'd planned on giving her when he told her he loved her.

Unable to help herself, she pulled the band from the box and slid it on. A perfect fit—just like the man who had walked out the door moments ago.

As she studied the ring on her finger, Cassie knew there was no way she would go down without a fight. No way at all. Emily would come first, as always, but who said she couldn't have the man of her dreams *and* her family?

If Derek wanted to fight dirty, well, bring it on, because Cassie had just gotten a whole new level of motivation to fuel her fire. And there was no way in hell Derek would take her child or the dreams Cassie had for a future with Ian.

The depth of Ian's love was so far beyond what she'd dared to imagine. His strength as a man and father was exactly what she needed, wanted…deserved. She wouldn't let his sacrifice go to waste.

Chapter 21

Ian wasn't sure why he didn't book a trip somewhere exotic to just get away. He'd come back to L.A. after breaking things off with Cassie. Max had more than understood his need to leave, but his friend had also had some choice words for him regarding the stupidity of his decision.

Ian wished there'd been another way. He'd had many sleepless nights looking for another way to protect Cassie and Emily, but it was because he loved them so much—because they *were* his family—he knew he needed to remove himself from their lives.

The pain after he'd left was unlike anything he'd ever known. Sharp, piercing pain had settled into the void in his heart that Cassie and Emily had left. But he also knew, in the long run, this was the best for the ladies he'd quickly grown to love.

Now, back in his beachfront home, he saw Cassie and that precious baby. How had two females he'd known only a short time infiltrated every single corner of his life? There wasn't a spot in his house, his mind or his heart that they hadn't left their imprint on.

He'd been home almost a month, and in the phone calls and texts between Max and Lily, he knew the filming was nearing the end. He hadn't asked about Cassie.... He just couldn't. The thought of her possibly playing house with Derek to keep the peace for Emily nearly crippled him.

Ian sank down onto the sand and pulled his knees up to his chest. The orange glow from the sunset made for a beautiful backdrop and not for the first time was he elated to have all of this for his backyard.

But he'd give it up in a heartbeat for a chance at happiness with Cassie. Letting her go was hands down the hardest thing he'd ever done in his entire life.

He hadn't been lying when he'd said this decision was better for Emily in the long run. When he'd been younger he would've given anything for his parents to have stayed together. Perhaps his father would've been a little more relaxed and his mother not so much of a free spirit always seeking attention from men.

Ian couldn't alter Emily's future by coming between her parents. His broken heart was minor in comparison to their safety. All that mattered was that sweet Emily wasn't a pawn, that he gave her the best chance to know her father. A chance he'd never had.

Damn it, he loved that little girl. He missed those little fingers wrapped around his thumb as he gave her a nighttime bottle. He missed that little two-toothed grin she'd offer for no apparent reason.

He missed everything...even the diaper changes.

"Beautiful place you have here."

Ian jerked his head over his shoulder, his heart nearly stopping at the sight of Cassie in a little green sundress, her hair whipping about her shoulders and Emily on her hip.

"I was just in the neighborhood and was curious if you had room for two more," she went on, not coming any closer.

In an instant, Ian was on his feet. "Room for two? Were you wanting to stay here?"

Cassie shrugged, her face tipped up to hold his gaze as he moved in closer. "Your house, your heart. Wherever you have room."

Ian's knees weakened. She'd come for him. When he'd thought they were finished, when he'd thought he'd done the right thing by setting her free, she'd come to him.

"I'll always have room in my heart for you and Emily." Ian reached out, slid a crimson curl behind her ear. "But my house? That depends on what's going on with you and Derek."

Cassie grabbed his hand before he could pull away from her. "Derek is being taken care of by my team of attorneys. I hired three to make sure he didn't blackmail me, you or use Emily as a bargaining chip. He's agreed to supervised visitation because Emily is young and would view him as a stranger. He's not allowed to take her from the state for any reason and I have approval over any and all visits."

Shocked, Ian merely stared. When Emily reached for him, his heart tumbled. Pulling her into his arms, he held her tight, breathing in her sweet scent.

"I've missed you," he whispered into her ear. Her little arms came around his neck and Ian had to physically fight back tears.

"We've missed *you*," Cassie told him. "But I had to make sure Derek was being handled before I could come to you."

Ian lifted his head, slid his arm around Cassie's waist and pulled her against his side. This right here was worth everything. The heartache he'd felt, the worry, the sleepless nights.

"If you ever try to be noble again, I'll go to the press with horrid lies." Cassie smiled up at him. "I know why you left—I even admire your decision on some level—but being without you for weeks was a nightmare. I never want to be without you again."

Ian slid his lips over hers. "What about your family? What about the school?"

Reaching up to pat his cheek, Cassie smiled. "Emily and I are staying here for a while. As for the school, I'd really like to open it on the estate, but I'll move it to California if you're needed here."

Ian couldn't believe what he was hearing. She was willing to part with her life, live across the country from her family, her rock, all because of him.

"I'd never ask you to leave your family," he told her. "I actually want to be near them. What do you say we keep this home for our getaways and vacations? We can live on the estate or build nearby. The choice is totally up to you, but I want you to have the school at Stony Ridge."

Cassie's smile widened, those sparkling blue eyes glistening. "Sounds like a plan. Of course, we're missing something, you know."

Curious, Ian drew back slightly. "What's that?"

"Well, I've worn my ring since you left." She held up her left ring finger and the sight had his heart jumping. "I assumed that this ring had a question that went along with it. I mean, I'm assuming the man I've fallen in love with plans on carrying out his intentions."

Ian looked to Emily. "What do you think, sweetheart? Should I ask your mommy to marry me?"

Emily clapped her hands and grinned. "Mom-mom-mom."

Laughing, Ian glanced back to Cassie. So many emotions swam in her eyes. So much hope and love, and it was all for him.

"How did I get to be so lucky?" he murmured.

Shrugging, Cassie said, "I'd say fate has been pushing us together since the moment I fell into your arms."

Pulling her tighter against him, he held the two most precious ladies. "This right here, in my arms, is my world. Nothing will come between us again. Not an ex, not my tendency to be noble, nothing. You're mine, Cassie."

Easing back to look down into her eyes, Ian saw his entire future looking back at him. "Tell me you'll marry me. Tell me you'll let me be Em's dad. That you'll even teach me all about horses. I want to be part of everything in your life."

"I wouldn't have it any other way," she told him, wiping a lone tear that had slid down her cheek. "Besides, I still owe you that horseback ride you've never been on."

Ian laughed. "How about we lay Emily down for a nap and we'll discuss other plans for our family?"

The gleam in her eye told him she hadn't missed his

hidden meaning. "*Our family.* Those are two of the most beautiful words I've ever heard."

He kissed her once again. "Then let's get started on building it."

* * * * *

WE HOPE YOU ENJOYED
THIS BOOK FROM

HARLEQUIN
DESIRE

*Luxury, scandal, desire—welcome to
the lives of the American elite.*

Be transported to the worlds of oil barons, family dynasties,
moguls and celebrities. Get ready for juicy plot twists,
delicious sensuality and intriguing scandal.

6 NEW BOOKS AVAILABLE EVERY MONTH!

HDHALO2021

Get 4 FREE REWARDS!

We'll send you 2 FREE Books plus 2 FREE Mystery Gifts.

FREE Value Over **$20**

Both the **Romance** and **Suspense** collections feature compelling novels written by many of today's bestselling authors.

YES! Please send me 2 FREE novels from the Essential Romance or Essential Suspense Collection and my 2 FREE gifts (gifts are worth about $10 retail). After receiving them, if I don't wish to receive any more books, I can return the shipping statement marked "cancel." If I don't cancel, I will receive 4 brand-new novels every month and be billed just $6.99 each in the U.S. or $7.24 each in Canada. That's a savings of at least 13% off the cover price. It's quite a bargain! Shipping and handling is just 50¢ per book in the U.S. and $1.25 per book in Canada.* I understand that accepting the 2 free books and gifts places me under no obligation to buy anything. I can always return a shipment and cancel at any time. The free books and gifts are mine to keep no matter what I decide.

Choose one: ☐ **Essential Romance**
(194/394 MDN GNNP)

☐ **Essential Suspense**
(191/391 MDN GNNP)

Name (please print)

Address   Apt. #

City   State/Province   Zip/Postal Code

Mail to the **Reader Service:**
IN U.S.A.: P.O. Box 1341, Buffalo, NY 14240-8531
IN CANADA: P.O. Box 603, Fort Erie, Ontario L2A 5X3

Want to try 2 free books from another series? Call 1-800-873-8635 or visit www.ReaderService.com.

*Terms and prices subject to change without notice. Prices do not include sales taxes, which will be charged (if applicable) based on your state or country of residence. Canadian residents will be charged applicable taxes. Offer not valid in Quebec. This offer is limited to one order per household. Books received may not be as shown. Not valid for current subscribers to the Essential Romance or Essential Suspense Collection. All orders subject to approval. Credit or debit balances in a customer's account(s) may be offset by any other outstanding balance owed by or to the customer. Please allow 4 to 6 weeks for delivery. Offer available while quantities last.

Your Privacy—The Reader Service is committed to protecting your privacy. Our Privacy Policy is available online at www.ReaderService.com or upon request from the Reader Service. We make a portion of our mailing list available to reputable third parties that offer products we believe may interest you. If you prefer that we not exchange your name with third parties, or if you wish to clarify or modify your communication preferences, please visit us at www.ReaderService.com/consumerschoice or write to us at Reader Service Preference Service, P.O. Box 9062, Buffalo, NY 14240-9062. Include your complete name and address.

STRS20R

SPECIAL EXCERPT FROM

ⒽHARLEQUIN
DESIRE

*Looking to settle down, Alaskan CEO Garth Outlaw
thinks he wants a convenient bride. What he doesn't
know is that his pilot, Regan Fairchild, wants him. Now,
with two accidental weeks together in paradise, will the
wife he needs be closer than he realized?*

Read on for a sneak peek at
The Wife He Needs
by New York Times *bestselling author Brenda Jackson.*

"May I go on record to make something clear, Regan?" Garth
asked, kicking off his shoes.

She swallowed. He was standing, all six feet and three inches
of him, at the foot of the bed, staring at her with the same intensity
that she felt. She wasn't sure what he had to say, but she definitely
wanted to hear it.

"Yes," she said in an almost whisper.

"You don't need me to make you feel sexy, desired and wanted.
You are those things already. What I intend to do is to make you feel
needed," he said, stepping away from the bed to pull his T-shirt over
his head and toss it on a nearby chair. "If you only knew the depth
of my need for you."

She wondered if being needed also meant she was indispensable,
essential, vital, crucial…all those things she wanted to become to
him.

"Now I have you just where I want you, Regan. In my bed."

And whether he knew it or not, she had him just where she
wanted him, too. Standing in front of her and stripping, for starters.
As she watched, his hands went to the front of his jeans.

"And I have you doing what I've always fantasized about, Garth.
Taking your clothes off in front of me so I can see you naked."

She could tell from the look on his face that her words surprised
him. "You used to fantasize about me?"

"All the time. You always looked sexy in your business suits, but my imagination gets a little more risqué than that."

He shook his head. "I never knew."

"What? That I wanted you as much as you wanted me? I told you that in the kitchen earlier."

"I assumed that desire began since you've been here with me."

Boy, was he wrong. "No, it goes back further than that."

It was important that he knew everything. Not only that the desire was mutual but also that it hadn't just begun. If he understood that then it would be easier for her to build the kind of relationship they needed, regardless of whether he thought they needed it or not.

"I never knew," he said, looking a little confused. "You never said anything."

"I wasn't supposed to. You are my boss and I am a professional."

He nodded because she knew he couldn't refute that. "How long have you felt that way?"

There was no way she would tell him that she'd had a crush on him since she was sixteen, or that he was the reason she had returned to Fairbanks after her first year in college. She had heard he was back home from the military with a broken heart, and she'd been determined to fix it. Things didn't work out quite that way. He was deep in mourning for the woman he'd lost and had built a solid wall around himself, one that even his family hadn't been able to penetrate for a long while.

"The length of time doesn't matter, Garth. All you need to know is that the desire between us is mutual. Now, are you going to finish undressing or what?"

Don't miss what happens next in…
The Wife He Needs
by Brenda Jackson, the first book in her
Westmoreland Legacy: The Outlaws series!

Available November 2020 wherever
Harlequin Desire books and ebooks are sold.

Harlequin.com

Copyright © 2020 by Brenda Streater Jackson

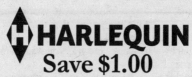

HARLEQUIN

Save $1.00

on the purchase of ANY Harlequin book
from the imprints below.

*Heartfelt or thrilling, passionate or
uplifting—our romances have it all.*

PRESENTS   INTRIGUE

DESIRE   ROMANTIC SUSPENSE   SPECIAL EDITION

LOVE INSPIRED

Save $1.00

on the purchase of ANY Harlequin Presents, Intrigue, Desire,
Romantic Suspense, Special Edition or Love Inspired book.

Valid from December 1, 2020 to November 30, 2021.

Canadian Retailers: Harlequin Enterprises ULC will pay the face value of this coupon plus 10.25¢ if submitted by customer for this product only. Any other use constitutes fraud. Coupon is nonassignable. Void if taxed, prohibited or restricted by law. Consumer must pay any government taxes. Void if copied. Inmar Promotional Services ("IPS") customers submit coupons and proof of sales to Harlequin Enterprises ULC, P.O. Box 31000, Scarborough, ON M1R 0E7, Canada. Non-IPS retailer—for reimbursement submit coupons and proof of sales directly to Harlequin Enterprises ULC, Retail Marketing Department, Bay Adelaide Centre, East Tower, 22 Adelaide Street West, 40th Floor, Toronto, Ontario M5H 4E3, Canada.

U.S. Retailers: Harlequin Enterprises ULC will pay the face value of this coupon plus 8¢ if submitted by customer for this product only. Any other use constitutes fraud. Coupon is nonassignable. Void if taxed, prohibited or restricted by law. Consumer must pay any government taxes. Void if copied. For reimbursement submit coupons and proof of sales directly to Harlequin Enterprises ULC 482, NCH Marketing Services, P.O. Box 880001, El Paso, TX 88588-0001, U.S.A. Cash value 1/100 cents.

52617010

5 65373 00076 2   (8100)0 12493

© 2021 Harlequin Enterprises ULC

HSERIESCOUP0221